MAGICIAN'S CHOICE

by

Todd A. Gipstein

First published by Dog Ear Publishing
4010 W. 86th Street, Ste H
Indianapolis, IN 46268
www.dogearpublishing.net

ISBN: 978-1-4575-2013-6

This book is printed on acid-free paper.

Printed in the United States of America

Cover photograph by
Marcia Roby Gipstein

Dedicated to:

My mother, who gave me my first magic set
and always encouraged me to pursue my dreams,

Russell Delmar, proprietor of the Magic Center,
a life-size magic set of a store in New York,

Marcia, the magic in my life,
who adds wonder to all my days.

FOREWORD

Magic is about wonder, wonderment, and believing. It speaks to the secrets and mysteries of life. Having seen magic from the inside, I know it holds a special place in life and the world of entertainment. Magicians may make women float in the air or cut them in half, rabbits appear from hats, and all manner of things appear and disappear, but in truth they are really showing us that the impossible is possible and that dreams can come true. They give us the gift of believing in miracles, if only for a few hours in a theater. Yet it is a gift that can last a lifetime.

The story told in "Magician's Choice" is one that is repeated over and over in the history of magic. A young child sees a magic show or is given a magic set, or even a rabbit, and then they are bitten by the wonder of magic. For some, it becomes a hobby or avocation. For a few, it can become a career and a way of life.

Like Guy, the main character in this novel, my father-in-law, Harry Blackstone, Sr., experienced his first magic show as a young boy. He saw the reigning world's greatest magician, Harry Kellar, perform in Chicago, and Harry knew his destiny. He, too, would become a magician and, as it turned out, the leading magician and illusionist in America for over half a century.

As this adventure unfolds, Guy encounters many magicians of the 1930s and 40s. At first an outsider, he is eventually embraced by the fraternity of magicians. As he tries to become a professional himself, Guy sees the good and the bad side of the business. Though his path is not always easy, he never loses his passion for the art of magic. And those who mentor him, notably Harry Blackstone, Sr., Lou Tannen, and the great close-up artist Dai Vernon, never lose their faith in the young man who wants to dedicate his life to magic no matter what.

There are lots of twists and turns in this story. Many mysteries within the world of mysteries. Things are not always what they seem. People are not always who they seem to be. The story itself is like a magic trick, an illusion grounded in reality that yet partakes of dreams.

I believe that if my late husband and his father were alive to read this tale, they would both smile and see their life stories somewhat mirrored by Guy's. So sit back and get ready for the show. The lights dim. The orchestra plays the overture. The curtain rises. A single spotlight illuminates the stage, and the wonder is about to begin!

Gay Blackstone

BLACKSTONE
WORLD'S GREATEST
MAGICIAN
1001 WONDERS
SOUVENIR
PROGRAM
AND
GILBERT
Mysto Magic
EXHIBITION SET
BE A MAGICIAN
DEVELOPED AT
THE GILBERT HALL OF SCIENCE

MODERN MAGIC
A PRACTICAL TREATISE ON THE ART OF CONJURING
PROFESSOR HOFFMANN
MUMMY ASRAH
A real beauty for effect and mystery. There are two very clever ideas involved - to throw off those who know!
A full dimension wood mummy about 12" high is shown freely and placed on a thin bench that stands several inches above your table. Mummy is placed on the bench and covered with a fancy cloth. Magician waves his hand over it, and it floats up off the bench, under cover of the cloth, then away from the bench and over to one side of the table, then almost down to the floor - then back up to fingertips.
Magician takes corner of cloth and tosses it in the air. The Mummy vanishes completely. The thin bench can be picked up and shown underneath and all around.
Can be worked under almost any conditions; no assistant necessary. You can feature this as the miniature of an effect you saw performed in a strange country with a real Mummy.
Complete with Mummy, Bench, Cloth, etc. price: $10.00
GONE!

1

Light from the theater marquee flooded the darkness of the sidewalk below, captivating Guy Borden and firing his imagination with its promise of the night's glamour and enchantments. "1001 Wonders," read the billing, "Harry Blackstone, The World's Greatest Magician."

On this October night in 1935, twelve-year-old Guy and his mother, Ruth, were just two in a crowd of hundreds, jostling to get into the Garde Theater, to their seats, to the evening of wonder that awaited.

In one hand, Guy clutched his ticket; in the other, his mother's hand. There were lots of kids in the crowd, all a bit wide-eyed with anticipation. The adults were, too, though they might have appeared nonchalant.

Magic shows did not come to New London, Connecticut often. When one did, it was a unique draw, and the arrival of a headliner like Harry Blackstone, the world's greatest magician, was something special.

Magic is not like other performances. It has the unique ability to invert the laws of nature, to topple our assumptions of what is possible or impossible. In doing so, magic creates wonder. For adults, whose sense of wonder has been eroded by the harsh realities of life, a magic show offers a return—if only for a few hours—to a time when *all* the world was a place of discovery and enchantment. Looked at this way, it was hard to tell if it was the adults leading the children to Blackstone's show or the other way around. Or perhaps, at a magic show, there are no adults.

Guy looked at the marquee jutting out of the theater's facade, the large black letters distinct on the bright illuminated background. He had never seen anything like it. It was like a giant newspaper headline, beaming out into the darkness, and the crowd was drawn to it like moths to a flame. They all lifted their eyes to the marquee as they milled about the sidewalk, their faces lit by it. "1001 Wonders."

Guy heard snatches of conversations in the crowd, things like: "He performed for the president, you know," or "My cousin saw him in Boston and said it was the most amazing night of his life." The comments fueled Guy's excitement and his expectations.

His mother had gotten the tickets for his thirteenth birthday, in just a few days. He had seen an ad in the local newspaper, *The New London Day*, for the upcoming show, and had not let up. She had succumbed to Guy's pestering. The tickets were her birthday gift to him.

It was a gift—an experience—that would change his life.

The doors to the theater opened. The crowd surged forward. Guy and his mother were swept inside. In a blur, their tickets were taken, and they made their way to their seats in the tenth row. As his mother studied the program, Guy gawked at the theater itself.

The Garde was a magnificent place. It was used for movies and concerts, musicals and all manner of performances. It held about fifteen hundred people. A balcony hung halfway across the orchestra seats below. The decor was a mix of Arabic and Art Deco themes. Paintings of sultans and tents, harem girls and camels, adorned the walls. The box seats were gold, their wood fronts carved into geometric shapes. Moorish accents, blue tiles, and the red velvet seats gave it an air of refinement and grandeur.

Though its ornate decor would fade when the lights dimmed and the show began, until then, the Garde Theater itself was a spectacle to behold. It made the evening special even before the evening began, like the prologue to a great drama. It was a perfect setting for a magic show, hinting at secrets and exotic, distant lands of mystery.

"Wow," was all Guy could say as he looked around. He had never been in the theater, and the Garde was not like anything he had ever seen, maybe even imagined. It was as if he was in a waking dream, and the magic had yet to begin.

The orchestra was tuning up. They played bits of oriental music and hypnotic dances, drum rolls and sparkling bells that hinted at the wonders to come.

He looked at his program, which told stories of Blackstone's life and adventures, offered some tricks to learn, and listed the tricks for the evening—55 in all! Guy supposed that there just wasn't enough time for 1001 wonders. No matter; 55 would do.

Some of the titles were enigmatic: Here, There and Somewhere Else. The Hindu Rope Mystery. A Girl Without a Middle. A Possible, Impossibility. Others were more clearly descriptive: The Pinup Girls. Pigeons from Nowhere. Levitation. They promised an evening of spectacle and stories, a journey around the world, through time, and into life's mysteries.

The lights dimmed. The crowd slowly quieted.

"Happy birthday, Guy," his mother whispered to him. And as she did, she studied his face for a moment. He was smiling, his eyes wide, a cute boy about to be transported to another world.

"This was a good idea," she said to herself. "He's in for a treat." Then she thought: "So am I." She regretted that his father hadn't wanted to come. He considered a magic show a frivolous entertainment.

The huge velvet curtain slowly rose, revealing a stage bathed in spotlights, full of cabinets and backdrops, tables of props, and objects whose purpose could not be known. The orchestra played a lively overture and then on walked the master magician himself, Harry Blackstone.

Blackstone was a striking presence on stage. Though not tall, he carried himself with a regal bearing. His head was large, crowned by a shock of white hair. He had a prominent nose, small mustache, and large hands. He wore a tuxedo and white gloves. He bowed slowly to acknowledge the applause that rolled through the theater like thunder.

The world's greatest magician made his way to center stage. All the stage lights dimmed except for a single brilliant white spotlight that formed a cone against the darkness. Blackstone walked into that light and stood there. He and he alone was the center of attention. As the orchestra played a dramatic piece that built the sense of expectation, Blackstone slowly removed his gloves. When they were off, he waited a beat, then tossed them into the air where they suddenly transformed into a white dove that flew up and over the balcony, circled the chandelier at the top of the theater, then swooped down to Blackstone's waiting finger, where it landed gently.

"Wow," said Guy.

The crowd gasped then cheered then applauded, and the orchestra hit a "ta-da." A young assistant walked on stage and took the bird from Blackstone, who bowed to the ongoing applause. He held his hands up asking for quiet.

"Ladies and gentlemen: it is my pleasure to be here in New London to bring you my show of 1001 Wonders. I hope in the next few hours to transport you to other worlds and show you miracles that will amaze, surprise and delight. I invite you to join me on a journey into the unknown. Together, and only together, we will make the magic happen. So now, without further ado, let us continue our night of wonder!"

Again applause, and another bow from Blackstone. He spun around and strode to a large box, now bathed in light.

The next few hours were extraordinary. For Guy. For his mother. For the hundreds of people who'd come to see Blackstone's wonders.

Though he sometimes told stories in front of the main curtain, Blackstone was silent during much of his big stage show. He presented illusions with broad gestures of great theatricality.

Blackstone levitated a woman beneath a gossamer shroud, then made her vanish into thin air. He took a pocket handkerchief, tied a knot in one end, waved his hand, and the white hanky began to dance between his hands and about the stage. He sawed another woman in half with a menacing circular saw. She survived the trick unscathed. A gentler illusion was his "Vanishing Bird Cage." Two dozen children joined him on stage, put their hands on a small bird cage with a canary inside, then squealed in surprise and delight as Blackstone made it vanish.

"The Garden of Flowers" was a beautiful trick where dozens of bouquets of brilliant feather flowers appeared all over the stage in a vast kaleidoscopic garden of color.

As he always did, Blackstone invited a young child onstage and after some light banter, produced a rabbit from a crumple of newspaper. He gave the bunny to the delighted child as a gift, smiling as he did like a doting grandparent.

Blackstone's act was a tightly orchestrated presentation, full of colorful props, young men in smart outfits, and pretty women in fantastic garments that ranged from Oriental to Arabic, from gauzy to bizarre. In one trick, a young woman was transformed into a moth. In another, a woman disappeared from a box on stage only to appear at the back of the theater.

Guy was struck by how graceful Blackstone was, how delicately he held the hand of a lovely assistant aloft at the end of a trick, inviting applause.

And then it happened.

For a card trick, he needed help from the audience. Maybe it was just chance, or perhaps a more determined working of fate, or perhaps a magician's choice, for as Blackstone scanned the crowd, his eyes came to rest upon Guy.

"How about you, young man?" said the world's greatest magician, pointing to Guy. "Would you care to come up here and help me with my next bit of wonder?"

"Go on, Guy," said Ruth, prodding him with her elbow. He nodded. Blackstone continued: "Yes? Let's give him a round of applause folks."

The crowd applauded as, in a dream, Guy stood, squeezed his way down the row of seats, down the aisle, and up the stairs to the stage, a spotlight following him all the way.

Blackstone greeted him: "Welcome, young man, and what is your name?"

"Guy. Guy Borden."

"Pleased to meet you Guy. Are you enjoying the show? Have I made you a believer in wonder?"

Guy nodded "yes," and Blackstone turned him to face the crowd. Guy could not see it, as the spotlight was blinding. He squinted into the darkness, knowing hundreds of people were out there, though he could see not a one. It is the odd thing about being on stage standing in that cone of the spotlight. You are in the light surrounded by a world of darkness. You are the center of attention, the focus of hundreds of eyes, yet you can feel utterly alone.

Blackstone smiled at Guy and said softly: "Don't be nervous, lad. Just do as I say and you will be a star."

Turning to the audience, Blackstone boomed out: "Young Guy Borden here will now help me with a special card trick."

He turned to Guy, cupped his hands together, and when he slowly opened them, a deck of cards had appeared. Blackstone fanned them with a flourish so their faces were clearly visible.

"As you can see," he said, "a deck of cards. Fifty-two. All different. Guy, would you be so kind as to pick a card, any card?"

Guy studied the fan a moment and then chose the Jack of Diamonds.

Blackstone took out a pen. "Would you be so kind as to sign this card, Guy, so that you know it is yours. It will be unique, and easily identifiable."

Guy signed his name on the card, and, using a bit of showmanship, held it up high, drawing a smile from Blackstone.

"A natural showman!" he said, and the crowd chuckled. "Now, Guy, please put your card back in the deck and hold on to them for me." Guy did as he was told.

At the edge of the stage, a spotlight came on and illuminated an assistant holding a gleaming sword. The orchestra began to play a mysterious Middle-Eastern tune. Blackstone left Guy standing in the center stage spotlight and strode to the assistant. He took the sword and turned to show it to the audience.

"As you can see, a sword. A sharp sword given to me by the Sultan of Ybor. Now with this sword, and Guy's help, I will do something extraordinary."

Blackstone swung the big sword around in an impressive flurry. Guy could hear the whoosh as it cut through the air. Blackstone walked over and stood a few feet from Guy.

"Guy, when I count to three, I want you to throw the deck of cards in the air, towards me. Do you understand?"

Guy nodded that he did.

"Okay, young man, get ready."

The orchestra brought their hypnotic tune to an end. The drummer took over, doing a slow roll as Blackstone began to count, the sword poised.

"One ..." The drumming got louder. "Two ..." Louder still. "THREE!"

Guy threw the cards in the air. The drummer hit a cymbal crash. Blackstone waved and jabbed the silver sword into the flurry of cards that cascaded around him like snowflakes. Blackstone was wild-eyed as he lunged. Guy recoiled. The cards fell to the stage. All except one. Blackstone held the sword up in the air and a single card was skewered on it.

A murmur of surprise rippled through the vast theater. Guy's eyes widened.

"A single card, speared by my sword," boomed Blackstone, then after a beat, "could it be yours, Guy?" He let the question hang in the air and penetrate the minds of the audience. "Could it be?" Showman that he was, Blackstone drew out the anticipation. He held the sword high, brandishing it, showing the card.

"You threw the cards at me, Guy. I lunged at them with my sword. In that instant, could I possibly have found your card? Let us see, Guy. Let us see."

Building suspense, Blackstone slowly, dramatically, lowered the sword and held it toward Guy, the spotlight following him as he did, the white card glowing. He stopped when the card was eye-level.

"Now, Guy, now is the moment for you to show us all if this is the same card you chose and signed. Time to show us if I have performed a miracle."

The drummer began a slow roll.

Guy reached up and carefully pulled the card from the tip of the sword. His eyes widened. It was the Jack of Diamonds with his signature on it!

"Which card is it, Guy? Say it loudly!"

"It's the Jack of Diamonds, and it has my name on it!" Without prompting, Guy held it up and showed it to the audience.

The drum roll hit its crescendo with another cymbal crash. There was a moment of stunned silence and then the audience erupted into wild applause.

Guy and Blackstone were frozen in a tableaux in the spotlight, a moment of astonishment in an evening of wonder.

"Thank you, ladies and gentlemen! How about a round of applause for my assistant Guy!" Guy turned and took a bow, savoring the applause, the moment of being the center of attention. Blackstone watched and smiled, and as the applause began to die down, he said to Guy: "Thank you for your help young man. Keep that card as a souvenir." Blackstone led him to the stairs at the edge of the stage. Guy walked back to his seat, clutching the card.

There were a few more tricks to wrap up Blackstone's 1001 Wonders. When the show was done and Blackstone and his assistants had taken their bows, people began to leave, shaking their heads, talking about their favorite illusions, speculating about how the tricks were done. Guy remained seated.

He held up the card that Blackstone had given him, a tangible connection to wonder.

"You were quite the star," said his mother. "I guess you liked the show?"

"It was amazing, mom. Thanks. Thanks a lot. I'll never forget it!"

Ruth Borden smiled. They were almost the last in the theater. "You know we have to leave, Guy."

It was with reluctance that twelve, soon to be thirteen-year-old Guy Borden got up and left the Garde Theater with his mother. He did not want the evening of magic to end. He wanted to stay in that enchanted place of wonder forever.

Guy fell asleep that night to images of dancing handkerchiefs, colorful flowers, young men handling props and beautiful women floating or becoming moths or vanishing from

Chinese cabinets. The wonders continued, merging in the mysteries of sleep into startling new combinations.

On Guy's bedside table was the Jack of Diamonds, pierced with a hole and with his signature on it, tangible proof that the evening of 1001 Wonders was not itself an illusion but a reality. A reality that would become the foundation of Guy Borden's dreams.

2

"Happy birthday, Guy," said his father, Sam, handing him a small box. It was the day after the magic show.

Inside the box was a gleaming gold pocket watch, with a running horse embossed on the cover. Guy pushed the button on the side and the lid popped open revealing the clock face. Inside the lid was a miniature portrait of Guy's parents. They looked out at him from some sepia world, smiling.

"Gee, thanks, dad!" said Guy, turning the beautiful watch in his hand.

"That's an expensive watch, Guy. I saved for it for a long time. I saw it at Mallove's Jewelers about a year ago."

"It's a beauty, Dad."

"Now you take care of that. Don't lose it."

Guy and Sam were sitting side by side on barber chairs in his father's small shop at the Crocker House Hotel on State Street, a few blocks down from the Garde Theater.

Guy went to Harbor School on Montauk Avenue on the banks of the Thames River. Every day after school, Mrs. Levinson, his homeroom teacher, would give him a ride downtown to the Crocker House where Guy would work a few hours. His father thought it was good for the boy to learn the value of hard work. He paid him ten cents for his efforts. They included sweeping up hair, sharpening scissors and razors, filling up the shaving cream containers, stacking towels, and tidying up the magazines and newspapers.

Guy liked the work. The barbershop was cozy. He liked the jazz on the radio, the smell of the Mennen's and Aqua Velva after shaves, Vitalis hair tonic, and Pinaud Clubman Talc. He liked the leather barber chairs, the old brass cash register, the mirrors. He liked to read the newspapers that came in every day, and to sneak a peek at the pulp girlie magazines Sam kept under the towels in the corner.

Guy had tried giving shoeshines, but that enterprise was short lived. Besides being in his father's way and scrambling to follow the chair as it rotated his clients' feet out of his reach, their hair got stuck in the polish. After one customer stood up, looked at his hairy boots and complained, "The kid's made me look like I have monkey feet!" Sam put an end to the shoeshines.

Most of all, Guy liked to listen to the conversations of the patrons his father groomed.

Though Sam had his share of local regulars—Merrill Dreyfus, the lawyer; Phillip Beshany, the Admiral; Charlie Glassenberg, the newspaper guy; Ralph Martin, the pastor; Caleb Bowen, the lighthouse keeper—he also served many customers who were staying at the hotel and just passing through. Guy loved to hear them talk of their lives and work. As his father snipped and spun the chair, Guy heard tales of a photographer on his way to Africa, a steamship captain heading to China, a vaudeville singer readying for his big night at the Garde, an author researching New London's whaling history, a strange foreign man named Tesla who claimed he'd invented something that sounded like a death ray, and even the great Boston pitcher Lefty Grove, in town for a friend's wedding and on his way to a spectacular 20-12 season.

For a half hour, men from near and far came to Sam's shop. Their chatter filled Guy's mind with glimpses of the great world beyond the confining mirrored infinity of the cozy barbershop. The entertainers in particular struck a cord with him. Their tales of theaters and crowds, circuses and trains, and trips on ships to exotic places thrilled the young boy. Sam never knew that the patrons of his shop were sowing the seeds of wanderlust and show biz in his young son. The boy sat and listened, or swept the floor and listened, or cleaned the combs and listened. He was a sponge, soaking up the details of other lives and other worlds.

Sam was a kind man who wanted nothing more than a good life for his family, and a better life for Guy. Not that there was anything wrong with being a barber. But he had dreams of Guy going to college and becoming a doctor, architect or engineer.

Guy was a little kid, skinny as a rail. He had an easygoing nature. He was too small to be athletic, though he had the competitive drive to excel—at something. An only child, he was the vessel for all his parents' love and expectations and dreams. Guy was more clever than smart. He was creative and a dreamer, neither attribute things schools of the day much cared about. And he was a showman. Even at an early age he liked to recite poems for relatives or tell corny jokes. He was not shy. Guy had a streak of gullibility that made him the butt of his classmates' jokes and pranks. The kid trusted people by nature and had yet to learn that not everybody deserves trust.

When he was in fourth grade, some his classmates told him they were all going to meet at Indian Rock in Mitchell's Woods to build a fort. To be included, he had to give Bruce a quarter to help buy supplies. He did. Indian Rock was a big rock in the middle of the woods. Someone had once chalked a big drawing of an Indian's head on it. The chalk washed away but the name endured. Guy arrived. Nobody was there. He waited. And waited. And waited until it got dark, when he at last caught on and trudged home to his anxious parents.

"You can't believe everything people tell you, Guy," Sam had said.

"How do I know when they're lying?" Guy had asked.

Sam had no answer. "Well, it isn't easy," was all he could say.

Sam had become a barber as a young man and taken over the shop when the original proprietor, an Italian man named Tuti, had retired. In slow times, and there were plenty, Guy and Sam would listen to baseball games on the radio or shoot the breeze. It kept them close. Once a summer, Sam, Ruth and Guy took the train to New York, usually in the swelter of early August. They rented a cheap room and had their vacation. Since New London had beautiful beaches, it was the city itself that was the draw.

They wandered around going to museums and to the top of the Empire State Building to gawk at the ever-growing skyline.

They went to Yankee Stadium to watch Babe Ruth, Red Ruffing and Lou Gehrig play. They walked across the Brooklyn Bridge, a journey that always thrilled Guy. They roamed Central Park, looked at the caged animals in the zoo, and bought ice cream from street vendors. They shopped. Sam would always buy Guy's mother a new purse (she was always sure it was, at last, the perfect one) and himself a new set of cuff links. Guy got something, too—usually a memento from Yankee Stadium or a souvenir from a museum.

For the Bordens, life was a comfortable routine. For young Guy, that routine had been fine until the night he saw 1001 Wonders. It had been his first exposure to something so exotic, his first inkling that the world could have such glamour and glitz and … magic! Even the movies he had seen had failed to make such an impression on him. Flat and remote as they were, they did not seem like real worlds. But Blackstone had been there in person, just twenty feet away, creating a world of wonder. It had been a waking dream. When Blackstone invited Guy up on stage to help with the card trick, when Guy had been in the spotlight and the audience had applauded him, something had happened inside him. It was real, no illusion. In corny Hollywood movies they'd say he'd been "bitten by the showbiz bug." Well, indeed, he had been. Bitten and infected.

But the show had ended and with it Guy's moment of glory. Blackstone was a memory, once again just a name on a marquee up the street.

Until he walked into the barbershop.

It was just two days after Guy had seen the show when the door opened and Harry Blackstone walked in. Guy was sweeping the floor and he stopped, stunned. There was the magician himself! Sam Borden had no idea who he was, greeting him in his usual way and seating him in the barber's chair.

"Sam Borden," said Guy's dad as he shook a striped white cloth and laid it carefully over Blackstone. To Guy, it looked like his father was about to perform a magic trick himself. Maybe levitate Blackstone and then make him disappear.

His father asked: "And you are?"

Before Harry Blackstone could answer, Guy blurted out: "He's Harry Blackstone, the World's Greatest Magician!"

Sam and Harry turned to look at Guy.

"That's right," said Blackstone. "I am the magician. As for being the world's greatest, well, I guess that's what the marquee says. I hope I live up to it."

"You the fella who's got the show up at the Garde?" asked Sam.

"That's me," said Blackstone, smiling at Guy. "For three more days. I'm staying here at the hotel."

"What'll it be?"

"I need a trim. Not too short. And a shave."

Sam nodded and stared at the man's hair. Harry Blackstone had a big head of white hair, so much so that it made his head seem way to big for his body. Sam was a little flummoxed. He wasn't sure just how much to cut. He figured he'd go slow and let the man tell him if he wanted more taken off. That was always a good way to work. You cut hair off and you cannot put it back on, though, in a few weeks, it would be back anyway, any errors erased.

"He's amazing, Dad. I told you, you should have seen the show."

"So you saw it, ah …"

"Guy. I'm Guy. Yes, sir, I did. I really liked it. I helped you on stage. Remember?"

"Hmmm, well let me think, maybe I do. A few nights ago, right? With the card trick?"

"Yup. Look: I have the card you gave me." Guy pulled out the Jack of Diamonds and showed it to Blackstone.

"Ah, the Jack of Diamonds. Do you know, Guy, that every card in a deck has meaning?"

"Really?"

"Yes. For example, the Jack of Spades means change. The Six of Diamonds means anxiety, losing control of things. The Two of Hearts means romance is in the air. The Seven of Spades means betrayal. And so on. Now the Jack of Diamonds … that's a good card. It means patience. It means that if you stick with things they may eventually go your way."

"What should I stick with?"

Blackstone laughed. "That's not for me to say. That's up to you. What're you interested in?"

Sam was turning Blackstone left and right to cut his hair and, Guy thought, to discourage this talk. He didn't know why, and he didn't know why his father hadn't said much of anything. He had finished clipping Blackstone's hair and was lathering him up for a shave.

"Magic!" said Guy. "Ever since I saw you, I haven't been able to think about anything else!"

"Well, I'll tell you Guy, magic is ..."

"Mr. Blackstone, if you don't want me to nick you while I'm shaving, you better be quiet."

Blackstone looked at Guy a moment, smiled, and settled back into the chair. It was Sam's time to talk.

"Guy said you put on quite a show, Mr. Blackstone. I'm sure it was something. A nice bit of diversion. Sort of thing to catch a young boy's fancy. But Guy's a practical kid. He's got college in his sights. He really wants to be a doctor or architect. Or maybe an engineer. He's clever and good with his hands. He has a knack for inventing and making things. I'm sure the wonder of your show will fade with time and he'll get his feet back on the ground. Right, Guy?"

"Yes, Dad," he said a bit dejectedly. He looked at the Jack of Diamonds a moment, put it carefully in his pocket, and went back to sweeping up the hair on the floor. He did a turn around the chair Blackstone was in, piling up the great magician's white locks in a tidy pile. To Guy they looked like feathers, maybe from one of the doves Blackstone had used in his act.

Sam finished the shave. The magician stood up and let Sam brush him off with a small broom. Sam powdered him with a little Pinaud's.

"Shave and a haircut: two bits," said Sam, and Blackstone paid him.

"Well," the magician said, "I think I'll grab a bite and a cup of joe at the coffee shop. I do it every day about this time. Wakes me up for the show at night."

He looked over at Guy.

"Be seeing you, Guy," he said with a wink. And then the great Harry Blackstone, star of "1001 Wonders," left the barbershop. The bell on the door tinkled a moment. Sam turned to Guy.

"Magic might be something fun to see, Guy. But as a career, forget it. Maybe one-in-a-million ever makes it like Mr. Blackstone. I suppose that's what he was about to tell you before I told him to be quiet. It's like being a concert musician. It's not enough to like to hear pretty music. To play it, you have to have talent. You have to practice until your hands bleed. And you have to be lucky. A lot of folks waste their lives chasing after things they'll never catch. Or are disappointed in if they do catch them. You have to be practical. Find a profession that will guarantee you work and money. Like me. Folks always need their hair cut."

"What about wonder?" Guy asked.

"Wonder?"

"Yes, what Mr. Blackstone does. He said in his show he gives people the gift of wonder."

Sam smiled. "Wonder's nice in life, Guy. But not essential." He picked up a newspaper and started looking at the sports page, anxious to see how his beloved Red Sox were faring.

Guy thought about what his father had said. Then he turned and looked at himself in the mirror. There were mirrors in front of him and behind him, and he saw himself reflected again and again, growing smaller and smaller, Guy Bordens lined up to infinity.

He lost himself in the illusion, wondering which one of his selves was real.

3

The next day, at about four, Guy told his dad he wanted to meet a friend for a milkshake. Business was slow. Guy had been exceptionally industrious all afternoon, doing all his normal chores and then some. There was nothing much for him to do, no ball game on the radio to listen to. Skipping out for a shake seemed reasonable.

"Okay, Guy. Don't be too long."

"I won't, dad."

Guy left the barbershop, walked around the corner, through a side door, and into the Crocker House coffee shop. He was anxious. He hoped Mr. Blackstone would be there. He would be leaving town the day after tomorrow, and this might be Guy's only chance to see him again.

Blackstone was there, hunched over a cup of coffee, reading a newspaper. He looked up when Guy walked in and smiled. He did not seem surprised to see the boy.

"Would you care to join me, Guy?" he asked.

"Yes, sir," said Guy and sat down in Blackstone's booth.

"Does your father know you are here?"

"Not exactly. I told him I was going to meet a friend for a milkshake."

"I see," said Blackstone and motioned for a waitress. She came over.

"A milkshake for my friend," said Blackstone.

"More coffee for you?" she asked.

"No, thanks. Don't want my hands to shake." He winked at Guy. "A shake with a friend, just like you said. I don't like to promote lying."

Blackstone put the newspaper down. Guy peered at it. *Variety*. Seeing Guy's interest, Blackstone commented: "*Variety* is a trade newspaper about show business. I like to keep track of what the competition is doing. Who's playing where, the gossip—that kind of thing."

"Mr. Blackstone, my dad said the life of a performer is really hard. He said you have to practice until your hands bleed and you need luck, and that hardly anybody ever makes it big to have their name on a marquee like you do."

"All true," said Blackstone. "Except maybe the hands bleeding part. That might be a bit of an exaggeration. But it does take a lot of hard work and practice. And luck. That's true. Sometimes, the only difference between a fella with his name in lights and one you've never heard of is a bit of luck. A twist of fate. They say you make your own luck, Guy, but sometimes luck makes you."

Out of the spotlight, sitting across the table from him, Blackstone just seemed like a regular man. Yet Guy knew he was the greatest in the world, so he listened attentively to everything Blackstone had to say.

"Guy, magic is like anything really: no matter how good you get, you can always get better. You have to keep working hard and practicing."

Guy nodded.

The waitress arrived with Guy's milkshake.

"Mr. Blackstone?"

"Yes?"

"How did you do that trick where you had that lady choose a card and it was the only one turned backwards?"

"You work on making that disappear, Guy, and I'll tell you a little bit more about magic, okay?"

"Sure." Guy unwrapped his straw and stuck it in the shake and began to suck it down as Blackstone spoke.

"Now that trick, Guy, used what we call Magician's Choice."

"What's that?"

"Well, Magician's Choice is when a magician wants a certain result, but he wants to make you believe that getting to it is all your idea. So he cleverly interprets your choices along the way to lead you to his goal. You think it's your choice, but it's not. It's the *magician's* choice. It's the basis for a lot of magic tricks. The magician gives you the illusion of free choice when, in fact, you have no choice at all."

"It sounds complicated."

"Yes and no, Guy. It takes a while to learn how to do it well so it's not obvious. It's all in the words you use and when you use them. You have to think quickly. It's kind of a planned improvisation."

"What's improve-a-vization?" asked Guy.

Blackstone smiled. "Same as winging it."

"Oh."

Blackstone reached into his pocket and took out a pen. He tore off a piece of his paper napkin and wrote something on it, then folded it. He put the little packet in front of Guy.

"Guy, I'm going to name four cards in the suit of spades. Let's see ... how about the Two, Ten, Jack and King. Now I want you to select two."

"The Two and the Jack," said Guy.

"Good choices. Those will be yours. Mine are the Ten and the King. Now select one of mine, please."

"Hmmm. The King."

"The King of Spades. Do you want to change to the Ten or stay with the King. It's your choice, Guy."

"Okay, I'll change to the Ten."

"Fine. Now where are we, Guy? We have arrived at the Ten of Spades, and you have made all the choices along the way, correct?"

"Yup."

"Would you kindly open that little packet of paper in front of you?"

Guy unfolded the bit of napkin. Written on it: "You will pick the Ten of Spades."

Guy looked up at Blackstone with a surprised smile.

"How'd you know?"

Now it was Blackstone's turn to smile. "Magician's Choice, Guy. A crude example, I'm afraid."

"But wasn't I choosing the cards?"

"Yes and no, Guy. You made choices, but what I *chose* to do with your choices led to the outcome I wanted, the Ten of Spades. The Magician's Choice is a powerful tool Guy. You stick with magic and you'll learn all about it and its variations."

Guy didn't really understand how Magician's Choice worked. It sounded complicated. "I think I like tricks with things better."

Blackstone laughed. "Fair enough. But if you ever want to learn about it, read this book." He scribbled the title on another piece of napkin. "Meanwhile, how about I teach you something more visual, then? Something with a single coin?"

Guy's eyes widened and he smiled.

"Sure!"

Blackstone reached into his pocket and pulled out a shiny 1904 Morgan silver dollar. He turned it over in his hand a few times. Then, he opened his left palm, slowly put the coin in it, then curled his fingers into a fist as he withdrew his empty right fingers.

Guy watched closely, focusing on Blackstone's hands with intense scrutiny. This is called "burning" in the parlance of magic. And when someone is burning a magician's hands, it is usually the hardest—and worst—time to do a secret move or "sleight."

Blackstone gestured to his left hand with his right, and Guy caught a glimpse of his empty right palm. Nothing there. Nothing tricky yet.

"Now watch, Guy," said Blackstone. He gently blew on his left fist, and slowly, very slowly, uncurled his fingers.

His hand was empty. The coin was gone!

Guy gasped.

Blackstone held both hands up, backs to Guy, fingers spread. And then he slowly turned them around to show his palms empty.

"Where did the coin go?" he asked.

Blackstone sat back in the booth and relaxed. He smiled, then leaned forward and reached over to the basket of rolls at the edge of the table. He picked it up.

"Pick one, Guy."

Guy pointed to a roll.

"Are you sure?"

"Yes, sir."

"Fine," said Blackstone. He picked up the roll and slowly broke the roll so that it opened up, then reached in with his fingers and started to pull something out.

"Here, I'll let you do it," he said, handing Guy the roll.

Guy saw it immediately. The edge of a coin. He pulled it out. It was the 1904 Morgan Dollar.

Guy was dumbstruck. Something utterly impossible had happened, right in front of his eyes. Just a few feet away. He had watched closely. He never saw anything remotely odd, yet the coin had vanished from Blackstone's hand and appeared inside a roll!

"Would you like to learn how to do that, Guy?"

"You mean I could do that?"

"Certainly, Guy. It's not that hard," he paused a moment. "No, that's not quite true. The basics of the trick are simple, like most tricks. It's pretty easy to do. But to do it well—*that's* hard."

Guy nodded.

"So if I showed you, Guy, you have to promise me you will practice it and practice it a lot, and that you won't show it to anybody until you can do it perfectly. Agreed?"

"Yes, sir!"

"Fine. What I showed you was a combination of two moves, or "sleights." The first is fiendishly effective. It's called the Retention Vanish."

"What's that?" asked Guy.

"It's when you don't really put the coin in the hand, you *retain* it in the hand that's putting it in the other hand."

"And nobody sees it?"

"You didn't. Why? Well, the Retention Vanish relies on another type of retention: the lingering image on the retina of the eye of that shiny coin on the palm. You know, like the after-image you get if you look at the sun or a flash bulb or lightning."

"Yeah, you still see it even when it's gone."

"Exactly. Now when you do it with a shiny coin, it's a timing thing, and if you time it right, it's a completely convincing illusion. People will swear they see the coin in your palm because, in a way, they do. Just not quite as long as they *think* they do."

As he was explaining this, Blackstone was doing the Retention Vanish over and over, and though Guy knew exactly what was happening, his eyes told him differently. Blackstone was right. He would swear that the coin was still in his left hand inside his curled fingers. No matter how he burned the magician's hands, the illusion held.

It was the most beautiful thing Guy had ever seen.

"I'll break the trick down into two parts, Guy. Making the coin vanish, then making it appear inside the roll. Now, let's start with the Retention Vanish."

It took a few minutes. Blackstone showed Guy the sleight, doing it in slow motion, showing him exactly how to hold the coin, move his fingers, get the timing down so the illusion worked.

Once Blackstone had explained the mechanics of the Retention Vanish, Guy could not believe something so simple could be so wondrous.

Blackstone smiled and explained.

"Even the simplest trick can be a miracle, Guy, if you present it well. Slow down, draw it out, make it clear, make it magical. Just before you reveal the magic has happened, pause. Build the suspense. Then show that something impossible has happened and hold that moment so there is no doubt you have created a miracle. It's that simple." He paused a moment. "And it's that difficult."

Blackstone put the shiny coin on the table.

"Want to give it a try, Guy?"

"Okay." Nervously he picked up the dollar. It seemed big in his hands. He tried to do what Blackstone had done but the coin dropped onto the table with a clatter.

"They don't like to be dropped, Guy," said Blackstone with a smile. "Try again. Relax. Don't hold the coin in such a death grip. Be gentle. Soft hands, Guy."

Guy tried again. He didn't drop the coin, but his handling was clumsy, his timing was way off and there was no illusion.

"No. You rushed it. I saw the flash of the coin, but not where I should see it. Try it again, Guy."

Guy did. A little better.

"Again."

Guy did the vanish again. A little better.

"The Retention Vanish is probably the most beautiful vanish of a coin there is, Guy, but it's a funny sleight. Most of the time, you try to direct someone's attention away from what you are doing when you do your move. You look at them so they will return your gaze, and when they are distracted, *that's* when you do the sleight. We call that misdirection.

"The Retention Vanish is different. You invite people to watch you closely. That makes it harder. They are burning your hands with their eyes. If you don't do it well, you're dead. They'll catch you every time. No magic.

"But if you do it well, really well, it's a miracle. And it's a miracle *because* they are watching so intently that the afterimage of the shiny coin is etched on the retina, making the sleight work."

Guy did the sleight a few more times, each time a little slower and a little better. He was getting a feel for the timing.

"Not bad, Guy. Don't be afraid to do it slowly. That's what makes it work. You have good hands. A knack for this stuff. You'll get it."

Guy did the Retention Vanish a few more times. He was still tentative and clumsy, but he had the basics down.

"Now let me tell you about the roll part," Blackstone said. "After you've made the coin vanish, the spectators are in limbo. They have one question in their minds: where did it go? So you move on to the next phase and give them the answer. You make the coin appear inside the roll. You have just performed two small miracles building on one another. That's called a routine, and that's what makes magic.

"How do I get it to appear inside the roll?"

"That's pretty simple, too, Guy. But it takes a little acting. Here, I'll explain it."

Blackstone went through the second part of the trick, Guy watching him like a hawk. He explained how the two phases of the routine fit together, how gestures and eye contact created misdirection, and the moves needed to get the coin to appear in the roll. Though in performance it appeared simple, it was in reality more complex, more nuanced than Guy had imagined.

Blackstone noticed that as he explained the second part to Guy, Guy was practicing the Retention Vanish over and over. He wasn't even aware that he was doing it. The kid was a natural.

Blackstone explained how you could have something concealed in your hand but imply it was empty by how you positioned your fingers and casually gave the spectator a glimpse of your palm. He called this a "subtlety."

"Are there names for everything?"

"Pretty much so, Guy. All the arts have their names for things. In magic, for things like coins, we have the Classic Palm, the Finger Palm, the Fingertip Rest, the French Drop, the Retention Vanish, the Shuttle Pass, the Thumb Clip and the Back Clip. Just to name a few. You learn them as you need them. And magicians are always inventing new sleights."

"Let me try the roll part," said Guy.

Blackstone nodded.

Guy again did the retention vanish, then grabbed another roll. As he broke it open, the coin again dropped to the table. Blackstone frowned.

"I know, I know," said Guy. "They don't like to be dropped!"

Blackstone smiled. "Try it again."

Guy did, and managed to complete the trick. He did it poorly, obviously, but he did it.

"Do that a few thousand times, Guy, and you'll have it down."

"A few thousand times! Boy, that's a lot of rolls!"

"There are no shortcuts to skill, Guy. You have to practice and practice and practice to master even the simplest sleight."

"Until my hands bleed!"

Blackstone laughed.

"Not quite. You have to practice until the sleight becomes completely natural. Until what you do when you are doing the trick looks the same as when you are doing it without any moves."

"What about the tricks you do on stage Mr. Blackstone. Are they hard?"

"In their way. But it's different. It's a performance for hundreds, maybe thousands of people. It's got to play big. But truth be told, it's a lot easier to strut and pose up there with a bunch of big colorful props and animals and pretty girls than to fool somebody two feet away. To me, the mark of a real magician, a real artist, is how he does close-up.

"You should see somebody like Max Malini, Al Baker, Ross Bertram or Dai Vernon—the masters of sleight of hand, of close-up. You can sit across the table from them, and they will make your jaw drop with what they can do with cards and coins and some balls and little cups. Theirs is a ballet of the hands, miracles done on the stage of a tabletop.

"Magic like that is something, Guy. The audience is so close they can feel your breath, see the slightest tremor in your hand or the nervous sweat on your brow. When you do close-up there's no place to hide. No smoke. No mirrors. No pretty girls to distract attention. Just your hands and your skill and your nerve."

"Why do you do a big stage show, Mr. Blackstone?"

"Well, Guy, while close-up is all about intimate miracles, a stage show is all about theater. About glamour. 1001 Wonders. Think about it! That's a big promise. My big show is all about creating a whole fantasy world in front of a thousand people. There's nothing like hearing their gasps, or feeling the weight of their stunned silence. And, of course, the applause. I love the sound of their applause rolling like thunder through the theater, washing over me. That's a thrill. You can't get that sitting at a table with five people."

Blackstone sat back.

"How did you happen to come to my show, Guy?"

"My mom took me. It was a birthday present. I turn thirteen next week. My dad gave me a pocket watch. It has a picture of mom and dad inside."

"Tell me, Guy … were you thrilled when you saw my show?"

"You bet! It was the most amazing thing I've ever seen. Better than a movie."

"Why?"

Guy thought a moment. "Because you were right there doing it, for real. And because I got to be in the show."

"Oh yes. The sword stab. I almost forgot. You liked being up there in the spotlight?"

"Sure. Wouldn't everybody?"

"Not necessarily, Guy. Some people would be scared to death. As I recall, you had fun."

"I sure did. I still have the card."

"Yes, you showed it to me yesterday. The Jack of Diamonds. Like I told you, it signifies patience. So important. You need to take your time in life. Stick with things. See how they unfold. If you do, lots of times, things will work out for you. Who knows … maybe someday, your name will be on a marquee."

"Did you always want to be a magician, Mr. Blackstone?"

"From pretty early on. When I was eight, I got a magic trick for my birthday. I became fascinated with magic and started to play with it. Then, when I was your age, I saw the world's greatest magician, Harry Kellar, perform. Ever heard of him?"

"Nope."

Blackstone smiled, but there was little humor in it.

"Well, *he* was once the greatest magician in the world. I saw him at McVickar's Theater, in Chicago. He had a big stage show. I was amazed at what he did. And I knew that's what I wanted to be: a great magician with a big stage show. I fell in love with magic and devoted myself to it. Love can take you far, my boy. It can break your heart, but it can also make it soar."

"Do you think that will happen to me?"

"It might, Guy. You never know what destiny awaits you."

Guy looked up at the clock.

"Oh boy! I gotta get back to my dad! Thanks for the milkshake, Mr. Blackstone."

"You're very welcome Guy. I hope we meet again." Guy got up to leave. "One more thing, Guy."

"Yes?"

"Here, take this Morgan dollar. You practice the Retention Vanish with it. Your hands are a little small, but that's fine. Practice it with a big coin and you'll be a master with a small one."

Guy took the Morgan. It was a beautiful coin.

"Keep that shiny. It'll work better that way. Don't spend it or lose it, Guy. Make that your magic coin."

"Yes, sir, Mr. Blackstone. Thanks!"

And with that, Guy scurried out of the coffee shop.

Blackstone thought about the boy. The lure and love of magic ... from Kellar to Blackstone to Borden? Maybe it was fated. Maybe Guy Borden was destined to be the next "world's greatest magician." Or at least a good one. Harry had a feeling he might. He'd just bet a dollar on it.

4

Guy practiced the Retention Vanish with the Morgan silver dollar a lot. He'd do it a few dozen times in front of the mirror in his bedroom. He'd do it in his lap on the bus to school or in front of one of the mirrors in the barbershop. It was, indeed, hard to do with his small hands, but he kept at it. He was determined to perfect it, and he was determined not to show it to anybody until he had done so. He had promised Blackstone.

Sometimes, he'd do the Vanish and, as he watched himself in the mirror, surprise himself with it. Done right, it fooled the eye and the mind followed.

After a while, he moved on to combine the vanish with making the coin reappear in a roll. At dinner, he never ate his roll, and always gathered any left in the bread basket at the end of the meal.

"Guy, don't you leave those lying around your room! You'll attract mice!"

When he went shopping with his mother, he'd bug her to buy him a bag of dinner rolls.

"What on earth are you doing with all these rolls, Guy?" Ruth asked one time in exasperation as he loaded an extra bag into the shopping cart.

"A trick, mom. I told you. I'm trying to perfect a new magic trick and I need rolls to do it."

So she bought rolls. Lots of rolls. Bags of rolls. And Guy practiced breaking them open so the coin could be seen inside or, sometimes, dropped out dramatically. He even practiced with the halves of rolls. When he was done, when the bread was broken and ragged, he tossed it out the window for the birds and squirrels. His father noted one day at breakfast as a well-fed squirrel lumbered across a branch: "We have fat squirrels."

Many young boys, when they are eight or ten or twelve, discover magic. Especially those who are not particularly athletic, who want a little attention, who want to be special. They dabble with it as a hobby, learning a few tricks, impressing their friends. But then they leave it behind, a passing fancy.

For a few, the hobby endures. They practice and become better at their sleight of hand, their storytelling, their command of wonder. They seek out more difficult tricks. Magic may be a lifelong hobby, even a way to earn a little extra money doing shows at parties.

For those with the passion and dedication, magic may become a profession. An elite few find fame and fortune. They may even become the world's greatest magician. For a while. They cannot work their magic on the sad reality that fame is fleeting. It can vanish as quickly as one of their rabbits.

A few weeks after Blackstone's 1001 Wonders show, a box arrived in the mail for Guy. When he opened it, there was another box inside, about the size of a shirt box. It was sturdy cardboard, bright red, with a drawing of a somewhat scary looking magician on the cover. "Gilbert's Mysto Magic Set" read the big letters. Below them: "Complete Magician's Show Including Poster and Makeup." And below that, smaller still: "Developed at the Gilbert Hall of Science. New Haven, Connecticut."

A small envelope was taped to the corner of the lid. Guy opened it. Inside was a handwritten note:

"Guy: Happy Birthday. I thought you might find this set of interest. Remember, study the tricks carefully. Practice, practice, practice! Don't perform a trick until you are sure you have mastered it, and do it all with passion. Remember the Jack of Diamonds: Patience. All will come to he who has patience. I hope our paths may cross again. Yours in magic, Harry Blackstone."

"Wow!" exclaimed Guy.

He opened the Mysto magic set. And gasped. Inside was an assortment of balls, rings, cards, coins, a wand, some pamphlets and a few other things he could not identify. It was a box of wonder. Maybe not 1001, but wonders aplenty.

Watching Guy as he looked through the box, Ruth marveled at how her gift of Blackstone's show at the Garde had led to Guy helping him on stage, which had led to this gift of a magic set. Life was unpredictable. Full of surprises.

"It was awfully nice of Mr. Blackstone to send you that," she said. "I guess you made an impression on him. And, I think, he on you."

She looked at Guy. She knew the other kids teased him because he was small. Maybe magic would give him some confidence, something special that would impress the other kids. No harm in letting him try.

"Guy, you have to promise me you won't fool around with any of this until you've finished your homework, okay?"

"Sure, mom."

"I mean it, Guy. I don't mind you learning about magic, but your studies come first."

"I know. I promise."

"As for your father, well, I'll tell him it's just a hobby and will do you some good."

"How so?"

She thought a moment, not knowing much about magic.

"I think it will teach you how to practice something. I don't think you can become very good at magic unless you practice a lot. Like the piano. You'll have to be patient if you want to be any good."

"That's what Mr. Blackstone said. To be patient. And to practice a lot."

"Well, you do that. Maybe you can even do a show for your cousin Rosalie's birthday."

"Yeah, maybe." That sounded pretty awful. But then, on second thought, maybe not so bad. He took the Mysto set to his room. He carefully piled up his books and homework papers, put them on his bed, and put the magic set on his desk.

He stared at the box. He tried to imagine himself the magician on the cover in top hat and tails, wielding a wand like a sword of mystery. He opened the box slowly, reverently. Again he took in the fascinating, exotic objects arrayed across the inside of the lid and nestled into custom-made holders in the bottom. These were the props with which he would create wonder.

The set included a letter from Mr. Gilbert himself. In it, he wrote:

"I think it will interest my boy friends to know that magic has been a hobby of mine all my life. Herrman the Great asked me up on the stage at one of his performances when I was a small boy. From then on I began to practice magic tricks, later became a professional magician and finally started the Mysto Manufactoring Company."

He went on to talk about various facets of magic and gave advice, including: *"Practice, practice, practice."*

The inside of the lid had five packets of cards visible in little holders, centered on a drawing of a smiling Joker. Below it three holders contained pamphlets. One was Gilbert Knots & Splices: With Rope Tying Tricks of Famous Magicians. Another was Handkerchief Tricks. Guy wondered if he would learn how to make a hanky dance as Blackstone had done. The final was the Mysto Magic Instruction Book.

He took out the Mysto pamphlet. The cover depicted a red devil and three imp minions rapturously looking at a cauldron. From it a cloud of smoke curled up and became a magician in top hat and tails holding a wand in one hand and a rabbit by the ears in the other. He opened to the first page. It read: "The Wonderful Secrets of Magic." The next page got down to business.

"Advice to Young Entertainers!"

"Hello boys! Here's fun. With your set of Gilbert's Mysto Magic Tricks you can do some of the very same tricks you have seen done by magicians on the stage. If you have never worked any magic tricks before, you have no idea of the fun you can have. The directions in this Manual of Instruction will enable you to give a really fine show, starting with the simplest trick, and ending with a splendid big illusion such as is used by professionals. Appearing before audiences will give you self-confidence which, when you grow up, will stand you in good stead in talking at big business meetings. When a boy, Mr. Gilbert

learned to do magic tricks, and the practice he got talking to audiences knocked all the bashfulness out of him."

The rest of the instruction book comprised just two pages, with a paragraph about each of the main things to be learned: "What Magic Is." (A brief history). "About Practice." (No mention of bleeding hands) "Misdirection." "Something to be Remembered." "If Something Goes Wrong." (It will happen. They will laugh. Stay cool.) "Patter."

After these brief discussions of the theoretical underpinnings of magic, the rest of the instruction book explained, with text and illustrations, how to do each of the tricks in the set. These included the Multiplying Billiard Balls (which were actually the size of large marbles), the Vanishing Handkerchief, the Cups and Balls, the Vanishing Rabbit, the Latest Four Ace Trick, the Mysterious Linking Rings (were there any other type?), the Ball and Vase Trick, and the Mysto Thumb Tip.

He set the instructions aside for the moment. He wanted to handle the props. They were not fancy. Most were made of plastic or tin or wood. No matter. To Guy, they were magnificent. He played with the cups and balls, the paddles and rings, cards and tin thumb tip. They represented so much potential. He savored the moment, and indeed, it would be a memory that would last him a lifetime.

After he had examined all the props, Guy read through the book again, each trick in hand, familiarizing himself with the workings of the effects. Some were a bit of a disappointment: there seemed so little to them. Others amazed him with their cleverness. They played with assumptions and perceptions to create effects that seemed impossible. Some of the best tricks were based on the simplest of principles.

Guy did not fully understand yet that the prop was merely a small portion of a trick. True magic was a blend of the mechanical effect—the prop—the dexterity of the performer, and his ability to create a mystery through presentation. The Mysto magic set provided the props. Practice would create the dexterity. But only time and experience could create true wonder.

Guy read on. A section on patter—what a magician says—concluded that it could be both essential and negligible. Guy recalled how so much of Blackstone's show had been done to music only. The great magician had said nothing. Gesture and timing had created mystery. When Blackstone had spoken, his stories had been enchanting, spellbinding. Guy supposed it all depended on the trick.

Guy did a few of the tricks silently, watching himself in the mirror. For a few others, he whispered improvised stories. He started with a classic: the Ball and Vase.

"This is an ancient vase passed on to me by mystics from the East." Somehow, though, the little plastic vase didn't look ancient.

Another tack: "This strange little vase was given to me by a mysterious man in China ..." Except, Guy thought, nobody would believe he'd been to China. Hmmm. Not so easy.

"This vase, just a little plastic container holding a ball, has some strange and wonderful properties ..." Yes, better. Talk about the magic, not how he came to have the vase.

He played with the Ball and Vase for half an hour, mumbling his patter, developing and revising his story, practicing the moves and routine, turning a puzzle into a bit of wonder.

Guy put the trick back and turned his attention to the poster that had been included in the magic set. It was about 10 by 20 inches. It had a blank box to put in his name, followed by the text:

IN HIS NEW AND STARTLING EXHIBITION
OF GILBERT'S MYSTO MAGIC

Below that was a circle with a devilish figure, and below that more text:

AN INTERESTING AND FASCINATING
ENTERTAINMENT FOR YOUNG AND OLD
MYSTIFYING ILLUSIONS, SLEIGHT-OF-HAND
CARD TRICKS, ETC.

PREMIER ACTS OF THE WORLD'S FAMOUS MAGICIAN
A REGULAR CARNIVAL OF FUN
WIZARDRY, LEGERDEMAIN,
AND PRESTIDIGITATION!
COME AND BRING YOUR FRIENDS!

Below the final line was another empty box to write in the location and date of the big show.

Guy liked the idea of a carnival. It sounded exotic. He could not pronounce and did not know what "legerdemain and prestidigitation" meant, so he got down his dictionary (seldom used for his homework) and looked them up.

legerdemain, *noun*
skillful use of one's hands when performing conjuring tricks.
• *deception; trickery.*
ORIGIN late Middle English: from French léger de main 'dexterous,' literally 'light of hand.'

prestidigitation, *noun formal*
magic tricks performed as entertainment.
DERIVATIVES
prestidigitator | - *noun*
ORIGIN mid 19th cent.: from French, from preste 'nimble' + Latin digitus 'finger' + -ation.

The words were interesting and impressive sounding, and he had learned a little history, too. His mother would be happy. Learning magic was as good as homework. Maybe better.

He thrilled to the broadside. He especially liked the line about the "premier acts of the world's famous magician." That sounded a lot like Blackstone's billing. Guy opened his bedroom door and carefully taped the poster to it. He stood back and admired it.

It was his first marquee. It didn't light up, and nobody would see it except his folks, but there it was in black and white, a banner proclaiming that behind this door was a real magician, soon to be world famous!

The Mysto magic set would become one of Guy's most treasured possessions, right up there with the gold pocket watch his dad had given him. The watch was practical and sentimental. The magic set fanciful and imaginative.

Guy went to bed that night and dreamt of himself in top hat and tails, wielding a wand, making billiard balls and silver rings, playing cards and hankies do his bidding. In his sleep, the wind outside rustling the leaves transformed into the applause of an audience watching the "Premier Acts of the World's Famous Magician," also known as "Guy Borden."

5

The years passed. Guy went to school, where he excelled in geometry and shop, building all sorts of intriguing things. He remained too small to do much with sports, and was awkward around girls. Guy practiced his magic, especially the Retention Vanish and reappearance. He wowed his classmates with tricks from his Mysto set. He got invited to a lot of birthday parties where he would do a few tricks.

He found the book Blackstone had recommended, and read up on Magician's Choice. As he grew to understand it, he marveled at its cleverness. Giving the illusion of free choice while, in fact, leading someone to a desired outcome was a masterful mix of psychology, verbal skills, and timing. He wondered if anyone but magicians did it.

In the summers, he worked at the barbershop, where the walls of mirrors were excellent for practicing magic when things were slow. Occasionally he'd perform a trick for a patron, sometimes earning a tip. His father watched, and though fascinated by Guy's dexterity and perplexed by the tricks, he still considered magic a trivial pursuit. He never wavered in his desire to see Guy go to college and become an engineer or an architect. That was his dream. A kid with hands as dextrous as Guy's should put them to good use. And magic was not good use. He didn't talk to Guy about it much, only saying, "You've got a surgeon's hands, son." Guy would nod and continue practicing his sleight of hand.

Guy's interest in magic grew. He read *Hoffman's Modern Magic* and other books. The deeper he got into the art, the more it fascinated him. It had such a colorful, rich history. While magic might be, on one level, trivial, on another it spoke to life's deepest desires and mysteries. Who would not want to float like a feather? Pluck money out of thin air? Be resurrected after vanishing in a flash of fire? Magic, Guy was discovering, was not just disbelief. It was also, like religion, belief.

Sometimes, his mother would walk by his room and see him practicing in front of the mirror, whispering his patter, intently watching his reflection. She would stand and watch him as he did the one thing that really seemed to make him happy in life. Magic. She wondered if he was wasting his time, or building the foundation for his future. Time would tell.

While most of his classmates dreamed of going to New York to see the Yankees play, Guy dreamed of going to Martinka's and Tannen's, Manhattan's two pre-eminent magic stores. He had a catalogue from Tannen's, and had spent countless hours studying the drawings and descriptions of the tricks. He knew these far better than geography or mathematics.

His dream was realized when Guy was sixteen. The family took a trip to New York. They took in some of their old favorites—the Museum of Natural History, Broadway and the Brooklyn Bridge. When Ruth said she wanted to do some shopping, Guy pounced on the opportunity. He suggested he could go off to Tannen's magic store. He wanted to go alone, to venture down the rabbit hole without impatient parents along for the journey. He convinced his folks he'd be okay and promised to take a taxi back to the hotel.

They finally agreed.

So Guy made his way to 45th Street where a small doorway offered a register of business names. He found Tannen's on the 13th floor, which was actually the 12th floor. Superstition, Guy supposed. Or maybe just the first of Tannen's illusions.

Guy rode the elevator in breathless anticipation. He had never been to a magic shop, and he was beyond excited. The ascent was slow. The suspense built. Finally, with a jolt, the old elevator stopped. No explorer ever felt a greater thrill of discovery as did Guy when the door opened and he found himself right inside the store. The elevator had taken him from the gritty streets of New York to a magical world of wonder.

He blinked in awe. The place was small and cluttered. Glass cases and shelves were full of boxes, decks of cards, bouquets of feather flowers, bottles, shiny rings, coins, wands, fake birds, colorful silks, devil heads, gleaming brass pans and canisters, and countless other props, big and small, many colorfully painted with top hats or rabbits or Chinese characters.

"Wow!"

Being at Tannen's was like being inside a life-sized Mysto magic set.

That magic set was ostensibly a benign gift for a young boy. But it was really the start of a lifelong addiction to props. Props were the agents of wonder, and no one really interested in magic could ever get enough of them. More props meant more magic. The *next* trick was the *ultimate* trick, the one that would turn the garden-variety magician into a miracle worker. This was seldom true, but the addicted magician was helpless to resist the temptations of tricks. And Tannen's was a devil's lair of temptation.

For a delightful afternoon, Guy watched trick after trick demonstrated. A few older men stopped in, and Guy thought he even recognized one. After bantering with Lou Tannen a moment, they ignored the display cases and shelves and went behind some curtains into a back room. Guy heard talking and laughter and arguments and the riffle of cards and clink of coins. Lennie, one of the men who demonstrated tricks at the store, said it was the "inner sanctum," a place where the pros gathered, a place where few were ever allowed. It thrilled Guy to think some famous magicians might be so close.

Guy bought a few carefully selected tricks, then headed back to the hotel. For the rest of the weekend, he played with his new props and relived his hours at Tannen's.

Slowly, his repertoire grew. He still had the Mysto magic set, supplemented by other tricks he'd acquired. Some he performed. Others he discarded, disappointed by them. One was the Mummy Asrah, a trick he mail-ordered from Tannen's. The drawing said it was a "real beauty for effect and mystery" and "cleverly combined two methods to throw off those who know."

He wasn't so sure.

The Mummy Asrah, for all the mystery and charm in the ad, was a lot more mundane in reality. It was hard to do and not very convincing: it looked like something vaguely mummy shaped under a cloth dangling in midair from his hand. If the light wasn't perfect, the black thread from which the cloth hung was obvious. Guy thought that maybe it was a matter of practice and finesse. He remembered what Blackstone had told him about patience and the meaning of the Jack of Diamonds (which he still had, tucked into a corner of his mirror). Guy stuck with the Mummy Asrah for months. But in his hands it never got beyond "dangling" to "floating."

Guy had discovered one of the great truths of magic. The ads for tricks, and the glowing descriptions by dealers, painted a picture of wonder and mystery that was not always within reach once the trick was in hand. The charming drawings, done by masters like Ed Mishell, portrayed tricks in a way that fired the imagination and seduced the magician. They played to his addiction to props. The ads for magic tricks promised "mystery and wonder and amazement." They boasted, "You won't believe your eyes." Or, as in the case of the Mummy Asrah, "a real beauty for effect and mystery." But advertising is advertising. It is designed to sell. Performance is not guaranteed.

The Mummy Asrah was one of the great disappointments of Guy's young life. He had dreamt of a person swathed in cloth floating above the stage—just as he'd seen it in Blackstone's show. Instead, he got a crappy balsa-wood mummy and a cloth with a string. He felt betrayed.

Guy put the Mummy Asrah in a shoebox in his bedroom closet. It joined other miracles that had fallen short of their promise. All magicians have a box or a drawer where they discard tricks—a graveyard of shattered dreams. But as bad as the tricks may be, magicians cannot bear to throw them away. Perhaps they hope that left alone in the dark, and given time, the tricks will emerge someday and live up their promise of wonder. One of the greatest illusions all magicians perform is the triumph of hope over disappointment. Guy thought that maybe someday he would master the Mummy Asrah. So he kept it.

In general, the years between 1935 and 1941 were fairly uneventful for Guy. He kept up with his magic. He would practice it endlessly in his room. Sometimes he would wander into the living room while his folks were reading or listening on the radio to The Shadow, Jack Benny, Benny Goodman or Orson Welles and his Mercury Theater on the Air.

"Wanna see a new trick?" he'd ask. His dad would put down the newspaper or the National Geographic magazine, and Guy would show them the trick, usually stumping them completely. Sam would sometimes spot a sloppy move and tell Guy, perhaps thinking it might discourage him, but it had the opposite effect: it just made Guy practice more.

Guy would head back to his room.

"You know, Sam, he's quite good," his mother would often say, to which Sam would invariably reply: "Yes, but he can't earn a living making money disappear."

When Sam's brother Louie visited, Guy was thrilled because Louie loved magic tricks, or "magics" as he called them.

"Show me some magics," Louie would say, chomping on his cigar. And Guy would.

A few times, Guy gave little shows when relatives visited. He would proudly move the sign that came with the Mysto magic set down to the living room and paste on a note card with the day's date. His shows were a mix of tricks from the magic set and ones he'd bought. He never ceased to baffle the relatives, one of whom paid him the great compliment of saying to his father: "He's good enough to perform on Broadway." Guy floated through the rest of the day, dreaming of his name in lights.

One day, Mrs. Levinson, his old grade-school teacher, called and asked Guy what he'd charge to do a show at her son's bar mitzvah.

Guy was stunned. He had never charged for a show and had no idea he could. He stammered "ten dollars" and Mrs. Levinson agreed. "It's in a month, on May 14th. Is that okay?"

Okay? Guy was thrilled.

Then Guy was terrified.

To be paid for a show meant he had to be good. Really good. He wasn't sure he was up to it.

May 14 loomed. Guy practiced his tricks a lot. He quickly realized that small coin and card tricks might not be so good for fifty kids. So he took some of his allowance and sent in an order to Tannen's for a couple of bigger tricks, which included the Mystery Spots Canister, The Ghost Rise Chest, and the Square Circle Production Cabinet. He added in some things that he could produce from the production cabinet, stuff that looked real but squished small: foam rubber bananas, a long link of hot dogs, and a slice of watermelon. He added some bright silk scarves, a feather bouquet, and a fake rabbit that had a big spring inside to give it "incredible lifelike action."

His total bill was $16. So, he realized, even if he pulled the show off, he would lose money. But, he reasoned, he would have some really nifty props!

As he waited for his new tricks, Guy looked at the pictures in the catalog over and over, trying to imagine himself the elegant magician in tails, doing tricks, assisted by a scantily clad girl with a big chest, just like in the drawings. Tails!? He didn't have tails! Did he need them to perform the tricks? He hadn't thought of that. He hoped not. Well, he wouldn't know until he got them and read the instructions. And a girl? He knew a few, sure, but they didn't look or dress anything like the ones in the drawings. Guy began to realize that there was a big difference between "doing tricks" and performing a "regular carnival of fun."

He had a vivid dream about his bar mitzvah show. In it, he arrived at the Levinson house, where a giant marquee illuminated their whole front lawn. Huge black letters proclaimed "Guy Borden, Mitzvah Maestro." Inside, the Levinson living room was not a cozy place with a wooden RCA radio and lumpy couches, it was a huge theater. And there weren't just fifty kids, there were five hundred. There was an orchestra, too, and Regina, a girl he had a crush on, now with a big chest, dressed in a skimpy sequined outfit. In his dream, this magic show business was looking pretty good.

In his dream.

But upon waking, he was back in his little room, and there were no gaudy tricks, no marquee, no slinky assistant—just his Mysto magic set and a box of tricks.

He waited in agony. Three days. Four days. Where was the postal truck with his package? At school, his mind drifted as he imagined the delivery truck rumbling its way north from New York.

Finally, after a week, it arrived. The package was sitting in his room when he got home from school. He tore open the box and stared wide-eyed at the bright treasure within.

Magicians never lose this thrill. No matter their level of skill or their age, they never lose the giddy intoxication kindled by a box of new tricks. A box of magic tricks is a box of potential. A box of miracles just waiting to be unleashed. It has the allure of the unknown. A magician of eighty will look like a kid of eight if you plop down a package of new tricks in front of him. His eyes will sparkle with that mischievous joy magicians feel when they are about to give an audience the gift of wonder.

Guy unpacked the box of magics with great care, almost reverence, and put them in a neat row on his desk, swept clean of notebooks and textbooks. He was mesmerized.

"Wow!" he whispered to himself. These were *real* tricks, brightly colored, the Square Circle and Ghost Rise Chest decorated with exotic Oriental writing. The Mystery Spot Canister looked pretty neat, too. He wasn't so sure about the foam-rubber production items, but maybe from a distance they'd fool people.

The spring-rabbit was a bundle of white fur with two ears and red button eyes. When Guy held it and pushed its rump with his thumb, compressing the spring inside, it squirmed and wiggled like a real bunny. An excited, somewhat spastic bunny, but a bunny nonetheless. He had a rabbit. He was a real magician! He hadn't figured out what he would do with it. He didn't have a top hat to make it appear in and wasn't sure how he'd do it if he did. Maybe the production cabinet? He tried to stuff the bunny into the load chamber. It was a tight fit. Guy pushed harder and in so doing, the spring ripped a big hole in the bunny's back, rocketed out, and bounced off the ceiling.

"Oh no!" he yelled, as the spring bounced around the room and the bunny withered into a shapeless puddle of white fur.

That was the end of Guy's bunny. He hadn't even used it in a show, and it was ruined. He held it up by its ears. Without the spring inside, it looked like a white furry glove with eyes, not a bunny at all. Guy was crushed. Two dollars wasted on a spring bunny that had lost its spring. It was a devastating moment.

Bunny or no bunny, the show must go on.

Guy read the instructions that came with each trick. He had high hopes he'd ordered some good ones. But you never know. The disappointment of the Mummy Asrah haunted him, like a ghost from the beyond.

6

Finally the day of the Levinson bar mitzvah arrived. Guy's mother dropped him off at the Levinson house an hour early so he could get ready. There was no marquee on the lawn.

Guy carefully set up his props, checked everything, checked everything again, and then a third time just to be sure. He didn't have tails or a top hat (nor a slinky assistant), but he did have a dark blue blazer, and that was the best he could do to look like a real magician. He had the wand from the Mysto set. He had the broadside, too, with a piece of paper pasted at the bottom: "Levinson Bar Mitzvah. May 14, 1938." He taped it up.

He found a bathroom and spent twenty minutes in front of the mirror practicing a few moves. He was in there so long it prompted Mr. Levinson to shout, "Are you okay?"

At five, the kids gathered. The boys were especially keen on the table of props, and Guy had to keep shooing them away. He hadn't counted on that. Sometimes several came up, like a pack of wolves. "Hey, what's in the box?" "You gonna pull a rabbit out of a hat?" "Aren't you kinda young to be a magician?" Guy formulated an answer to all their questions: "All will soon be revealed." He repeated it over and over, sounding like a mystic seer. Or maybe just a broken record.

Mrs. Levinson introduced him and there was applause from the fifty kids seated in the crowded room and the parents standing at the edges and in the doorway.

All eyes were on Guy.

He was faced with a real live audience, not just his mom and dad or Uncle Louie or Cousin Rosalie. No, this was about eighty people, all looking at him, expecting him to perform miracles.

What had he gotten himself into?

After a second of panic, he reminded himself that this is what he wanted. This is what he had sought out, had spent countless hours in front of a mirror practicing for.

"Showtime," he muttered to himself.

He had planned to start with a simple, foolproof trick to get himself settled. So he picked up the square-circle production cabinet and tube and got started. He showed both the box and the tube that fit inside it empty, nested them, then produced his foam-rubber banana, watermelon slice, hot dogs, some silks and a bouquet of feather flowers.

He got some polite applause, but also a few shouted spoilers: "That's a fake banana!" and "Those flowers are feathers!"

He smiled and moved on.

The next trick involved a small wooden ball that was connected to a strong elastic string. The string was attached to the inside top of his coat. Guy would reach inside and grab the ball and pull it forward as he turned to get his wand from the table. He would hold the ball out, resisting the elastic that wanted to snap it back. He did this, presenting the ball at his fingertips. Nobody could see the thin black elastic string. He waved the wand over it and shook his hand, covering the moment when he let go of the ball and the string quickly yanked it behind his back. A quick and startling vanish.

Guy had practiced the simple trick hundreds of times and it worked flawlessly. But practice is not performance. This time, as he let go of the ball, it got caught on the edge of his coat and stayed there, wobbling oddly at the edge of the buttons.

"I can see it!" yelled one kid. "It's there on his coat. It's on a string!"

Busted!

Guy quickly yanked at his coat, freeing the ball, which shot back behind him. Too late. The effect was blown. He had failed miserably. Magic is unforgiving. If you do a trick well, you are a miracle worker. If you screw up, you are a fool—just a guy with a red ball dangling from the edge of his coat.

Guy got rattled.

In his next trick, the Ghost Rise Chest, he forgot his patter and mumbled his way through the climax, diminishing it. When he did the Mystery Spot Canister, he got all out of sequence and only recovered by turning his back to the audience and rearranging his silk loads. Very inelegant, very bad showmanship, and not in the slightest mystifying.

The kids were only too happy to announce his lapses. "It's in your pocket!" "You have two of those!" "Show us the other side!" And so on. Thirteen year olds get sadistic glee out of making someone, anyone, feel bad. Claim to do the impossible and they ratchet up their predatory instincts.

Guy realized that he had not practiced his new tricks nearly enough to make them truly magical. He hadn't developed good stories. He was going through a series of moves, more or less telling them what he was doing. "Here I have a tube. Nothing in it. And here a box. It's also empty. Now I put the tube in the box and I wave my wand...."

He was mindlessly explaining the obvious. He was presenting puzzles, not wonders. People were starting to fidget. After a trick that had gotten a smattering of applause and a few jeers, he went back to his table to get the next trick and stopped.

It came to him in a flash: there was one trick he *had* practiced enough. It used a simple coin and a roll. He reached in his pocket and pulled out the Morgan dollar Blackstone had given him. He had taken it along for luck. He needed that now.

But it wasn't luck that came to his rescue. It was skill.

He turned and walked to the front row. Holding up the coin, he started to speak:

"I am now going to show you a real miracle. Something you will never forget. Please, those of you at the back, come closer. Fill in the sides. I will show you something I learned from Harry Blackstone, the world's greatest magician."

He had no planned patter. He had no idea what he was about to say. But it was coming naturally. He was telling a story, a real story, and he felt at one with the trick. He was calm and in command.

"After his show here in New London, Harry and I dined together, just the two of us. We talked magic. And he showed me this trick. I will do it with this dollar coin, a coin he gave me. One dollar. One miracle. Watch!"

He held up the dollar and slowly turned to show it to everybody. Blackstone's words drifted back to him:

"Even the simplest trick can be a miracle, Guy, if you present it well. Slow down, draw it out, make it clear, make it magical. Just before you reveal the magic has happened, pause. Build the suspense. Then show that something impossible has happened and hold that moment so there is no doubt you have created a miracle."

Guy did his Retention Vanish. He did it slowly. More slowly than he'd ever done it, more slowly than he thought was possible. The dollar caught the light and glinted brightly as Guy deliberately placed it in his palm and slowly curled his fingers around it. He pulled away his hand and casually showed the palm empty as he did so. He fixed his stare on his closed palm and walked along the front row, his arm outstretched.

"I grip the coin as tightly as I can in my hand. Watch closely. No funny moves. No strings attached. No, right in front of your eyes...."

He began to uncurl his fingers, slowly, very slowly. First his pinky, then after a second his ring finger—each uncurling finger revealing a bit more of his empty palm.

"I open my hand...."

His middle finger and finally his index finger opened. He now showed a flat, empty hand. He let the moment sink in. He waited an extra beat.

"And there is nothing. The coin has vanished."

There was an audible gasp. Some kids, and the adults, too, frowned in surprise. Others opened their mouths, eyes wide.

"The coin has vanished," Guy repeated for effect.

His vanish had been perfect, the coin catching the light and burning its shiny image into the eyes of everybody in the room. They all knew he had put the dollar in his hand. They had seen it there. And then he had opened his hand and it was gone. It was astonishing.

Now the comments were different: "No way!" "Impossible!" "I don't understand!" "Wait a minute!"

"But, my friends, the coin hasn't gone far," Guy continued. "Could someone kindly pick one of those bagels from that bread basket and give to me?"

A kid did. It was passed down to Guy. He had someone place it on his outstretched palm. He reached over with his right hand, flashing his empty palm. He tore a small hole in the side of the bagel and showed it to a girl in the front row.

"Do you see anything inside this bagel?" he asked.

The girl gulped. She could not believe her eyes. She blinked. Stared. Finally found her voice.

"A coin," she whispered. "A coin!" she shouted.

Guy reached in and slowly pinched the edge of the dollar and pulled it out a bit. Then he held it up and showed it around.

"A coin. A silver dollar. Inside a bagel. How impossible! How wondrous!"

The audience was murmuring.

"If you please," said Guy, bending over and offering the girl the chance to remove the coin. She did so and held it up squealing. "It's the dollar!"

The room erupted into applause and whistles.

"Thank you," said Guy, bowing. Beaming. Thrilling to the applause washing over him.

He had the good sense to end his show there.

Nobody would ever remember the tricks he had done poorly. They would only remember the moment when a kid named Guy performed a miracle.

For Guy, it was a revelation. It was the moment when he became a performer, a true worker of wonder.

It was the moment when Guy Borden became a magician.

7

After the hurricane of 1938 wiped out much of the coastal area of New London, the city decided to build a grand amusement park. It featured a boardwalk a third of a mile long, rides, a pool, a beautiful beach of silky white sand, and a penny arcade full of games of chance, a fortune teller, and shooting galleries. A large clock tower, a bandstand, ballrooms and various gift and food concessions completed the park, known as Ocean Beach. Dedicated in 1940, it quickly became a favorite with local folks and tourists seeking a less crowded alternative to Coney Island or Atlantic City.

Ocean Beach was the place to go on hot summer days to sit in the sand and swim in the ocean. Teens spread out blankets, took in the sun and flirted. Older folks brought folding lawn chairs and umbrellas and coolers full of cold drinks and snacks. Radios created a tapestry of music and sports—a Yankees game floated on the strains of Glenn Miller and the carousel's calliope. People took long strolls along the boardwalk, young couples holding hands and falling in love, the elderly holding hands and sharing memories.

Out on Long Island Sound, ferries went back and forth to Fishers, Long and Block Islands. Sailboats drifted by. At night, two lighthouses, Race Rock and Ledge Light, swept their beams across the sea.

In the arcade, boys tried their hands at the shooting range, hoping their skill would win them a huge stuffed teddy bear or bunny that could impress a girlfriend. They played skee ball and pinball machines, gobbled candied apples and cotton candy.

They thrilled to rides on the Ferris wheel, roller coaster, Tilt-a-Whirl or the Bullet. Parents watched as their toddlers laughed and swirled by on the merry-go-round, its calliope playing popular songs of the day.

The hot, hazy days of summer unfolded like a wonderful, glittering dream at Ocean Beach. The amusement park amused. There was always a big fireworks show on the 4th of July, and big bands played frequently. People danced on the boardwalk and lost themselves in a carefree world of amusement and indulgence.

To grow up in New London was to grow up at Ocean Beach. Guy was no exception. With a few friends he would go there to while away a summer day. He no longer worked at his father's barbershop. For several years, he had made money doing magic shows on weekends and during the summer when school was out. He performed at birthday parties, anniversaries and bar mitzvahs. Small shows, but he earned more than he ever had working for his father. The shows gave him experience. With it came confidence and polish to his act. He always did his Retention Vanish and coin-in-roll as a show closer. It never failed to astonish. Guy loved to perform it, for himself and as homage to Blackstone, his inspiration and first teacher.

What Guy liked most about Ocean Beach was the arcade. It was dark, lit by gaudy bulbs and the glow of pinball machines and games. It smelled of gunpowder, sweat and popcorn. The arcade was a cacophony of small caliber rifles going off in the shooting gallery, bells, whistles, people laughing, skee balls rolling and bouncing, pinball machines playing snatches of music, and barkers trying to entice players to their booths.

"Step right up. Shoot the duck and win a doll!" "Say, young man, how about you show that pretty girl how strong you are!" "Put your money down and win a clown!"

Guy loved the theatricality of it. The noise, the lights, the confusion all fascinated him. It was like a carnival, a place of dark indulgences. Most of all, he liked the Gypsy Fortune Teller.

She was an automaton, made of wax, dark-complexioned, eerily lifelike. She was tucked in a corner, almost lost in the shadows. The Gypsy Fortune Teller sat in a glass case, visible from her waist up. A turban of patterned silk swathed her head, a large chipped ruby in its center. Her hands encircled a large crystal ball. Whenever Guy went to Ocean Beach, he would sneak away from his friends to visit her. The fortunes she dispensed hinted at truths and destinies; she seemed an agent of fate. He took her seriously.

On a hot August day in 1940, Guy stood before her dimly lit cabinet. The Gypsy stared at him. She seemed in a trance, lost in a mystical dimension. She sat there motionless, waiting for a nickel to be dropped in the slot at the base of the cabinet, which was adorned with stars, astrological signs and cryptic writings.

Guy fumbled in his pocket for a nickel. He twirled the coin in his hand absent-mindedly, rolling it around his knuckles and back into his palm as he studied the Gypsy in her glass case.

As Guy took a step forward toward the Gypsy Fortune Teller, a young couple stepped in front of him and jammed their nickel in the slot. The gypsy came to life, breathing, slowly nodding her head. Her eyes blinked. The crystal ball between her hands glowed. She swept her right hand over a pile of fortune cards and ticked one off and down a hole. It appeared in another small hole in the base. The boy picked it up and showed it to the girl, whose eyes widened. He shook his head, stuffed the card in his pocket, and they walked off.

Guy wondered what the fortune had been. Had it been meant for him? He wondered if it mattered when he chose to get his fortune from the Gypsy Fortune Teller. Other people slowly moved toward her. Should he wait? Should he step up now? If things in life were fated, preordained, it wouldn't matter. *Whenever* he stepped up and got his fortune was when he was *meant* to do so. The fortune he got was the one fate had determined he should get. He had no real choice in the matter, no free will. Just like the Magician's Choice.

If, on the other hand, nothing was predetermined at all, then it *would* make a difference when he chose to get his fortune from the Gypsy. *He* would pick the moment and *his* choice would determine his fate.

Or maybe it was random? Maybe nothing was predetermined nor was there any meaning to his choice. That could be.

Then again, randomness might just be an illusion. It might mask the true workings of fate. Maybe it was just misdirection.

Guy stood there and thought all this over. And over. Going in a circle of reasoning and speculation. Free will? Predetermination? Randomness? Fate?

It was giving Guy a headache.

While he was thinking, another couple, older, stepped up and got their fortune. "Oh, Bernie," said the woman, "I hope that's true!"

He could wait no longer. He walked up to the Gypsy Fortune Teller. He put his nickel in the slot. She came to life, stared into the crystal ball, swept her hand to the side, and the fortune—Guy's fortune—dropped into the base. The small white card appeared in the receptacle. Guy looked at it a moment, then took it out and read it:

"You never go so far as when you don't know where you are going."

He pondered the enigmatic message. It could be taken in many ways.

He tucked the card into his wallet, near where he kept Blackstone's Jack of Diamonds. Both would influence his choices for years to come.

8

A few days after his visit to Ocean Beach, Guy told his folks he didn't want to go to college but rather to New York to try his hand at magic.

Sam did not take the news well. He told Guy he hadn't worked hard to save up for college to throw it away on a "crazy show biz gamble."

"You study, find yourself a good profession."

Guy countered that he already had a profession, and they began to argue until, exasperated, defensive, angry, and confused, he excused himself and abruptly left the table. He stormed out the front door into the night.

Ruth and Sam did the dishes in awkward silence. Sam lit a cigar and walked out into the backyard and sat on the swing that hung from an old maple tree. Ruth thought that Sam looked like a train the way he was puffing on his cigar. She came out a few minutes later and sat next to him, slowly rocking them. She hoped it would calm Sam down.

From a radio somewhere, the strains of Duke Ellington playing "Mood Indigo" wafted across the heavy summer night.

"It's crazy," Sam growled. "Going off to New York to make it in show biz. Magic no less. Does he know how few make it? What kind of life it is? He's done a few shows. Is that an act? A career? He's smart. Good with his hands. He could be an engineer. Or a surgeon! He should go to college. That's been my dream since he was born."

"Your dream, Sam. But what about Guy's dream? Doesn't it count? We're old, Sam, in our forties. We know many of life's dreams don't work out, but he's young. Shouldn't he get a chance to live *his* dream?"

Sam said nothing. He just puffed his cigar, sending little blue clouds of smoke into the night.

"You see how hard he practices," she continued. "You yourself say he's good. Maybe he's good enough to make it. Who knows? Maybe it's worth a try."

"Maybe. Maybe not. He could waste years."

"Maybe. Maybe not. What's the rush? Let the boy get some seasoning, find out if he has what it takes to make it in magic. He seems to love it. Everyone should get a chance to pursue their love."

She squeezed Sam's hand. He sat silently for a while. His puffing slowed.

"I don't know, Ruth. I don't know. It would be a shame if he failed and wasted his time and ended up a stagehand or something."

"No, Sam. It would be a shame for us to stop him and for Guy to live his life regretting not trying. If it doesn't work out, he'll get it out of his system. And he'll know he gave his dream a shot. You know what it's like when you don't get a chance to do that."

Sam did. As a young boy, he had loved to play the violin. He was good at it. It was his passion, and he dreamed of playing for a symphony someday. But his father had persuaded him to follow in his footsteps and become a barber. He enjoyed the work. He made a comfortable living. Still, when he listened to the radio and heard a violin concerto, there was always a twinge of regret. The violin had been left behind, and with it a dream. He had never tried to play again, even after Guy heard the story and urged him to.

Sam had told him. "Sometimes, you just have to let things go and move on."

Ruth and Sam sat watching the summer stars, listening to the jazz on the radio. Crickets chirped like an audience.

"Think it over, Sam. He needs your support. He wants your blessing." She kissed him and left him on the swing. As she reached the back porch she turned to look at him. Just then, a bright shooting star streaked by. She knew Sam had seen it. She waited a moment and then called to him:

"If you just made a wish on that shooting star, Sam, you're still a dreamer."

Then she went inside, the screen door banging behind her.

9

Sam finally agreed to let Guy go off to New York. He had had to face his own regrets and admit he did not want Guy to suffer the same fate. Still, it had been a bit of a negotiation. Guy just wanted to go; Sam wanted to put some limits on it. First he tried six months, but Guy protested that breaking in and building a career would take some time. Maybe a few years. Sam shook his head, saying that if there was no deadline, things could drift along forever. Ruth suggested eighteen months. If Guy hadn't gained a real foothold in the world of magic, if he wasn't performing regularly and supporting himself in that time, he would try college.

It turned out to be a compromise everybody could accept.

A few weeks later, Sam and Ruth drove Guy to Union Station. He had two suitcases. One held his clothes, the other his Mysto set and magic props. He was wearing a new sweater Ruth had knitted. She was giving him suggestions on meals to cook, straightening his collar, talking quickly, burying her emotions in trivial things. It was hard to see her baby leaving home. She was having second thoughts. Sitting on the swing, talking of dreams and regrets was one thing. Now, seeing him with his suitcases and knowing that, for the first time in over eighteen years he would not be sleeping at home, was another. She worried that he was a naive small-town boy about to walk into the maw of a big city. They had been to New York; she had seen for herself the city's crazy crowds and frantic pace. She was scared.

Sam sat quietly, letting her fuss at Guy. He, too, was nervous, but he hid his anxiety in a mask of calm.

Guy pulled out the pocket watch Sam had given him and popped it open.

"Nine-thirty. The train should be here in a few minutes," he said. As he closed the watch he met his father's eyes, and Sam gave him a brief smile. Guy held the watch out a moment, acknowledging that he knew what his father was thinking, then put it back in his pocket.

The stationmaster announced the train. Sam and Ruth walked Guy out to the platform. The train chugged in and stopped in clouds of hissing steam.

"Well, I'm off," said Guy.

"Promise you will call tonight when you are settled in at the hotel, Guy."

"I will, mom."

"And be careful." She gave him a big hug, tears in her eyes, then stepped back.

Sam stood in front of Guy and again their eyes met.

"Good luck, son. Make the best of this opportunity. Whatever happens, we're always here for you."

"Thanks, dad."

Sam shook Guy's hand, slipping a folded piece of paper in his palm as he did. Without looking, Guy put it in his pocket and boarded the train. He stowed his two bags overhead and sat by the window, waving to his parents as the train pulled out. They vanished into a cloud of steam, like an illusion in a magic show.

He took out the piece of paper his father had given him. It was a hundred dollar bill wrapped in a note: "Play your violin."

10

Guy spent a few days in the hotel and devoted his time to finding an apartment. He learned quickly that the classified ads, like the ads in magic catalogues, tended to shade the truth a bit. One particularly inventive ad boasted a "view of the city." He went to take a look. It *did* have a view of the city. If one dragged a mirror by a window and angled it just so. A tiny sliver of skyline—a smoking chimney—appeared. Like a magic trick, it used smoke and mirrors to create its effect. Guy was not fooled and continued his search.

Eventually, he found a cozy place on 10th Avenue, then he started to look for a job. From the start, he was determined to work in the theater. He reasoned that being around a theater he would meet people in the entertainment business. He could make contacts, maybe do a few shows for parties, get some momentum going, get his name out there. So it was to theaters he went, offering to do anything: be an usher, a janitor, a stagehand, a clerk.

"Look," he would say, pulling out a coin and doing a few quick tricks. "I'm good with my hands."

One manager watched, chomping on a cigar, then looked up at Guy. "That's swell. You can make money disappear. I had a partner who did that a while back. He made a lot of my money disappear. Get the hell out."

Guy learned from that. The next manager he met, he tried a different tack.

"Watch," he said. He took a dollar bill, carefully folded it, blew on it, then unfolded it and it had changed into a five dollar bill.

The manager looked up at Guy.

"Quite impressive. Since you can make money so easily, I guess I wouldn't have to pay you."

Guy left. Maybe doing magic tricks wasn't the way to get a job in the theater. On and on it went, day after day. He knocked on doors, finagled a talk with the theater or stage manager, told them he could or would do anything, and was ushered out. He was just about to give up and try another line of attack, when fate smiled on him. He walked into the Morosco Theater on West 45th. Somebody rushed by and almost knocked him down. A group of people were huddled on stage, surrounding a man on his back who was moaning.

Guy walked to the edge of the stage.

"Is somebody getting a doctor?" one man yelled.

"Yeah, Barney's going for one."

"How badly is he hurt?" someone asked.

"Broken arm, for sure," said a woman.

"Maybe his back, too," said someone else.

The doctor arrived and a few minutes later an ambulance crew. They put the stricken man on a stretcher and rushed him down the aisle and out of the theater. A man in a rumpled suit who had been watching the scene spoke.

"Great, just great. We open in two nights, and our best stagehand is down and out! Shit!"

Guy guessed he was the director or manager.

"I can do the job," said Guy. In the confusion of the injured stagehand, nobody had noticed Guy standing at the edge of the stage.

"Yeah? And who are you?" asked the Rumpled Suit Man.

"I'm Guy Borden. I came here looking for work."

"You want to work in the theater? You look young. You know anything? Where you worked?"

Guy was on the spot. He had never worked in a theater. He'd only been in one theater, in fact. The Garde, in New London.

"I've been in the theater a while now," he blurted out. True, he had been standing in the Morosco a good five minutes. "You know the Garde Theater, in New London, Connecticut?" he continued.

"Can't say that I do," said Rumpled Suit Man.

"Well, I performed there," said Guy. True, he had helped Blackstone on stage. "I could go on and on." He had been inspired by the classified ads and their interpretations of reality. In New York, it seemed, truth was what you made it.

"You got any references?" asked Rumpled Suit Man.

"Well, I'm sure the World's Greatest Magician, Harry Blackstone, if you could find him, would vouch for me. He's seen how I handle a roll."

"I don't need an actor, I need a stagehand."

"I'll do whatever needs to be done. I'm a magician. Good with my hands."

Rumpled Suit Man looked at Guy a moment and then waved his hand. "Okay, what the hell. I don't have time for this. I got a theater to run and a show to put on. I'm Jon Thompson, manager of the Morosco. Rosco, come over here."

A short man in baggy pants, a blue shirt and suspenders ambled over.

"This is Rosco. He's the stage manager. Rosco, this guy will take over for Tony. He's young, looks strong. Show him around. Teach him the ropes. Make sure he knows his ass from his earlobe by rehearsal time tonight." Thompson walked down the steps and shook Guy's hand. "Welcome to the Morosco, kid. Don't screw up or your career in the theater will be a short one." He walked down the aisle, followed by several people asking him questions about schedules and problems and so on.

It was a masterful performance by Guy. His patter had been good. He had fooled Thompson. Or maybe, as in many tricks, Thompson had fooled himself. We believe what we want to believe. In magic, in life.

"What did you say your name was?" asked Rosco.

"Borden, Guy Borden."

"Well, welcome to the Morosco, Guy. I hope you have a better day than Tony. He fell off a ladder. Probably drunk. Tony is a good stagehand, to be sure, but he can't keep away from the bottle. Boss don't know that. You don't drink, do you?"

"Not around ladders," said Guy.

"Good. Well, let's get to work. 'Clash By Night' is a tricky show with lots of props and scenery and cues. I hope you're a quick study."

Guy was. He learned the ropes, literally. He helped raise and lower the scenery. It required perfect timing and coordination with Bobo, the guy on the other side of the stage. They had to work together to unhook the rope, lower a huge scenery flat, tie it off, then raise and secure the flat behind it. He also helped prepare props and put them on stage between scenes.

The show went off without a hitch that night and for weeks thereafter, and Guy was quickly adopted by the Morosco Theater family. After the show, he delivered flowers, drinks, telegrams and sometimes call girls to the dressing rooms.

Whenever he met someone and was asked what he did, he said, "I'm in theater." It always seemed to impress people.

Guy had taken the first step toward a career in magic. He was in a theater, and on a stage. As yet, behind the curtain, in the darkness, far from the spotlight. But he would get there. He had determination. He had patience.

11

Guy loved working at the Morosco. It hosted a kaleidoscope of acts and shows, an ever-changing spectrum of performers.

He admired their skill, their nerves, their showmanship. It was intoxicating to see it night after night, week after week. Singers, dancers, comedians, actors, and magicians—especially magicians. He saw Dante perform his Sim Sala Bim revue, Theodore Annemann, who seemed a nervous wreck, do uncanny feats of mentalism, and Cardini astonish with his silent manipulations of cigarettes, cards and billiard balls.

Sometimes, when a show was over and the stars had left, when the musicians and lighting guys and stagehands and ushers had all gone home, Guy had the theater to himself. He would stand there on the stage, in an empty house, and imagine an audience of hundreds watching him. Loving him. Rising to their feet in a thunderous ovation for the wonder he had given them.

He would recall that night when Blackstone had come to the Garde and called on him to help with the card trick. For those brief few moments he had been in the spotlight, he had tasted its sweet intoxication.

To be at the Morosco in New York was to be in the heart of the world of showbiz. For a young man in his late teens, it was a heady experience. He liked the showgirls, too. A lot. Young beauties his age who sometimes wore very little, they flirted with Guy constantly. He was flattered and scared, having never been intimate with a girl.

But showbiz in New York City is nothing if not a place to learn about girls. Guy was, as always, an eager study. So it was to Ginger, a stunning, nubile redhead who was part of a dance revue, that he lost his innocence one night in a prop room in the back of the theater.

As he was stowing away a cardboard sea, part of the revue's scenery, Ginger appeared in the doorway. She wore a very tight white-lace body stocking and had big feather wings attached to her shoulders. She had appeared in a number called "Angels in Heaven." She was gorgeous.

"Can you help me unhook these wings?" she asked, turning her back to him.

Guy obliged, unhooking the clasp to her wings.

"I'm not an angel," she said, looking at Guy with her bottomless green eyes.

"You're not?" said Guy, falling into those eyes.

"No," she purred. "But I'd like to show you heaven."

Before he knew it, she was all over him, pushing him back onto a muslin tree, yanking at his pants, shedding her body stocking, kissing him, wild and wanton. He had no choice, and that was fine with him. His glimpse of heaven turned out to be pretty nice.

Afterwards, she took her angel wings and left him, exhausted and happy.

"Boy," he said. "That was some angel!"

He was in love.

She was gone the next day as the show moved on. Guy moped. He asked Rosco if he knew the next stop for the revue.

"I saw that gal go back there," said Roscoe. "Forget her. You had your fun."

"But I want to see her again."

"I don't think she'll give you an encore. But don't worry, kid," Rosco said. "They'll be plenty more. Just watch yourself. Don't let Thompson catch you foolin' around. He don't like that kind of stuff going on in his theater."

Guy shook his head. "I liked heaven," he said.

"Take it from Rosco, kid. When it comes to dames, there's a fine line between heaven and hell."

Guy had much to learn. He picked up a program for the night's show: "All-Girl Chinese Acrobat Circus."

"Wow," he muttered.

12

Guy had been in New York only a few weeks before he went to Tannen's Magic Store on a rainy Saturday morning. It was as he remembered it from his visit years earlier: a life-sized magic set.

Only about the first quarter of the space was the store. The rest was storage space, a workshop, and a small performance area where some of the great magicians of the day would gather to talk, show each other tricks, invent new moves and try out routines. They'd also eat, smoke and drink. It was not something just anybody could be a part of. It was, as Lennie had told Guy years earlier, the inner sanctum, reserved for those Tannen deemed worthy of admission. It was an exclusive club. Patrons of the store, like Guy, might be up front watching Lou demonstrate a trick while just a few feet away, behind a curtain, masters of the art were holding court.

The rainy day Guy ventured into the store, a few magicians had already gathered in back for coffee and some spirited "sessioning" as they called it. Guy could hear their muffled voices, the shuffling of cards, the occasional burst of laughter or a cuss or two. He wondered who was back there. He wanted desperately to go behind that curtain. But he knew he'd have to prove himself in the front room before he'd get to go to the back room. Patience.

Most of the kids and men at the store—hobbyists and amateurs—cared little about the back room. They were far more interested in the tricks sold up front. The shop owners knew all about magicians' addiction to tricks, of course, and played to it without mercy. "Hey, Scott … I know you have a million decks of cards already, but have you seen this new one? The gaffs are really something new. I know you won't use it and don't need it, but let me just show it to you anyway, just for the hell of it."

Lou would show Scott the trick, then act a bit surprised when Scott bought three. "And, by the way, you know, Owen just came out with a pretty slick card case that would work really well with that deck...."And so on, the cash register going ca-ching, ca-ching all the while. They preyed on the weakness of magicians for "just one more trick." And the magicians knew it, but could not stop themselves any more than a drunk can stop himself from wanting "one more drink."

Many a time, a magician would walk out with a bag of new stuff, get about a block away and mutter "Damn," knowing he had a bag of new stuff he didn't need to add to the last bag of stuff he didn't need, both of which would probably end up in the drawer of stuff he didn't need.

Their wives had their shoes. The magicians had their decks, coins, silks, card gaffs, flash paper, chop cups, Okito boxes, shells, slippery Sams, flippers, pulls, clips, reels, coils, topits, changing bags, rattle boxes, dye tubes, thumb tips, sixth fingers, coin droppers, packet tricks, Lippincott boxes, Himber wallets and spring loaded bunnies. Sure they used some of it. But not all of it. It's a rare magician who has a single deck of cards and a few coins to his name.

In truth, as the great Max Mailini once observed, a magician needed only six tricks to make an act. And they need not be exotic or complex. In the hands of a good magician, even the simplest effect, maybe something out of a magic set like the Mysto, could become a miracle.

Some guys who came to Tannen's were really passionate about magic, loving to play with the tricks, to understand the secrets, to belong to the mysterious fraternity of magicians, even though they seldom performed.

These guys (and they were almost all guys) might practice for hours in front of a mirror, then show a trick to their wife or kid or cat. A no-pressure audience. Sometimes, an opportunity might come up when they could perform, say after dinner with some friends. Then they either did not have a trick with them or froze in fear at actually performing. Or did a trick or two, probably in a daze, forgetting their practice and their patter, mumbling, fumbling, then later lying awake full of regret and recriminations. If they managed to do the trick well, they would be puffed with pride for months. Their names were on the marquees of their egos.

"I killed 'em!" they would say to themselves over and over, and head right back to the magic shop to buy yet more tricks, emboldened and inspired by their rare moment of proffered wonder.

Guy became a regular at Tannen's. He was there every Saturday morning. He loved to kill time talking with the guys at the counter. Unable to resist, he bought tricks. He shared moves and routines, maybe not in the back room, but with other magicians and hobbyists who shared his passion for the art. He kept an eye on who went behind the curtain to session. He started to recognize them, and the regulars were happy to fill him in.

"That's Dai Vernon. Great close-up guy. That's John Scarne, that's Okito—actually Theo Bamberg—and Cardini." And so on. Tannen's, like Martinka's Magic shop and a few others, was a hub of magic. Their proprietors had created welcoming little worlds where men who loved the honest deception of magic shared their love and lore, their smiles and their sleights.

Lennie was one of several men who demonstrated tricks at Tannen's. He was in his sixties, heavyset, and did the tricks without much flare or competence. He often exposed the method in his clumsy handling.

"Got to work on that before my big show," he said to Guy one day after flubbing a move.

"What show is that, Lennie?"

"My one-man show on Broadway, Guy."

"You have one?" Guy asked incredulously.

"Not yet," said Lennie. "But I will."

Later that morning, Guy asked Lou Tannen about Lennie.

"Lennie's a sad one," said Lou. "He's got problems. Mental problems. He lives in a dream world."

"He told me about his show on Broadway."

"Yes, his big show. He's been working here for ten years and he's always about to get that Broadway show. You know and I know that's not going to happen. Lennie's best illusion is that he will make it big someday. But the biggest stage he'll ever work is that counter top over there. A man should have dreams, Guy, but when they are totally unrealistic, it's sad."

Guy watched Lennie perform the egg bag for some kids. At one point, he dropped the wooden egg and it rolled across the floor.

"It's nice of you to keep him on," said Guy.

Tannen shrugged. "I feel sorry for him. You know, 'there but for the grace of God' and all that. He's harmless. He sells a few tricks."

"Speaking of tricks, Mr. Tannen, I ordered a trick from you when I was a kid, the Mummy Asrah, and it's terrible. There it is on the shelf. I can't believe you still sell it."

"Well, Guy, maybe it's a bad trick. Maybe it isn't. You know, it's not always the prop's fault. A hundred guys can do a billiard ball routine and it can be clunky. Uninspired. Boring. Then one guy will come along and turn it into a thing of beauty, of poetry, of art. Some guys can take the simplest trick, a vanish or a transposition—something that takes thirty-seconds—and turn it into five or ten minutes of mystery. It's not just the apparatus or how fast your hands are. You've got to wrap the effect in a presentation that creates wonder. So, son, it might not be the trick. It might be the guy doing it. Maybe you need to practice it. Find a way to make it work."

"Maybe," said Guy, unconvinced. It would take a lot of work to make it look like more than just a cloth with a cut out shape of a mummy inside dangling from a thread in his hand. A sudden burst of laughter emanated from behind the velvet curtains in back.

"Hell, Charlie, you'll never get away with that, they'd have to be blind!" someone yelled.

"Do they ever buy new stuff?" asked Guy, still looking at the curtains.

"Not much, Guy. Pros find tricks they like and master them. Not to say that I can't persuade those guys to buy something new, but it isn't easy. They're generally more interested in technique and creating routines. That's what they're doing back there now. Inventing and sharing moves and routines. Up front here I sell props.

"Can I go back there?" asked Guy.

Tannen studied the young man a moment.

"Show me a trick."

"Got a roll?"

"Just a second." Tannen parted the curtain and went into the inner sanctum. He returned with a bagel with a bite out of it.

"It's Isadore Klein's. He likes his bagels. It's all I could get from back there. Now show me your trick."

Guy did his retention vanish and appearance of the coin from inside the bagel.

Tannen whistled.

"Pretty good, Guy. Actually, very good. It would fool most folks. But you flashed the coin between the fingers of your right hand when you picked up the bagel. Not much of a flash, but I caught it. Those guys back there have seen the best coin guys who've ever lived do that vanish. In fact, some of them *are* the best coin guys who have ever lived. You go back there, you better do it better than anybody, *ever*, or they'll eat you alive."

Guy was crestfallen. He thought his retention vanish was so good!

"Where'd you learn that, Guy?" Tannen asked.

"From Harry Blackstone."

"No kidding? Hmmm. Well, if Harry were here he'd tell you what I just told you. You do it very very well. But not quite good enough to show to that crowd back there. No, Guy. Not yet. You're not ready."

Before Guy could say anything, Tannen put up his hand.

"You keep coming in here, Guy. You keep showing me your stuff. I'll tell you when you're ready to go back there and session with the greats. Now, would you like to see this new effect from P&L?"

Guy started to say “Yes,” then stopped.

“No, Mr. Tannen. I don’t need another trick today. I think I’ll go home and practice my Retention Vanish and the Mummy Asrah. I’ll practice until my hands bleed.”

Tannen looked at Guy in the eye.

“You do that, Guy. Work on the roll part of the Retention. And give the Mummy Asrah another try. Believe me: someday you’ll find just the right occasion to do it and you’ll be happy you mastered it.” Then he paused, perhaps worried that Guy was serious about the hands bleeding part.

“Take care of your hands. Put on some lotion to keep ’em supple. Do some finger exercises to keep them strong and nimble.”

Guy stayed at the counter a moment, listening to the laughter and insults being thrown around behind the curtain, to the sound of cards being shuffled and dealt. Then he got into the elevator and pushed the down button.

“By the way, Guy,” Tannen said as the door closed, “you owe Klein a bagel.”

13

Guy was restless. He wanted to think. To reflect. It was a clear, warm night. He decided to take the subway to Brooklyn and walk across the Brooklyn Bridge to Manhattan, as he had done years ago with his folks. He remembered the wonderful perspective on the city the bridge afforded. On the bridge, he could find freedom—an escape from the confinement of the city, a place to let his imagination loose.

As he walked to the subway he saw, ahead, a glowing storefront in the otherwise dark block. Its light spilled onto the sidewalk. He approached and saw an Oriental woman sitting at a table, folding small pieces of paper into figures—a cat, a heart, an elephant, the number six, a mushroom. She piled her creations in a little dish. The window was dirty, and bore no sign, so Guy had no idea what her purpose was. She did not seem to be aware of him, bathed in the glow of her light. She bent over her table and folded her little paper sculptures, alone in a shop window at night. It was dreamlike. Guy watched a few minutes and walked on.

He rode the subway to Brooklyn and began his walk. He stopped about halfway. Manhattan was spread out before him, a huge stage set on which a million dramas unfolded every day, every night.

He looked at the silhouettes of the buildings, dark and ominous, like slumbering giants. A galaxy of lights sprinkled across them in a random pattern. A glow radiated from the streets, and a distant hum, too, as if the city were a huge generator throbbing with energy. Which New York was. It was a vast dynamo fueled by hopes and dreams, ideas and interactions.

Guy could not see a single person. It was an illusion, of course, for millions lived in the jumble of buildings he looked upon. He thought about all those invisible lives, jammed together, some colliding, others never touching. He wondered how he fit into the world that was New York, the world that was magic?

He took a deep breath as if trying to inhale the energy of the city, to capture its muse. He didn't know how or where or when, but he knew his destiny lay in that universe of shadow and light that lay before him.

Guy resumed his walk toward Manhattan, toward that great city so vibrant with promises and illusions, knowing that he would have to find one and make it real.

14

Guy came home from his walk on the Brooklyn Bridge, his mind buzzing. He could not sleep. Images of the woman doing origami in the shop window floated alongside images of silhouetted buildings, a galaxy of lights, the towers of the bridge, the streaking trails of distant traffic. Perhaps he had tapped into the energy of the city, or perhaps it was just the flow of creativity that late night and insomnia can sometimes unleash.

Without knowing exactly what he was up to, Guy took down his Mysto magic set from the top shelf of the closet. He opened the lid and thrilled to the assortment of things inside. Every time he opened it he remembered the very first time he had opened it. He gathered some of his other tricks, too.

"You never go so far as when you don't know where you are going."

The fortune from the Gypsy Fortune Teller came back to Guy. Was it prophetic, or a statement of one of the basic beliefs of magic?

Guy began examining the tricks. Not as objects made from plastic or paper or wood, but for the underlying principles they embodied. What clever design made this simple box do something astonishing? What audience assumption was being slyly subverted by this set of coins? How was logic being fooled by the interplay of these cups and balls? How was this card handling done to seem natural while all manner of trickery was happening? Like the punch line of a joke, a magic trick lead the viewer down a path that only at the end suddenly became a different destination altogether.

Guy knew there were only a handful of core magic effects, including appearance, disappearance, transformation, translocation, levitation, animation, prediction. Like the notes in a scale, there were endless ways of using these fundamentals to create illusions.

Guy idly played with his old tricks, thinking, wondering, testing theories by imagining routines in his head.

Then he stopped.

He stared at all the paraphernalia spread out on his kitchen table. He picked up a pad and pencil and began to sketch. He stopped and looked at it. He returned to the Mysto set and tried combining elements from disparate tricks into something a little different. He played with some of his bigger effects, too. After a while and a few more sketches, he searched his apartment for some other things to try out and brought them to the table. A vague idea was forming for a new trick.

Inspiration is not always a bolt from the blue, a dramatic earthshaking moment of revelation. More often, it comes gently, like a wisp of wind, expressed as a quiet "Huh!"

The minutes became hours as Guy played, trying this and that, stopping, looking, shaking his head, sketching, erasing, modifying. He took what he was working on into his bedroom to examine it in the mirror, turning a bit to the left and right to check the angles, knowing that what looked good head-on could betray itself from the side.

He had come up with the idea for a trick that was extremely clever. It combined several principles and mixed simple sleight of hand with a complex mechanical prop. Guy revised a few bits of his design and routine, honing the effect, adding an element here, cutting a move there.

He worked until three in the morning, when fatigue finally won out. Before he turned off the kitchen light, he looked at what he had created. It sat there in the middle of the table, cobbled together. He didn't have all the things, nor the skill, to make a polished prop. But even in its rough form, he knew it was unique. Startling. Magical.

Guy would refine it and practice it and show it to a magician. Maybe to Chen Woo, currently appearing at the Morosco

Theater. Scaled up to stage size, his trick could be a stunning illusion. Guy thought it just might be his entree into the real world of performing magic.

It needed a name. He thought about it a while. He decided it should in some way be an homage to his Gilbert Mysto Set, his first collection of props. He wanted a name that was not merely descriptive, as so many were. Cups and Balls. Dove Pan. Production Cabinet. He wanted it to be more mysterious and evocative. Then it came to him: "Mysterium." No: "THE Mysterium." Yes, perfect.

He fell asleep thinking of how he would present The Mysterium, what patter he would use, how he would pace the trick and structure a routine for maximum effect.

Guy Borden, just nineteen, had created a magic trick. A *new* magic trick, unlike anything anybody had ever seen, ever performed. It was not an easy thing to do. It did not happen often. Most magic was a reworking of classic effects. To create something altogether new took insight, inspiration and inventiveness.

In his tiny apartment in the dead of night, Guy had had that insight, inspiration and inventiveness. He knew he had created a miracle of wonder.

What he did not know was that The Mysterium would lead him into the heart of another illusion, an illusion that went beyond the stage of magic to the theater of life.

15

Chen Woo was yet another Chinese conjuror. More than a few had appeared at the Morosco. Like most of them, Woo dressed in a silk outfit, had a long pigtail, and did not speak during his act. He was an older man, in his 70s. His act was modest. Guy watched from the wings, looking over Woo's shoulder out at the audience, and was not particularly impressed. The tricks were standard fare, delivered competently but without great flare or enthusiasm. The theater was never filled, and the audiences were not overly amazed by what they saw. Guy felt he was watching a performer past his prime, going through the motions.

Woo's two week run was winding down and there was talk it might end early. The manager had booked him to fill a gap in the schedule, and was now regretting it. Magic had to be good to create a buzz and fill seats in New York, where there was a great deal of competition. Woo's act was not up to the challenge. Guy pulled the ropes and readied the tables of props, props that were chipped and dirty from years on the road. Guy could not help but think that, given the chance, he could perform better than Woo.

Still, it was Woo on stage, in the spotlight, and Guy in the wings, in the shadows. Perhaps, thought Guy, if he showed Woo his prototype for The Mysterium, the man might be interested in buying it from him? Maybe he would let Guy become part of his act. And that, thought Guy, might be the way to work his way into the business. Surely Woo knew people. His act might be stale, but he was still getting bookings. Guy reasoned that it was better to be part of an established show than standing in front of his mirror at home practicing his sleights but fooling nobody.

A few nights before the end of Woo's booking, Guy was ready. The show ended. Behind the curtain Chen Woo swept off the stage toward the dressing rooms, his bright yellow silk gown billowing around him, its dragon design coming to life as the fabric rolled and swirled. Woo's face was made up for dramatic effect on stage. It was a kind of mask, his true self hidden and inscrutable.

Woo walked down a small flight of steps that led from the back corner of the stage to a hallway lined with small rooms. Guy waited for him there, nervously. He wasn't sure how to address the magician, so when Chen drew near he said, "Master, may I have a word with you?" Guy hoped the Chinese wizard understood English. Apparently, he did. Woo stopped and looked at Guy.

"Honorable Master Woo, my name is Guy. Guy Borden. I work here at the theater. I am a budding magician."

Suiting action to words, Guy took out his Morgan dollar and did his Retention Vanish and then made the coin reappear in his pocket. Woo's eyes widened just a bit seeing Guy's vanish. It was, indeed, startling, even for a Chinese wizard. Woo stood facing Guy, arms folded. He nodded his appreciation.

"Do again," said Woo.

Guy did. Even slower. Woo was riveted. Sensing his time with Woo might be short, Guy jumped in.

"Master Woo, I have invented a trick I'd like to show you."

Woo nodded again, his face expressionless, his thoughts a mystery.

"I call it 'The Mysterium.' I have only a small model of it. Not very polished. It still has some flaws, but it will give you the idea."

"Show me."

Guy opened a box and took out The Mysterium. Woo looked at it with great curiosity, his eyes narrowing.

"Show me."

Guy performed The Mysterium effect. It took time, and the working model was clunky. At a few parts, Guy could barely get it to work. "The Mysterium" was a complex mechanical wonder, but it also required sleight of hand, timing, and showmanship to pull off.

Throughout, Woo tried to remain impassive, but Guy could see the surprise in his eyes. When he was done, Woo stared at him.

"This is just an early version," said Guy. "And as you could probably tell, parts of it don't work perfectly. But they could be improved by someone with the right tools and skill. Imagine it bigger, on stage, in the spotlight. I think it could be a wonderful illusion. I have the plans for it."

"Show me," said Woo.

Guy nervously unfolded a sheaf of papers and held them out for Woo to examine. Woo took the papers and gazed at them intently, studying the drawings. Though Guy had tried to refine the design, it was still intricate. Woo put down the papers and grabbed the model. He examined it, turning it over, studying its design, trying its workings.

"Not sure," said Woo. "Not sure good for stage. Must think."

Guy was a bit deflated. Scaled up, he was sure the trick would mesmerize an audience and create an illusion of incomparable wonder.

"But Master Woo, if you imagine this trick much bigger …" Woo cut him off with a haughty wave of his hand. He thumbed through the diagrams again, studying them. After a moment he looked up at Guy.

"Must go now. Must think. I keep these to tomorrow. You come to hotel tomorrow. Algonquin Hotel. At four. Tomorrow. We talk."

With that he stuffed the plans in the pocket of his robe and, still clutching the model of the trick, turned and continued down the hall and into his dressing room. He shut the door with a loud bang.

Guy stood in the dark hallway and stared after him. He was sure Woo would see the potential in his trick. If magicians were addicted to new props, how could Woo resist the intoxication of The Mysterium? He knew he could persuade the Chinaman to hire him to build it for the stage. He would play to Woo's ego and his vanity. Like a magician's choice, he would make Woo believe it was *his* idea. He would sell himself on Guy's trick. Tomorrow at four at the Algonquin. Guy would create an illusion around his illusion.

* * *

As it turned out, Guy's illusion became disillusion at four at the Algonquin when the concierge told him: "I'm sorry, but Mr. Woo checked out this morning."

"Checked out?!" Guy was incredulous. "Are you sure?"

"Yes, sir. As magician's say, he has 'disappeared.'"

"Will he be back?"

The concierge shrugged. "Someday, perhaps. I believe he said he was off to South America."

"South America! Damn!" Guy walked out of the hotel and walked along 44th street toward Broadway. He went to the Morosco Theater where Rosco confirmed Chen Woo and his troupe had packed up and left, a day early.

"Screw him!" Rosco said. "He was a second rate magician anyway. "We get the night off. Fine with me."

Guy wandered out of the theater in a daze. He paid no attention to where he was going. He just walked, muttering to himself, trying to figure out what had happened. Had Woo seen the potential of The Mysterium and stolen it? It certainly seemed so. But, then again, maybe Woo simply forgot he was leaving when Guy had stunned him with his trick. Maybe in the morning, he had forgotten about Guy and the wad of papers in his robe. Though he thought his trick was impressive, Guy began to doubt himself. Maybe it wasn't. Maybe he had made a fool of himself to the seasoned old pro.

He found himself at Ralph's Place, a small bar he'd been to a few times. With nothing better to do, he went in, ordered a beer, and brooded.

Miserably, Guy put his head in his hands and wondered what to do next. He couldn't chase after Woo in South America. He didn't have the working model of The Mysterium or the plans. They were so complicated and it had taken him so long to figure it out he wasn't sure he could ever reconstruct it.

His father had once warned him that it wasn't easy to tell if people were lying. Guy had to agree yet again. Whether it was the ads in the magic magazines, or the ads for apartments in New York, or a gorgeous angel backstage at the Morosco, or now, Woo the Chinese conjuror, Guy had to admit he was easy prey for con artists. For a magician, he was blind to life's many deceptions.

16

Life went on at the Morosco Theater. Acts came and went. Guy did his job backstage. As the weeks rolled by, Guy tried to forget Woo, but could not. His hatred of the second-rate magician who had stolen his brilliant idea deepened.

It was his memory of The Mysterium that faded. It was like something in a dream, something only vaguely remembered. The Mysterium was a miracle that had become a mirage.

Guy did not give up on magic. He practiced his routines, did a few small shows, and visited Tannen's. He never mentioned Woo or The Mysterium to Lou. He was more interested in impressing him and getting into the back room with the boys. But Lou stubbornly refused him, pointing out the slightest flaw in any trick Guy did for him. He did not know if Tannen was trying to discourage him or trying to polish his skills. Just how good were those guys anyway? He began to wonder if the inner sanctum was just another trick, something Tannen dangled in front of Guy to keep him coming back and buying tricks. What if he went behind the curtain and found not the world's greatest wizards but a bunch of old hacks smoking cigarettes, eating bagels, and bungling card and coin tricks?

He could not entertain such a possibility.

Whether it was the betrayal by Woo or his frustrations at Tannen's, or just being surrounded by millions of people and feeling isolated and lonely, Guy hit a low point. He was growing weary of his work at the theater. His career as a magician was going nowhere. He felt adrift.

He went home for Thanksgiving. His mother worried about him alone in the big city. His father, though he said he still supported Guy's quest to make it in magic, also asked if he was "perhaps giving college a second thought?" Concealing his own doubts and gloom, Guy was vague. He still had some time left on their agreement.

"Just wondering," Sam had said. Perhaps Guy was not as good at hiding his emotions as he was at hiding a coin in his palm.

The day after Thanksgiving, he took a long stroll at Ocean Beach. Hunched into a chill wind blowing in from Long Island Sound, Guy looked out to sea, watched the ferries going by, and wondered where *he* should be heading.

His destination, at least for the moment, was clear. He walked from the bright expanse of the boardwalk into the dark pit of the arcade. He went to the corner where the Gypsy Fortune Teller sat in the shadows, motionless in her glass cabinet, waiting. There was nobody else there, nobody to cut in front of him and perhaps steal his destiny. Guy fished in his pocked for a nickel and dropped it in the money slot. The lights came on; the gypsy moved her head and eyes, her hand swept across the pile of fortune cards. His dropped into the hole and out the slot in front. Guy picked it up and read it.

"Change is in the wind."

Back out on the boardwalk, leaning against the railing that separated it from the beach, Guy looked out at Race Rock Lighthouse. He wished he had a lighthouse to navigate by. He did not. He had only an enigmatic fortune provided by a wax seer. It provided little direction.

"Change is in the wind." What sort of change? What would cause it? Would it be Guy's choice or, like a magic trick, would he be forced to a destiny he could little imagine? He had no answers.

He took the questions with him back to New York. On December 7th, a few weeks after Thanksgiving, Guy was at Ralph's Place. It was a quiet Sunday afternoon. He sat alone, staring into a beer, hoping it might provide an answer where the Gypsy's fortune had not. On the radio, the NBC Red network was broadcasting Sammy Kaye's Sunday Serenade with Sammy and his Orchestra, Tommy Ryan, Alan Foster, and the Three Kaydettes.

The day's broadcast was just finishing up when it was interrupted by a news bulletin. An agitated Robert Eisenbach reported that Japanese planes had staged an early morning surprise attack on Pearl Harbor, a navy base on the Hawaiian island of Oahu.

Guy had never heard of Pearl Harbor. He listened to the chaotic and horrific reports of the brutal attack. History unreeled in a series of news bulletins, each seemingly more dire than the last. The surprise attack had decimated the fleet stationed at Pearl. The death toll was staggering.

What would it all mean?

After a while, having heard enough, Guy walked out into the dark December night, wondering if the world had gone mad.

The next day, the events at Pearl Harbor consumed everybody. All day, everywhere, people were talking about the devastating Japanese attack. The number of men killed was mounting by the hour, and ever more harrowing details began to emerge. There was shock and anger and uncertainty. Everybody had an opinion they wanted to share. Strangers talked.

There was instant and venomous hatred of the Japanese. The evening show went on at the Morosco but was poorly attended. Most people were in front of their radios, still engrossed in reports of the events half a world away. The show wrapped up. The theater was put to bed. Guy was hungry and went to Ralph's for a late night bite.

As he ate, he read sensational reports of Pearl Harbor in the *Daily News*. Its whole front page was giant type: "Japs Bomb Hawaii." Much smaller, at the bottom: "Declare war on U.S. and Britain." Perhaps this was the change the Gypsy had foretold?

After a while, Guy turned to the entertainment tabloid *Variety*. He needed relief from the drumbeat of betrayal and war, indignation and revenge. He browsed through *Variety* every week to see who was performing where, wondering if there might be a magic show he could join somewhere. His eye was drawn to a small bold headline.

"Chen Woo A Star in South America."

Guy read on:

The oriental wizard, Chen Woo, has been wowing audiences on his tour of South America. With his lovely wife, Eleanor, assisting him, Woo unveiled a new trick that has audiences gasping. He calls it "The Mysterium." It has to be seen to be believed. It is an astonishing illusion of great ingenuity. The climax of Woo's act, it has pulled in audiences who have heard about this extraordinary new wonder. True to his mysterious nature, Woo will reveal little about the origin of the trick or even where he plans to appear next. He was quoted recently as saying, through an interpreter, that: "a man of mystery should always be shrouded in mystery."

"Shit!" Guy said loudly, drawing stares from the other patrons. "Goddamned thief!"

He was stunned. Woo! He had stolen the plans to The Mysterium, had it made, and was now amazing audiences with it. And no doubt earning a pretty penny as well!

It all came flooding back to him, and Guy kicked himself again for stupidly showing The Mysterium to Woo. For letting him snatch it away. Guy's eagerness to make an impression, to further his own career, had blinded him to the possibility that the old magician might appropriate his creation. What a fool he had been! What a fool!

The more he thought about it, the angrier he became. Damn Woo! Damn the Japanese! Betrayal was everywhere!

Guy looked up from the newspaper. Ralph's was busy, and the talk was all about the attack on Pearl Harbor. Everybody was speculating on what would happen. Their questions were answered when the radio announcer said that President Roosevelt was about to address a joint session of Congress and, at the same time, the people of the United States.

The bar grew quiet as the speech began.

"Mr. Vice President, Mr. Speaker, Members of the Senate, and of the House of Representatives:

Yesterday, December 7th, 1941—a date which will live in infamy—the United States of America was suddenly and deliberately attacked by naval and air forces of the Empire of Japan.

The thing about betrayal, Guy reflected, is that you never see it coming.

It will be recorded that the distance of Hawaii from Japan makes it obvious that the attack was deliberately planned many days or even weeks ago. During the intervening time, the Japanese government has deliberately sought to deceive the United States by false statements and expressions of hope for continued peace.

Guy shook his head. It was so hard to tell when people were lying. Not just for him, it seemed.

Japan has, therefore, undertaken a surprise offensive extending throughout the Pacific area. The facts of yesterday and today speak for themselves. The people of the United States have already formed their opinions and well understand the implications to the very life and safety of our nation.

"Change is in the wind," thought Guy.

I believe that I interpret the will of the Congress and of the people when I assert that we will not only defend ourselves to the uttermost, but will make it very certain that this form of treachery shall never again endanger us. Hostilities exist. There is no blinking at the fact that our people, our territory, and our interests are in grave danger.

"Revenge. The President is talking revenge," Guy thought, understanding how betrayal would ignite the anger that would fuel the fires of vengeance.

With confidence in our armed forces, with the unbounding determination of our people, we will gain the inevitable triumph — so help us God.

I ask that the Congress declare that since the unprovoked and dastardly attack by Japan on Sunday, December 7th, 1941, a state of war has existed between the United States and the Japanese empire."

The speech ended, and the absolute silence that had overtaken the bar exploded into a cacophony of voices. The bar was noisy with speculation, calls for revenge, with swagger and bravado.

The radio played Kate Smith singing "God Bless America" and, after finishing their last beer and paying their tabs, most of the young men decided to enlist. They left the bar misty eyed, with jaws clenched in patriotic determination. They would defend America and teach those Japs a lesson!

Betrayed himself, seething with anger, vowing vengeance, Guy joined them.

17

The bullets were flying. It was North Africa, 1942. Guy hunkered down behind a stone wall with two other guys. They kept their heads low. The damned Kraut shooting at them with the machine gun was spraying the area back and forth, like he was trying to exterminate ants. He was in the shadows just inside the door to a small deserted house. A sniper off to their left took aim from a roof, keeping hidden behind a chimney. At least that's where he was now. The bastard had been moving about for an hour, shooting from a rooftop, from behind a wall, from one angle or another. Sniping was like magic: it was all about angles. The sniper had already wounded Curly. The sniper was spooking everybody. There was no telling where he'd shoot from next. There were plenty of places to hide. No one was going anywhere until someone killed him and the machine gunner or it got dark, and that was still hours away.

They had walked into an ambush as they advanced toward Oed Zem Boujad, in Morocco. Already, Lester and Sonny lay dead, both cut down when the machine gunner opened fire as they approached the small adobe building, trudging through the desert, bending forward as the wind whipped up the sand and drove it into them like buckshot. They'd thought the village was deserted, but they were dead wrong. As far as they could tell, there was only one machine gunner and one sniper lurking. Together, they effectively covered the area and stopped Guy's squad from advancing. Their best route was through this small village and on, where they would meet up with the rest of their battalion. But for the moment, they were pinned down—out in the middle of nowhere, going nowhere, trapped in a deserted village.

Guy had been in the war for two weeks. He'd seen enough death in that time to last a lifetime. Basic training hadn't prepared him for the real thing. They could teach him to march and fire a rifle and make his bed and take orders. But they couldn't simulate the terror of being in battle. They couldn't get him ready for seeing a pal cut in half by machine-gun fire or having his head blown into a grey pink mist or the stench of innards spilling out of a gaping belly wound. In training, nobody lay on the ground, slowly dying, screaming in pain, pleading for help, praying, or calling for his mother.

No. War had to be experienced first hand. Only that could make it real. Forget the tactics and training. He acted on instinct. Kill or be killed. That was the choice. No choice at all, really.

Guy had enlisted just days after Pearl Harbor, upsetting Sam and Ruth. Like many parents, they understood their son's desire to fight for his country. Like many parents, they were terrified of what might happen to him. He was their only child, little Guy. They could not picture him at war.

Guy went through basic training at Fort Dix in New Jersey. Then he waited around a lot, playing poker, getting drunk, marching, firing and cleaning his rifle, playing more poker, practicing his coin and card tricks, and so on. Then, in March, he'd shipped out to Africa, where the action was. He had expected to see elephants and lions, but encountered only endless miles of sand, small villages of stone and adobe, and a lot of crazy Krauts, Arabs and Italians trying to kill him. No Japanese. He wasn't sure why there were Italians in Morocco, but when he asked he was told to shut up and try to kill them.

Fate had taken him to this stone wall in Oed Zem Boujad where he sat in the hot sands with Butch, a guy from Michigan, and Buck, a guy from Baltimore. They had very little in common except a patriotic desire not to get killed.

Sitting behind the wall waiting for night, or for someone to figure out a way to kill the machine gunner and the sniper, gave Guy plenty of time to practice. As he idly played with a coin, going through his sleights, he thought about bullets and the "Bullet Catch" trick, a classic of magic.

For generations, magicians had had a bullet signed and loaded into a rifle. The magician stood on one side of the stage, the man with the rifle on the other. Holding up a dish, talking about the danger of standing in the line of fire, the magician would build the suspense and drama. Drum rolls and nervous assistants would add to the theatricality of the trick.

Finally, the brave—or foolhardy—magician would give the signal. The man would fire the rifle. The magician would stumble backward as if wounded. The audience would gasp. Then the magician would smile and show a bullet in his teeth. He'd spit it onto the dish and show it was the original signed bullet.

It was a great trick—and a deadly one. Several magicians had been killed doing this feat of daring, none more famously than the marvelous Chinese conjuror Chung Ling Soo. Soo was not what he seemed to be. He was not Chinese at all. He was William Ellsworth Robinson, from New York, who dressed up as a Chinaman and played his part convincingly: he never uttered a word onstage and always used an interpreter when he spoke to journalists.

Everybody believed Chung Ling Soo was an authentic Chinaman until the moment in 1918 when his bullet catch trick went horribly wrong. He was shot for real, and as he crumpled to the stage mortally wounded he gasped: "Oh my God! Something's happened. Lower the curtain!" The audience was stunned by both his misfortune and his sudden command of English.

Chung Ling Soo died the next day.

Yes, thought Guy, the bullet catch was a dangerous trick. Men were not meant to catch bullets in their teeth or anywhere else. As he sat behind the stone wall and bullets whizzed above his head, he could not imagine voluntarily standing in the line of fire for a magic trick. He looked down at the shiny Morgan dollar in his hand. A coin trick was less dramatic, but so much safer. Guy kept that Morgan with him always, both as a good luck charm and to have a coin handy to practice with. Practicing making a coin vanish and reappear was Guy's way of burning off his nervous energy.

He was not the first magician to do so. During World War I, a fellow named Richard Valentine Pitchford passed time in the trenches by practicing card manipulations. He honed his ability to perform card tricks while wearing gloves. After being injured in battle, Pitchford continued to polish his magic skills in a hospital, and went on to become one of the world's greatest card manipulators, performing as "Cardini." Guy had seen him at the Morosco.

From the Morosco to Morocco. Change had certainly been in the wind that had swept through Guy's life. He and Butch and Buck were in a state of bored terror. Boredom from sitting behind the wall for hours, and terror of the sudden death a false move could lead to. Sarge, Snuffy, Doc and Tyler were behind another nearby wall, arguing over the best way to cook meatloaf.

"Do it again," said Butch. He was speaking of the coin trick Guy had done at least a hundred times since they'd taken refuge behind the wall. It was his Retention Vanish. Butch was rapt as over and over Guy make the coin vanish and reappear, sometimes in his top pocket, sometimes in Butch's. Nothing very fancy, but in Guy's hands, after years of practice, astonishing. "Do it again," Butch would say each time, a broad smile on his face. He was mesmerized by the trick, and it calmed the big kid down.

Butch was not too bright, but loyal and a great shot. Guy was happy to have him nearby when the fighting started. Guy liked him. Butch had grown up on a cherry farm in northern Michigan. He knew a lot about cherries. More, in fact, than Guy cared to hear. He was about six two, muscled like a prizefighter. He dreamed of marrying his high school sweetheart, Sue, having lots of kids, and managing the family farm. If Butch survived the war, Guy had a feeling that this one trip to the desert of Africa might be the only time the kid would set foot outside the United States. Or maybe even Michigan, for that matter.

Buck, on the other hand, was a street-smart kid from Baltimore, which was pretty much his world. He knew a lot about cars. He fixed Jeeps and trucks for the Army. He dreamed of opening an auto shop someday. He wanted to be his own boss, maybe put his kids to work for him so he could restore old cars. He was small, stocky, talked slowly, and looked around a lot, wide-eyed. He was nervous about getting shot. They all were, of course, but Buck kept swiveling his head around as if he could see an incoming bullet and dodge it. The other soldiers would sometimes yell "Duck, Buck!" when they saw him doing this, and he would, pulling his head down into his shoulders like a turtle. A very quick turtle. Then they'd all laugh and Buck would shoot them the finger and say, "Screw you!"

So there they were. The farm kid. The city kid. And Guy, a small town boy who dreamed of being a famous magician someday. Destiny and the U.S. Army had thrown them together, and now they huddled behind a low wall in Oed Zem Boujad, in North Africa, fighting Italians, Germans, and Arabs, hoping to win the war.

At the moment, the other guys were winning. As Guy's squad had approached the village, three men had been cut down. Two had died instantly. The third, though mortally wounded, had lingered for several hours. At first, he had shouted "Don't let me die! Don't let me die!" They couldn't get to him. He was out in the open, and anybody trying to help him would have been killed. As his life ebbed away and his strength faded, his shouts dimmed to a muttered monologue, a delirious ramble about his life. Finally, they could only hear him whispering to his mother.

Then silence.

Buck had said a prayer for the man.

That was hours ago. Now, the occasional rat-a-tat-tat of the machine gun or a shot from the sniper were the only sounds around them. It was nerve wracking. It was hot behind that wall out in the desert sun. They'd taken their helmets off.

"Do it again," said Butch. Guy did. As he pulled the coin from his pocket, Guy looked at Butch who was smiling again, utterly delighted by the moment of wonder, as if it was the first time he'd experienced it. Guy smiled at him, waiting for the inevitable "Do it again!"

He heard a distant gunshot.

The wonder and the life blinked out of Butch's eyes. A smile still on his face, he toppled forward into Guy's lap, a bullet hole in the back of his head, gushing blood.

"Sniper!!" screamed Buck, *his* eyes wide in horror. Guy was frozen in shock. He looked down at Butch, dead, slumped into his lap.

In a daze, without thinking of the machine gunner or sniper, Guy stood up to get away from the corpse on him.

Buck yelled: "Down, Guy! Get down!"

But Guy wasn't going back to the horror at his feet. He pulled out his gun, and started running toward the machine gunner at the farmhouse, taking a crazy zigzagging path so the sniper couldn't easily draw a bead on him. In a blind rage, he began shooting as he ran. Lucky for Guy, the gunner was at the far end of his deadly sweep. Guy ran and dodged around some brick walls, firing in a mindless fury of adrenaline, fear and anger.

His foot exploded in pain and he went down. A good thing, too, as the machine gun sprayed it's deadly arc of hot lead just above him. He looked down and saw his boot ripped open and bloody. He glimpsed muscle and bone.

The sniper stood up on the roof, next to the chimney, thinking he'd killed Guy. Guy saw him. Fighting the pain, he sighted on the silhouette of the man and squeezed off a few rounds. His aim was true. The sniper fell to his knees then slid down the roof and dropped to the ground with a thud. Dead.

Guy crawled a few feet to the edge of another stone wall. He was very close to the house now, and the machine gunner couldn't get a good angle on him. The soldier picked up his machine gun to move it. It was a careless moment. Guy had a clear shot at him, no more than twenty feet away.

The German was just a kid, maybe 18, shoved into this damned war, ordered to be a murderer, left behind to slow down the Yanks as they tried to advance. He was Guy in a different uniform, speaking a different language. For a second, their eyes met. He was the enemy, but he was scared. Guy could see it in his eyes.

Guy pulled the trigger. He shot into the doorway until his gun was empty. When the smoke cleared, he saw the gunner lying dead in a creeping pool of blood. Single handedly, Guy had killed the sniper and the gunner. Butch's death had pushed him to act in mindless fury.

As he lay there in the sand, his foot was agony. It looked like some toes were missing, and the sight made him nauseous. He was bleeding profusely. He saw sparkles dancing in front of his eyes. He dropped his head onto the sand, hot and gritty against his cheek. He vaguely heard men yelling. Or maybe it was the wind.

Then the bright desert day turned to night, and Guy tumbled into the darkness.

18

Guy's eyes flickered open.

Sunlight streaked across a white wall. A curtain blew in a lazy breeze. He looked around. Everything was white. A pretty girl dressed in white leaned over and looked into his face with a smile.

"Am I in heaven?" Guy asked.

"Not quite, soldier boy. Bliss."

"Bliss?"

"Bliss Hospital. Welcome home," said the nurse, whose nametag read "Sigrid Schuetz."

"I don't remember a Bliss Hospital in New London," said Guy.

"New London?"

"Yes, m'am, New London, Connecticut. That's where I'm from."

"Soldier boy, I hate to tell you but you're about as far from Connecticut as you can get in the United States. You are a guest of the Bliss Army Hospital at Fort Huachuca in Arizona. Almost in Mexico. At the bottom of the country. Some call it 'America's Ass.'"

"Arizona! It doesn't make sense. Why didn't they send me to a hospital in New England?"

"This is the army. It's not supposed to make sense," said Nurse Sigrid.

Because of the morphine they kept giving him, Guy had only vague memories of being in a field tent, in the back of a truck, on a plane, in a hospital, on another plane and so on, until he awoke in this sunny room in a hospital in Arizona where a buxom and smiling nurse welcomed him home, even though he was far from home.

His wound ended the war for Guy. He had been in combat for two weeks. He had gone from the deserts of Morocco to the deserts of Arizona. They'd patched up what remained of his foot, just his big and pinkie toes. He had to learn to walk without the missing digits. He had a bit of a funny step, but that was about it. If you are going to get a body part shot off, it turns out toes are probably the best. He stayed in the hospital convalescing and chatting with Sigrid, who called him "soldier boy" and flirted mercilessly.

To relieve the tedium, he asked for a deck of cards and practiced his magic. He was amazed that his lucky Morgan dollar had made it all the way with him, tucked into his top pocket where he was reaching for it when Butch got shot.

"Show me a trick, soldier boy," Sigrid said one afternoon as she watched him practice his moves. Guy smiled and took his Morgan and did his Retention Vanish.

"Where could it be?" asked Guy. "Ah, I know." He motioned Sigrid over. "There it is," he said, and reached into the pocket of her nurse's uniform, held taught by her ample breasts. He thrilled to the feel of them against the white fabric.

"Do it again," said Sigrid. Apparently she'd liked the conclusion of the trick, too.

Guy froze. He dropped the coin. For a moment, he was not in a hospital in Arizona but behind a wall in the Moroccan desert doing magic for a big farm kid.

Butch.

He would never forget him or the moment he died. To see his expression go from wide-eyed wonder to the blank stare of death in an instant was a haunting memory. It would take Guy a very long time to be able to perform the trick without thinking of Butch dying. It was another wound—the infection of his favorite trick with a tragic association.

"You okay?" Sigrid asked. "You look kinda ashen."

Guy took a moment to compose himself. He shook off the images of death in the desert.

"I'll be fine, Sigrid. I just have some bad memories I need to forget."

Sigrid nodded. A lot of the young men who came back from the war were haunted by their experiences. She could only imagine what horrors they'd seen. She knew there was no medicine that could help. It would take time and compassion to heal them.

She picked up the dollar and gave it back to him.

"That's quite a trick, Guy." He wasn't sure if she meant his Retention Vanish or his trying to forget. She sat by his bed, and they said nothing for a while.

"Sigrid, I've been wondering about you," Guy said at last. "Your name. Sigrid Schuetz. It sounds German."

She smiled. "It is. My folks immigrated to America after World War I. You know, the war to end all wars."

"They were wrong."

"Yes, they were. But I'm about as German as you are, Guy. I don't speak German. I don't like German food. I've never even been to Germany."

She gave a rueful laugh.

"It's a tough time for us now. People don't like anything German, though we have it better than the Japs. At least nobody is rounding us up and sticking us in camps. At least not yet."

She paused, shook her head.

"It's strange. We're the same people we were a few years ago. Patriotic, God-fearing Americans. But people look at us differently now. Like we're freaks or something. Sometimes I wish we could wear masks. Hide who we are."

"War's crazy, Sigrid. I killed a German. He was probably 18. He was the enemy, or so they told me. I was the enemy, or so they told him. But, really … what did either of us know what the damned war was about? We were just trained to kill."

"Don't think about it too much, soldier boy. It's over for you now."

"Maybe. Maybe not. I'm not sure it will ever be over."

"You gotta get on with life. What's done is done."

Hearing her, Guy remembered what his father had once said. "Sometimes, you just have to let things go and move on."

Easier said than done.

19

A few weeks into Guy's convalescence, a general walked in with some aides. He stood at the foot of Guy's bed, made a brief, perfunctory speech, and took two medals out of a box. Guy received a Purple Heart for his wound and a Bronze Star for heroism for single-handedly taking out the sniper and machine gunner. It had enabled his squad to meet up with the battalion for more fun in the Moroccan desert. His few seconds of mindless, murderous rage had earned him the gratitude of his country, an honorable discharge, and status as a minor hero. At least in the eyes of Nurse Sigrid, about the only person he knew at Bliss.

After six weeks, Guy was discharged from the hospital and the army. He was walking pretty well, though still in some pain. He was given enough money to travel home, along with his pay and some compensation for his wound. Not a lot, but enough to last him a few months. Guy thought about spending some of it on Sigrid. He thought they could have a good time together. Maybe take a trip or two to heaven. But he was self-conscious about his maimed foot, so he settled for some tasty steaks washed down with large glasses of beer.

Guy indulged himself for a few days, then hitched a ride north to the train station in Benson. He wanted some time to get used to life, to his half-foot. He figured the small towns of the South would be a good start, so he bought a ticket all the way to New Orleans. He would get off at anyplace that looked interesting.

He wrote a letter to his folks telling them he would be home eventually, but that, for now, he was traveling and exploring life. He hoped the mention of his medals would make them proud and buffer their disappointment that he was not running back to them.

Guy was adrift. No longer a soldier, not really a magician. He didn't know where he was going and, for the moment, that was fine with him. The army had provided enough structure, regimentation and direction for a while. A long while. The war had provided more than enough excitement and trauma. He didn't want to see any more death. He wanted to forget. He wanted to fill his mind with new experiences and memories.

So he got on the train in Benson and headed east to New Orleans, days away. He hopped off at El Paso but didn't much care for it. He next tried Marathon, Texas. It was there he finally overcame his shyness about his foot and spent a lovely night with a girl named Susan who did her patriotic duty to keep a hero's mind off his suffering. He met her at a bar, dazzled her with a card trick, got her sympathy with tales of his time in the war and his wound, and discovered that she knew a little sleight of hand herself.

He didn't want to get entangled and neither did Susan. After a few sweaty days together, living up to the name of the town, he left her behind and boarded the train again.

Guy liked the trains. He liked the clackity-clack of the wheels, the gentle sway of the carriage, the coziness of a sleeper cabin. He liked the lounge and restaurant cars where he had chance encounters with strangers. They came from all walks of life. They all had stories or were in the midst of making new ones. On a train, people's lives intersected for an hour or an evening, never to cross paths again. Guy could only wonder what became of them, how their little dramas played out.

He met an old couple from Madison, Wisconsin, on their way to Florida to see the alligators. He dined with a young soldier, just out of boot camp, and his pregnant wife. The boy was excited and nervous, about to go off to war, young and ignorant of the horrors that awaited him, just as Guy had been. The kid kept asking Guy about the war, and Guy kept telling him he didn't have much to say. He didn't want to scare them with the truth.

Guy spent an evening in the club car listening to a daredevil pilot tell of his barnstorming days in Ohio and the time he met the Wright brothers. He listened, bewildered, to a man named Shivers, who seemed a bit crazy and harbored a tremendous fear of the sea. He met a photographer named Jim who worked for National Geographic and was on his way to shoot the cotton fields of Mississippi.

For his part, Guy realized he was free to adopt any persona. Sometimes he wore his uniform and talked about war, as he had with the young soldier and his wife. Sometimes he wore street clothes and told them he was a barber. Or a writer. Or a scientist. Once, hoping to seduce a sultry young woman, Guy told her what he did was "classified." He hoped to sound mysterious, maybe even dangerous. It didn't work.

A few times, Guy even did a magic trick or two, though his props were limited to coins (including his beloved Morgan), a deck of cards, and whatever wonders he could create with match books, cigarettes, silverware, and dollar bills. He enjoyed giving little impromptu shows after dinner, when a few diners and waiters would gather around and watch him.

Guy loved to be snug in his berth as a train rocketed through the night, through the landscape of America, blowing its mournful horn. If he was awake when the train stopped, he would raise the curtain and watch as a passenger or two departed or embarked from tiny stations in sleepy little towns.

After dinner one night, heading across southern Texas into Louisiana, Guy, in uniform, went to the club car for a beer. It was full of businessmen in suits sipping drinks. The air was thick with blue cigarette and cigar smoke. Guy sat at a small round table and idly watched a wine cork roll around, to and fro, in time to the swaying of the train. A big man with a pointy noise, walrus mustache and mutton-chop sideburns muscled his way back from the bar. The only seat open was the one across from Guy, and spotting it, the man stopped.

As he sat down he asked, "Mind if I sit here?"

"No, go ahead," said Guy, though he had no choice in the matter.

The man took a sip of his drink, put it on the café table. He watched as the clear liquid sloshed up toward the rim and the glass slid a few inches across the table. He thought better of it and rescued the drink. With a smile, he looked up at Guy.

"Jenks is the name. Willie Jenks. And whom do I have the pleasure of sitting with?"

"Guy Borden."

"Guy. Guy Borden," Jenks said, saying his name as if he were studying it. "Where ya headed, Guy?"

"I'm not sure," said Guy. And he wasn't.

"My type of guy, Guy. My type of guy. I like a fella who doesn't have a goal." Jenks paused and took a sip of his drink, then motioned over his shoulder with his thumb.

"Look at all these guys. They know *exactly* where they are going, I'll bet. Exactly where, exactly when. But where's the fun in that? Where's the adventure?" He leaned over toward Guy and continued in a hushed, conspiratorial tone. "You got to take some risk and break away, right? Push the limits. Dance at the edges, if you know what I mean."

Guy didn't exactly. Willie Jenks had blown in from the bar like a squall, and now he seemed to have stalled at Guy's table.

"Now the truth of it is, Guy, I don't know where I'm going, either. That will depend on the next few hours. There are a number of possibilities." He took a long swig of his drink. He licked his lips and sighed. He eyed the martini like it was a miracle. In one of his big hands he idly played with the cork that had been rolling around on the table.

As Jenks took another sip of his martini, Guy thought about multiple outcomes. Life was like that. Many possible outcomes, as Willie had just said. Could life be like a cosmic Magician's Choice with God bending our decisions to His will?

"I can't help but notice, Guy, that you're a soldier. Been in action yet?"

Guy said he had and told Willie Jenks the story of his brief stint with the U.S. Army fighting Germans, Arabs and Italians in the deserts of Morocco. When he was done, Willie Jenks whistled, and shook his head.

"That's quite a story, Guy. Here's to you and your bravery!" He raised his glass and Guy did the same. They clinked them together and drank.

"I myself have not served my country. Not that I didn't want to, mind you. Hell, I am as patriotic as the next fella. But the good Lord cursed me with flat feet, asthma, and a heart murmur. Nobody wanted Willie Jenks to defend his country and keep the world free." He sighed and took another sip of his martini.

"So I have been doomed to sit out this current war and watch the exploits of others like yourself."

Willie Jenks looked very sad as he said this. Guy didn't know quite what to say. He took a sip of his beer and suppressed a burp.

"Let me ask you, Guy. What's the most valuable thing you have?"

Guy thought about it. "A gold pocket watch," he said. "With a picture of my mother and father in it."

"Yes?" said Jenks. "Got it with you? Can I see it?"

Guy reached into his pocket and took out the watch. He unclipped it from his pants loop and handed it to Jenks.

"My father gave it to me on my thirteenth birthday," said Guy.

Jenks studied it. Opened it, checked the time on his own watch, and looked at the miniature picture of Guy's folks.

"Handsome couple," he muttered. Then he shut the watch and gave it back to Guy.

"It's a fine watch, Guy. I'll give you that. I'd be proud to own it. But it's not the most valuable thing you have."

"It's not?"

"Hell no, boy. Hell no. The most valuable thing you own is your own free will. Your ability to choose what you want to be. Where you want to go. *That's* priceless!"

Guy nodded.

"Look at these guys, Guy," Willie Jenks continued, again motioning over his shoulder. "You think they have free will? Well, no, they don't. They have jobs and schedules and wives and kids, and they gotta be where they gotta be and do what they gotta do. They have about as much free will as a dog. But you know what?"

Guy shook his head "no."

"They *think* they have a choice. But it's a delusion. A myth. A falsehood. Oh, sure, they can take this train or that train or order steak or chicken. They can buy a striped tie or a checked one. Darn, those choices don't matter. Not really. Not in the big scheme of things. But you, Guy, and me: we have *real* choice! We can go where we want, do what we want, be *who* we want! Why? Because we don't know where we're going, that's why. We have the freedom of uncertainty. Soon as you start making too many choices you end up finding out you have no real choices at all. So the trick is to choose your choices with the utmost care. Are you following me?"

Guy wasn't sure he was following Willie Jenks exactly, except, in a way, he knew there was some truth in what he said. He thought about it. Then he decided that perhaps he could make Willie Jenks think a bit as well. Do a trick for him that would get Willie chasing his tail thinking about free will and choice.

Guy took out his well-worn deck of cards. After removing the deck from the box, he took out a single card at random. He glanced at it but did not show it to Jenks. He put it face down on the table.

"If you mean to suggest a game of chance," said Willie Jenks, "I must tell you that I am not a gambling man. Money is too hard to come by to risk losing it on games of chance. There are no shortcuts to wealth." Willie picked up the cork that kept rolling back and forth across the table and over the card.

"No, no, Mr. Jenks. I am not proposing any gambling. I'd just like to show you a little demonstration about choice, since you have brought it up."

"Well, Guy, that's fine. I am intrigued." Willie leaned forward and looked at the back of the card intently, sipping again on his martini.

"Mr. Jenks, as you see, I have chosen a card from this deck. I won't show it to you yet. Now, I am about to give *you* some choices. Free choices. Are you ready?"

"Yes, son, I am. Shoot."

"Okay, Mr. Jenks. Cards come in four suits. Clubs. Diamonds. Hearts and Spades. Two are red, two are black, correct?"

"Of course."

"Now, which do you prefer: black or red?"

"Hmmm. Red I suppose."

"Okay. You selected the red. They are yours. That leaves me the blacks. Now in the black suits, we have spades and clubs, correct?"

"Yes."

"Do you have a favorite? Is it clubs? Or do you like spades?"

Willie thought a moment. "Spades, I believe. I like spades."

"Me too, Willie. Okay, there are thirteen spade cards, as there are in all suits. To make this simple, let's choose just four, say, the Two, the Seven, and, I don't know, how about the Ten and the Queen. Fair?"

"Eminently."

"Now, Mr. Jenks, please select two of those four."

"Hmmm. Let me say the Two and the Queen."

"Any particular reason you chose those two?"

"Well, I'm not sure, Guy. The Two, maybe, because it's so low. And the Queen because she's so powerful. Make sense?"

"Good reasons, Willie. You keep what you choose. As for me, you leave me with the Seven and the Ten. Not very exciting cards, really, though there are a lot of pips on the Ten. They make a nice pattern, if you can imagine it. Anyway, of the two cards we have left in play, the Seven and the Ten of Spades, one of those two is special. Which one do you think it is?"

"The seven," said Willie.

"Though some may think the Seven of Spades is perhaps unlucky, you choose it? You're sure?"

"Yes!" said Willie, quite fascinated with Guy's experiment.

"You don't want to change your mind?"

"No."

"Let me review, Mr. Jenks. We started with a deck of cards. Fifty-two of them. You have made choices all along the way. Free choices, yes?"

"Yes."

"And from that whole deck of possibilities, you have arrived at a single card: the Seven of Spades, right?"

"Right!"

"Well, of course you have, Mr. Jenks. Of course you have. And I knew you would. I knew it with absolute certainty. How? Because I took one look at you and knew that you were a man who would choose the Seven of Spades if given the choice."

"Really?" asked Jenks, startled.

"Really," said Guy. "And I can prove it. I looked at you, I knew the card you would choose, and I took it from the deck."

As he said this, Guy very slowly lifted the card he had selected and put on the table, keeping its back to Jenks.

"The Seven of Spades," said Guy as he slowly turned the card around so Jenks could see it.

Willie Jenks stared at the card in amazement. He blinked a few times. Then in a single gulp he finished his martini.

"Well, my God, Guy. You are a wonder! Can you really predict what card a man will choose?"

Guy smiled, enjoyed the astonishment on Jenks' face. He waited a moment before answering.

"Not really, Mr. Jenks. I used a technique called Magician's Choice that gives you the illusion of free choice when, in fact, I am interpreting your choices in a way that leads to what I want." Guy paused. "Without your knowing it," he added.

"How?" asked Jenks, picking up the Seven of Spades and turning it over and over.

"Oh, I can't say. That would betray the oath of secrecy I've taken. Besides, once you know, the magic would be gone. Believe me: you're much better off with the wonder than with the explanation. You'll remember the wonder. You'd forget the explanation."

Jenks shook his head. "Goodness, Guy. From now on, every time I make a choice, I'll wonder if someone else might be calling the shots. Maybe that's what happened to these guys," Jenks said as he gestured to the men at the bar.

"Well, Magician's Choice is fine for a card trick," said Guy, putting the deck back in his pocket. "But I doubt it would work in life."

"You never know," said Jenks with a smile. "Life is full of surprises."

"That it is," said Guy, who had had plenty.

The train chugged along, its whistle blowing across the empty Texas flatlands. Willie smiled and shook his head, still amazed by Guy's trick. Over the hubbub of the bar, the conductor announced the next stop coming up in a few minutes. A few men finished their drinks and paid up. After a moment, Jenks spoke.

"Say, Guy. I couldn't help but notice that that watch of yours was mighty dirty. I guess it's been through a lot. I can show you a quick, easy way to clean it."

"Yeah?"

"Sure. Let me see it a minute."

Again Guy took out the watch and handed it to Jenks.

"Now here's how you do it. Watch closely. Give me your napkin. Thanks. Okay, you wrap the napkin around the watch nice and tight, like this, see. It's gotta be tight or it won't work. Now, Guy, give me some aftershave."

"Aftershave?"

"Yes, you shave don't you?"

"Well, of course. But I don't carry aftershave with me."

"No, of course not. How stupid of me. What do you use?"

"Aqua Velva."

"Hmm. Nice. Spicy. I like Mennen's Skin Bracer myself. Here, hold the napkin with your watch and I'll be right back. My cabin's right next door and I have some Mennen's there. The trick is, you wrap the napkin tight around the watch, pour on the aftershave, and rub the napkin so the alcohol cleans the watch. In a few minutes you won't recognize it. I guarantee!"

Jenks got up and was gone. Guy sat holding the napkin with his watch inside.

Just then, the train rumbled to a stop, the breaks squealing. Guy gazed out the window at the station platform. The sign read "China," which confused Guy for a moment. He watched as the people milled about and boarded. He watched as passengers left the train, squeezing between those trying to board. The conductor yelled all aboard. Just as the train started to move, he saw Willie Jenks on the platform, suitcase in hand. He stood watching the train leave, checking the time on his pocket watch.

With sudden dread and realization, Guy unwrapped the napkin. Inside was the cork that had been rolling around on the table and Jenks had been playing with. Apparently Willie Jenks knew sleight of hand, too.

"Hey! Hey! Jenks! Shit, he stole my watch!" Guy yelled. He tried to get out of the café car, but there were too many men who knew exactly where they were going in the way. The train picked up speed. Desperately, Guy tried to muscle his way to the door. By the time he got there, it was too late. The train was moving fast and China, Texas, Willie Jenks, and Guy's watch were left behind.

Guy had just been conned out of the second most valuable thing he owned, right behind his free will, which, Jenks had explained, was priceless.

A few minutes later, the conductor came through and Guy told him what had happened.

"That so? Well, kid, the rails are full of con men and grifters. They come on and get involved in card games or prey on trusting folk. They're confidence men. They run their scam, make their sting, then get off. Find another train or another poker game or some other con. Looks like you just met one. Sorry, kid, but he's long gone. Even if I called back to the station, nobody'd ever find him or your watch."

Glumly, Guy returned to his seat and ordered another beer.

The Mummy Asrah. Chen Woo. Now Jenks. They were all scams or cheats, and Guy had fallen for them time and time again. Guy wondered if all life was like this, full of con men and liars and cheats. Was he doomed to be the victim, the hapless mark for them all? He thought about Willie Jenks. About the magician's choice trick he had played on the man who would turn around and trick him.

Guy's eyes widened a bit.

The Seven of Spades! Each card had a meaning, as Harry Blackstone had told him that day in Sam's barbershop. Guy had later learned them all. The Seven of Spades meant betrayal and theft. Guy had chosen that card out of the deck randomly. Or so he thought. Yet given how Willie Jenks had made off with his watch, Guy had to wonder if it was destined.

The train rumbled on through the night.

20

Guy sat with his head against the window of the lounge car, hypnotized by the rush of countryside going by, the lulling sounds, the gentle rocking. He was a bit hung over from his night in the club car and his unfortunate encounter with Willie Jenks. Thoughts drifted by like clouds. They were just fragments of his life, a kaleidoscope of images and faces. Sam and Ruth. Blackstone. The Gypsy. Ginger. Woo. Tannen. Butch and Buck. Sigrid. Susan. Jenks.

"You never go so far as when you don't know where you're going."

"Well," thought Guy, "I sure as hell don't know where I'm going so maybe I'll go very far." He sat back in his chair and sighed. His eyes drifted to a crumpled piece of paper on the seat across from him, perhaps left by the man who had been sitting there a while back. Guy picked it up and unfolded it. It was a broadsheet. He smoothed the creases and began to read:

STREETER & HALE'S
Carnival of Curiosities, Oddities and
Perilous Performers
1943 SEASON

Playing one & two-week engagements in

TEXAS: Milano, Wallis, Sugar Land

LOUISIANA: Sulphur, Thibodaux

MISSISSIPPI: Picayune, Derby, Enterprise

ALABAMA: Cuba, Oxford

GEORGIA: Tallapoosa, Lula

SOUTH CAROLINA: Liberty, Arcadia, Cowpens

NORTH CAROLINA: Ruffin, Hurt

VIRGINIA: Culpepper

MARYLAND: Havre de Grace

PENNSYLVANIA: Chester

NEW JERSEY: Princeton, Jersey City

He was still reading it when the conductor came through and announced they would be pulling into Sulphur, Louisiana, in fifteen minutes. Sulphur! It was on the broadside. He wondered if the carnival would be in town. It was worth taking a look. A carnival might be just the thing Guy had been looking for. Something exotic, adventurous—show biz on the road.

He did not hesitate. He rushed back to his tiny cabin, No. 6. He started packing up his belongings, stealing quick glances out the window by his berth. The train slowed and stopped. Guy was ready. He got off the train.

Perhaps Jenks was right. Maybe Guy was just exercising his free will. His priceless ability to choose where he wanted to be. Or maybe, like the men in the club car, Guy really knew exactly where he was going. He just didn't know it yet.

A few minutes later, Guy was standing alone, enveloped in the steam of the departing train, a world as white and full of possibilities as a blank canvas. As the cloud slowly dissipated, the details of the scene materialized like a new idea. He stood at a small depot. It was quiet, like a storm had passed. He reached into his pocket to check the time and only then remembered his pocket watch was gone. Jenks, the son-of-a-bitch! Guy clenched his teeth in anger. He'd find that bastard someday and get his revenge. Right after he took care of Woo. Guy turned and went into the creaky wooden depot.

His questions about the carnival were quickly answered. Posted on a wall, the Streeter and Hale broadside had a date filled in in a box at the bottom, just like his Mysto Magic Set poster.

"Opening May 14."

Tomorrow. It was fated. Guy was sure of it. His life and the carnival's were meant to intersect. What happened next was up to him. He wandered out of the depot and down the street, and booked a room at the Brimstone Hotel for the night.

21

The train whistle tore into the silent night like a nocturnal animal hunting its prey. The carnival arrived in the dead of night, creeping into Sulphur on the back of a chill spring wind.

In his hotel room, Guy heard it. He lay in bed listening. He could hear the rattle of the train as it came into town, the hiss of steam as it braked, then silence once more. It was here. And he knew that his life and the carnival's would be entwined.

He stared at the cross-shaped shadow of the windowpanes on the ceiling. He tried to imagine the carnival. He knew he wanted to work in it, if they hired magicians. If they didn't already have one. He started to plan what he would do. He had no tricks with him. Just a deck of cards, some coins and a few other small props. Not much, but maybe enough. He could get or build what he needed.

He rolled over and drifted off to sleep.

When he awoke in the morning, he quickly showered, ate breakfast, and headed over to the carnival. It tugged at him with its own peculiar gravity, irresistible, and Guy felt himself falling toward it.

By the time Guy arrived at the carnival, it was halfway set up in the dry dusty earth of an abandoned field at the edge of town. Roustabouts were hard at work pounding in stakes for the tents, attaching ropes, hauling canvases, moving barrels, opening crates, setting up small stands and stages and signs. It looked chaotic, but given how frequently the carnival moved, it was really an efficient, tightly choreographed process.

Guy wandered about and gawked at the activity and at the strange apparitions that walked by. A giant who must have been over seven feet tall, a woman or maybe it was man covered in hair, like fur. An enormous fat lady and alongside her, smoking a cigar and yammering, a midget no more than three feet tall. Guy tried not to stare as they passed him. There were other performers—a muscle-bound man bickering with a lithe beauty speaking some foreign language, a man carrying a violin, another dressed garishly in a checked suit and bowler hat. From what Guy could see as he walked around, the carnival lived up to its billing as one of curiosities, oddities, and perilous performers.

Three men were walking toward him, and Guy could hear one of them speaking.

"I tell you, Mr. Streeter, we need to be sure we have enough chickens. You know that. We need a couple of dozen, and last town, we ran short!"

The man named Streeter stopped and turned to the third man.

"What do you think, Hale? Can we get enough? Do they sell live chickens in a town like this?"

Hale, shorter and bald, with a cigarette dangling from his mouth, shrugged. "I dunno. I'll check. Do they have to be alive or can they be frozen?"

The man who had been pleading for chickens answered: "Live, frozen, I don't care. I cook 'em either way and Bruno eats 'em. I just need plenty!"

The three men had started walking and a few paces brought them to Guy, who stood blocking their way. They stopped, and Streeter looked at him.

"Can we help you?" he asked.

Guy figured he had better make it short. He had learned in his attempts to get a job in theater that managers were not patient men. He said what he'd rehearsed at breakfast.

"Yes, Mr. Streeter. Mr. Hale. My name is Guy Borden. I'm a war hero, a magician, and I want to work in your carnival."

The three men looked at Guy. Hale said to the third man: "Cooky, I'll get you your chickens. Now scram."

Cooky clapped his hands, spun in a circle, shouted "Yowza!" and scampered off.

"A magician, eh?" said Streeter.

"Yes, sir," said Guy.

"Hale," asked Streeter, "do we need a magician?"

"Do we need a Monkey Girl? A Fat Lady? A nasty little midget?" answered Hale. "You know how it is: we lose some acts; we get some acts. Any of our acts might be gone next town."

"Hmmm," said Streeter. "Can you show us something?"

Guy thought he had his foot in the door, so he decided to do something quick and dramatic. Before Hale had a chance to react, Guy reached out and snatched the cigarette out of his mouth. The man was surprised, and that surprise grew to wide-eyed amazement when Guy slowly formed his left hand into a fist and pushed the lit cigarette into it. Smoke curled out. Both men leaned forward to get a closer look. Guy pushed the cigarette deeper into his fist. Then he held his fist right up in front of Streeter's eyes.

"Say: 'go!'" Guy said.

"Go," said Hale.

Guy blew on his fist, held the moment, then very slowly uncurled his fingers.

"Gone," said Guy.

His hand was empty. The cigarette was, indeed, gone. He pointed to his empty hand with his other hand, also clearly empty.

"Son-of-a-bitch!" exclaimed Streeter.

"No way!" said Hale.

Before either man could recover their balance from the tilted world that magic tends to thrust people into, Guy took out his shiny Morgan silver dollar.

"Now watch," he said, "watch very closely, because this silver dollar that you think you see here …"

Matching action to words, Guy slowly put the coin into his hand and curled his fingers around it, "is not here at all." He opened his fist and the dollar was gone.

"Not here," he said pointing to his empty palm, "but here." And as he said this, he reached into Hale's shirt pocket and slowly removed the silver dollar.

"Son-of-a-bitch!" exclaimed Streeter.

"No way," said Hale.

"Just a small demonstration, gentlemen. My serious tricks are home in New England. I could have them sent and be ready with a show in a week or two. And let me tell you, when a crowd sees a magic show, they come back again and again, hoping to figure out how it's done. That's good for business. They tell their friends of the wonders they have seen, and *they* come, and *that's* good for business." Guy thought that sounded good.

"Give us a second, kid," said Streeter.

He and Hale walked off a few steps and talked. They came back to Guy.

"Okay, we'll give you a try," said Streeter. "Hale here will go over the schedule and you can figure out where to send your tricks. He'll get you set up with a tent and a sign. You can work with Archie on the ballyhoo."

"Archie? Ballyhoo?"

"Yeah. He runs the show and is one of our best ballyhoo men. He talks up the act, promises them the moon—that's what we call ballyhoo. Your act flies and we'll talk about a contract. We need three shows a night and matinees Saturday and Sunday. Until then, you can help out where needed. We pay eighteen bucks a week. Deal?"

Guy was thrilled. "Sure. You bet."

"Let's introduce you to Archie," said Hale. The three men walked around a tent. Streeter called out to a group. "Hey, Archie, get over here!"

Guy had seen Archie earlier. He was the man dressed in the garish checked coat and bowler hat. He was hard to miss. Streeter and Hale told Archie they were going to give Guy a shot as a magician, and that he'd have to work up some ballyhoo for the act. They had Guy do his coin vanish and appearance for Archie, using a dollar of Streeter's.

After the trick, as the men talked, Guy absent-mindedly rolled the coin along his knuckles, the silver glinting in the sunlight. Suddenly, a red blur emerged from the shadows of the tent. Something small and furry and very fast grabbed the coin and vanished back into the darkness.

"Hey! What the hell!" yelled Guy.

Streeter and Hale and Archie Walters burst out laughing.

"That's Arrigo!" said Walters, when he was able to speak.

"Arrigo?" asked Guy, still stunned.

"Arrigo the Monkey" said Hale. "He was part of an act. Mazzucchi the Organ Grinder and Clown. You know, dancing and screwing around while the music played. When Arrigo's part was done, he'd roam around the crowd. They were still watching Mazzucchi do his clown stuff. Arrigo was a pick-pocket. He was short and quick and had a knack for lifting shiny stuff from folks. Apparently he learned it back in Palermo. We didn't encourage it, but how do you reason with a monkey? One day, Mazzucchi vanished. He left Arrigo behind."

"Must have been close to a year ago," said Hale.

"You owe me a dollar," said Streeter.

"Hey, give me a break. The damned monkey has it," said Guy.

"Sorry son," said Streeter, "that's between you and the monkey. You owe me a buck. I'll take it out of your first week's pay. Archie, show the kid around, introduce him to folks and find him a berth somewhere. He'll need some room for his crap, too. Work it out."

Hale turned to Guy. "Welcome to the Carnival, kid. And by the way—you owe me a cigarette."

Then Streeter and Hale were gone, off to oversee and troubleshoot the set up of the carnival.

"You better watch out for Arrigo," said Archie. "He likes shiny stuff. Money, certainly. But he'll take a watch or anything he can lay his paws on that isn't bolted down. Cooky locks up the silverware because that little monkey was taking it. Took a corkscrew and cigar clip of mine before I wised up to him."

"Where does he put it?" asked Guy.

"Nobody knows," said Archie.

"Why don't you get rid of him?" asked Guy.

"Bad luck."

"Bad luck?"

"Ask Irena," said Archie.

"Who's Irena?"

"Trapeze girl and tightrope walker. Real looker. You'll meet her soon enough," said Archie.

"So Streeter told me you do the ballyhoo?"

"That's right. We got a bunch of guys who do it, but I'm the best, if I do say so."

"What is it, exactly?"

"Basically, it's a sales pitch. Most acts have them. My spiel is called the ballyhoo. I embellish your act with a description of spellbinding excess. I try to make folks think they're about to see the most unique and amazing thing they're ever gonna see in their life." As he said this, the giant, the fat lady and the midget walked by and waved. "And it just might be true. But ballyhoo only starts with the truth. And generally leaves it pretty far behind. Whatever I'm talking about, it's 'the best,' or the 'most amazing,' or 'something you will only see here and only this one time.'"

"A real beauty for effect and mystery," Guy thought, remembering the ad for the cursed Mummy Asrah.

"My job is to get the tips all fired up," Archie concluded.

"Tips?"

"The suckers. The marks. The nice folks of Sulphur, Louisiana, or wherever we happen to be, who'll pay a nickel to see a freak or a dime to see the trapeze artists. My job is to seduce them with what the carnival has to offer. Sometimes I stand at the front gate and weave my web of words to trap the townsfolk. You'll hear me soon enough. Anyway, let's show you around, let you meet some of the oddities and perilous performers."

Archie Walters took Guy on a tour of the carnival. Their first stop was at a small tent. Outside, a huge sign hung:

300 Pound
Man Eating
Chicken

Guy tried to imagine a chicken that big. There was a small stand set up outside, a lantern hanging in front of the entrance, and some chickens scurrying about. None of them looked to be anywhere near 300 pounds.

"This is Bruno's act," said Archie. "Though it's not much of an act." Archie ducked into the tent and Guy followed. Inside, there was a table. A kitchen table behind a rope to keep the audience back. A man, a large man, sat reading a newspaper. In front of him was a plate of fried chicken.

"Hey, Archie," said the man, glancing up from the paper.

"Hi, Bruno. Getting ready for the opening, I see."

"Yup."

"Bruno, this is Guy. He's a magician. A new act we'll be trying out."

Bruno nodded hello. Guy was getting a sinking feeling that he understood the act all too well.

"I guess you have it figured out," said Archie. "Like the sign says, they get to see a 300 pound man eating chicken. Though, of course, they convince themselves they're gonna see a 300 pound chicken eating a man. The sign don't lie. Could be the way the lines are written it's a little confusing, though.

"Some folks get pissed off at the con, but most just chuckle. You'll note they come in here, get their fill watching Bruno here getting filled, then they gotta leave back there behind him. They go right into the tent with the hoochie girls. That way, they can't warn off the folks waiting to get in here. And once they see the girls, they forget about Bruno."

"It's a bad joke," said Guy.

"Yes it is, son," said Archie without remorse. Then he turned to Bruno. "How's Cooky doin' your chicken these days, Bruno? Frying it like you like?"

"It's fine," said Bruno. "But for a change, how about we try a '300 Pound Man Eating Lobster?'"

"Hell, Bruno," said Archie with a chuckle. "Nobody'd believe that."

He waved Guy forward and around Bruno's table and through the back flap into the adjoining tent. There, the tamest of the Hoochie Girls, Bodacious Bettie, plied her trade.

Bodacious Bettie was puttering about, pulling slinky garments out of a trunk and hanging them on lines strung across the back of her tent.

Archie introduced Guy. Bettie was a young beauty, and her act was a striptease. She didn't end up naked, though. That was reserved for the Forbidden Hoochie Girls (admission twenty-five cents) who had their own tent a bit away from the midway, and to which only adult men would be admitted.

Bettie's act was far less risqué. She had a small wind-up Victrola and a glass record with her bump-and-grind music—Ravel's Bolero. They chatted a few minutes as she hung her costumes, which started as billowing diaphanous silk gowns and harem outfits and ended up as pasties and G-strings. Guy learned she liked to do watercolors and had painted her own scenery. Indeed, she stood before a backdrop that depicted a log cabin and a Civil War soldier who seemed to be standing on a tree stump.

Bettie giggled and confessed she had "a thing" for Charlie. Charlie was known as the "Colonel."

"He's not a real Colonel," Bettie explained. "It's just pretend. He puts on makeup to look like a really old man. He says he's the oldest living Civil War veteran. He tells a bunch of stories 'bout riding to Gettysburg with Jeb Stuart. Sometimes he recites the Gettysburg Address. Then he does some sharpshooting. It's quite an act and very educational."

"I'll have to see it," said Guy.

"He's my sweetheart," said Bodacious Bettie. "And I'm gonna marry him someday."

Archie and Guy left her tent and went from its cool darkness to the blinding sunlight. The change made Guy recoil and long to be back inside. It was, no doubt, calculated. Get them in a tent where it was cool and they could see something exotic or erotic, then back out into the blazing sun before enticing them back into soothing shade. The carnival offered "the shade and the shady," thought Guy.

The midway stretched before them for a hundred yards, lined on either side with tents, small platforms for the ballyhoo man to stand on, a little podium for the ticket takers, and the tents housing the various games and sideshows. The game tents were shallow and had a counter where the tips would try their luck. The games were traditional carnival fare: pitching balls at milk bottles, tossing hoops over the heads of plaster clowns, shooting BB guns at little bears and duckys that lurched across a bright diorama, chucking darts to pop balloons. Of course, the games were all rigged. The milk bottles were made to stick to each other with glue; the rings fit over the clown heads only when thrown with almost impossible precision; the balloons were under-inflated and hard to pop. But folks would try, because occasionally somebody—most often a shill working for the carnival—*did* knock over the bottles or crown the clown or shoot the bear or pop the balloon. They would be rewarded with one of the huge stuffed cats or bunnies or doggies that hung from the tops of the tents like a bloated furry audience.

Archie veered over to the milk bottle game. He introduced Guy to the man who ran it.

"Give it a shot, Guy," said Archie, and the man handed him three softballs. The balls were big and the bottles only about eight feet away. There were ten bottles, set up in a pyramid. It seemed easy. Guy wound up and threw. His aim was a bit off and he just nicked the bottom bottle. The pyramid shook but held. Guy's next shot was spot on to the center of the row of three. The ball bounced off it.

"Shit, Derwood," said Archie. "Lighten up on the glue, will you? You got them so bound together a sledgehammer wouldn't knock 'em down. You gotta be crooked with a little finesse, know what I mean? Give 'em some chance to win. A little one, but some chance. Christ, you keep it like that and we'll end up with a mob with flaming torches wanting their money back."

Archie turned away from the game and strode away in disgust. Guy followed him.

"It's hard to get a good con man anymore," said Archie. "Derwood there is typical. Ya gotta mask the deception, you know? Folks have gotta believe they have a chance. And that means that once in a while, they win. Shit, he's got them bottles so glued together you'd have to drive a truck into 'em to knock 'em over. The cheat is obvious. You gotta have some subtlety. I hope your magic is better than his game, you know? Streeter and Hale leave it to me to make sure all these games run, and the acts go off okay, and the freaks do their thing, and the Hoochie Girls don't start a riot. It's all very complicated and a lot of work for old Archie."

They strode down the midway, Archie nodding at various concessions and games and acts, calling out instructions and warnings as they went.

"Your sign's as crooked as your game, Delbert!"

"Get those candy apples out of the sun!"

"Gates open in three hours, Orville, get that pig in costume!"

"Hey, Pugsy, where's your tutu?"

Archie bellowed and cajoled, ordered and scolded, shook his head and muttered a lot. It was clear that if Streeter and Hale were the brains of the carnival, Archie Walters was the heart.

They passed a woman who had tattoos covering every inch of her exposed skin.

"That's Edith, the Tattooed Lady," said Archie. "One of our oddities."

Edith was very pretty and waved as they passed.

"An oddity," said Archie, "but also quite educational."

"Educational?" asked Guy. He couldn't imagine.

"Oh, yes. All her tattoos are great works of art. Masterpieces. You can learn about the Baroque era on her belly, the Renaissance on her back. You'll find Greek and Egyptian on her legs, and Impressionism on her buttocks. She has Modern art on her arms. And though nobody's ever seen it, we all know where we'd find Venus Rising on the Half Shell."

Guy swiveled his head to look back at Edith. He could only imagine.

They had arrived at the freak show.

22

The freak show was a series of small tents. Lurid signs spoke of the oddities within. "The Fat Lady." "The Giant." "Priscilla the Monkey Girl." "Major Midget." "The Human Torso." "The Alligator Man." "Zero, The Pinhead." Embellishing the signs of these acts were artistic fantasies—montages of creations Guy doubted could ever exist: a head on a platter, something that looked half human, half fish, a man with five eyes, a three-headed woman. These were meant to stoke the fires of the imagination. There was no shame in the sign that promised "the most disturbing specimens of aberrant humanity on this earth." Guy wondered how that made the freaks feel.

"Want to meet them?" asked Archie.

"Sure," said Guy. He had already seen a few walking around. He and Archie ducked into the first tent. Guy saw no one. At first. Then he lowered his gaze and saw Major Midget. He was a perfectly proportioned and quite handsome man. He was three feet tall, dressed in a natty suit, smoking a cigar. He was a walking illusion: he looked like a very normal man of about 30, seen at a distance.

"Major Midget, this is Guy. He's a magician joining the carnival."

He stuck out his tiny hand and Guy shook it. Carefully. He was afraid he'd break the little fella.

Midget said in a high falsetto voice: "We are such stuff as dreams are made on."

Guy frowned, bewildered at the midget's odd phrasing.

"Shakespeare," said the midget. "The Tempest."

"Major Midget is quite the student of the Bard," said Archie. "He is always quoting him."

"Why not?" said Major Midget. "Shakespeare was the best ballyhoo man that ever lived, bar none!"

"True enough," said Archie.

Just then, the Fat Lady squeezed into the tent. She lived up to her name. She was enormous. Guy guessed maybe six hundred pounds. Archie introduced her as "The Fat Lady."

She smiled sweetly at Guy. "Welcome to the carnival," she said. "I am the resident fat lady. And, in case you're wondering, I'm seven hundred pounds."

"Now, now," scolded Archie. The Fat Lady rolled her eyes.

"Sorry. Seven hundred and twenty."

When the giant ducked in, Guy was faced with a tableau of stunning oddities that seemed like something out of a bad dream. A seven-foot, six-inch man standing next to a seven-hundred pound woman standing next to a three-foot man.

"In case you haven't guessed, this is Clarence, the giant."

"Hello," said the man quietly, extending an arm that looked like a tree branch.

Archie and Guy wandered into a few more tents, where Guy met Priscilla the Monkey Girl and the Alligator Man.

"I married them," commented Archie. "I'm a Justice of the Peace."

Guy tried to imagine their offspring. He could not.

They met Willis, a Negro with pitch-black skin, a wary look, and no arms.

"He can do just about anything with his toes," said Archie. "Shuffle and deal cards, tie knots, write, roll and light a cigarette, hold his harmonica—he's quite amazing."

"Well, I guess he's had his whole life to learn," said Guy as they left the tent. Archie stopped. "No, Guy. Willis wasn't born that way. Not like most of the freaks. He was *made* who he is."

"Made?" asked Guy. "I don't understand."

"It's quite a story. Horrible, really. Willis had the bad luck to be born a black man in Alabama. The story I heard is that when he was about 16 or so, he was accused of stealing something. I don't remember what, but I don't think it was much of anything. The sheriff investigated and couldn't prove anything against Willis. And that was that. Or it was supposed to be. But some men didn't agree. They were *sure* Willis was the thief, even if they couldn't prove it. So, as they sometimes do down here, they took the law into their own hands. They found Willis and hacked his arms off with axes. Told him he'd never steal again. It's a miracle he didn't die. Someone found him and got him to the hospital. He had to learn to do everything he used to do with his hands, with his feet. That's his act now."

Guy shuddered, imagining the violence.

"Hatred blinds people, Guy. Those bastards didn't care if Willis was the real thief or not. They hated him because he was a Negro, and they had their vengeance. God forgive them. I know I couldn't."

"I had no idea," said Guy.

"Well, how would you? He's just another freak, now. A wretched soul who entertains because he is flawed."

Archie spat into the dusty ground in disgust.

"The real flawed humans are the monsters who did it to him."

They walked on in silence, through the tents of the sideshow. They waved to the Human Pretzel, the Goat Boy, Zero the Pinhead, and Mr. Electro.

They passed one tent with a handwritten sign posted on its flap:

***"The local doctor has determined this exhibit is too horrific for viewing.
This tent is closed."***

Archie watched as Guy read it. After a few moments, Archie asked: "What are you thinking, Guy?"

"I'm trying to imagine what could possibly be in there."

Archie lifted the flap. In the dim light, Guy saw a large crate with a chain around it fastened by a huge padlock. There were air holes on the top of the crate.

"Still wondering?" asked Archie.

"Yes, still trying to imagine what it could be."

Archie chuckled. "Exactly, kid. Exactly. This was Hale's idea and it's brilliant."

"But it's not an exhibit. It's closed today."

"Yep. Today and tomorrow, and next week when we get to Picayune and the week after in Derby then Liberty and Cowpens and all the rest. It's *always* closed."

"I don't get it."

"It's simple. There is nothing we can really show anybody that is as shocking and horrific as what they conjure up in their imaginations, like you were just doing. We post that sign and it just invites folks to wonder, to speculate, to try to imagine something so horrific we aren't allowed to show it to them. My God, what could that possibly be? We leave the flap loose. We know they peak in. We want them to. They see that crate with its chains and its lock and they imagine something even worse. My God, it has to be locked up! It's a great part of the freak show. And we don't have to pay it or feed it or put up with its moods."

"The power of suggestion," said Guy.

"Yes. The power of suggestion, the allure of the forbidden, the fascination with the unknown. It's pure carnival."

Magic, too, thought Guy. He realized these carny folks had a very good understanding of human nature and preyed ruthlessly upon it.

The Fat Lady and Major Midget walked by, and Archie stopped them.

"Fats," said Archie, "how about you show Guy the rest of the carnival? I got a lot to get done before we open tonight."

"Sure thing, Archie," said the Fat Lady.

"Kid, I'll find you a cabin on the train. I think No. 6 might be open. Meet the rest of the oddities and performers, grab some dinner. Then you come to the main gate at seven. You'll see ol' Archie in action."

With that, he turned and walked away.

"Come with me, Guy," said the Fat Lady. "You can meet the rest of our strange little family."

"We are but poor wretches, abandoned and forsaken by the creator who mismade us," said Major Midget.

"The Bard?" asked Guy.

"No, the Midget," said the tiny man.

Guy met Zero, a pinhead with a tiny IQ but an uncanny ability to sing any song with heart-wrenching beauty. He met all of them; then the Fat Lady turned Guy loose to explore the carnival for himself.

He explored the midway and came to a tent with a big sign: "Cabinet of Curiosities." He went inside. When his eyes grew accustomed to the gloom, he saw the tent was full of shelves and tables and display cases, all filled with the strangest assortment of things Guy had ever seen or even imagined. It was like walking into a nightmare, into a painting by Hieronymus Bosch. A man was busy at work at a small table.

Hi," said Guy. "I'm Guy Borden. I'm new to the carnival."

The man looked up. "Pleased to meet ya, Guy. I'm Rufus King, master of the world of curiosities. What's your act?"

"Magician."

Rufus nodded. "A fellow illusionist," he said.

Guy looked around. Here was a murky jar with a tiny baby with two heads. Next to it, a strange stuffed animal that looked like a woodchuck with antlers. "Jackalope," read the sign. There was a block of glass with a mummy inside. "Frozen for Eternity in a Tomb of Ice," read the label (why the ice never melted was, perhaps, part of the mystery). A glass case had a human hand inside, one of the fingers slowly tapping at the glass: "The Living Hand." A sunflower with a human eyeball in its center was "The Vision Flower." A sharp, shiny dagger was "Jack the Ripper's Knife." A vial of green liquid was labeled "Blood of a Martian." And so on. The Cabinet of Curiosities lived up to its name. Guy was fascinated by the objects on display, objects that showed incredible inventiveness and a shameless knack for exotic narrative.

"1,000-Year-Old Newt." "Finger of Moses." "Winged Frog." "Tooth of a Werewolf." "Spoor of a Dinosaur." "Splinter of Noah's Ark." "Muffin from the Titanic." "Skeleton of a Clamacat." "Cleopatra's Eyelash" And Guy's favorite: "Penis of a Caveman."

Some just had labels, while others had little explanations attached or stories about daring expeditions where the objects were found. Many were plausible if one was inclined to believe a set of false eyelashes might actually be Cleopatra's. Who could say? It's not like there were experts on much of this stuff or, if there were, they would waste time coming to the carnival to expose the fakes. Guy thought that the most amazing thing was the imagination responsible for the curiosities. It was the work of a kind of mad genius.

"Is any of this stuff real?" he asked.

Rufus King laughed. "Well, of course, Guy. All of it. You can see it, touch it."

"No, I mean, is any of it real in terms of being authentic."

Rufus laughed again and shook his head. "You *are* new to the carnival, aren't you! Guy, there is *nothing* authentic about the carnival. It's all a concoction. You know: 'It's only a paper moon, sailing over a cardboard sea,' like the song they play on the calliope says. People know it. They come here to escape reality, to tiptoe through a waking dream.

"It so happens the carnival is a dark dream. It's unsettling and odd, and that's why folks love it. Same reason they like horror movies. For a few hours, they are seduced by the evil charms of the carnival. The freaks. The curiosities. The hoochie girls. The crooked games and thrilling rides. They shudder, they avert their eyes, they get a little spooked, they laugh nervously. Then they go home. They probably have nightmares about the dreams they have just seen."

Guy thought that in its way, the carnival was just one big magic show, and the Cabinet of Curiosities was a perverse version of Tannen's Magic Store.

Guy bid Rufus good day. On his way out he stopped a moment to look at a small box in which a shrunken head lay nestled in cotton. "Shrunken Head from the Amazon," read the label. Smaller text read: "Missionary, 1884." It looked a bit like a shriveled up monkey's head with eyeglasses on it, which, Guy supposed, it probably was. He left the tent thinking that Rufus King might just have been the most creative person he'd ever met.

As Guy sank into the world of the carnival, he began to realize how inventive it was. The carnival created its own world, like Rufus had said. A theater of the mind. A magician might seem prosaic in this surreal world.

23

A few days after Guy joined the carnival, he was wandering around late at night. The carnival was sleepy, most of the performers back in their railroad cars. Voices drifted in the darkness, a poker game, perhaps. In the distance he heard music, a solo violin. He wandered into the main tent and was surprised to see Irena the Russian aerialist, practicing. Her partner in the trapeze act, Ivan, had left. She was working on her tightrope act, alone, high up in the tent.

A single spotlight shone from in front of her, along the wire, catching her small form. She glowed in the darkness like an angel. Irena looked straight ahead as she walked, oblivious to Guy. Her arms went through graceful movements as she walked, her steps assured. Usually when she performed there was music, but not now. It was eerie to watch her, as if she were in a movie with the sound turned off.

Guy watched her, mesmerized. She seemed to float up there, a sleepwalker in a dream. Then she did a front flip followed by a back flip. She landed on the wire with no wobble. She did a handstand and a split, then a spin back to upright.

Guy could see she was breathing a little heavier from the exertion of her moves. She lifted her head high, bent her legs, and leapt into the air, using the springy wire to catapult her upward.

She did two quick flips on her way down, then spread her arms into a swan dive and rode it into the net, curling in at the last minute to land on her back. She bounced high and did another flip and came to rest in the net.

Irena got to her feet and bounded to the edge of the net, reached down and grabbed the edge rope in her hands, then flipped herself onto the ground, extending her arms as she did so.

Guy could not help but applaud her as she did.

Irena jumped, surprised, puckered her face a bit, then walked over to a chair and grabbed a towel from it. She patted her face as she walked over to Guy. She had close-cut black hair and dark, dark eyes. Very Russian.

"You watch long?" she asked.

"A few minutes," he said.

"Why?"

"No reason. I was just taking a walk, wandered in here and saw you alone up there. You are beautiful to watch. You're Irena, right?"

"Yes, Irena. Now. Was Ilyana back in homeland, but Irena here."

"Why the name change?"

"Mistake. Man at counter off boat not bright and spell wrong. So now I Irena. Ilyana still me, but not here."

She paused a moment to let this sink in, not that it did.

"You new guy, right?" Her Russian accent was thick, and Guy found it sexy. That and her sweaty, tightly athletic body, which showed off all its assets in her skin-hugging outfit. He gulped. Her wings were probably nearby.

"Yes, I am," he said.

Nodded. "What do you?" she asked.

"I'm a magician."

"Magic! Lady floating? Cut in half? Bunny in hat?"

"Well, more or less, yes. No bunny."

"No bunny? How come no bunny? Magician always have bunny."

Guy didn't really know why he didn't have a bunny in his act. He just didn't. Maybe it was the trauma of the fake bunny he'd gotten as a kid, the one with the spring inside he'd ruined the first time he used it. He wanted this conversation to go someplace else, but it was a little hard talking to Irena. Her English didn't seem so good. And he had a hard time keeping himself from looking at her nipples. They poked against her tight outfit, which was almost transparent in places from her sweat. He made up an answer.

"Bunny got away. So I cut him from the act." He moved on. "So you do both trapeze *and* high wire, I see."

"Yes. I fly from trapeze and Ivan catch. He is strong. We be together much time. After trapeze, Ivan go and I walk the rope that is tight. Sometimes I flip. Balance one foot or sit in chair."

"I see," said Guy. "Do you always use a net?"

Irena looked shocked. "Yes! Wire much high. I fall, no net, go splat!"

"Makes sense," said Guy. "I'm sure I'll see your whole act soon. I look forward to it."

"I love to fly off bar, soar like bird. And I love to walk wire. I don't care of crowd. One person, one hundred, one thousand. All same to me. I way up in air, on wire. I do it for me." She was patting the sweat off her face, about the only part of her that wasn't covered in skintight nylon. He could see ... a lot of Irena's contours. He liked her contours. She seemed more naked than if she had been naked.

"Don't tell Streeter that," said Guy. "He'll think he doesn't have to pay you."

She snorted. "Streeter. Streeter! Deshevyj ubljudok!"

"Deshev ubjudok?" asked Guy, trying to get his tongue to twist around the Russian.

"Yes. Mean, how do you say, 'cheap bastard.'"

"Really?"

"Yes. He mean. Not pay well. 'Cheap' is right word?"

"Yes," said Guy.

"And 'bastard'?"

"Well, that might be a bit harsh," said Guy. "What about Archie Walters, do you like his ballyhoo?"

She snorted again. "Walters! Walters! Predurok!

"Predurok?" asked Guy.

"Yes. Russian. Means, how you say, man who is not much with brain."

"Stupid?"

"No."

"Idiot?"

"Yes! Idiot! Walters is idiot." Irena smiled.

"Why is Walters an idiot?" Guy asked.

"Because he not much with brain," Irena said, as if it was obvious.

Talking to Irena was like hacking through a thick underbrush. Guy plunged ahead.

"Do you train here every night?" he asked.

"Yes. But some nights not." Guy didn't quite know what she meant.

"You? You all time practice?"

"A lot," he said. "It's hard. You can always get better."

"Yes, better always. I agree to that," she said. Guy wanted to kiss her and shut her up. He had a fleeting image of them locked together in passion, her sweaty body entwined with his, her muscles rippling, her …

"Guy, you here?" she cut off his reverie.

"What?"

"Your eyes glass. You look like predurok. Okay?"

"Fine, Irena, very good."

She looked him over. She reached out and squeezed his upper arm.

"You young. Fit. You like make love?"

"Uh, well, yes, of course, when I have someone to make love to."

He was flummoxed and felt a little dizzy.

"You got girl?"

"No girl."

"No bunny. No girl. Too bad but good," said Irena.

Guy was adrift again, and he just couldn't take his eyes off this sweaty athletic Russian who suddenly grabbed him and gave him a very passionate, deep kiss.

"Now we go," said Irena. "Now we go and make like bunnies."

Grasping his hand, she led him out of the tent toward her cabin on the train. Under the spell of this brazen Russian, Guy had little choice but to follow.

Neither of them saw Ivan, watching from the shadows.

24

Ivan was a bear of a man who also spoke halting English with a Russian accent and who happened to be Irena's lover. Or one of them now that she and Guy had found passion.

Whether Irena went for Guy to get back at Ivan for some slight was hard to say. But when the triangle was created, it came with the problems love triangles always come with: jealousy, deceit, anger, tension and danger. Irena was walking another tightrope.

Guy didn't know that Ivan knew until a few days after his first encounter with Irena, when Ivan strode up to him and, without saying a word, punched Guy and sent him tumbling to the ground.

"Hello," said the big man. "I am Ivan. You stay away from Irena. She's mine. Good night." Then he stalked off back into the darkness. Irena hadn't introduced Guy to Ivan. He had made his own introduction. A rather unforgettable one.

Guy sat there on the ground rubbing his jaw. It wasn't broken, but it had started to swell and he'd have a nasty bruise.

Well, what did he expect?

If Guy hadn't been so smitten with Irena, he would have done the wise thing and left her to Ivan. If for no other reason than to avoid bodily harm. He was certainly no match for the man, whose hands were twice the size of Guy's, and whose arms bulged with muscles. But the truth of it was their lovemaking had been so wonderful, so intense, that he wanted it to continue. Irena had devoured him with her body. Her athleticism was truly amazing and yielded truly amazing pleasure.

Guy stood up. Brushed the dirt and sawdust off his pants. He wandered around, rattled by Ivan's punch and the dilemma he found himself in. It was during these musings that Major Midget came by.

"Hi, Guy. Say, you look like shit."

"Thanks, Major," said Guy, still rubbing his jaw.

"What happened to you?"

"I met Ivan. Or should I say, I met his fist."

"Oh, it is excellent to have a giant's strength, but it is tyrannous to use it like a giant," said Midget.

"Midget?" asked Guy.

"No, Shakespeare."

"Well, Ivan must be a tyrant. He certainly didn't pull any punches," said Guy.

"Why did he hit you? What happened?"

"I think he took exception to my being with Irena."

"Yes, I guess he did. They're a strange couple. Always arguing. But she's quite the looker. I don't blame you. Still, you gotta watch out. Ivan's mean. He has quite the temper. He could break you in half."

"What's up with him, anyway, Major? Why is he so mean?"

"From what I've heard, he was a scrawny kid. And he stuttered. He was tormented and bullied. Some kids might laugh that off. But not Ivan. He vowed to become strong, to get vengeance on his tormentors. He somehow got rid of his stutter, and he lifted weights until he was very strong. I guess he beat them up at some point. But the hurt never left him. It was like a poison inside. It made him angry and cruel. A little crazy. He became what he had hated—a bully."

Guy rubbed his jaw.

"Ivan doesn't like us freaks at all. You'd think having gone through what he did, he'd have some compassion for those who are a little different. But he doesn't. He's a big man with a small mind. So be careful, Guy."

"Thanks for the advice, Midget."

"I'll watch out for you, Guy."

Guy almost laughed. It seemed an absurd offer from such a tiny man. Ivan could kill him with a single punch. But it was said in all sincerity.

"Thank you, Major. I appreciate that."

"You're welcome, Guy. Anyway, I've been looking for you. Archie wants to see you."

"All right, I'm on my way."

"Make haste into the night, be swift afoot and keen of ear lest the tyrant take his wrath on you."

"Shakespeare?" asked Guy.

"No, the Midget."

25

Guy found Archie in his train cabin, wearing only a sweaty undershirt and shorts, hunched over a pile of papers.

"Hello, Guy. Gee, you look like shit."

Wearily, Guy flopped into a chair. Here we go again.

"A story not worth telling, Archie. You wanted to see me?"

Archie stared at him a moment, clearly weighing whether to prod or not. He shrugged.

"I hate Mississippi," he said. "It's too goddamned hot and humid. I feel like I'm melting. I'll end up a freak in the sideshow. The Amazing Melted Man. I hate Mississippi."

"It *is* hot, Archie. I don't care for it either."

"Hale told me you told him your magic stuff is on the way?"

"Yes. I've had it sent. Should be here in a few days. Then I can get it sorted out, practice a bit, and be ready to go. Maybe next week."

"Swell. So I gotta work up some ballyhoo for your act. I'll make a few notes and then figure it out. You'll be 'the best, and the most amazing,' and so on. But can you tell me a bit about what you'll be doing?"

Guy wasn't sure what he'd be doing, actually, but he knew what tricks he had, so he described them to Archie, who busied himself making notes.

"You gonna float a dame?" he asked.

"No, that takes a big stage."

"Cut her in half?"

"No, same problem."

"Hmmm. Okay. I can work around that. What about a bunny? I assume you have a bunny in your act?"

"Sorry, Archie. No bunny."

"Well, shit, Guy. What the hell *do* you do? No dame, no bunny. You just gonna make a damned coin disappear?"

"No, Archie, I promise you, I'll do more than that. The fact is, most magicians don't pull bunnies out of their hats. That's just a myth, the stuff you see on posters."

"I want a bunny in your act," said Archie, sounding like a petulant little kid. Guy had had enough. "Okay, Archie, okay. You get me a goddamned bunny and I'll figure out something to do with it if it will make you happy. Maybe I'll cut it in half."

"Now you're talkin'!"

"Anything else?" asked Guy.

"No, I got enough. I can spin something for all of this."

There was a pause.

"Care for a drink, Guy?"

Realizing that Archie was only trying to help, and having pissed off Ivan already, Guy decided to stay on Archie's good side.

"Sure."

Archie took a bottle and some glasses out of a drawer and poured them drinks.

"Sorry," he said. "The ice melted."

"So tell me, Archie. How did you happen to be a part of Streeter and Hale's Carnival of Curiosities?"

Archie stared into his glass a moment, as if it were a window on his past.

"I'm kind of a natural showman, Guy. In case you haven't guessed. I was born Archibald Walchinsky, but changed it to Walters when I started performing. Easier to fit on playbills. And not so ethnic. I did well in music halls and then in vaudeville. A variety act—some jokes, a little singing, juggling and puppets. I had a way of making people happy with the foolish crap I did. My star was on the rise."

"Was? What happened?"

"Not what you might think, Guy. Not the usual. Not booze or women or gambling. No, my career was undone by something I had no control over: light."

"Light? I don't follow, Archie."

"I was done in by the flicker of light telling stories in a dark theater. Movies. They came along and killed vaudeville. Pretty quickly. I was on top of the world one week, and out of work the next. Well, not quite that quickly. It took maybe a year. But it happened. The shows and revues dried up. Lots of talented people were left by the side of the road. I found the only work I could. As a ballyhoo man at a carnival. Streeter and Hale threw me a lifeline, and I love 'em for doing it."

Guy nodded. He knew that some of the big magic shows had been undermined by the movies. Some great magicians, who once had full evening shows, faded away.

Archie went on: "For many of us, the carnival is kind of the end of the road. It's an asylum for those whose dreams have been shattered. Or maybe for those who never had them. Hell, what could a girl covered in hair like Priscilla ever hope to do in life? We're a family of misfits, united by our despair."

Archie took a sip of his drink. Then another. He swirled the amber liquid around the glass then looked Guy in the eye.

"You know, Guy, you're pretty young. You may be a little naive, but you seem pretty normal. A few toes missing. That don't count for much around here. Won't even get you into the freak show. Listen: you have a lot of life ahead of you. Be careful you don't get trapped here. It's really not a place to start a career; it's a place to end one."

"You make it sound so sad, Archie. You all perform. You're not losers," said Guy.

"Maybe not, Guy. But we aren't exactly winners, either. We're hanging on, maybe hoping for another chance, but knowing we probably won't get one. Life doesn't give many second chances, Guy. Wish it would. Knowing we're heading to a dead end makes us a little crazy, I guess. But that's okay. A carnival runs on crazy."

Archie shook his head as if in regret, then again as if to clear away the thoughts he'd been talking about.

"Let me know when your act is ready, Guy. I'll work on the ballyhoo. And I'll find you a bunny."

"Will do," said Guy. He finished his whisky, stood, and left Archie to work on his ballyhoo—the final, flamboyant expression of his thwarted talent.

26

While he waited for his props to arrive, Guy helped the tent men and the cook and the riggers. He did whatever he could to make himself useful.

He tried to remember what tricks he had and scribbled down various ideas for an act. Walters found him a bunny, which Guy named Lou, after Lou Tannen. He modified a box he found into a trick that would vanish the bunny. Irena was thrilled with Lou.

"Got bunny. Now real magician," she said approvingly.

It was with a sigh of relief when, a few days after his talk with Archie, Guy went to the post office in Derby, Mississippi, and found a package waiting for him. After he'd enlisted, he had sent all his tricks back home. His mother had simply sent everything on to him. She had included a note:

"Guy, we are so proud of you for your service to our country and the medals you received. It pains me to think of you without three toes, but from what you wrote, it is not causing you problems. If I could, I'd give some of mine. All is well here, though New London seems a bit empty with so many young men off to war. We know you are working your way back to us, and hope you are enjoying your well-earned vacation. I don't know what you plan to do with all this magic stuff. I hope I have sent everything you wanted. We were surprised when you told us to send it to Mississippi! Your father sends his love and wonders if you have given any more thought to college. Please keep in touch and let us know when we might expect you home. Your bed is waiting in your own little room. It will be so good to see our young hero. All my love to our sweet, wonderful Guy. — Your mother."

"Vacation?" Guy wondered. Well, probably better than them knowing he was traveling with a carnival. As for college, he was learning plenty, though his folks might be shocked if they met his classmates.

Guy took the box of magics back to his train cabin and began to unpack it. It had been a long while since he had seen his tricks. He got that old familiar thrill when he opened the box and saw them.

There they were: his linking rings, production cabinet, milk pitcher, miser's dream bucket, nested boxes, silks, chick pan, ghost rise chest and all the rest. Old friends. As he unpacked them, he held each in his hands, lovingly turning them over, brushing dust off a few, checking the mechanisms of those that had moving parts. He even unpacked the shoebox with the Mummy Asrah. He'd keep practicing it, almost out of spite, hoping to master it and finally allay his anger at being duped by the ad. Maybe someday he would use it.

His mother had included his Mysto magic set. The tricks in it were better for close up than the parlor-style effects warranted by the crowd in a tent. Even if he couldn't use them, he was happy to have the set. It always reminded him of his earliest days falling in love with magic.

Though it wasn't with the set, Guy recalled the poster from the Mysto set. He had looked at it so much he remembered every line. He smiled when he remembered:

**PREMIER ACTS OF THE
WORLD'S FAMOUS MAGICIAN
A REGULAR CARNIVAL OF FUN**

Perhaps that poster had foretold his being with the carnival, though he wasn't quite world famous yet. That was his first marquee.

His second would be put up that day.

Hale had asked him what he wanted on the sign outside his tent. Guy hadn't thought about it. He needed a stage name, or at least a name for his act. The man who painted the signs came over as Hale was speaking to Guy.

"Mr. Hale, I have the board and my paint. Who's this sign for?"

Hale jabbed a finger at Guy.

"It's for him, the magic guy."

"Oh." The man turned to Guy. "So what do you want your sign to say?"

Guy had an idea. "How about: 'The Magic Guy'? What do you think, Mr. Hale?"

Hale thought it over. "Hmmm. The Magic Guy. Not very exotic, Guy. Shouldn't you be something like that Chinese guy, what's his name?"

"Chung Ling Soo? Chen Woo?"

"Yeah, like one of them Chink sorcerers."

"Do I look Chinese, Mr. Hale?"

Hale considered this. "Naw. You look American."

"Right. But if you have some other ideas ..."

"How about Guydini?" suggested Hale.

"Not original."

"Screw it. Use whatever name you want, Guy. It's your act. Ben here will paint your sign and we'll hang it up on the tent. Archie will have his ballyhoo ready. When will *you* be ready?"

"Give me a few days, Mr. Hale. I need to put together the act and practice. You want it to be good, don't you?"

"Yeah, kid. At least as good as the 300 Pound Man Eating Chicken. You gonna saw a woman in half?"

"No, Mr. Hale."

"What about a bunny? You gonna pull a bunny out of your top hat?"

"No, sir. I don't have a top hat. But I will make a bunny disappear."

"Well, then I guess we'll have to settle for you making a bunny disappear."

"I won't disappoint. I'll do some great magic and there will be a bunny."

"Okay, kid. Swell. I'll come to your first show and see what you've got. I don't care so long as you get the crowds in, wow 'em and send 'em out happy. Got it?"

"Yessir."

"Good, Magic Guy. See you later." Hale walked off.

Ben the painter looked at Guy.

"I think we should feature the bunny," he said. "People like bunnies."

Guy rolled his eyes. "Sure. Maybe you can show a bunny pulling *me* out of a hat!"

Ben shrugged. He had a wooden board about six feet long and three feet high. He'd already painted it white. He rested it on top of two oil drums. He had buckets of red, black and yellow paint.

"So you gonna settle for the Magic Guy?" Ben asked.

"You don't sound like you like it."

"I don't. It's stupid."

"You have a better idea?"

"How about Merlock?" said the painter.

"Merlock? What sort of name is that?"

"It combines Merlin, a great wizard, with Warlock, who was a sorcerer in league with the devil."

Guy was taken aback. He didn't expect a sign painter to be quite so versed in history.

"Did you just think of that?" he asked Ben.

"Pretty much. I was listening to you and Hale and got to thinking."

"Merlock. Merlock," said Guy. "Could work."

"I'd drop the 'k'. Spell it M-E-R-L-O-C," said Ben.

"Why?"

"Looks better on a sign. Shorter. Simpler."

"Can you put 'The Magician' under it?"

"Yeah, sure."

"Okay, Ben. Merloc, The Magician it is. I kind of like it."

Ben pried open a can and dipped in his brush. He took it out, dripping bright red paint like blood.

"Don't look over my shoulder," he said. "I can't paint with someone looking over my shoulder. No artist can. Go away. I'll find you when I'm done."

"Okay," said Guy, walking away. Then he stopped and turned back to Ben. "Don't forget the bunny. People like bunnies."

Guy left Ben to his work. He wandered around the carnival, watching it being set up.

He returned to the painter after about an hour. The sign was done. Ben had done a good job. The letters were nice and big, in red with black and yellow outlining that gave them depth and drama. There was a black and white bunny, too, its paw outstretched and pointing to the words "The Magician."

Guy told Ben how much he liked the sign. Ben beamed with pride. "I especially like the bunny," he said.

"Yes," said Guy. "The bunny really pulls it all together."

They took it over to the tent where Guy was to perform and, standing on chairs, tied it above the entrance.

They stepped back.

"What do ya think?" asked Ben.

"Very nice, Ben," said Guy. "Very professional."

But truth be told, Guy was kind of let down. It was his new stage name, big and bright, but it was hardly a glowing marquee. While it was his act, it was in a ragtag carnival, not a real theater. Archie's words about the carnival being the end of the road came back to him.

"No," Guy thought to himself. "Not for me. For me, this is the start, the beginning of my real career."

He brought his tricks into the small tent, which featured a bunch of folding seats and a tiny elevated stage set above the dirt floor. A single bare bulb dangled overhead, like in every tent. It was his spotlight. There was a small table in the center of the stage. It all looked a bit sad, hardly setting the scene for mysteries. He'd have to make the best of it. He spent the next several days and nights practicing. He even stayed away from Irena.

On a hot June afternoon in Derby, he felt he was ready to give it a go. He told Streeter and Hale and Archie that he would do an evening show.

That night, about 7:15, Archie Walters arrived at his tent, decked out in his flamboyant outfit, and as a small crowd gathered, he began his ballyhoo for Guy's act.

"Step right up, ladies and gentlemen. Pay your dime and see the most amazing and mystifying feats of conjuring, legerdemain and prestidigitation this side of Casablanca. Come in and see Merloc the Magician, a young man who has traveled the world in search of timeless mysteries, the magi's secrets, the conjuror's art. He will amaze you with miracles learned from a shaman in Peru, the court magicians of Europe, the fakirs of India, a blind monk in Tibet.

"In this tent, reality is a stranger. It is dreams that live here. Your eyes will see but your minds will not comprehend the impossibilities this young man will show you. He will dazzle you with boxes and rings, coins and cards, and even the world's smartest bunny! If you live to a hundred, you will never forget what you will see here. Step right up! The show begins in minutes!"

Archie would repeat the spiel, word for word, speaking with more and more urgency and fervor. Like all the ballyhoo men, he had a cadence to his words, a lilting, hypnotic rhythm that pulled listeners along. A good ballyhoo man, like a good preacher, could hold a crowd in thrall and make them true believers. He delivered an audience already half convinced and amazed. It was up to the performer to close the deal.

Listening, Guy wondered where on earth Archie had gotten all that stuff about Peru and China and India. And he had to smile that he didn't just have a bunny, but the world's smartest! Archie made exaggeration a fine art. He was a beguiling huckster.

So Archie gave his ballyhoo about the most amazing magic anyone had, could, or would ever see, and at 7:30 Guy began his show. His first real show in years. He shook off his jitters and concentrated on being a man of wonder.

Guy's act was a balance of classic parlor tricks that played well to a crowd in a tent.

He began by removing his hat, waving a wand over it and producing a bouquet of flowers. It was an opening flourish that surprised the audience and got them in the mood for miracles. Then he moved on to a classic: the Miser's Dream. Guy grabbed a silver bucket and started to pull coin after coin out of thin air, dropping them into the metal can with a loud clink. Over and over he reached up with an empty hand and plucked a coin from nowhere. He even found them behind the ears and in the pockets of spectators—everywhere! After a few minutes, he had a bucket full of shiny half dollars that he spilled out onto his table to the gasps of the delighted crowd.

He moved through his repertoire. He made the damned bunny vanish from a tip-over box he'd put together. The crowd applauded. Ben was right: people like bunnies. He did tricks with silks and boxes, cards and ropes. He even did a trick like Blackstone's with jumbo cards that used Magician's Choice. He ended with his Retention Vanish and the reappearance of the coin inside a roll, always a crowd pleaser. He was a bit rusty, his patter not very polished, but he got through the act without any major problems. There were plenty of "oohs" and "ahhs" during his tricks, and nice applause when the act ended after thirty minutes.

Hale came up and spoke to him. "You're all right, Guy. You fooled me and the tips liked it. Work on your patter, it was confusing at times. I liked the bunny."

Streeter, who had also been watching, came up to him.

"Not bad, Guy. A little rough around the edges, but I know it's been a while. Maybe a little more joking around with the crowd, and with your volunteers for tricks. And keep it moving. Pick up the pace a bit. All in all, okay. Have Archie watch you and see what he thinks. He's a master showman. He'll give you some tips."

"Thanks, Mr. Streeter, Mr. Hale. I know I can do it a little better. I'll settle in."

Streeter nodded. He reached in his pocket and took out a silver dollar.

"Okay, Guy. Show me."

Guy took the dollar, did his Retention Vanish. Pulled the coin from Streeter's pocket as always. Streeter shook his head.

"How many times have I seen that, Guy? I just don't get it! It's in your hand. I can see it. But then it's not."

"No, Mr. Streeter, it's not," said Guy, doing the trick again, almost mockingly slowly, and reached into his shirt pocket and pulled out the dollar. "It's here." And instead of keeping the dollar, he rolled it over his knuckles and held it out to Streeter.

Streeter smiled. "Thanks, Guy, but you keep it." He turned to leave and then turned to Guy again. "Is it true what I hear that Arrigo the Monkey keeps swiping your coins?"

Guy frowned. It was not the reputation he wanted.

"He's made off with a few."

Streeter shook his head. "Makes you wonder where he puts all that money. Maybe he spends it on whisky and women." That thought set Streeter to laughing as he left Guy's tent.

In the days that followed, Guy did what Streeter had suggested, loosening up, playing to the crowd, keeping the act moving briskly.

Archie watched a few times and gave him some pointers. He offered some off-color jokes that Guy ignored. He had some other ideas for Guy's patter.

"Listen, Guy, I spin quite a tale for your act in my ballyhoo. You know, all that stuff about India and China and shamans and whatnot. You ought to pick up on that. Instead of telling them you have a box, tell them it is a box the emperor of China gave you when you performed in his court. And your bunny is not just a bunny. No, it's a smart bunny. It's a magical bunny blessed by a shaman in the jungles of the Amazon with extraordinary powers of intelligence. Tell them the bunny helps you with the predictions in your act with some secret bunny code or something. That kind of thing. Make it more exotic. *Embellish* it!"

Guy wasn't sure if they had bunnies in the Amazon, but he understood Archie's point. Archie's best piece of advice was to scan the crowd at the start, spot the prettiest girl, and call her up to help in a trick.

"Never underestimate the appeal of a beautiful gal, Guy. Guys just can't help but staring at 'em. You know, like Irena."

In the carnival, Guy had what every magician wants: steady work, lots of shows in which to polish and refine his act, and a guarantee of good crowds. What it lacked was respectability. A carnival magician, like everything to do with the carnival, was tainted with a whiff of the seedy, the con. Nonetheless, whenever Guy approached his tent to perform, he got a little tingle of pride when he looked up and saw his sign.

"MERLOC. The Magician."

Modest, yes. Seedy, perhaps. Still, it was his sign, his tent, his act.

27

Streeter and Hale's Carnival of Curiosities, Oddities and Perilous Performers played its shows throughout the South, moving slowly through the heat, as if stuck in molasses. Guy settled into his show, giving dozens of performances, polishing each trick, refining his patter, growing as a magician.

He became a regular at the freaks' Friday night poker games. They sometimes called him "Two Toe" to make him feel part of the gang. Whenever there were coins on the table, someone kept watch lest Arrigo swoop in and make off with the pot. Guy knew well Arrigo's prowess for larceny. Once Arrigo learned Guy played with a lot of shiny coins, he tormented him. The monkey would stalk him and steal Guy's coins if he turned his back or dropped one while practicing. When Guy wanted to work on the Miser's Dream, he did so in the middle of an empty field so Arrigo couldn't sneak up on him. They even posted a guard at his shows to keep the monkey out.

One day the Fat Lady, Guy and Irena were ambling along. Fats observed that Arrigo must be one rich monkey. "Where does he put the loot?" she wondered.

"Damned if I know. But I'll find it. And I'll get even with him."

"No hurt monkey!" Irena admonished.

"No?" said Guy.

"No. Old Russian proverb: 'Circus monkey good luck.'"

"There's a proverb about a circus monkey?" asked Guy.

"Yes!" said Irena. "Very old."

"What, are thieving monkeys common?"

"Yes, happen all time. Be nice to monkey. Monkey good luck."

"He's a thief," said Guy.

"We all thieves," said Irena. "Be nice to monkey. No bad luck."

She wandered off. The Fat Lady shrugged. Guy shook his head. They fell into step together, walking very slowly, as The Fat Lady's enormous size gave her a ponderous gait, like an elephant. Guy was amazed she could walk at all.

"Tell me," said Guy, "what's Major Midget's story?"

The Fat Lady chuckled. "Midget is a real piece of work. His real name is David Cohen. He was a smart kid. Went to a fancy private school. That's why he knows so much Shakespeare. His father was a big shot stockbroker in New York. Midget wanted to follow in his father's footsteps, if not in his shoes. Or at least he did until the day his dad took a swan dive off a building when the market crashed back in 1929. The family lost everything. Major Midget became a midget with diminished prospects. It's not easy for a Jewish midget to get work, so he ended up here. He still likes to invest, though. I think he bought into a gold mine a while back."

"He has a lot of swagger for such a little guy."

"That he does. Some of the carny folks call him the 'NLB'"

"NLB?"

"Nasty Little Bastard." Midget has a temper. He doesn't like to take crap from anybody, which he often does, being so small. Especially from Ivan."

"I can imagine."

"Yeah, those two are like oil and water. They're always needling each other."

"How did he get the name Major?"

"Archie. When Streeter pointed him out when he first joined the carnival, Archie said: 'Wow! He's a major midget!' The name stuck."

They had arrived back at the train. The Fat Lady was huffing and puffing. "Time for me to get some rest, Guy. It's hard for me to walk very far, especially in this heat. I like the night better. See you later."

Guy watched as she slowly lifted her bulk up the few stairs into the train. He was by the Giant's railroad car and decided to say hello. He walked up the stairs and opened the door

"Hey, Clarence, I was passing by and …" Guy stopped.

Clarence was there, hunched on his bed, a hypodermic in his hand, a shoelace tight on his other, bared arm. Clarence looked up at him, and they stared at each other a moment.

"Don't judge me, Guy. It's my only solace. The only thing that dulls the pain, you know. What do I care? What future do I have? The damned Lord who made me this way can have me back. Maybe he'll do better by me next time. Go away. Go screw Irena. Have your fun. Leave me alone to mine."

Clarence jabbed the needle in his arm. He pushed the plunger in and the drugs surged into him. The giant closed his eyes. Guy couldn't watch. He turned away and left the man to escape to wherever the drugs took him.

"So much pain," thought Guy. Archie Walters had said the carnival ran on crazy, but it was pain that really fueled it.

It was late afternoon. Time to have some dinner and get ready for the evening's shows. He did four or five every night. It was tiring, but he loved astonishing people. He loved the look of wonder in their eyes.

Occasionally, he was able to see Ivan and Irena perform their trapeze act. What really thrilled him, though, was her solo turn on the high wire. He liked to see her perform, thinking of their lovemaking as he watched. He was wary of Ivan. He knew he might be lurking in the shadows, watching and waiting. Between Arrigo and Ivan, Guy spent a lot of time looking over his shoulder.

One night, Guy asked Irena about her relationship with Ivan.

Her answer was, as always, a kind of demented ballyhoo.

"Is okay but sometimes problems. Ivan think he own me, but no man own me if I not want and sometimes so. As lover he good and we have much fun, but anger too, so sometimes we part after we together and then he mad and I mad and fun no more, together no more unless we are again. I pick man, not man pick me, though sometimes man not man I pick even if I pick him."

Guy blinked. Then he rolled Irena over, kissed her, ran his hands down her shoulders to her hips, and they made love again. It was much easier than trying to talk.

28

When the carnival hit Cuba, Alabama, Willis was missing from the Friday night poker game. Guy went searching for him. He walked around and finally heard the soft, sad sounds of a harmonica coming from one of the baggage cars. Guy went in. It was dark. Some boxes lay around. In the middle of the car was a cage, usually used to keep some of the small animals used in the acts. Tonight, it held Willis.

Guy pulled up a box and sat near the cage. Willis made no sign of noticing him. He kept on playing his harmonica, held with his toes. Guy recognized the tune. It was "Swing Low, Sweet Chariot."

"We missed you at poker tonight," said Guy.

Willis played on to the end of the song. He put the harmonica down and only then could Guy really see him, or at least his bright eyes and teeth, oddly luminous in the shadows.

"I locked myself in here, Guy. They ain't gonna git me agin."

"Who isn't going to get you?"

"The bastards what chopped my arms off. They live in this state. They got me once but they ain't gonna git me again." Willis spat.

"No one is going to let anyone hurt you, Willis."

"I ain't so sure," he said. "Leave me be. I ain't comin' out 'til we be out of here. 'Til 'Bama be behind us. I's locked in and in I stay. Cooky can bring me some food."

Guy could not blame Willis. To have done to him what had been done was so unthinkable it made Guy shudder again. But he thought he'd try to reason with the man.

"Come on, Willis. That was long ago. You've locked yourself in a cage of fear."

"And them who done this to me locked themselves in a cage of hate. We both trapped."

Willis grabbed a bottle with his foot and took a big swig.

"You know what they say about hate, Willis?"

"What, Guy?"

"Holding on to it is like grasping a hot coal meaning to throw it at someone. You're the one that gets burned."

Willis snorted. Took another swig.

"You ever hate anybody, Guy?"

Guy thought about Woo and Jenks. "Yes, I have."

"Then you should know it ain't easy to let go of that ember even when it's burnin' you. In a funny way, you don't mind the pain. It lets you know you're alive."

Guy sighed. He could not argue with the man whose hurt and hatred were palpable in the dark train car. The cage could not contain them.

"Okay, Willis. Have it your way. I'll come by for a visit tomorrow. We can play some cards."

"You do that, Guy. And you tell Streeter I ain't gonna leave here 'til we're out of 'Bama."

Willis grabbed his harmonica with his left foot and began to play again. Guy left the man in his cage. He didn't feel like playing poker anymore so he just walked around in the suffocating Alabama heat.

Across the hot summer night, the garish lights of the carnival bathed the sky like an earthbound aurora borealis. The sounds of the calliope, of giddy laughter and the pop of the arcade guns drifted across the evening. The carnival called out across the darkness, beckoning with the sweet temptations of evil. The old and the young, the vain and the virtuous answered the call. Wherever the carnival came to town, the town came to it.

Guy made his way to the front gate where Archie was standing on a platform. Dressed in his gaudy checked suit, streaming sweat in the hellish heat, Archie was shouting out his ballyhoo like a reverend giving an impassioned sermon. His congregation, the curious townsfolk, stood in a crowd listening to him, swaying to the rhythm of his spiel, one by one reaching in their pockets for coins and paying their way into Streeter and Hale's carnival of oddities, curiosities and perilous performers.

"Life is short, friends. Life is short. Here are diversions and pleasures for every taste. Here you will find the brave and the beautiful, the wicked and the cursed.

"Now I know you've been good Christians, been to church on Sunday. But now it is Friday. Night is upon us. It's time for a visit with … the devil. My God, yes … the devil! That mischievous chap who knows our true hearts. He is here; his spawn are here; his minions are here.

"Now, my friends, remember what it says in the Bible. 'And yea, they looked upon the face of the devil and saw that he was evil and shuddered and closed their eyes lest they be tempted!'

"Well, open your eyes, my friends. Give in to temptation, because here it is harmless. We have tamed the devil, yes, tamed him for your amusement! Step in to our world and play our games of chance. Thrill to our rides. Gaze upon curiosities and oddities that you have never seen and did not think were possible. And remember: no sins last beyond this night or outside this gate.

"Come in, come in, come in one and all and see our show. It's wonderful to experience. Hard to describe. Impossible to forget. Streeter and Hale welcome you to their world of dreams. Step right up!!!"

And they did.

Guy marveled at Archie's ballyhoo. It fit perfectly the dreamlike atmosphere of the carnival, its vivid and sometimes grotesque visions. Guy walked to the edge of the carnival, where he came upon a single booth, a bit apart from the rest of the activity and noise. It was a small glowing island in the darkness. The booth was like most others. A game. Toss a ball at a pyramid of stacked boxes. Knock them down and win a prize. Here, the prize was a rubber mask. The masks were lined up, row after row of faces peering out from under the awning.

But these were not like any rubber masks Guy had ever seen. There were no Frankensteins or Mummy or Wolfmans—

none of the classic horror characters. No Cyclops or green aliens, or even horrid faces with drooping eyes and half-revealed skulls. No clowns. No, these masks were realistic and lifelike.

All the masks were disturbing in the subtle way they distorted normal features. A frowning brow, a sneer, thin slits for eyes—every one seemed molded to express an inner evil. Subtly, but unmistakably. These masks *were* monster masks, the monsters of real life. Here was the face of the criminal, the bully, the sadist. It was a spectrum of the dark side of human nature, molded in rubber.

Guy had never seen masks like them. They made him shudder.

The masks were blank, lifeless, waiting for the twinkle of real eyes to give them life and animate their souls. Guy stood back a ways, in the shadows, watching two teenage boys whose wanderings had taken them to the booth. The carny man began to chant his ballyhoo:

"Take yourself a shot, boys, take yourself a shot
Nickel buys a chance, boys, take yourself a shot!
Win yourself a mask, boys, win yourself a mask:
Choose who you're to be, boys—anything you want!
What you are you are, boys, the mask that fits is you.
Win yourself a mask, boys, the rubber is the truth!"

The boys hung on his rhyme, powerless to stop their hands dipping into their pockets to cough up a nickel. They eyed the masks that eyed them.

"Choose who you're to be, boys—anything you want!"

He had them and would not let them go. The rows of rubber masks peered down at them like an expectant jury.

"Win yourself a mask, boys, the rubber is the truth!"

His words floated on the sound of the calliope and laughter. Guy realized that the whole carnival was like those masks. It was a grotesque and empty caricature of life, waiting for innocent souls to wander in and inhabit it. Only then would its lifeless heart beat and its dark impulses find expression.

29

The carnival moved on through Alabama, pushing through the oppressive summer heat. Guy and Irena added to the heat with their passionate lovemaking. One night, when Irena had drifted off to sleep, Guy stole back to his cabin. He breathed a sigh of relief when he closed the door behind him.

In a blur, Ivan stepped out of the shadows and pinned Guy against the wall with a strangling grip to his neck. He was holding Guy a foot above the floor with his chokehold. Leaning in so his face was just inches from Guy's, Ivan hissed:

"I tell you leave Irena alone, but you no listen. She is *my* woman. I catch her in air; I love her in bed. I warn you, magician, but you not listen. Why you not listen?"

Guy could not breathe, let alone answer. As it had in the deserts of Morocco, his vision began to tunnel in on him. In the darkness of his cabin, sparkles danced before his eyes, and behind them, a mask of rage, was Ivan's face.

"Maybe you do your last trick and just disappear tonight, magician. Happens all time in carnival." Ivan tightened his grip on Guy. He was losing consciousness, his legs hanging limply, as if made of lead.

"Ivan say: 'goodbye, Guy.'"

The door to the cabin slammed open.

"Put him down!"

Guy looked beyond Ivan, who turned his head to look at the doorway. Neither saw anything.

"I said put him down!"

Ivan and Guy lowered their gazes, and lowered them still more until they spotted the tiny figure of Major Midget. He was holding an enormous gun, pointing it at Ivan.

"Put him down now or I'll blow your head off, Ivan!"

"You damned dwarf, stay out of this!" snarled Ivan.

Containing his rage, cocking the gun, Major Midget hissed back: "I...am...not...a...dwarf! I am a midget!"

"Dwarf, midget, what's the difference?" Guy was turning blue.

"A dwarf has distorted proportions. A big head and stubby fingers. Grotesque. A midget has perfect proportions. Everything is normal but scaled down. *That's* the difference. NOW PUT HIM DOWN OR I'LL SHOOT!" he shouted.

With a growl, Ivan let go of Guy, who slid down the wall, gasping for air.

"You shoot that gun, dwarf, and recoil knock you to next county!"

"Midget, you lead-headed idiot! Midget, not dwarf!"

Ivan snarled.

"Get out of here!" Major Midget yelled, stepping into the cabin and off to the side, the gun still aimed at Ivan.

"If you don't have gun, I crush you like bug."

"But I do have the gun, Ivan. It's my great equalizer."

Ivan looked down at Guy. "You stay away from Irena, magic man. And you watch out for Ivan!" He turned and headed for the doorway.

"And you, too, damned dwarf!" Ivan stomped down the stairs and into the night.

"MIDGET, YOU ASSHOLE! MIDGET!" yelled Major Midget after him. He slammed the door and went over to Guy.

"Are you all right?"

"I think so."

"Jesus, Guy. You can see his handprints on your neck!"

Guy got to his feet, a bit wobbly.

"Thanks, Major. Thanks a lot. I owe you my life."

"Aw, just call me your guardian midget," said Major Midget with a smile. "I told you I'd watch out for you. But you better do what he says, Guy. Stay away from Irena and be careful. He's out to get you."

Guy nodded. "Would you have shot him?"

Midget shrugged. "Who knows? If he had called me 'dwarf' one more time, probably."

"You ever fired that thing?" asked Guy.

"Nope."

"So you don't know what would happen from the recoil."

"Well, actually I don't. It's a big gun. A .45. And I'm a little guy."

"Then it might have knocked you into the next county," said Guy.

Major Midget smiled. "Well, that's where we're headed anyway."

30

The carnival was in Lula, Georgia. Guy could not sleep. Irena was busy with Ivan. As he lay in his bunk, Guy heard the most beautiful music wafting in the distance, riding the heavy hot air of the summer night. Curious, he dressed and left the train. He walked in the direction of the music, a solo violin. He passed the dark concessions and the lifeless rides and went on, out into the empty fields of the countryside. The moon was bright, the air still.

He saw a solitary figure sitting on a tree stump. It was Alberto, a member of the small band of musicians who played on the center stage of the carnival. Alberto played a gentle, melancholy melody. It was romantic, reflective, and so emotional that it brought tears to Guy's eyes. He kept his distance, sensing it was a private moment. He listened for a while until it became almost unbearable. Clearly, Alberto felt deeply the music he played.

Guy made his way to the rides. They were huge menacing silhouettes against the moonlit sky. They looked like the dinosaur skeletons Guy had seen at the Natural History Museum.

The open doors of the rides beckoned, but no thrill seekers approached. A carnival after hours was an empty stage awaiting its actors and their dramas.

Guy lit a cigarette and sat on the footrest of one of the Tilt-a-Whirl cars, leaning back against the face of a painted clown. He thought about how he had come to be here, of all places, traveling with a carnival, somewhere in rural Georgia, so far from New London, so far from the barbershop, so far from the glitter of Broadway and the horrors of the African desert. His path through life had been so unpredictable. How much of it had he chosen? How much was fated? How much of it was the random interplay of people and opportunity and happenstance? His reverie was broken by approaching footsteps. It was the Fat Lady. She lumbered by and saw him.

"Can't sleep either?"

"No. Too hot."

"Imagine how I feel, Guy, under all these layers of fat." She squeezed into one of the seats of the Tilt-A-Whirl, meant for three people. The ride creaked. Something rattled. She looked over at Guy.

"Heard there was quite the confrontation the other night between Major Midget and Ivan."

"There was. I was there. Midget saved my life, actually."

"Well, I told you he was a tough little character."

"That he is. He lives up to his nickname." Guy took a long drag on his cigarette. He let the smoke out, watching it in the moonlight. They listened to Alberto's distant music.

"Beautiful, isn't it?" said the Fat Lady. "He makes you want to weep. He does that most nights. Plays on the bandstand all day, full of smiles and energy and joy. Then late at night he wanders off and plays like this. I think somebody hurt him once. Very badly. He has a lot of pain to get out."

They listened a while longer to the sweet sad music of the distant violin, accompanied only by the chirp of crickets.

"I've learned a lot about some of the folks in the carnival, but I don't know much about you," said Guy. "What's your story? How did you come to be here?"

The Fat Lady leaned her head back. She looked up at the starry sky, at the moon.

"My story? Well, when I was a young girl, before this happened to me, I dreamed of becoming a ballerina. I guess all little girls do at some point. I wanted to be on stage, to entertain people ... but not like this.

"I hate being trapped in this body. It's a prison, and I'll never get out. It's a life sentence. Nobody really knows me. The real me. I'm just the Fat Lady. A sideshow act. A freak. That's who I am, and not who I am at all. It kills me sometimes." She waved her hand as if to clear something away. "Ah well. No use wallowing in self pity. I am who I am."

"Who are you really? What's your real name?"

The Fat Lady looked surprised.

"Nobody here has ever asked me that, Guy. Nobody. I'm just the Fat Lady. Or Fats."

"Well?"

"Lily," she said. "Lily Lavierre. Thank you for asking, Guy. Thank you very much." She smiled.

"That's a very pretty name," he said, and smiled back at her. Guy shook his head. Asking her her name. Such a simple thing. It had meant so much. Guy reached over and gave her hand a gentle squeeze. She looked up and he saw the sadness in her eyes. She mustered up a weak smile.

"I like you," said Guy.

"That's sweet. But would you want to hold me? Make love to me? No. You'd be revolted. It's okay. I understand. Why me when you have Irena? Not an ounce of fat on her."

"Not much brains, either."

She laughed." Maybe not, Guy. Maybe not. But men don't really care so much about brains, do they?"

There was an awkward silence.

"You don't have to be my lover Guy. A friend is enough."

Guy nodded. "I'd like that, Lily."

Again they grew silent and listened to Alberto. After a while, Lily said: "Tell me about the war, Guy. What was it like?"

"Like? It's not like anything else, Lily. It is its very own nightmare. A lot of it is just crap. Waiting around. Marching. Doing mundane stuff. Boring stuff. But when the fighting starts, it's a whole different story. Nothing boring about dodging bullets. Or seeing friends get ripped to shreds by them."

"You lost some friends?"

"Yeah. A few. I wasn't in that long, you know. Just a few weeks. But one guy—Butch, a sweet kid from Michigan—died in my lap. Not something I'll ever forget, though I'd like to."

Guy paused, took another long drag on his cigarette, then flicked it away.

"I was doing a coin trick for him. One second he was watching, happy and amazed. Then a sniper got him. I saw the life go out of his eyes. In a second. Here, then gone. I wish I could have done something for him."

Lily shook her head.

"You did, Guy. Think of it: the last thing Butch experienced in life was wonder, and what a gift that was, to go out not in pain or fear or doubt, but in joy. We should all be so lucky."

"I never thought of it that way."

"Still, someone dying like that, in my lap … God, I can't imagine it."

"Everything you imagine about war falls short, Lily. You miss the anxiety, the terror. You miss the sense of luck. Ten guys can be charging the enemy. Three get taken out, the rest live. Why? An inch here, an inch there, a moment when you flinch or your foot hits a little depression in the ground and the bullet whizzes by your head instead of through it. You realize you have no control over your fate. No choice. None at all. And that wears on you. Makes you crazy."

Guy shook his head and continued to stare at the moon, but his mind was elsewhere. Someplace he didn't want to be. This time, it was Lily who reached out to rest a comforting hand on his.

"They gave me a medal for being a hero, Lily. But I barely remember what I did. Things happened so fast. The kid died in my lap and I just wanted to get away from him. I snapped. I jumped up and ran. Next thing I know I'm on the ground, my toes blown off. I took a shot at the sniper and killed him. Luck. Then I killed the machine-gunner. Most of it's a blur. Just fragmented impressions. All except the look in Butch's eyes and the look in the young Kraut's eyes. I remember the eyes, Lily. I'll never forget them."

"Whatever happened, you came out a hero," said Lily.

"I don't feel like one. I was more angry than brave. I wanted revenge so I shot those guys. That's not being a hero."

"What is?"

Guy looked out into the deep dark night, listening to Alberto play. After a long pause, he turned to Lily.

"Being a hero is when you are in your right mind and know that danger—maybe even death—is around the corner and you don't flinch. You do something for others without thinking of yourself. That's being a hero in my book."

"Sounds like you've thought about this a lot, Guy."

"I have. In the hospital. On the train. In bed when I can't sleep. I try to make sense of what happened. I try to make sense of war."

"And?"

"I can't. War is madness, Lily. And you can't make sense of madness."

"I'm sorry, Guy. I didn't mean to bring up painful memories. Let's talk about something else."

Guy nodded and shook his head again as if to rid himself of the war, but it never worked.

"How did you happen to end up with Streeter and Hale?" asked Guy turning the talk back to Lily. She kept her eyes on the stars as she spoke.

"When I started to get really big, I was a history teacher. High school. A tough age to teach. They're cruel. Cruel to each other. And cruel to me, their fat, fat teacher. I got bigger and bigger and finally I was asked to leave. I was disruptive to the classroom. I was a good teacher, Guy. I loved to teach the kids. But that didn't count.

"It was hard for a seven-hundred-pound girl to find work. One day, someone called me a freak. And I got to thinking that maybe I could get work at a circus or carnival. A few months later, when summer came along, so did Streeter and Hale. I talked to them and they gave me a job. As a freak. Which is what I am to most folks. It's easy work, you know. I get paid to do nothing, really, except be my fat self. Not bad so long as you don't mind the humiliation of being gawked at like an animal in a cage."

Guy could see the tears in her eyes.

"There's nothing you can do? No medicine?"

"No. Too late. I'm beyond the reach of medicine. There's nothing anybody can do, Guy. Unless, that is, you can work some magic and turn me into a slim beauty."

"I like you just the way you are," said Guy, but it sounded like a lie.

"Well, I don't much care for me, but I'm all I got." Lily laughed.

"I guess a lot of us could say that, Lily."

She was quiet a moment, staring at the moon. When she spoke, it was almost a whisper.

"It's a tough world. Especially now. There's war; people are struggling. They're scared. That's why they like the freak show, Guy. They know they'll find someone with more problems. Someone with no arms or half a brain. Someone all skin and bones or fat as a whale. Bad as they got it, they come here and find someone who has it worse. That's what we are: the worst."

Lily sighed, shifted around in her seat.

"But you know what? We're not all that miserable. We have work. We get fed. We have each other. We're a little family. Though the Giant and the Monkey Girl and Major Midget might not admit it, we love each other. At least a little. The way I see it, the people who come here, they're the ones really hurting. I can see it in their eyes."

Guy thought about Clarence in his cabin, dulling his pain.

"There's a lot of pain everywhere, Lily."

"There is. You have to judge people not by what they do or don't do, but by what they suffer."

Guy remembered what Clarence had said about not judging him.

"Some folks can handle their pain, some can't," said Lily. "And some get to a point where they don't even want to try anymore."

"What about you, Lily? Still able to cope?"

"For the moment. But I don't think I'll live too long, Guy. I don't much care. I got a raw deal this time around. Maybe next time, I'll be lucky. I'd like to come back as a bird. I'd be lighter than air! I'd soar on the wind. That'd be nice. I can hope."

She looked over at Guy and cocked her head.

"Tell you what, Guy. If I do come back as a bird and I'm not in Africa or China or someplace far away, I'll find you."

"Sounds good to me, Lily," he said quietly.

With a groan, Lily stood up.

"Thank you, Guy. It was nice to talk to you. You listen. And thank you for caring enough to ask me my name."

Guy stood up, too.

"I enjoyed talking, too, Lily. It was interesting to hear your side of things."

"You know, Guy, you should treat the freaks like anybody else. We're different, but we're not. Some of us are nice; some of us aren't. Our problems don't make us noble."

They looked into each other's eyes a moment, understanding well each other's loneliness.

"Walk me back to my railroad car, Guy?" Lily asked.

"My pleasure," said Guy. He took Lily's hand and the two of them, the magician and the Fat Lady, slowly made their way back to the carnival, lit by the moon, warmed by their friendship, serenaded by the sad strains of Alberto's distant violin.

31

The carnival was abuzz. They were in Tallapoosa, Georgia.

Major Midget had been knocked senseless the night before. He had been walking along, minding his own business, when the business end of a fist came out of the night and clocked him. Cold-cocked.

The Alligator Man found him. Midget's pockets were turned inside out, his jaw swollen the size of an apple. He'd lost a tooth. Some thought it was locals who mugged him. Major Midget thought differently.

"It was Ivan," he told Guy. "I'm sure it was. He's been waiting to get a shot at me since I pulled that gun on him. Now *I* have to be careful. Look over my shoulder for that creep."

Later in the day, Midget saw Ivan and strode up to him.

"You hit me you Russian bastard!" he hissed.

Ivan just looked at him and sneered. "I not bother. Hitting you beneath me," he said.

"Not last night. But now I know and I'll be ready for you next time, Ivan. I'm gonna keep my 'equalizer' with me. You get near me and I'll blow your head off."

Ivan snorted. "Not scared of dwarf," he said, and walked off.

"Midget, damn you! I'm a midget not a dwarf!" Midget yelled, as best he could with his swollen jaw. Irena heard him and offered advice.

"Watch for Ivan. Don't make angry. He much mean."

"Well Ivan better watch out for me, Irena. I much mean too."

"Yes, I know. NLB."

"What?"

"No mind. But listen to Irena: small man not as big as big man, but big man smaller than small man if big man more mean."

Midget blinked.

Irena walked off. Guy came by.

"What's wrong, Midget. You look dazed."

"I was talking with Irena."

"Oh. That'll make your head hurt more than getting hit in the jaw."

Midget looked around.

"I'm nervous, Guy."

"Scared of Ivan?"

"Yes, he's after me."

"What about your gun?"

"I have it with me as much as I can, Guy, but there are always chances for the big jerk to surprise me. I gotta sleep, you know. I need a plan."

"A plan?"

"Yes, Guy. I need to plan how I'm going to survive a pissed off giant who wants to crush a midget."

"Maybe you need several plans, so you're prepared for different situations." Guy was thinking about Magician's Choice.

"I don't follow you, Guy. You're starting to sound like Irena."

"God forbid. Listen, Midget, sit down and I'll explain."

Guy told Major Midget all about Magician's Choice, about having many possible pathways that would lead to the solution the magician wanted.

Midget nodded, asked some questions. When Guy was done Midget stood up. "Thanks, Guy. Something to think about. Your magic comes in pretty handy. Seems like you could make just about any problem vanish."

"I wish, Midget. A magic show is one thing, real life another."

Midget gestured around at the carnival.

"Real life? Where the hell is that, Guy? This is a carnival, a world of make-believe. One big show. If Magician's Choice could work anywhere, it could work here."

32

"*You never go so far as when you don't know where you're going,*" the Gypsy Fortune Teller had foretold, but as they seemed to be going nowhere week after week, except to the next small town, Guy had no expectations when the carnival pulled into Liberty, South Carolina. They set up for a two-week engagement. He did his show, as usual. He had added some of the exotic patter Archie had suggested, and he was pleased to hear some gasps when he mentioned Chinese emperors and Amazon shamans and Indian fakirs.

Early in the show, Guy had spotted a young beauty who was staring at him intently. Not only was she beautiful, she was unusual: her eyes were different colors, one blue, the other hazel. So when he got to his torn and restored card trick, he smiled at her and asked: "How about you, miss? Would you care to come up here and help me with my next miracle?"

"Yes," she said, smiling, and came to the edge of the stage. Guy extended his hand to help her up the three steps, and the audience applauded her. She introduced herself as Rachel Dowd. She was tall, thin, with long blond hair and an easy smile. Guy guessed that she was about nineteen or twenty.

Rachel beamed on stage. She was a natural. She had presence. And unlike so many he invited up, she wasn't shy, didn't freeze up and forget the simplest instructions. No, she bantered with Guy, flashing him a knowing smile, her eyes sparkling.

Walking behind her on his way to pick up the card frame, Guy could smell the faintest trace of perfume. He saw the fine hairs on the nape of her neck, glowing in the light. For a moment, he could imagine himself nuzzling that neck. It was the trance of but a few seconds, but in those seconds, Guy felt a powerful attraction to Rachel Dowd.

And then he was past her, on the way to his table. The audience chuckled. Perhaps she had made a face. Guy picked up a small picture frame, showed it empty, and covered it with a cloth. He put it back on the table. Then he took out a deck of cards. He fanned them to show they were all different, both to Rachel and the audience.

"A deck of cards. All different, right?"

"Yes."

"Good. Now Rachel, I'll spread them out and I want you to pick one. It's your choice."

Guy held the fanned cards toward Rachel. She picked one.

"Ah, the Two of Hearts. A wonderful choice. Do you know what that card means, Rachel?"

"No. What?"

"Romance is in the air." Guy decided to take it a step further. "Are you perhaps engaged? Or is there a new boyfriend?"

"No," said Rachel, smiling. "Neither. But I'm always on the lookout for a handsome, talented man." She said it staring right at Guy. His knees buckled a bit. The crowd laughed. A few applauded. Guy just smiled and nodded at her remark. He was distracted, and that could be disastrous when doing a magic trick.

The great French conjuror Robert Houdin had once observed that a magician is "an actor playing the part of a magician." Among other things, this implies a continual awareness of patter, gesture, character, movement, position on stage, anticipation, the mood of the audience, a sense of the moment. Added to all this, a magician had to be ready to do his sleights, to work his props, to conceal and misdirect.

Guy couldn't afford to let this pretty girl distract him, break his concentration. Of course, a pretty girl was a great asset. She drew attention, and that lessened the attention on him. That's why so many magicians have pretty assistants. Or call upon pretty girls from the audience. But during a performance, Guy knew he had to keep his wits about him, pretty girl or not.

"Rachel, would you please hand me the card you chose. Thank you. I am going to tear a piece off the corner. Here, you hold it." Guy tore off the corner, showed it to the audience, and handed the piece to Rachel.

Guy tore the remainder of the card into pieces, put them in a dish and lit them on fire. When they were ashes, he made some gestures over them and at the cloth-covered frame. He walked over and unveiled it. There was a Two of Hearts missing a corner.

The crowd gasped and applauded. He removed the card from the frame, walked back to Rachel and showed it to her.

"A piece of my heart is missing," she said with a smile. Guy couldn't have scripted a better line himself. He smiled back and said: "Yes, but I can fill that in." He gave her the card. "See if they fit," he said.

Rachel took the card and fit the corner to it. She showed them dramatically to the audience.

"A perfect fit!" she said.

The crowd in the tent broke into applause.

"You may keep the card as a souvenir," Guy said. Then, turning to the audience: "Let's have a hand for Rachel Dowd, who helped me with this impossible miracle."

The applause swelled louder, and as Guy held Rachel's hand and helped her down off the platform, their eyes met for a second. The gaze of her mismatched eyes was bewitching. He thought back to when he had picked her from the audience and wondered if she had somehow plied the Magician's Choice on him. Did she need to? When faced with a pretty woman, does any man have free will?

When the show ended and the crowd had left, Guy busied himself putting away his props. It was the last show of the evening and he was in no rush. He couldn't stop thinking of Rachel Dowd, of her beautiful eyes, the curve of her neck, her subtle scent.

"I enjoyed your show."

Guy spun around and there she was. Rachel Dowd. She smiled, and so did Guy.

"Thank you. You helped make it a good one," he said.

Rachel started to laugh. Guy didn't understand why until she pointed at his table. Lou the bunny was pushing his nose out of the secret compartment that hid him in the tip-over box.

"I think your bunny wants to get out," said Rachel.

"Yes, he certainly does," said Guy.

Rachel came forward and sat on a chair in the front row, watching as Guy fiddled with his tricks. Guy was more nervous than if he had a full crowd watching him.

"I hope you don't mind my being here," she said, "I mean, I don't want to see any of your secrets."

"Don't worry," said Guy. "These are just the props. Only part of the magic." He folded up a feather bouquet and emptied the coins from the bucket he used for the Miser's Dream, glancing around to make sure Arrigo wasn't on the prowl. "Are you from Liberty?" he asked Rachel.

"Yes, from the other side of town. My father is a pastor. At the Liberty United Methodist church. My mother and sister are teachers. We're a small, loving family."

"I have family back in Connecticut," he said. "Just a mother and father. I'm the roaming son."

"Can I ask a question, Mr. Merloc?"

"Guy. My name is really Guy. Guy Borden. Merloc is just a stage name."

"Oh." Rachel fished in her purse and pulled out the Two of Hearts with the missing corner. She looked at it, smiled, and showed it to him. "Tell me, Guy, when you had me pick that card for the trick, the Two of Hearts. Was that my choice or yours?"

"Does it make a difference?"

"Maybe."

"Well, if I told you, Miss Dowd, *that* would be telling you a secret. Which I can't do." He winked. "But I'll say this: I'm glad it was that card."

"And why is that?"

"Because of what it means."

"Romance is in the air."

"Right."

They looked at each other. Two young, vibrant people dancing around a strong mutual attraction.

"I just wanted to check," said Rachel, standing up. She took a step forward and held out her hand. Guy took it and she shook, gently, slowly.

"I hope to see you again, Miss Dowd. We're in town for a few weeks. Why don't you come to another show? Maybe we can have some ice cream afterwards, or take a walk, or even get away from the carnival for dinner?"

"Your choice," said Rachel with a wink of her own, then turned and left the tent.

Guy stared after her. He freed Lou from the tip-over box and stroked the bunny's soft fur.

"Lou," he said, "I think I'm going to need some patience."

33

On the Sunday after the carnival came to town, Reverend Dowd gave a sermon. Its title, posted on the small sign outside the Liberty United Methodist church, was "The Gravity of Evil."

Guy waited until services had begun to sneak in and stand in the back, listening through an open door.

After the usual invocation and singing of hymns, Reverend Dowd strode to the pulpit. He was an imposing figure, tall, thin, straight-backed, wearing wire-rimmed glasses. He had a deep, mellifluous voice. He took command when he spoke, and Guy could not help but think of Archie Walters. Though their aims were different, Dowd and Walters were both superb orators who knew how to manage an audience. With their words and the force of their personalities, both men made believers out of people.

Dowd looked out from his pulpit, slowly sweeping his gaze, pulling in the attention of his congregation. There was silence, and then he began.

"Temptation. So much a part of life. It is temptation that tests our belief, our fortitude, our moral purity.

"We are tempted by that which is forbidden, by that which we know is only an indulgence, by that which promises pleasures that are shallow and fleeting. It is human nature, for we are flawed, and, like water finding a crack in a rock, temptation finds its way to our weaknesses.

"A few days ago, a carnival came to town. It brought with it a host of temptations. Now, my good people, I am not preaching against fun. We need levity in our lives. There is no harm in the excitement of thrilling rides, of performers dazzling us with their feats of daring. No, there is nothing bad about a little harmless fun.

"But there is more to the carnival. A sinister side. The carnival offers evil temptations that appeal to our darker impulses, our prurient interests.

"When we see the naked hoochie girls, we are succumbing to forbidden pleasures of the flesh.

"When we look upon the freaks, we witness the devil's spawn.

"When we play the crooked games and watch the strange acts, we trade our freedom for the slavery of illusion.

"Resist those temptations at the edge of town, at the edge of goodness. For while there may be harmless diversions there, they are merely to entice you to enter a more sinister realm, one that preys upon the weak. The gravity of evil will pull you off the path of righteousness and hold you down with its lies.

"A carnival is the devil's game. Beware: lose to him and he wins your soul. But you have a choice. Stay with the Lord, our God in heaven.

"The Lord rewards believers, but only if the believers are unwavering in their belief! God works in strange ways, sometimes testing us. We must accept His challenges. We must know that whatever befalls us, it is part of His plan. It is not for us, mere mortals, to judge the divine. We must bend to His will, hope for His mercy, and accept His judgment.

"If you be tempted, turn away.
If you be seduced, reject false love.
If you find yourself in the darkness, seek the light.
If the Lord calls you, answer Him with service and belief.
It is your choice.
Now let us pray."

Guy left the church. He was impressed with Dowd's oration. Thinking about what the pastor had said, Guy couldn't totally disagree with him. There *was* something dark about the carnival. Something that chilled even as it thrilled.

Guy wondered if the sermon would keep people away from the carnival or drive them to it to satisfy their curiosity about what was so forbidden. Sometimes the best way to get people to do something is to tell them not to. That made Guy smile. Perhaps Reverend Dowd, unwittingly, had become a ballyhoo man for the carnival.

34

Rachel came back.

The next day. And the day after that. Guy wondered if the pastor knew his daughter was spending so much time in the realm of the devil.

Rachel sat and watched Guy's show. He didn't ask her up on stage again. He wasn't sure why, but he had a feeling it was for the best. After the fourth time she saw the show, she lingered in the tent, and when she was alone with Guy, she spoke.

"I've figured out how you do most of your tricks. They're very clever. And you're very good."

"Thank you, Miss Dowd."

"Rachel."

"Rachel. Thank you, Rachel." He busied himself resetting his props for the evening show. Rachel watched him.

"Don't you get tired of doing it over and over? Of the traveling? Setting up. Staying a bit. Then tearing down. Moving on?"

"I do," said Guy. "But that's life in the carnival. Here today. Gone tomorrow."

Rachel nodded.

"In your act, when you do the trick where you pull the coins from the air and put them in the bucket ..."

"The Miser's Dream. That's the name of the trick."

"Yes, that one. When you get to the part where you pretend to pull the coin out of the kid's ear, you should draw it out a bit more. It would be funnier."

Slightly offended that this girl would presume to critique his act, Guy answered, a bit coldly, "I'll try to remember that advice." He busied himself carefully folding up a bouquet of feather flowers and putting them into the load chamber of his production box.

Rachel sensed his annoyance.

"Sorry. Just trying to be helpful. It's a wonderful trick. You got a great reaction to it."

Guy thought for a moment about what Blackstone had told him about slowing down and drawing out the magic moment. In truth, the repetition of his act had probably dulled his enthusiasm a bit, and maybe he had been rushing that part. Rachel was right. And, he thought, quite perceptive.

"No, you are probably right. Maybe I could do that a bit slower."

"A little like the bunny box," she said.

"The Tip-Over Box? What was wrong with *that*?"

"Well, you rushed the end of that a bit, too. Just tonight. You did the first part really well. All that talk about mystery and China and how the bunny was good luck. It was very convincing. Then when he disappeared ... I don't know exactly ... maybe you should react more—do a double-take or something. You just lost your good luck, after all."

Guy turned to her and was about to speak when she cut in.

"Mind you, I doubt anybody would notice. But I've seen your act over and over, and I see how a little variation can change the effect. It's quite interesting. Magic is more subtle than I thought."

Again, Rachel's critique was right. Guy was quite charmed by her. By her interest in his act, her perceptive observations of the nuances of performance. And he liked her mismatched eyes.

That night, she accepted his invitation for a stroll around the carnival and some ice cream. They repeated it the next night and every night thereafter. She came to watch his show, offer a little advice, and then join him afterwards. They were both aware the carnival would leave in a week. Neither talked about it. They were just getting to know one another.

And falling in love.

They walked by the calliope. Among other tunes, it played "Paper Moon," a song Guy knew well from his days at the

Morosco. Its lyrics fit the carnival—and their budding romance—perfectly.

"Do you know this song, Rachel?"

"Yes, it's 'Paper Moon' isn't it?"

"Right. Do you remember the lyrics?"

"No, not really."

Guy sang along with the calliope:

Say, it's only a paper moon
Sailing over a cardboard sea
But it wouldn't be make-believe
If you believed in me

Yes, it's only a canvas sky
Hanging over a muslin tree
But it wouldn't be make-believe
If you believed in me

Without your love,
It's a honky-tonk parade
Without your love,
It's a melody played in a penny arcade

It's a Barnum and Bailey world
Just as phony as it can be
But it wouldn't be make-believe
If you believed in me

"A nice song," said Rachel with a smile. "The truth of love in a world of illusion."

Guy mused that in the make-believe world of the carnival, in the world of illusion that was magic, perhaps Rachel and his feelings for her were the only truths in his life. She seemed to think so, too. "Paper Moon" became their song.

They walked on a bit, watching people play the games, listening to the ballyhoo, adrift in the crazy dream of the carnival.

"I'd like you to come over for dinner, Guy," Rachel said. "Tomorrow night, before your show. We always eat early on

Friday. I'll bet it's been a long time since you've had a real home-cooked meal."

Guy thought about it. It had been a long time. Years, in fact. But then he thought about the sermon. He had told Rachel he'd been there listening.

"I don't know, Rachel. I don't think the pastor would care for me. He would probably think of me as a minion of the devil."

Rachel smiled.

"He does have strong beliefs, Guy. But he may be more open-minded than you think. He likes to talk about things and hear other views."

"He seemed quite close-minded in his sermon about what the carnival had to offer."

"Well, that's his job, you know. If he didn't come across as confident in his beliefs, folks wouldn't think he was much of a preacher. Like you, Guy: you have to believe in your magic for it to work, right?"

"True."

"And Guy, you and father are more alike than you might think."

"Oh? How so?"

"I've been thinking about it. You both make people believe in miracles. Father does it with scripture. You do it with cards and coins."

Guy thought about it a minute. Why not? He was falling in love with Rachel, and her desire to have him meet her family was a good sign. It was happening quickly, but the nature of their situation had turned up the heat. They didn't have the luxury of time.

"Okay, Rachel, dinner it is. I'll hide my horns and cloven hooves."

Rachel laughed.

"Don't worry, Guy. Just be yourself. My family will like you. Even father."

The sights and sounds of the carnival washed over them. They strolled, and Guy gently took Rachel's hand.

"I meant to tell you earlier, Rachel: I like your dress. I've never seen anything quite like it."

"Thank you, Guy. I designed it myself."

"Really?"

"Yes, I have a flare for it. Mother encourages me. I've even designed some dresses for weddings and the annual charity ball. It's my dream."

"Your dream?"

"Someday I'd like to go to New York, work in the fashion world there. See if I could make my mark. I'd at least like to try. But, I don't know. It's a long way from Liberty to Fifth Avenue."

"Life's funny, Rachel. You never know how it will unfold. I was in New York, joined the army, went to Africa, woke up in a hospital in Arizona, stumbled upon the carnival, met you."

"Tell me about New York, Guy."

Guy told her about his time at the Morosco Theater (he left out the angel), his visits to Tannen's, his betrayal by Woo.

"My God," she said when he was done. "I envy you. It sounds so exciting."

"I want to get back there someday," he said. "Maybe have my own show. With a pretty assistant."

Rachel just smiled.

"You never know how things might work out, Rachel. Sometimes we choose. Sometimes life chooses for us."

"True," she said. "Life is full of surprises."

35

Early Friday evening, Guy found the Dowd's house, on Clover Street not far from the church. It was small but attractive. He was happy to be visiting a real home; it had been ages since he'd been in one. His had been a life of hotels, barracks, a hospital, and trains. He realized how much he missed a home with a yard, a place where people had put down roots.

Rachel met him at the door, looking radiant in another lovely dress.

"Your design?" he asked gesturing to it.

"Yes," she beamed, pleased. She gave him a kiss on the cheek and invited him in. He had two bouquets of flowers—real ones—for Rachel and her mother. And a box of chocolates for Rachel's sister, Angela.

"A good start," whispered Rachel.

Guy met Rachel's mother, Mae, who took his flowers with a big smile and twinkling eyes. Guy liked her immediately. Some people are like that. They exude an aura of warmth and openness.

Rachel introduced Angela. She was tiny, like her mother, with bright red hair and freckles.

"Angela is an English teacher at the Roby Elementary School."

"Pleased to meet you," said Guy.

"And I you," said Angela. "I hope you'll show us a few tricks tonight."

"Maybe," said Guy.

Then the pastor. As he shook the man's hand, Guy did not mention that he had already seen the pastor. He just said,

"Pleased to meet you, Pastor." The pastor was tall, quite a contrast to his diminutive wife and youngest daughter. Clearly, Rachel had gotten her willowy height from him.

As Mae and Angela finished making dinner, Guy, Rachel and the pastor sat in the living room.

"Rachel tells me you're with the carnival," said the pastor. "A magician?"

"That's right. I've been doing magic quite a few years. In New York and then after the war, in this carnival."

"She tells me you're very good." The pastor's tone was neutral. Not dismissive, as Guy had expected, but neither was it overly warm.

Patience.

"I work hard at it, pastor. To me, it's more than frivolous entertainment." Guy had the advantage of knowing what the pastor had said in his sermon, and he hoped to navigate through the man's preconceptions.

"How so?"

"Pastor, people come to a magic show, or, I suppose, to the carnival, to escape their worries for a little while. They want to leave their troubles behind and experience something different."

"No doubt about that," said the pastor. Guy knew that the pastor was thinking dark temptations. Guy was thinking something much more positive.

Just then, Mae came in and said dinner was ready. They all went into the dining room. Dinner—ham, potatoes, beans, salad and rolls—was passed around. The smell of home-cooked food was delightful. A true temptation, Guy mused to himself.

"Guy was telling me why people come to the carnival to see his magic," said the pastor.

"Go on, Guy," urged Rachel.

"Well, as I was saying, they come to escape their problems for a while. What I offer them is wonder."

"Wonder isn't found just in magic, Guy," said the pastor. "Why in my life, I've seen a few wonders."

"I've seen 1001," said Guy, thinking of Blackstone's show.

There was a pause, then Guy continued.

"I don't doubt there is wonder everywhere, pastor. But it's unpredictable in life. It's a surprise and a delight when we encounter it. At the carnival, at a magic show, you are guaranteed of it. When people come to see me, they *expect* wonder. And they get it."

"But Guy, what you do are tricks. You deceive them."

"No, pastor. I make them believe."

"Believe? In what?"

"In the impossible. My hope is that when they leave, they will take that belief with them. If I can make a rabbit disappear, then maybe they can get rid of some pain they have. If I can restore a playing card, then maybe they can fix a broken relationship. If I can turn a glass of water into wine, then maybe they can turn a dream into reality."

"So," said Reverend Dowd, an edge to his voice, "do you think when Jesus changed water into wine he was just doing a clever parlor trick?"

"Not at all, pastor, not at all. And believe me, I'm not comparing myself to Jesus. What I mean is that when people see a miracle—wherever they see it, whoever is doing it—they are inspired. They have new hope that what they thought was impossible might be possible. That's all. What they do with that hope is up to them."

Reverend Dowd looked at Guy and seemed to be considering what he'd said. Rachel was smiling, as was Mae. Guy had danced around blasphemy and defended what he did persuasively. And, as Rachel had said, the pastor was willing to listen. Guy thought of Butch dying as Guy did his retention vanish and what Lily had said about that moment.

"Let me ask you something, pastor."

"Go ahead."

"If one of your congregants was dying, and you were at their bedside in their final moments, and you could say or do something that would usher them into the afterlife in a state of joy and wonder, would you be happy?"

"Yes, of course. One always hopes that the moment of death be one of calm, even rapture, rather than fear. Why do you ask?"

"Because of something that happened long ago and far away. When I was in the war. A friend died. It's painful to remember, to talk about. I've been haunted by his death, but I've come to look at it differently."

The pastor nodded. "Death haunts us all, Guy. The end of life, it's a big part of life. We must all make our peace with it. I had two brothers. One died as a child, the other in the war. I know how difficult it can be to understand. To accept."

The Reverend had a somber look on his face, and for a moment, he was lost in thought. Then he closed his eyes as if closing a book on his memories. He opened them, back with them, and looked at Guy.

"I have another question about the carnival, Guy," said the pastor, "don't you think that there are elements of the carnival—the crooked games, the naked women, the freaks—that appeal to our darker sides? That are evil?" Dowd was back to his sermon.

"Yes, pastor, I do. I don't like all of what goes on there. But the carnival is just a reflection of life. It has light and it has shadows. And as in life, people must choose what to embrace, what to reject. Just because there is darkness, it doesn't mean we want to walk in it. But I take issue with one thing you said."

"What is that, Guy?"

"Including the freaks in your list of evils. That they are evil. They are not children of the devil. They are just poor souls who are different. It is not their choice to be who they are. If you were a blind man and met them, talked to them, got to know their hearts, you would see they are just like you and me. No different. They don't deserve our fear or scorn, and they don't want our pity. They just want dignity. And love. The sad part is, they seldom get either."

All eyes at the table turned to the pastor. Chastened, he said, "I suppose you're right. After all, Jesus loved the afflicted."

"Exactly, pastor. Your daughter has two different color eyes. Someone might think she's a freak. I think she's beautiful."

Guy paused. Enough of this serious talk and philosophical sparring. He had made his points to the pastor. It was time to move on.

"Could you pass the butter, please?" he asked.

The talk turned to other things as Guy asked Angela about her teaching and told Mae how much he liked the dresses Rachel had designed. Mae was a proud mother and smiled at Guy throughout the meal.

"You promised us a trick," Angela said. All eyes turned to Guy. He stood up. He took out his Morgan silver dollar and did his Retention Vanish and the reappearance of the coin in a roll Mae selected from the bread basket. They were all delighted, even the pastor, who exclaimed: "Good Lord!"

When they had settled down, Mae asked: "What are your plans, Guy? Do you want to stay with the carnival? Do you want to go somewhere else to do your magic?"

"I'll leave the carnival at some point, Mrs. Dowd. Like anyone in the business, I'd like to have my own show at a theater in New York. That's my dream. But, who knows if it's in the cards? We'll see."

"You are drawn to the glamour of Broadway?" Mae asked.

"Not so much to the glitter, though being in a spotlight like that would certainly be wonderful."

"Then what?"

"What draws me is that in New York, or in any show in a real theater, you get a big audience. Not just twenty or thirty like I get in the carnival, but hundreds, even thousands of people. Every show. Show after show."

"Does it make a difference?" asked the pastor.

"Well, if my goal is to spread wonder, it does. When you preach, pastor, don't you like to see a full congregation? Isn't it better when you can get your message out to a crowd of people rather than a few?"

Dowd nodded "yes."

"Same with me. But there's more. When I perform for big crowds, there's an energy in the theater, an electricity. We're sharing something special together, all those people and me. I draw inspiration from them, and they draw it from me."

"Isn't it scary?" asked Angela. "I get nervous in front of just fifteen kids."

Guy thought back to the Levinson bar mitzvah.

"So do I," said Guy. "Believe me, kids are the toughest audience of all. My hat's off to you standing in front of them every day. It'd kill me."

Angela smiled at his praise. He looked over at Rachel who winked at him. This dinner was going okay, Guy decided.

Guy and the Dowds chatted into the early evening. For Guy it was wonderful to be with a family, in a real living room in a real home, full of family pictures and knickknacks, full of humor and love.

"Your wedding picture?" asked Guy, pointing to a photograph of a young beaming couple.

"Yes, it is," said Mae. "I was very happy that day. It was our wedding of course, but I was happy I had finally gotten the preacher to the altar to do something besides pray!"

"Now come on, Mae, it didn't take that long," the pastor protested.

"Nearly a year," said Mae, laughing. She turned to Guy and whispered "Francis doesn't like to rush things."

"I heard that!" said Francis as Mae went into the kitchen to get more coffee. He turned to Guy. "I just like to be sure of things."

"Watching you two this evening," said Guy, "I'd say you chose well. You love her very much, don't you?"

"Even more than God," whispered the pastor, in case God was listening. "I'd be lost without her."

About seven, Reverend and Mrs. Dowd announced that while they were enjoying the evening, they had to get to church to run the Friday night bingo game, and Guy had his shows to perform.

"You're okay," the pastor told Guy. "I like how much you care about what you do, and I think your motives are good. I'll think about the carnival some more. And I'm sorry for what I said about the freaks. I suppose some of them are your friends?"

"They are, pastor. It's okay. Most people have a hard time accepting them. But get beyond how they're different and you see how they're the same as us. Just people, trying to survive, to find a little happiness."

Everybody said their good nights and left. Rachel wrapped her arm around Guy's as they walked in the balmy summer night.

"I told you my family would like you, Guy. What did you think of them?"

"I liked them, too, Rachel. I really did. Your father is, like you said, more open-minded than I'd have thought, especially from his sermon. Angela is sweet. And your mother's a doll. I really liked her."

"Yeah, she liked you, too, Guy. She told me in the kitchen. She said that even though you're a magician, you're not an illusion."

36

Can a man fall in love in two weeks? Can a woman? If it's love at first sight, it takes only seconds. Compared to that, two weeks is an eternity. The love that connects two people changes the course of their lives. They head off, together, in a new direction.

For the two weeks the carnival was in Liberty, Guy and Rachel saw a lot of each other. She came to his shows often. He enjoyed seeing her out in the audience, winking at him and noting any flaws in his performance. He was too focused on his act to notice Irena standing at the back of the tent watching. She had seen Guy with Rachel and knew he was falling in love. She missed his visits to her cabin, their lovemaking. But she always had Ivan. She even confronted Guy about it.

"You got new girl from Irena?"

"Maybe. I'm not sure. We've just met. We're just getting to know each other."

"No love making?"

"No love making, Irena."

"Good but I not so much care. I know our hearts not as one."

"Okay, then. Everybody can be happy."

"Old Russian proverb agree: 'making love not always love in the making.'"

"Of course," said Guy, "You Russians are smart."

"Right damned," said Irena, walking off in search of Ivan.

The dinner at the Dowds was not repeated. Though Mae had suggested it, their time together was so short that Rachel wanted Guy to herself. They met for walks and picnics. For quiet dinners and ice creams in the park where they could just talk. There was an urgency, an edge to their encounters. Both knew that in a matter of days, like a soldier shipping out, Guy would move on with the carnival.

Or would he?

One day, waiting for Rachel in the city park, Guy stood on a small white bridge over a glassy calm pond. Dragonflies flitted like fairies over the lily pads. Frogs belched their throaty songs. Bluebirds flew overhead. He heard the distant crack of a baseball bat and kids yelling. He looked out over a gentle landscape of grass and trees, small buildings and bright skies.

Guy wondered if he could stay. Could he jump off the carnival train and land … where? Could Liberty provide a living for a magician? He doubted it. If not magic, what would he do? He knew enough about cutting hair to become a barber. But he knew that he could never be happy in a job where, when he looked up, he saw only himself reflected in a mirror. Him watching him. No, Guy needed an audience. From an audience he drew his strength and his courage and his inspiration. Their astonishment, their applause was the energy that drove his act. His life.

Could Rachel's love replace that? Could he turn his back on show business and embrace a quieter life? Would he ever be happy living far from the spotlight, with little chance of ever being back in it?

Standing on that bridge, looking out over the quiet park, Guy did not think he was ready to give up his dream.

And there was something else.

Rachel was holding something back. He didn't know what, but he sensed it. She seemed guarded at times. Her smile could vanish in a blink, and he'd catch her lost in thought, a slight frown lining her pretty face. Being so newly acquainted, he had no idea what that meant. Perhaps she had doubts. Maybe it really was too soon for love. Maybe she already had a love, and her time with Guy was just a slight wandering away, as if drawn off a path by an interesting view. Soon enough, she'd pull away, back to a man she already had. Or was it fear? Perhaps the religious morality of her father had made her afraid of falling in love, as if it were a sin.

What troubled Rachel troubled Guy.

"Hi, Guy!" Her voice was happy, and when he turned to see her on the bridge, she was radiant, her golden hair backlit by the summer sun.

Guy bowed slowly.

"You look beautiful," he said. Rachel beamed.

Is there anything sweeter than the first days of love, when the world fades away to a background blur and all your focus is on another? It is intoxicating.

"You looked lost in thought," she said.

"I *am* lost when you are not with me," he said, realizing as he did that it was a bit heavy handed. Rachel just smiled, whether pleased or indulgent, he couldn't tell.

They walked and talked of their lives, their dreams. In the backs of their minds, both wondered what a life including the other might be like. Which part of whose dream would endure; which part would be discarded or compromised? Love always requires a leap from the known into the unknown.

As it turned out, two weeks together was not enough to change the course of their lives. That change requires the most exquisite timing and alignment of circumstance. For two destinies to merge into one is like two birds soaring across the sky toward each other, circling, then veering off together, side by side, beating their wings in perfect rhythm. At the end of two weeks, Guy and Rachel had come together, but they would fly off in different directions.

Their last night together was tense. They had dinner, but both were thinking that tomorrow the carnival would pull up stakes and leave Liberty, and Guy would go with it. He had not said as much, but they both knew it. She wished he would stay, stay so they could see if the love they felt would blossom. Rachel knew that to ask Guy to leave the carnival was asking a lot. Guy might resent her for taking him from a love he already had. Not Irena. No, there was no love there; they were just lovers. His true love was magic.

What about herself? Could she join the carnival and travel with Guy? What life awaited her with him? He didn't know where he was going. Could she take the leap of faith and follow him to destinations unknown? Could she possibly leave the family she loved?

After dinner, they walked through the park. Neither wanted to bring up the inevitable. They circled around it, both about to crawl out of their skin with the tension of it.

It was Rachel who finally got to the heart of the matter.

"Guy, this isn't easy, so let's not try to make it so. There is something special between us. I know it. I think, I hope, you know it, too. There's love here, Guy. Here in my heart. Here in Liberty. But I know you want to move on, to stay with the carnival. If you left it now, you would regret it … right?" The last word was tinged with a tone of uncertainty, with the hope that maybe it was the wrong word.

Guy listened, and when she stopped, when he looked in her glistening eyes and thought about what she had said, his love for her deepened. She had spoken from her heart and touched his. He almost told her he would stay. That thought, that desire was in his mind. She was in his heart. But something in him said: "no." He listened to it.

"You could come with me, Rachel. Be my assistant. We'd be together."

She, too, was tempted. But like Guy, she felt the timing was not right. Or was it fear? Fear that she would uproot herself for a man she did not know that well for a life she could not imagine. She turned from him and looked out at the street, feeling the quiet comfort of her hometown. She looked back at Guy.

"I can't leave, Guy. Not now." She stared into his eyes. "Promise me we will meet again. Pick this up where we leave it now."

"Rachel, I would like that to happen. Truly I would. But I can't promise that. You know how life is. You can't promise the future."

"Why not, Guy? Don't we set our own course to the future?"

"Sometimes. Not always."

He took her in his arms. She cried quietly against his shoulder. He smelled her hair. He looked at the back of her neck, glowing in a streetlight as it had that first night on stage.

Why shouldn't he stay? Why shouldn't he trust his fate to their love? Maybe the path to what he wanted lay here in Liberty, with Rachel. Or could he get there only by staying the course he was on, resisting anything that would push him from it? But *was* he on a course, or just drifting along?

After a few minutes she pulled away from his embrace. They walked on, both lost in thought, in sorrow, the warm night cold.

37

He did not see Rachel the next morning. They packed up the last of the carnival, and the train pulled out at eight o'clock. In a few minutes, Liberty was left behind, and with it, Rachel.

He was back on course again, meandering through small towns, the places always changing yet always the same. It was like a drugged sleep, at once intense and vague.

He thought of Rachel often. He wondered what she was doing. He wondered if he had made a mistake not staying with her, or if she had made one not coming with him. Other pretty girls smiled at him from the audience, but they were not Rachel. She was different. He had fallen in love with her. Yet magician that he was, he could not vanish her memory.

Though he pined for Rachel, Irena was a force to be reckoned with. Now that the carnival had moved on, and Rachel left behind, Irena had Guy to herself, even if Guy didn't have Irena to himself. No, there was always Ivan.

The triangle continued.

Guy saw Irena some nights, but it was Rachel who was constantly on his mind. Irena was sex, Rachel was love, and Guy had discovered the difference.

Some nights he preferred his own company. On Fridays, he played poker with the freaks. Willis had left his cage when the carnival left Alabama and was back shuffling and dealing with his feet. Guy lost a lot to Major Midget, who chomped a big cigar, constantly needled the other players, and piled his chips with smug glee whenever he won, which was often. "Read 'em and weep," he liked to say as he laid down a winning hand. He was indeed a NLB.

Like the marks who came to the carnival, Midget and the rest of the freaks were hardly immune from the lure of dreams the carnival offered. One of the most dreamlike attractions was the funhouse.

It was a corridor that twisted its way through a tent, doubling back on itself. Lining the corridor were all manner of odd and disturbing things, including glow-in-the-dark skeletons, distorting mirrors, scary dummies and eerie lighting effects. The floors and walls were canted at disorienting angles. A window looked into a room where a live cat roamed about, growing and shrinking as it did—a clever optical illusion.

It was at the funhouse where, late one night, Guy heard laughter. He quietly opened the door and stepped inside.

Around the first bend of the corridor, Guy heard Lily and Major Midget talking and giggling. They were at the distorting mirrors. Midget stood in front of one that made him look very tall; The Fat Lady stood in front of one that made her thin. It was ironic. For most people, the mirrors distorted their bodies. For the Fat Lady and Major Midget, they made them normal.

"You'd be able to look the Giant in the eye," Lily laughed looking at Midget's reflection.

"You'd be the sexiest of the hoochie girls," said Midget, looking at hers.

All too soon, Guy thought, they would have to leave their illusions. But for a few silly moments, the Fat Lady and the Midget escaped the curse of their true selves and saw themselves as they dreamed of being. Guy turned and quietly left them to their fantasies.

Some nights, Guy walked around the carnival and just let it wash over him. He liked to observe people as they took in the attractions. He liked to look in on the sideshow acts and the freak show. Sometimes he loitered in the main tent, watching the Perilous Performers. Not just Ivan and Irena, but the acrobats and sword swallower, the fire eater, the man who ate glass, the cowgirl sharpshooter and all the rest of them. As he had at the Morosco Theater, Guy studied the performers and their effect on audiences.

Guy liked the rides, too, the swirling blur of lights and faces. He'd hear the screams, the thrum and whir of machines in motion. He had noticed a loud rattle coming from the machinery of the Tilt-a-Whirl. The guy who ran it was Purvis. He sat on a stool near the controls. He had a few days' stubble, a cigarette dangling from his mouth, and greasy hair.

When Guy approached, Purvis looked at him with hooded eyes, like a snake.

"You know, I couldn't help but notice this thing is making a lot of noise," Guy said above the racket of the ride and its riders.

"There's a rattle somewhere in the machinery. You know what it is?"

"Nope."

"Don't you think you ought to check it out?"

"Nope."

"What if it is a problem? Something dangerous? Aren't you worried?"

"Nope."

Purvis just smoked his cigarette. Thin, full of tattoos, mean looking, the man was probably fresh out of prison. His job went no further than taking a ticket, slamming the safety bars down, and running the ride. It was three minutes of tilting, whirling, stomach-churning thrills.

If there were pretty girls aboard and they screamed a lot, Purvis might extend the ride a bit. He liked the way the young women came off the Tilt-a-Whirl: weak-kneed, wobbling, glistening with sweat, panting, breasts heaving, eyes wide. If they had boyfriends, he'd just watch. If they didn't, he'd try to flirt. He'd smile and tell them to come back for another go. "I got the biggest machine here," he'd say, thinking he was being clever. The girls would wander off, giddy and giggling with adrenaline excitement. He'd follow them with his half-closed eyes and think impure thoughts. What did he care if the machine rattled?

Guys like Purvis floated into the carnival for a few months or a season then floated away. They were like rats—scavengers who saw the carnival as a place to earn a little money, steal a little more, have some fun, and then move on. The men who ran the rides were seedy drifters. Often criminals. The carnival regulars kept their distance from them. Without a trace of irony, Archie Walters had once told Guy, "Guys like that just give the carnival a bad image."

Wandering around late one night, after listening to Alberto play his violin, Guy stopped at the Tilt-a-Whirl. The rides were shut down. Their lights were off. Everything was quiet and still. Purvis was long gone. Guy had pinpointed the rattle to a small gearbox that hung below one of the cars.

He knelt down and turned a little knob that opened a hatch on the box. To his utter astonishment, forks, knives, spoons, bottle caps, a corkscrew, cigar cutter, razors, jewelry and all manner of junk tumbled out. Along with them, like a jackpot paying off on a slot machine, hundreds of coins spilled out. He had found Arrigo's secret hiding place.

"Well, I'll be damned," said Guy. "I found it!"

Just then, hearing the rattle and clink of the falling hoard—*his* hoard—Arrigo came charging out of the darkness. He stopped a few feet away from Guy and looked at him with wide eyes, long tail twitching.

"I found your stash of stolen goods, you little thief," said Guy.

Arrigo ran in and tried to swipe some of the booty. Guy reached out to grab him. The monkey grabbed a fork and took a swipe at him. Guy grabbed a spoon and they briefly dueled, silverware flashing in the moonlight. Finally, Guy swatted Arrigo, sending him tumbling head over heels. Arrigo got up, looked at Guy with anger in his eyes, chittered something in monkey talk, and ran off into the night.

Nobody ever saw him again.

Irena was upset when she learned that he was gone.

"Is no good."

"Is there an old Russian proverb for a missing monkey?" asked Guy.

"Yes: Carnival without monkey is carnival without luck."

38

It was a hot August day, the kind of day that makes men and dogs mean. There was no escape from the heat, but the carnival tents, both big and small, at least provided some shade. They were in Cowpens, South Carolina.

Guy ran into Major Midget, who was holding a letter in his hands and shaking his head.

"Well, hell!" he said.

"What's wrong, Major?"

"I just got this letter from the Gilmore Mines. They said the vein I'd invested in wasn't gold after all; it was lead. Lead! Can you believe it! I'm a damned reverse alchemist, Guy. I managed to turn gold into lead! Shit! I'll lose a lot of money on this goose chase."

Major Midget crumpled the letter and threw it on the ground.

"Shit! Not my lucky day!" he fumed and stalked off.

It seemed that everyone was in a foul mood. The mood had spilled over to a bunch of locals. There was an argument outside the "300 Pound Man Eating Chicken Tent." Some of the rubes didn't appreciate the joke of being conned out of their dimes to see a man eating fried chicken. Six of them were arguing with Archie, and one began to push him. That's when the Giant came to Archie's rescue. He put his massive body between Archie and the angry men.

Their anger overcame any fear they may have had of the imposing giant. First one and then several starting pushing and punching him. None could come close to his head, so they pummeled his body. Though big, Clarence was clumsy. He tried to fend the angry men off, but they kept at him like a pack of dogs. He staggered back and his head hit the lantern hanging from the tent post above the sign. The lantern swung wildly and then fell to the ground spilling kerosene on the straw. The flame of the lamp jumped to the straw and in seconds a small fire had started. The giant stepped away. Archie jumped back. The angry men took a few final swings, then stopped.

In less than a minute, the fire had spread and touched the canvas of the tent. Soaked in oil to keep out rain, the canvas was like a giant wick. The flame shot up it and a great swath of the tent was quickly aflame. Another minute and it had spread to the adjoining tent where a packed crowd was watching Irena perform her tightrope act.

The local men fled, leaving Archie and the giant to deal with the fire. They stared in horror at the conflagration that had erupted so swiftly. For a moment, both men were paralyzed. They didn't know what to do.

Inside the tent, Irena performed high above the crowd and the net. She didn't see the fire or notice the smoke. But those in the grandstands did. With sudden screams of "Fire!" they tumbled out into the middle of the tent, out under the net, looking for a way out.

Pandemonium broke out as the fire and panic quickly spread. People were running about wildly. Parents held their children and ran, or screamed frantically looking for them. More and more of the tent caught fire, a great canopy of burning oil and canvas. Those who urged calm were knocked aside. The primal fear of fire took hold, and brave men turned cowards as they made for gaps in the tent where they could see daylight.

Irena dove off the high wire into the net. It, too, was aflame, but she managed to land and scurry off it before it broke from its tethers and crumpled to the dusty ground, trapping some people underneath it.

Guy and most of the carnival workers had arrived, running in to gather up the injured or grab children and take them to safety.

The massive poles that held up the tent began to burn. The whole tent was in danger of collapsing. In a big fire where there is a big crowd, chaos quickly takes hold, and it was chaos that spread through the burning tent of Streeter and Hale's carnival. People ran blindly, sometimes toward the fire rather than away from it.

"Head to daylight!" Guy yelled, pushing people to the edges. The heat grew. He heard screams and the fire's crackle. Strips of burning canvas rained down. Irena's tightrope, ablaze, snaked down trailing sparks. Guy saw Lily lumber by and Major Midget scurrying about. Archie Walters stumbled by, carrying an old woman in his arms, his ballyhoo now a soothing "I've got you, I've got you, it will be all right."

A pole had broken and crashed down on one of the grandstands, collapsing it. A man was trapped, his legs pinned. Guy, Streeter and Alberto struggled to lift the pole and free the man. They needed Ivan's strength, but he was nowhere to be seen.

"Don't let me burn!" the man cried in terror. "Don't leave me here to die!"

The three men pulled, fueled by adrenaline, knowing that if they did not free this man very quickly, they *would* have to leave him to die horribly. That was not something any of them could bear. So they pulled harder and finally lifted the pole and moved it aside. They dragged the man out, ignoring his shrieks of pain.

When the man was safely outside, Guy returned to the tent. People ran by, their hair and clothes smoking. Some lay writhing on the ground, hideously burned. A few did not move at all. Bits of flaming tent fell down, a deadly rain.

How long do nightmares last? They are eternities packed into minutes. Their horrors are vivid, unreeling in eerie slow motion as they rush to their chilling conclusions.

Guy stumbled through the fire and smoke, gasping, and found a boy standing in shock, not running, as still as a statue. His tattered clothes were starting to burn. Guy grabbed him and half carried, half pushed him toward a sunny patch that glowed beyond the smoke. They made it out, choking, blackened, hearts hammering and hair smoldering.

Guy turned back to the tent. He stopped. There was so much flame and smoke. He wasn't sure he could go back in. He saw Major Midget streak by. And then, through the smoke, he saw The Fat Lady, Lily Lavierre.

She scooped up a child, shielded him from the flames with her massive body, and carried him toward a fence at the edge of the tent. She moved with agonizing slowness. Pieces of flaming canvas dropped around her. She headed steadily towards the fence. She reached it and yelled at someone and handed the child up and over it. Then she turned back and headed toward another child whose skirt was burning. Lily picked her up, smothered the flame with her flabby arms and torso and lumbered back to the fence. Again she handed off the child to someone on the other side.

Guy watched as Lily headed back into the inferno, looking for someone to help. More and more of the tent was shearing away and falling. The poles were buckling. The whole thing was about to collapse.

"Lily, get out!" he screamed. "Get out now!"

Lily looked up and realized what was about to happen. She could not move quickly. She was far too heavy. She stopped. She took a step towards Guy. Their eyes met for an instant and he could see the fear in them. Lily looked up at the burning tent and poles above. Again she looked at Guy, and now he saw in her eyes not so much fear as a weary resignation. Her time was up. The smallest trace of a smile appeared on her lips. She might have nodded just a bit. She opened her arms wide as if to embrace the flaming death falling from above. With a thundering crack, the poles gave way and the burning tent fell on her.

Guy turned away. The dark scene turned bright as the sunny day was revealed. The tent was gone. There was no one left to save. The few who were beneath the wreckage were dead or dying. The flaming remnants of the tent became a funeral pyre. They could hear a few screams, but it was too late. To go into that fire was to die. They could do nothing but watch and listen. After a few minutes, there were no screams. Just the crackle of fire.

The stunned townsfolk and carny people stood in a circle around where the tent had been and watched as the fire burned itself out. They watched until there was nothing left but a smoking heap.

There were many injured. They lay scattered around where the tent had been. People were trying to help them. Ambulances began to arrive. Doctors and nurses. It looked like a battlefield.

Those who were not so badly hurt wandered around, many with half their clothes burned away. They were dazed, wide eyed. Some cried. Others mumbled the names of missing people. One man came up to Guy. "Have you seen my popcorn?" he asked. "I seem to have lost my popcorn." Then he sat on the ground, buried his head in his arms and began to cry.

Streeter and Hale moved about, trying to give comfort, trying to find out what happened. When they heard what had started the fire, they were shocked. It was hard to believe. All this because of a stupid joke. A silly con gone bad. The giant was weeping. He thought it was all his fault. It wasn't. Guy and Alberto told him it was an accident. But he could not be consoled. "I should have died!" he kept wailing, a huge man reduced to a blubbering, hysterical infant.

Guy stared at the smoking ashes of the tent. Pieces of the poles jutted out like giant bones. Somewhere beneath it all lay Lily and Major Midget. Tears streamed down his cheeks. Until his dying day, Guy would never forget that final moment when he and Lily had locked eyes. He replayed it now like a film clip, over and over. The look in her eyes! First abject fear. Then almost serenity. She knew she was about to die. And she seemed to accept it. Even want it. She knew in that instant that all the torment and humiliation and pain of her life was about to end. Her spirit, her wonderful spirit, was about to escape from the prison of her grotesque body. She gave herself over to the flames and the death they brought, hoping—maybe knowing—she would be freed at last.

And Midget? The Nasty Little Bastard. What was he doing in there? He'd have had a hard time finding someone smaller than himself to save. But Midget had been in there, and now he, too, was gone. It was too much to bear.

After a few hours, the locals drifted away home. The ambulances had taken all the injured away. The doctors and nurses were gone. The scene emptied. The sheriff had talked at length to Streeter and Hale. Nobody knew what would happen next. At the moment, nobody much cared. The sheriff stationed a few men to guard what he called the "crime scene." Then he left.

Finally, only the carnival folks remained. As the sun set, they stood and silently watched the still smoking pyre. The black smoke curled up above the smoldering ashes like a question mark before drifting away. Nobody said anything. Nobody could say anything, and there was nothing to say.

They stood a long time.

As twilight settled in, Alberto took out his violin and started to play Amazing Grace, and his violin, sweet beyond imagining, and too poignant to bear, did what his violin always did: it brought out the tears.

Zero began to sing in that beautiful voice of hers, and everybody joined in, singing as they wept, weeping as they sang. They weren't ballyhoo men or grifters or freaks; they weren't owners or perilous performers. They were just a family of shocked people united by sorrow. Zero's voice carried through the night, otherworldly, as if she was the voice of those who'd just died. It was sad, and at the same time, comforting.

When the song ended there was silence—the heavy, burdened silence that always follows tragedy. Nobody moved. They were rooted to the spot as if turned to stone, anchored by grief. They stood in the night until the embers of the fire finally faded into darkness, taking the carnival with them.

39

The next day, it rained. The weather matched everybody's mood. The carnival was closed, of course. Closed until the sheriff of Cowpens decided what to do. Policemen and the local coroner sifted through the wreckage, now a mucky stew as the rain mingled with the ashes.

Some of the carnival gang had gathered to watch the police go about their business. Guy and Irena watched in silence.

"Pechal'no proishodit'" Irena said quietly. For once her fiery nature subdued.

"Pechal'no proishodit?" asked Guy, struggling, as always, with the Russian.

"Sad happening," said Irena, translating.

"'A tragedy,' we'd say," said Guy.

Irena just nodded. What had happened was ultimately the same in any language.

Several policemen gestured for a body bag. Then another. Soon, a row of them lay beside the charred circle where the tent had been. The carnival folks stood and watched, some with umbrellas, some not, as if the rain that soaked them might cleanse away their grief. Clarence the Giant had retreated to his train cabin after the fire. He wouldn't come out. He had been crying when he went in, softly mumbling "It's my fault."

The townsfolk were kept away. It served nobody to let them see their loved ones' remains pulled from the ashes.

There were eight body bags. Then nine. Ten. Eleven. How high would the death toll go? A policeman gestured to Guy to come over and help him identify a body. Guy was afraid it might be Lily or Major Midget. He shook his head "no." He couldn't bear it. That horror fell to Streeter who walked over, took a look at what lay below a tarp and nodded "yes." Then he turned and vomited.

Hale relieved him when another body needed identification. This one took longer as Hale and the policemen knelt and examined the ground a while, picking things out of the ashes. Finally Hale nodded "yes" and left. Guy saw Major Midget's St. Christopher's medallion swinging from his clenched fist.

Guy kept replaying the moment of Lily's death over and over in his mind. The scene was stuck there, like a song, and he could not rid himself of it. That look when their eyes met, just before she died, would haunt him always, just like the look in Butch's eyes in the instant the bullet took him.

Guy watched as they searched through the ashes for the dead. At the end of the day, there were fifteen body bags. Thirteen from the town, two from the carnival. It was bad, but it could have been much worse. There were many injured. A rumor swirled that a few more in the hospital might not make it.

Streeter and Hale cooperated with the investigation. The sheriff was efficient. He wanted to find out what happened and get the carnival packed up and out of town as soon as possible. Nobody would go back to it. And he feared that some might seek revenge for their losses.

There were plenty of eyewitnesses, and the story had little ambiguity. The blame was shared by the carnival for running the stupid attraction and the local men who had overreacted to it.

The sheriff officially ruled it an accident. Tragic, stupid, but an accident. He told Streeter and Hale to get the hell out of town as quickly as they could. Reluctantly, he agreed to let them bury their dead in a far corner of the county cemetery. But he wanted it done immediately, before the thirteen dead from the town were laid to rest. The town needed to grieve without a bunch of freaks hanging around in their cemetery. His orders were succinct: "Bury them, pack up, and leave!"

Streeter and Hale were relieved to be cleared and agreed to do just as the sheriff had asked. They would bury the Fat Lady and Major Midget at dawn the next day and be on their way out of town by noon.

As he was leaving, the sheriff turned to Streeter and Hale. "I don't like carnivals" he said. "Never have. You're just a bunch of grifters. A bunch of con men, cheats and freaks. Losers all. Don't come this way again, you hear? Take your evil somewhere else."

He got in his car and left. Streeter and Hale stood in the rain and watched him drive off. They looked at each other, shook their heads. Then they turned and walked back toward the train, its bright colors and gaudy signs out of place in the gloom that had enveloped the Carnival of Curiosities, Oddities and Perilous Performers.

40

There were two caskets. One was ridiculously large, not a real casket but a large dark crate, holding the remains of the Fat Lady. Beside it was a tiny children's casket. They hadn't found much of Major Midget. He was so small, there wouldn't have been much of him left to find. So they filled the coffin with what they had: his scorched shoes, a belt, and his St. Christopher's medallion, which Hale had given to the undertaker. There were a few bones, too, ridiculously small, no bigger than chicken drumsticks. The two coffins sat there side by side next to the two graves waiting for them in the cemetery in Cowpens.

Archie Walters, Ballyhoo Man and Justice of the Peace, presided.

"Friends, we are gathered here to mourn the passing of the Fat Lady and Major Midget. A sister and brother of the ballyhoo. They died as heroes, helping others escape a terrible fire. And what of that fire? We may wonder if it was not, perhaps, a glimpse of hell. A warning that those of us who have evil in our hearts must embrace forgiveness and compassion and love, lest we, too, perish in the fires of Satan's eternal carnival. The Fat Lady and Major Midget: gone from our lives, but not from our hearts. May they find the peace and happiness that eluded them in this mortal life, and may the Lord welcome them into his fold, in that glorious heaven where He alone is the master of the ballyhoo."

Guy thought that while a bit bizarre, Archie Walter's brief eulogy had captured the essence of the situation. He liked the touch about Satan's eternal carnival. He had yet to wrap his mind around the concept of God as the master of heaven's ballyhoo. He shook his head. That was for later. At the moment, there was something else on his mind. Something that needed to be said.

"I'd like to speak."

Archie stepped back. Guy walked around to the head of the caskets. There was something so pathetic about them he started to choke up. He regained his composure and looked around at the carnival folks. He took a deep breath and began.

"Archie, in your eulogy, you said something that we all have been saying, and I'm sorry, but it's wrong. You said we are here to mourn the passing of the Fat Lady and Major Midget. Well, she was *not* the Fat Lady. She had a name. She was Lily Lavierre. She was more than an act, a name on a broadsheet.

"We of all people should have known it was not easy for her and shown her more compassion. She did not want to be as she was. It was not her fault. Everybody denied her her humanity, and at the end, she just gave up. Did any of you know that? I did. She could have made it out of the tent. But she stopped. She stayed. She embraced death. Why? Because life was too painful. Because she had lost hope. Because she had her fill of days of ridicule and pity."

Guy paused, choking up again. Poor Lily.

"Her name was Lily Lavierre. Not the 'Fat Lady'. Lily Lavierre. *That's* who we bury today. She was a kind, sweet, smart, caring person. Not just an oddity. She bore her pain with grace. And Major Midget: his real name was David Cohen. Sure he was small. And maybe he was an ornery little guy. But in his way he was caring and loyal. He was in that tent, too, trying to help. So let's say 'Goodbye and God bless you Lily and David.' Just this once, let's acknowledge who they really were! It's the least we can do for them."

Guy bowed his head, put a hand to his face and let the tears he had been trying to bottle up flow. There was silence for a moment as his words sank in. Then the carny folks began to whisper: "Goodbye and God bless Lily and David."

Archie nodded and some of the tent men lowered David Cohen's tiny casket into the waiting hole. They did the same for Lily Lavierre. When the two coffins were in place, Guy reached into his pocket and took out his Medal for Bravery. It glinted in the morning sunlight.

"This is my Medal for Bravery," he said. "They gave it to me for killing two boys in the war. I think Lily deserves it more than I do. She saved several kids in the fire. She went back in again and again. She showed a ton of bravery." He stepped forward and dropped his medal on top of her casket.

"This is for you, Lily. You died a hero. God bless you."

He lingered a moment, looking at the medal on top of the black box.

Then he turned and left.

He walked back to the carnival alone. A strong wind had whipped up. Close to the carnival grounds, two rubber masks from the game concession went skidding by. Guy recoiled as he saw them—flopping faces, grotesque and distorted. There were no twinkling eyes giving them life. He turned and watched them tumble down the road like lost souls. He shuddered. He felt he was in a twisted dream. The whole damned carnival seemed like a nightmare now.

It was time to wake up.

41

Nothing was quite the same after the fire. As Willis said one day: "What was ain't is." The carnival was always on the edge of unraveling, and now it seemed to be doing so. Guy stuck with it. He wasn't sure why. Maybe because it gave him a chance to do his magic, which he loved. To hone his act. Part of him felt, perhaps, that the wonder he gave with his magic helped offset some of the disappointment the cons and crooked games caused. He was an antidote of sorts. In the pathos and seediness that surrounded the carnival like a fog, he was a bit of sunshine. A man of honest deceptions in a den of thieves. He hoped, too, that by carrying on he was somehow honoring the spirit of Lily and David. But it wasn't the same. The carnival had lost its heart and soul.

They all wanted to put as much distance as possible between them and the horror of the fire in Cowpens. News of it had spread, and it drew people in. The carnival had an aura to it. He'd even heard a few people refer to it as the "Death Carnival." It made him sick.

The fire hung around the carnival like smoke that permeates a fabric. Just as it seemed to be fading, when the carnival seemed to have outrun its legacy, someone would bring it up or it would be mentioned in a newspaper article. It was a shadow they could not escape.

They were in Hurt, South Carolina. Clarence, the Giant, was missing from the freak show tent. Archie sent Guy to look for him.

Guy knocked on the door of the Giant's car. There was no answer. Guy knocked again. He tried the door handle and it opened. He stepped up and into the railroad car.

Clarence lay there, stretched out on his oversized bed, which ran almost the whole length of the car. A shoelace was tied around his arm just above the elbow, tight. A tourniquet. A syringe dangled from inside his elbow, its needle stuck in deep. The giant's eyes were wide open. Whatever he had injected to kill himself had acted quickly. Painlessly, Guy hoped.

"Oh, Clarence," Guy sighed. He knew the man had never forgiven himself for his part in the carnival fire, even though it was an accident. Clarence felt guilty over the deaths, and nothing anybody had said could change his mind, even when it was ruled an accident. Like Lily, the man had reached a point of despair where living had become too painful. Death was his only escape.

"Oh, Clarence," Guy said again, softly. "It wasn't your fault." He went over and looked at the poor man. Again he saw the blank stare, the lifeless eyes, the window to the soul closed forever. He reached down and closed the giant's eyelids. He knew they could no longer see in this world. He did it as much for himself. He was tired of the gaze of death.

They quietly buried Clarence a few days later in another oversized crate. Nobody had much to say. Not that they didn't like Clarence or mourn him. It was more that exhaustion had overtaken the carnival family. An emotional numbness had set in. The fire. The deaths. Lily and David. Moving on. Trying to forget. Now this.

What next?

42

Streeter and Hale's Carnival of Curiosities, Oddities and Perilous Performers pushed on, wrapped now in the numbing chill of tragedy. It moved up the Eastern seaboard, everything done in a resigned weariness, lacking energy and enthusiasm.

Business had been slow. Streeter asked Ivan and Irena to meet him in his railroad car after an evening show. The two performers arrived, still sweaty from their performance. Streeter sat behind his beat-up desk, smoking a cigar. He motioned them to sit.

"Irena, Ivan, it's no secret business has been slow of late. I'm looking for something to build a little excitement for the show."

Irena and Ivan exchanged a quick glance.

"You know that it says right on our signs, bright as day, that we have 'Perilous Performers.' That boils down to the two of you. We don't have lion tamers; nobody gets shot out of a canon around here. It's just you two up there on the trapeze and you on the high wire, Irena." Streeter fidgeted a bit, took a few nervous puffs on his cigar.

"So, long story short, I'm proposing we spice up your act a bit. Make it a little more perilous. Just for one night, mind you. We can get the word out, ratchet up the ballyhoo, bring in the rubes to gawk."

"What you mean more perilous?" asked Irena warily.

"Well, we've gotta inject a little, you know, danger into it. Right now, you miss a catch and you fall into a net."

"You say no net?" asked Irena.

Streeter puffed his cigar again. Tried to smile.

"Well, um, yes. Just for one night."

"I fall I go splat," Irena said with anger. "Only take one night to die," she added. "Russian proverb say so: 'Death come quick to those who fool with death.'"

"I want more money," said Ivan. "I got more responsibility."

Irena gave him a withering look. *He* had more responsibility! *She* was the one to go splat if he dropped her!

"Well, of course!" Streeter said quickly, sensing Ivan was in agreement.

"Twenty dollars more. For the one night." said Ivan.

"That's a lot," said Streeter.

Before Ivan could answer, Irena jumped in. "Not enough for me. It my life. If I agree, I want more."

Streeter's eyes narrowed. He hadn't figured on any negotiating with these two. He didn't like to negotiate. He liked to call the shots. "What do you have in mind, Irena?"

She thought a moment. "I fly with no net, risk going splat, I want ten percent of gate for night."

Streeter's eyes widened. "Ten percent!"

"Ten percent!" Irena shot back. "My life. My life worth ten percent. Might be zero. Might be hundred dollars. Maybe more. I take risk. I get paid. No pay, no risk. Ivan can catch Monkey Arrigo instead."

Streeter pondered her demand. He didn't like her tone. He didn't like her terms. But she had a point. She was the one who would go splat. Ivan looked annoyed. He had been quick to demand twenty dollars, a tidy sum. Irena had gone for the throat. But what choice did he have? No Irena, no act, no perilous performance, no big gate.

"If I agree, you will do your trapeze act *and* your high-wire act?"

"Yes," said Irena.

"How about five percent?" asked Streeter.

"How about ten?" Irena shot back, not budging on her demand.

Streeter rolled his cigar in his mouth, thinking. He was, no doubt, calculating the possible gate for the night. He was also thinking that if they did the act without the net and Irena did, indeed, go splat, it would be bad for business. Or maybe not. People had a ghoulish attraction to death and disaster. The fire had shown that, though an increase in attendance hadn't materialized.

"Okay," Streeter said. "Ivan, you get twenty bucks more for the extra responsibility of making sure Irena doesn't go splat, and Irena, you get ten percent of the gate for the risk of going splat. Agreed?"

"Yes," said Irena. "I fly. Risk splat. Ten percent."

"Yeah, sure," said Ivan a bit glumly. He had been too quick to negotiate. Not greedy enough.

"Okay then. I'll let you know when and where. We'll pick a town ripe for the picking and do some good advance work there. Build up the excitement and interest. And don't get too scared by what you hear. We're going to make it sound like the most perilous thing in the world!"

Irena leveled a cool stare at Streeter. "What more perilous than going splat?" she asked.

Streeter did not answer.

43

In Havre de Grace, Maryland, the night finally arrived. Streeter's advance men had done a good job pitching the "death-defying perilous performers who would be performing stunning feats high in the air, without a net, their lives at the very edge, death waiting below." In truth, of course, it was only Irena who was risking her life, or "going splat," as she bluntly put it.

The day of the show, Ivan and Irena were tense. They went through the afternoon show—with the net—without incident. Everyone in the carnival knew about the plan and most were against it.

Guy ran into Streeter late in the day.

"I want to talk to you," Guy said, falling into step beside him.

"Not now, kid. I'm busy. Big show tonight."

"That's what I want to talk to you about," said Guy. "This is crazy. Why risk Irena's life for a few extra dollars?"

"Cause we need 'em," said Streeter. "Attendance has been lousy. We're fading. We need a shot in the arm. Did ya see the newspaper from here today? We made the front page. Big headlines. 'Carnival Performers to Risk Death Tonight!' Hell, you can't buy publicity like that, Guy. You watch. We'll fill every seat. Maybe get standing room, too. This one night will make up for all the crappy ones we've had."

"What if she falls? What if Irena dies?"

"She knows the risks. She agreed to it. Theirs is a simple act, really. They don't push it, you know. They've done it a thousand times. I've kept track. They only missed one catch all season. Just one. And she's never fallen off the wire."

"If that one fall were tonight, she'd be dead."

Streeter stopped, looked Guy in the eyes.

"Kid, we all die sooner or later. Life is a perilous performance. The train may derail. A tent pole may fall on you. You could choke eating a steak. Or Ivan might strangle you. Yeah, I know about the bad blood between you two. Screwing around with Irena is a perilous performance. But you know the risks and you do it. No net. Life don't have nets, kid. Tonight, Irena's just living life the way it's meant to be lived." The discussion was over. Streeter turned and walked away.

Guy stood in the dusty field between the tents. "Son of a bitch!" he hissed. Then he went to find someplace to get a drink.

The tension between Irena and Ivan came to a head after dinner, about an hour before the evening show. He said something that sparked her anger, not a hard thing to do. She lashed out. Ivan stood his ground and let *his* anger boil over. Within a few minutes, they were having one of their loud arguments. The rest of the carnival tried to ignore them. People went about their business, but not without shaking their heads and muttering. Maybe it was a good thing to let the tension out, to bleed off some of their nervous energy. Or maybe it would rattle them and put them off their game. Time would tell.

The evening brought huge crowds. Streeter was right about people. They had a ghoulish fascination with disaster and death. If she survived, Irena had made a good deal. She'd pull in a pretty payday for her perilous performance. The marks gathered and paid their admissions—bumped up fifty cents because of the spectacular nature of the evening show. Streeter had scheduled Irena and Ivan as the final act of the evening. He knew the later it was, the longer folks would stay and spend money on games, concessions, rides and souvenirs. He strode around the carnival grounds beaming. If you looked closely in his eyes, you might have seen dollar signs.

In their car, Irena and Ivan dressed. Their argument had blown itself out, unresolved, both withdrawn in sullen silence. They heard the other acts and the sound of guns in the arcade, the calliope, the ballyhoo men—all the sounds of the crazy world that was their world. Ten minutes before their act, they left for the main tent.

Archie Walters was in the middle of the vast tent, resplendent in his outfit, glowing in the spotlight. He held a microphone, and his voice boomed.

"Laaaaadies and gentlemen. Streeter and Hale welcome you to tonight's climactic performance. You will soon witness two fearless, perilous performers risking their lives on the trapeze and high wire. Yes, RISKING THEIR LIVES! There will be no net in place for their performance tonight. NO NET! They have only done this once before, in St. Petersburg, for the Czar, and on that night it was a close call as the mighty Ivan lost his grip on lovely Irena. As the Czar—a mighty warrior and a fearless man himself—cringed and gasped, Ivan just managed to catch her again before she plunged to her death far below!"

This was all utter nonsense, of course. Irena and Ivan had never performed in Russia, much less for a Czar. In fact, the Communists were in charge of Russia, the era of the Czars long gone. But that didn't stop Archie from spinning his colorful tale.

"That night, after the show, the Czar bestowed upon them the highest award of Russia: the Czar's Gold Medal of Bravery, something but a few of the most courageous of the Motherland have ever received!

"Tonight, for only the second time in their long and storied career, they will again perform their acts WITHOUT A NET! If your heart is weak, you may want to leave now. If you are squeamish, if you are too young, if you fear the sounds of bones cracking, then I ask you to LEAVE NOW!"

Nobody budged. Archie had them in his thrall. He was building up the tension and the fear in the crowd. He was also doing a pretty good job of terrifying Irena. The part about bones cracking really got to her. She thought of backing out, of running up to Streeter and calling this madness off. But the moment had its own momentum, like a nightmare, and she felt oddly detached and powerless.

Ivan was dipping his hands into the bowl of rosin over and over. He'd get his hands and arms coated with the white powder, then slap his big hands together. The cloud that erupted looked like an explosion. He was nervous, and he did this over and over, though he had so much powder on him that it would take a week for the sweat to break the surface.

"Enough, already!" hissed Irena. "You'll choke us with that stuff."

Irena dipped hers in, too, carefully rubbing the white powder up to her elbows.

Archie was winding up.

"And so now, without further delay, I present to you these two perilous performers, heroes of the Motherland, worshipped by the Czar himself and soon to dazzle you with their brave feats of death-defying daring … IVAN and IRENA!!!!"

The crowd roared. The spotlight followed them as they made their way to the center of the tent to take a bow. Irena tried to draw energy from the crowd, to steel her nerves, but her legs were shaking. She would have to get herself under control. She took a deep breath. She bowed. She looked Ivan in the eye before they parted to climb their ladders on the opposite sides of the tent.

"No mess up," she said. "No drop me. I go splat, I swear on mother's grave I come back haunt you!" She smiled and turned and strode to the ladder. Ivan looked at her lithe little body in its tight outfit and tried not to think of it going splat. Of bones cracking. The band played a jaunty tune, vaguely Russian sounding.

Irena climbed her ladder. Ivan climbed his. The platforms were high above the crowd, very high. Spotlights picked the two figures out of the darkness.

Irena and Ivan unhooked their trapezes. The band started the trapeze medley. Irena looked at Ivan, nodded, grasped her trapeze and swung out into the air. Ivan, counting as she swung back and forth, timed his own jump so that they met at the apex of their swings in the middle of the tent. Like kids on swings, they went back and forth a few times, pumping their legs, building up momentum. Ivan curled his legs up and between his arms, locked his knees over the bar, and let go with his hands. He now dangled below it, arms free to catch Irena.

They swung back and forth.

Abruptly the music stopped. A lone drum roll sounded through the tent. The crowd grew silent.

Time for their first stunt. An easy one. Irena swung high and at the top of her arc, let go, did a graceful twist in the air, started to fall, brushed her arms gently down Ivan's body as he met her on his upswing, felt for his arms, slid her hands down them, then locked onto his wrists as he locked onto hers. A perfect catch.

The drummer hit a cymbal and the crowd erupted into wild applause. Irena and Ivan swung wide towards his platform, her extra weight adding momentum to his arc. On the back swing he let her go, she spun around and grasped her empty bar as it swung in toward her. Again a cymbal crash. Again wild applause.

They swung on their own bars, getting their rhythm in sync, their arcs just so. Irena kept telling herself not to look down. Not to think about the crowd or going splat or cracking bones.

They performed three more maneuvers, each more daring than the last. First Irena did a triple spin, her body a blur as she spun like a top before Ivan caught her. Then she did a graceful, slow, swan dive designed to look like Ivan would miss her but timed so she brought her arms together at the last instant so he could grab her. Her hands smacked his arms and sent up a puff of powder before she felt him clench her. Indeed, Ivan was so terrified of dropping her that he grabbed her as hard as he could, bruising her wrists. His arms and hands weren't sweating, but his face was. In the few seconds he held her during their swings, she saw his glistening skin, his wide eyes, the fear in his eyes. And he wasn't the one who would go splat if something went wrong!

Irena did a double somersault, drawing a gasp from the crowd, and it went off without a hitch. Then, apart, they rode their bars and pumped hard to get the most height they could in preparation for their final stunt. Below—far below—Archie took to the mic again.

"Laaaadies and gentlemen! You have witnessed what the Czar witnessed. Death-defying stunts by our perilous performers, fearless aerialists who laugh at death!"

"Laugh at death?" thought Irena as she swung. "Who's laughing!?"

"But these stunts you have seen are but child's play. Why, any number of brave trapeze artists, be they of sufficient skill and bravery and possessed of steely nerves, could perform them. But what you are about to see is something new. Something that has never been tried before!"

Again, of course, a lie. They were about to do a triple somersault. It was a standard move in Irena and Ivan's act. Not an easy stunt, but one they did well. As they swung overhead, Archie continued.

"It was Irena and Ivan who insisted they try this tonight. We begged them not to. It is far too dangerous. But they insisted. INSISTED! The winners of the Czar's Gold Medal of Bravery demanded that we let them try this trick. If they were to risk their lives, they wanted to do so trying something so dangerous, so impossible, that it was worth dying for! I remind you, there is NO NET to catch her if she falls! Again I implore you, I beseech you, I BEG you: If your heart is weak, leave now! If you are squeamish, if you are too young, if you fear the sounds of bones cracking, I ask you to LEAVE NOW!"

Leave it to Archie Walters to whip the crowd into a frenzy of fearful anticipation.

Irena and Ivan swung. The drum roll began. They swung for a good thirty seconds, building their momentum, building the anticipation. The damned tent was awash with adrenaline. The drummer brought his roll to a loud crescendo, as if they were about to do the triple, then brought it down. The crowd rode it like a boat in an angry sea.

Then the drum roll stopped.

Just before she hit the top of her arc, when her momentum was at its highest level, Irena let go of her bar. As she continued upwards, she did her first somersault. At the top of her arc, weightless, she did her second. As she started down, her third.

As she came out of it, she saw Ivan below her, and below him, far below, the ground. Both came up at her quickly.

The work of an aerialist is a precise thing. Though they carve broad paths through the air as they swing, the success of their tricks comes down to inches and hundredths of a second. Theirs is a world governed by a ruthless and unyielding physics. Their weight, their mass, their velocity, the instant of release, gravity, the humidity of the air—all are part of the equation that will result in a lovely woman's hands meeting a burly man's at precisely the right spot in space at precisely the right instant. The slightest variation in their swing or timing could skew that equation. The woman's hands and the man's would come close but miss.

The woman would fall for one, two, three, seconds. It would end in a sickening collision with the ground. The sound of cracking bones. It would end in death.

Maybe it was just the heavy summer air. Or the fraction of a second when Irena focused on the ground rushing up. Or maybe it was something more evil. Not her fault at all. Maybe anger had crept back into Ivan's mind, distracting him. Or pushing him to purposeful carelessness.

As she plummeted down toward Ivan, Irena was an inch farther away than she should have been. Irena reached for Ivan. She contorted her body to try to extend it that extra inch. But gravity was winning. She was accelerating downward quickly, moving away from him.

Ivan knew it. Archie and Streeter and Hale and Guy and the freaks and the whole tent full of people who had gathered and craned their necks to see this stunt knew it.

Irena was going to miss Ivan. He wasn't going to catch her. She was going to go splat. Irena did something she had never done in a performance.

She screamed.

It was a piercing, desperate, "I am about to die!" scream that pierced the night air like a knife. Ivan seemed frozen. The instant stretched out for an eternity, as if in slow motion.

Irena fell away from him.

Then, as if coming to, Ivan reacted. He did something he had never done in a performance. He unlocked his knees from the bar and let himself fall. As his legs brushed along the bar, he flexed his feet out and caught them on the bar ends where they met the chains. He winced in pain as the tops of his feet took his weight, but he held. That move, that instantaneous reaction to Irena's plight gave him a few extra feet of extension and a teeny bit more distance to his arc. As she dropped past him, he lunged as far as he could, twisting so his right arm was lower. His hand hit her elbow. Still she dropped. He waited just an instant until he felt her slim wrist slide by, then he clamped his massive hand hard on it.

He had her!

Irena came to a sudden stop. Something popped in her shoulder. She dangled from Ivan's hand. His feet were locked against the chains that now cut into them with Irena's extra weight. Ivan wasn't sure he would be able to hold on with them. If his feet came lose, they would both fall.

They would both go splat.

People started to scream. Ivan and Irena swung slowly, their arc decreasing, until they stopped. There was no momentum to get them back to the safety of a platform. They could go nowhere. They were helpless.

"Don't struggle!" Ivan groaned. Irena realized she hadn't been breathing. She took a breath. She was dead weight. Her shoulder was on fire.

"No let go!" she gasped.

Streeter and Hale were unable to move. Luckily, two of the tent riggers could. They quickly climbed the ladder to Ivan's trapeze platform. The trapezes trailed a slack line from their chains to the platforms. The two riggers got to the platform and started to haul in the line. With agonizing slowness, the men pulled Ivan and Irena back to the platform. When they were above it, one of the men grabbed Irena.

"You can let go of her now!" he told Ivan.

As if coming out of a daze, Ivan let go. The other man helped him off the trapeze. The tops of Ivan's feet were cut deeply by the chains and bleeding. Irena was holding her limp arm.

"Can you climb down?" asked one of the riggers.

"Yes. I get down. I get down on ground in hurry!" said Irena, trembling.

By now, the stunned crowd was on its feet applauding, cheering, stomping their feet. Guy turned to say something to Streeter, but the man had fainted. He lay in a heap on the floor.

Irena and Ivan climbed down the ladder slowly. Archie, shaken, tried to wrap up the act.

"Well, Ladies and Gentlemen, that was a close call. A very close call. Just like in St. Petersburg. Now you know why the Czar outlawed the triple somersault after he witnessed what you have seen tonight. Indeed, and you can look this up, over the centuries, a dozen performers have tried this trick. All have died. That is why we here at Streeter and Hale were so shocked, and now are so proud, that Irena and Ivan insisted on trying it here tonight."

Archie was laying it on thick, trying to turn a near disaster into a triumph. Judging from the cheering crowd, he was succeeding.

Ivan and Irena reached the ground. Irena bent over and kissed it. Whether out of genuine gratitude or pure theatricality, nobody knew. It was probably a mix of both.

"Ladies and Gentlemen, how about a special, HUGE round of applause for Ivan and Irena, eh?" Archie waited for the applause to swell. The ovation continued for several minutes as Ivan limped around the center of the tent bowing, and Irena, still holding her arm, did the same. They were two battered warriors who had survived the battle.

"As you can see, folks, Irena has hurt herself a bit during that death-defying stunt, so she won't be doing her high wire act. But I think you'll agree, she's given you quite a show for your money!"

The crowd cheered again. The band struck up "The Daring Young Man on the Flying Trapeze" and the spotlights went out. Ivan and Irena limped into the darkness of the backstage area.

Archie was waiting for them.

"Jesus!" he said. "Jesus, what a show!"

Irena kicked him in the groin. Archie crumbled.

"Have some cracking bones!" she shrieked.

Just then, Streeter, recovered from his swoon, jumped up and ran into the back tent area.

"Wow! That was quite a show! They loved it! I'll get your cuts to you in the morning! What a show! I thought you were gonna fall, I really did! Maybe we can try that again sometime?"

"Ubljudok!" Irena spat, and kicked him in the groin too.

44

The day after the perilous performance, the carnival was a mess. Irena's arm was in a sling. Ivan had bandages on both feet. Streeter and Archie were walking funny. The local newspaper had full accounts of the show, and some promoters had stopped by to beg Streeter to repeat the performance.

"No way, boys!" he'd said, holding firm, wincing as he sat in his chair, now padded with a thick pillow. "Last night was a once-in-a-lifetime thing. Well, twice if you count the show for the Czar. Besides, Ivan and Irena are pretty beat up. They won't be doing *any* show for a while. It was a near thing, you know. She almost went ... she almost died up there. No. No repeats."

They would be moving on, anyway. Word had spread ahead of them like a wave. Streeter knew that they'd be demanding the ultimate perilous performance at every town on their schedule. Too bad it was so late in the season. He wished he'd thought of it earlier. He could rake it in. He winced again. Jesus, no repeats! That Russian she-devil might kill him!

The carnival headed up the coast to New Jersey. After a show in Princeton, Guy noticed a vaguely familiar man in the front row. He had an unkempt mane of white hair, sad, droopy eyes and a thick mustache. He wore a cardigan sweater. One sock was down. The man made no move to leave. He sat quietly, smoking a pipe, apparently lost in thought.

"Do I know you?" Guy asked.

"Perhaps you has seen my picture somevere," the man replied in a German accent. He stood and held out his hand. "My name is Albert," he said. "Professor Albert Einstein."

"Yes!" exclaimed Guy. "Yes, you are! I remember reading about you in school. You invented the Theory of Relatives, right?"

Einstein laughed. "Not exactly. I came up vith the Theory of *Relativity*. It is about space and time and gravity and the speed of light. It explains much of how the universe verks. It vas difficult, yes, but a Theory of Relatives ... that vould be impossible."

"So, did you like my show?" asked Guy.

"Yes. Very much. I vas most fascinated by the trick with the boxes, young man. You took the smaller from the larger then put the larger back in the smaller. It defies all logic. And geometry. It vas not possible."

"None of my tricks are possible, Professor. If they were, they wouldn't be magic."

"I don't suppose you vould explain it?"

"I'm sorry, I can't do that, Professor. A magician never reveals his secrets. I guess we are more protective of them than the universe."

Guy was thrilled that he had fooled a genius, but the truth is, it is easier to fool a genius than an eight-year-old. Kids see things simply, and magic tricks are often accomplished by the simplest method. Smart people tend to make things much too complex, and get lost in that complexity. So Einstein would no doubt get hopelessly lost in intricate explanations and theories as he tried to unravel the mystery of Guy's trick.

"I'm surprised to see you here at the carnival, Professor Einstein. At my magic show. I would expect you to be in a laboratory doing experiments."

"I have alvays liked magic. It shows us things are not alvays as they seem. It is fun to see our vorld differently. To find out that the impossible is possible. It gives us hope. As for the laboratory, young man, most of my verk has been in my head."

"Your head?"

"Yes. Thinking, Doing vat I called 'thought experiments.' Trying to imagine things, trying to see them in my mind. More scientists should do this. They are very concerned vith their numbers and their tests, but imagination is more important than knowledge."

Guy was fascinated to hear about thinking from a man famous for it. Einstein walked over to the table where Guy's bunny sat, sniffing the air. He studied the bunny a moment.

"Still," Einstein continued, "the trick vith the boxes is beyond my imagination. I saw it vith my own eyes, yet I cannot believe it."

"Sometimes our eyes lie," said Guy.

Einstein nodded and patted the bunny. Guy caught the scientist looking at the table of props out of the corner of his eye, perhaps hoping to sneak a glance at the mysterious boxes and discover their secret. Guy casually walked over to the table, blocking Einstein's view as he started to putter around with his props.

"I vill figure it out," Einstein said. "Ve get answers, sometimes, by looking differently at things."

"True, Professor. Magic creates wonder because it makes people look at the world differently."

"Physics, too. You as a magician and I as a scientist are both interested in the perceptions of reality."

"I play with perception," said Guy.

"Me, too," said Einstein. "Vell, now I go and play the crooked games. I see the shows. I think about magic mysteries. Boxes that defy logic." Einstein's eyes sparkled. "And I have some ice cream. There is no mystery to ice cream."

Professor Einstein shook Guy's hand and shuffled out of the magic tent in a swirl of smoke, leaving Guy to his mysteries and taking his with him.

45

The carnival settled in for a two-week stint in Bayonne, New Jersey. After his evening show, Guy walked to the rides. Curly had just finished the last run of the Ferris wheel for the night.

"Hey, Curly," Guy said. "How about you spin me up top for a few minutes?"

Curly shrugged. "Climb in, magic man," he said.

Guy sat in one of the cars and clamped the safety bar down. Curly threw the switch and the wheel began to spin. When Guy was at the top, Curly stopped it.

"Don't leave me here all night, Curly," Guy called down.

"I'll let you down after a cigarette, okay?"

"Fine."

Perched up at the top of the wheel, about sixty feet above the ground, Guy gazed across the water to the glow of the city at night. His imagination roamed to Broadway and his dreams of his own magic show, his name on a marquee. He had been in New York before, visiting the magic stores, working at the Morosco Theater. It was there he'd met Chen Woo. There that the strange, exotic magician had stolen his trick. Guy had had plans back then. But then the war came along and his plans changed. After the war, he had stumbled into the carnival and that had taken him on its own strange ride. That journey had taken him back here, as if fate wanted him to return to New York. Could he deny what seemed his destiny?

The timing seemed right. His act had come along. He had learned a lot in the carnival about performing, about imagination, about human nature. He could pick up his plans again. Why not?

Sitting there, high above the ground, looking over at New York and forward to his future, Guy decided he'd work his two weeks in New Jersey and then leave the carnival. Leave Irena. Leave it all. He'd vanish into the maze of glittering skyscrapers and start anew.

His plan worked.

To a degree.

When he told Irena he was leaving, she blinked, thought for a moment and announced: "I leave, too."

"What?" said Guy.

"Tired of carnival. New York great city. We be together. Maybe I help in magic act, no?"

"No!" said Guy. "I mean, I don't have an act here yet. You can't throw away your career. And what about Ivan?"

"Tired of Ivan."

"But you and he are lovers. You have much in common. You share your Russian heritage."

"Ivan not Russian."

"What?"

"Ivan not Russian. From Philadelphia."

"Philly! But he sounds Russian!"

"Yes, but no Russian. Parents Russian. They teach him English so he sounds like them. He not Russian."

Guy blinked.

"Okay, so he's not Russian. But if you leave him …"

"Irena understand. You of him afraid."

"No … Yes. I just …"

Irena put her fingers on his lips to stop him.

"No panic. Bones tell me this good. Where you live?"

"Irena, I have no idea where I'm going. What I'm doing. I can't guarantee you anything. Not a job. Not a place to live. Not even me!" He *was* panicking. He had never dreamed Irena would want to leave the carnival and come with him. The wrong girl was following him.

She shrugged. "I have money. I make much night I almost go splat but not go splat."

Guy put his head in his hands. He had the feeling that no matter what happened, he was going to be walking the tightrope with Irena.

Ivan did not take the news well. His first reaction was predictable.

"I kill Guy."

Irena explained it was not Guy's idea but hers. She was tired of the carnival and tired of him. It was time to leave.

"I kill Guy."

It quickly blew up into a screaming argument—in Russian—that drew half the carnival to witness. Nobody wanted to intercede. It ended with a loud crash inside and Irena storming out of the train car. She had a black eye and her shirt was ripped. She strode out in a rage and turned and shouted something back at Ivan. The carny gang could see him through the open door, on the floor, holding his crotch and swearing.

Irena pushed a few people aside and stalked off into the darkness.

Guy had to spend several days avoiding Ivan, which was not that hard as, between his feet and his crotch, Ivan was not walking too well. The one time their paths did cross, Ivan was succinct in *his* plans.

"You leave. I find. I kill you."

"Listen, Ivan," Guy tried to explain, "I am not interested in Irena."

"Irena interested in you," said Ivan. Then he turned and waddled off.

Guy wished he'd found Major Midget's .45, his "great equalizer," but it had gone missing.

He spent his last day at Streeter and Hale's Carnival of Curiosities, Oddities and Perilous Performers saying his goodbyes. He would miss these people. Strange or shady as they may be, they were like family to him. They'd been through a lot together.

"You were a good act, Guy," said Streeter. "We'll have to look for a new magician.

"Yeah," said Hale, "along with a new high wire walker and some freaks. It's been a tough season. We've lost a lot."

They made some more small talk. Streeter gave him his last month's paycheck. It was only six dollars.

"Where's the rest?" Guy asked.

"You owed me sixty-four dollars, Guy. You made a lot of my coins vanish. I kept track. Good luck in the city."

Guy didn't tell him he'd found Arrigo's stash.

He found Archie Walters in his cabin, and they shared a drink. Guy gave him his bunny, Lou. The next magician could use him.

"I'm done here, Archie. My heart isn't in it anymore. It hasn't been for a while."

"Well, kid," said Archie, "at least you still got a heart. Most of us lost ours long ago."

"I'm taking your advice, Archie. I'm moving on. Like you warned me, I'm trying not to get trapped here."

Archie nodded.

"Remember, Guy, that all life is just a big carnival. It has curiosities and oddities and perilous performers. It's full of ballyhoo. And there are con men and cheats everywhere. Keep your eyes open."

Guy thanked Archie for his advice and his friendship.

"I hope our paths cross someday, Archie. I'll miss you."

"Ya never know," said Archie. "Life is strange."

After his final performance and a round of farewell drinks with the freaks, Guy took his bags of magic tricks and other possessions and made his way toward the ferry terminal. It was late; the carnival was closing down. He passed the concessions and the freak show, Bodacious Bettie's tent, the Cabinet of Curiosities and the funhouse. He walked by the crooked games and the rides. He came to the mask booth. A breeze blew up and the masks wobbled, mouths moving, a mute chorus. They were disturbing reminders of the carnival's empty promises. He'd be happy to never see them again. Guy left the carnival behind and headed toward New York and whatever fate had in store for him.

Best wishes
DAI
VERNON

46

Guy found a room at the shabby Sutherland Hotel and tried to get used to not moving on all the time. He had no schedule, no act, no friends. He was alone in a city of millions. He wanted to build his career in magic. Where or how he was not sure. But he knew where to start.

So, on a Saturday morning just a week after he arrived back in the city, he set out for Tannen's Magic Shop.

He rode the elevator up to the thirteenth floor, feeling the old thrill of anticipation. When the doors opened, he was back inside that magic set. Not much had changed in three years. The cases and shelves were still full of all manner of wondrous props, and Lou Tannen was still behind the counter. So was Lennie.

It took Lou a while to remember Guy, but when he finally did he exclaimed, "You were the fella with the remarkable Retention Vanish, right?"

Guy beamed. He had made an impression. He filled Lou in on where he'd been and what had happened along the way. He told Lou he had named a bunny after him. As he recounted his story, Guy himself marveled at how much he'd experienced in those years in the army, the War, the carnival.

"So you still want to be a magician?" Lou asked.

"More than ever," Guy told him. He heard the laughter and talk in the back room. "And I want to get back there," he said, pointing to the velvet curtains that shielded the inner sanctum.

"Yeah," said Lou. "I remember now. You always wanted to get back there. Why don't you show me some stuff, and I'll see if you're ready."

Guy only had his Morgan dollar. But he was in a magic shop full of any prop he could ever want. He asked Lou for a few things. Lou had to go in the back room to retrieve a bagel. When Guy had what he needed, he gave Lou and a few wide-eyed teenagers and middle-aged hobbyists an impromptu show. He finished with vanishing the Morgan silver dollar and making it appear inside the bagel. The teenagers, middle-aged guys and even Lou Tannen were dumbstruck.

"Guy, you're pretty good. And your patter … where'd you get all that stuff about the shamans and the fakirs and the Emperor of China?"

Guy told him he was taught by a master of patter, a ballyhoo man.

"He conjured in people's minds, Lou," Guy said. "His only props were words, and his only trick was the way he got people to pay to see the impossible."

"He taught you well, Guy," said Lou. "Do your Retention Vanish again."

Guy complied.

"Ya know, kid, I've seen that move done a thousand times, by some of the greats, but I've never seen it done that well. Whew! That's magic."

"Thanks, Lou. You told me to practice it and I did. In the war, in the hospital, on the train, while I was working the carnival. All the time. Maybe hundreds of thousands of times. I don't know. A lot."

"It shows," said Lou. "It's a thing of beauty. I could watch it all day, and you'd fool me all day. It's perfect."

Lou Tannen looked at Guy and smiled.

"I think it's time you came behind the curtain. The boys in the back have got to see what you can do. You game?"

Game? Guy almost fainted. Finally, finally, Lou Tannen had invited him into the inner sanctum. If the world ended tomorrow, Guy would die a happy man.

"Come on back, Guy. Lennie, mind the shop, will ya?"

Tannen turned to Guy. "As fate would have it, you picked a good day to reappear in my store. The whole gang is back there."

Tannen turned and walked toward the back. Guy followed him. He had waited for this moment for years. As he neared the velvet curtain, he tried to imagine what lay beyond. *Who* lay beyond. He pictured a room full of colorful props, a gilded table, and men in tails and sorcerer's outfits. There would be beautiful, slinky girls helping them conjure. It would be a mystical world of smoke and exotic incantations—a veritable dreamland of magic.

The curtains parted, and, heart pumping, Guy stepped into the darkness.

47

When Guy's eyes adjusted to the gloom, he saw he was in a dingy room thick with a haze of blue smoke. It smelled of cigars, cigarettes, bagels, lox, and coffee.

There were about a dozen men in their shirt sleeves smoking, some seated and some standing, the darkness lit by a few lamps and overhead bulbs. Boxes of magic tricks were stacked against the walls. Here and there, plates of food teetered on boxes and small tables. The ashtrays scattered about were full. Suit coats were thrown over the backs of chairs or hung on lamps. Hats were tossed here and there. At the back of the room, against a wall and next to a bathroom, a small stage made of two pieces of plywood resting on stacks of bricks was raised a foot off the floor. A single spotlight dangling from the ceiling was pointed at the stage. A large round table in the center of the room, covered with shabby green felt, was the main performance spot.

In a corner, a young man was busy packing a large box. Guy could see that inside it was a brightly painted magic prop.

"Boss," said the young man to Tannen when they came in, "I gotta pad this with something."

"Use some of those old Chung Ling Soo posters," said Tannen. "We have a pile of them. They're nice and thick."

"Okay," said the young man. He went into another room and returned with a pile of posters. Guy saw the top one. It showed the great magician on stage. The view was from behind, and the conjuror had his hands outspread. From a cauldron in front of him a wisp of smoke curled up, and a bat and a dove hovered near his hands. The poster showed the audience, wide-eyed in wonder at the magic unfolding before their very eyes. The name "Chung Ling Soo" was printed at the top and, on the bottom, "Spellbound they gathered far and near to scan the weird powers of this wondrous man."

"Spellbound." That's what Guy wanted people to be when they saw *his* magic. He wanted to transport them to a world of wonder. A world where time stood still as he made them believe in the impossible. The young man took a poster, crumpled it up, and stuffed it in the box, pushing it to the bottom.

"Perfect" he said, reaching for another. Guy smiled. King of the magic world one day, stuffing for a box another. The ebb and flow of fame and fortune.

The room was noisy with the soundtrack of magic. Over and over, the "brrrrrrppp!" of cards being riffled. Coin workers continually making coins appear and disappear as they practiced their sleights while watching the table. When someone dropped a coin, a wag would yell out: "They don't like to be dropped," and they'd all chuckle. Magicians are men of nervous fingers, always playing with something—cards, a coin, a pen, a peanut, a bottle cap, a cork, a piece of candy, a subway token, a ring, a key—anything handy with which they could practice their palms and passes, moves and flourishes. It was pretty much impossible for a magician to be anywhere for any length of time and not start to fiddle around with something. It was as if their hands had a mind of their own.

Guy was thrilled. Here were working pros who had seen it all, played vaudeville or traveled the world, done society parties or corporate dinners, performed for presidents and kings. They were guys who had their own shows or just found work where they could, itinerant workers of wonder.

Sometimes, intense debates broke out over a move, a bit of patter, the flow of a routine. They could spend an hour dissecting a tiny move and arguing over the position of a thumb or exactly when to execute a sleight: as the arm gestured? As it came to rest? As the body began to swivel to the left? Should it be masked by eye contact or a joke, by movement of the other hand or a bit of adjustment of another prop? Each magician had his own way of doing things, and each was ready to defend it. But they also watched and learned, trying some slight variation on for size. They were like jazz musicians jamming. They called it "sessioning."

Magicians share a wonderful fraternity. The old masters share war stories and secrets. There is competition, of course, and sometimes intense rivalries and bad blood. They mentor the young guys, bringing them along, nurturing their talent. When a young magician is invited behind the curtain to the inner sanctum, it is a rite of passage. It is tribal, the young warrior showing off his prowess not with swords but with sleights. The masters don't always make it easy, nor should they. They sometimes heckle or deride or scoff or brutally criticize. They are testing the mettle of the young magician, seeing how he responds to pressure. After all, if he can't handle it in the embrace of the fraternity, how could he possibly handle it at a table full of skeptical, eagle-eyed strangers or in front of a full theater? If they fail, they may be encouraged. If they prove inept or, worse, lacking in passion and obsession, they will be dismissed. It is up to the proprietors, men like Lou Tannen or Al Flosso, to weed out the pretenders, the hobbyists. Only those who have shown their "chops" and dedication might be given a chance to go behind the curtain.

This was Guy's chance.

The men had paid little attention to Guy and Tannen. Seated around the table and standing around the room, they were all watching a man who looked like Errol Flynn doing a card trick.

"Okay, Guy," said Tannen, "let me introduce you to the gang."

Lou directed his next words to the demonstration table.

"Dai, if you can stop dazzling the fellas for a minute, I want to introduce someone."

The man named Dai stopped shuffling the deck. The men seated at the table looked up. A few stepped forward, others remained in the shadows.

"Gentlemen, this is Guy Borden, a young magician with a lot of talent and promise. Guy, center stage here is Dai Vernon. Around the table are Charlie Miller, Faucett Ross and Ross

Bertram. Standing we have, Mandrake, Al Baker and Francis Carlyle. In the shadows over there are Theo Bamberg, Isadore Klein, and Doc Daley.

The men all nodded or said hello.

"Hello," Guy croaked back. The men of the "gang" were some of the greats of the day. He knew many of them by reputation. A few were unknown to him. Before Tannen could say much more, Vernon spoke up.

"Hey, Lou," he said to Tannen.

"Yeah, Dai?"

"I think I ought to break in a few new decks. Let me have a couple."

"Red or blue-backed?"

"One of each."

While Tannen rummaged through some cabinets for the decks, Vernon smiled up at Guy.

"How ya doin, kid?" he said.

"Fine," said Guy. "I came here to buy a trick."

"Makes sense," said Vernon. "This is a magic store. You a coin worker, card man, dove handler, mental maven or jack of all trades?"

"A little of everything," said Guy.

"I'm Dai Vernon," said the man, holding out his hand. Guy shook it.

"Pleased to meet you, Mr. Vernon. I'm Guy Borden."

"Here are your decks, Dai," said Tannen.

"Put them on my account," said Dai.

Tannen smiled. "Dai, you ever gonna pay me?"

Vernon smiled. "Sure, Lou, sure. I just don't have much with me today. How much I owe you, anyway?"

Tannen sighed and opened a ledger book. "Hmmm, let's see … looks like forty-two bucks."

"That much? Just can't help myself, I guess."

"It was those new brass cups for the cups and balls you got, mostly."

"Nice set."

"Expensive set, Dai."

Vernon looked at Guy. "Lou here sells the best stuff, you know. Not cheap, but good. Always buy good stuff, Guy. Folks don't expect miracles from stuff that looks like crap."

Guy nodded.

"You could learn a lot from Vernon," said Tannen. He's one of the best."

Vernon looked hurt. "*One* of the best? I'm *the* best! You told me so last week!"

"That was last week, Dai. This week, I'm not so sure. This young fella might be the best. Always new talent coming up, Dai."

It was clear Vernon and Tannen were old friends, and Tannen was just egging him on. Vernon took the bait.

"Show us something, kid."

"Yeah," said Charlie Miller. "Lou brought you back here so he must think you're good. Show us what you've got."

Nervous, Guy took out his ever-present Morgan dollar, the one Blackstone had given him.

"Go ahead, kid," said Tannen gently. "Don't be nervous. These guys will appreciate you."

"Okay, Mr. Tannen," said Guy. He took a deep breath. If Tannen thought he would impress them, he'd try.

"Now watch," he said.

And dropped the coin.

"They don't like to be dropped," said Charlie Miller.

"Pretty amazing," said Mandrake. "How'd you do that?" The men laughed.

"Come on, guys, give him a break. He's a little nervous. Not everyday a young guy gets to perform for some of the greats. And for Dai Vernon, too."

Tannen put a hand on Guy's shoulder. "Try again, son."

Guy picked up the coin. "Just wanted to get your attention," he said.

And then he did his Retention Vanish—very, very slowly.

Charlie Miller's eyes widened. Mandrake's cigar stopped wiggling in his mouth. A few of the other guys whistled. Vernon did a bit of a double take then quickly hid it.

"Does someone have a bagel I could use?" asked Guy.

A hand came out of the shadows and handed a bagel to Guy.

Slowly, Guy broke open the bagel. The Morgan dollar fell from inside it onto the table. It rolled in a circle and then flopped over in front of Vernon.

"Ever seen a retention that good?" Tannen said to the magicians. Then, to Guy: "Where'd you learn that? How long you been practicing it?"

"Harry Blackstone taught me how to do it. And gave me this coin. I've been practicing it for eight years."

"What do you think, Dai?" asked Tannen.

Vernon nodded. He appreciated talent and expertise when he saw it.

"Kid's good. Rough around the edges, but the basics are good."

Miller snorted. "Rough around the edges! Jesus, Dai, that's the best Retention Vanish I've ever seen and before you ask or say anything I'll tell you it's better than yours. Or mine."

"Thanks," said Guy, beaming.

Vernon bristled. "So he can do a good move. Big deal. Lots of guys can do a good move. What about his patter? His manner? His style? He showed me one sleight. That doesn't make him a good magician."

"He did it with finesse, Dai," said Ross Bertram. "He took care to do it slowly and convince us his hands were empty."

"Sure looked like that coin was in his palm," said Mandrake.

"And in the bagel," Carlyle piped up.

Vernon nodded. "I suppose. Let's see something else."

Guy did a few more tricks, using props supplied by Tannen. He did them well. The men weren't looking for anything new; they were judging his poise, his patter, his ability to turn a trick into miracle.

When he was done, they applauded.

Tannen said to Vernon, "Dai, you ought to take this kid under your wing. Tutor him a bit. Share all that wisdom of yours. Let him benefit from your expertise. He's got the talent. He used to hang out here all the time, a few years back, before he went off to war and became a hero and then got hooked up with a carnival. He's got the passion."

"Well, Lou, I don't know, I'm busy and I travel and ..."

"Geez, Dai, I'm not telling you to adopt him! Just spend some time with him. Give him some pointers. Polish those rough edges. Give him some advice about what it takes to do a sophisticated show like yours."

"Come on, Dai," said Baker, you're the best. We all know that. Help the kid. We have to bring along the next generation of magicians. Keeps the art alive."

"And keeps us old-timers always looking over our shoulders to see who's chasing us," mumbled Carlyle.

From the shadows, Isadore Klein spoke up.

"Share your love of the art, Dai. You live and breathe magic. It's all you think about. All you talk about, right guys?"

There was a chorus of agreement.

"Nobody knows more than Dai," someone said.

"Well, I don't know ... maybe I could ..." Vernon was still considering.

"Every great master needs an apprentice," said Bertram. "Not only do you pass on the art, but it makes you look at what you do and how you do it. You improve your own work."

Vernon liked all this talk of him being a master and knowing so much.

"I suppose I could help you out, kid. Give you a few tips."

"That would be great, Mr. Vernon. I promise I'll listen and practice. I want to be the world's greatest magician."

"There you go, Dai," said Tannen. Then he turned to Guy. "Guy, you gotta promise you won't steal any of Dai's gigs."

Another dig.

"Listen, Lou: by the time this kid is ready for the circles I perform in, I'll be an old man!"

"You're already an old man," said Miller.

"Look who's talking," said Vernon. All the time he'd been talking, his hands were constantly playing with a deck of cards, shuffling, palming, double-dealing, doing passes and double-lifts.

Without saying anything, he shuffled the deck, fanned it, showed that the four aces were dispersed throughout the deck.

Then he put it on the table. He slowly peeled off the top card. It was an ace. So was the second, third and fourth.

Now it was Guy whose eyes widened.

Vernon looked up at Guy, sizing him up. His cigarette did a slow pirouette between his lips. His hands still shuffled and cut the cards.

"So where have you performed?" Dai asked Guy.

"I was in a carnival for about a year. I gave hundreds of shows from Texas through the South and up the coast to New Jersey."

Vernon nodded. He knew about carnivals. He'd worked at Coney Island, mostly cutting silhouettes.

"So if you've given all those shows, you must know what you're doing. Why do you want my help?"

"Because I want to get better. Lots better. Other than Blackstone showing me the Retention Vanish, I've never had anyone teach me about magic. You know: the subtleties and things that make a difference. I can get by, but I want to be better than that. I want to perform here in New York. A little different than in a carnival tent."

"See, Dai," said a voice from the shadows. "The kid knows what he doesn't know. You always say a good magician is someone who knows what his weaknesses are and wants to improve on them."

"You guys act like I'm a professor or something."

"Well, you do know a lot, Dai. And you sure like to talk magic," said Mandrake.

"Yeah," laughed Miller. "Bore the kid a while. It'll give us a break." That drew a laugh.

Vernon was beginning to feel like it was all a card trick, that he was being forced. It was a Magician's Choice played on a magician by magicians. Finally he sighed.

"Okay, kid. I'm here most Saturday mornings sessioning with the boys. You get here about ten. I'll spend some time with you before I show these amateurs the real work."

This drew snorts from some of the magicians. An empty paper cup was launched in Vernon's direction.

"You're a good man, Dai," said Tannen. "Here, I'll throw in an extra deck. And I won't even put it on your account!" He winked at Guy.

"Dai's a bit crusty, kid, but he's the best close-up magician in the world. He's forgotten more than most magicians will ever know. So pay attention to what he tells you."

"Now you're talking," said Vernon who began another trick. The men turned their attention back to him, and the sessioning continued.

"Stick around," said Tannen. "Watch these guys in action. And don't be too scared by 'em."

He went back through the curtain to the front of the shop.

Guy stood watching Vernon hold court. The chatter grew louder as the other magicians jumped in with comments and suggestions. A heated argument ensued about the best way to hold a pinkie break.

As he watched, Guy practiced his retention vanish, as he always did, unaware he was doing so.

In the shadows, one of the men turned his attention from Vernon to Guy and watched him intently, intrigued either by the sleight or something else.

48

Vernon became Guy's mentor. They met in the back room of Tannen's and also at the nightclubs of New York. Dai loved them, performed at some of them, and never tired of a night out. Sometimes his wife, Jean, joined them. Or some of the other magicians. But usually it was just Guy and Dai at the Kit Kat or Stork Club. Vernon seemed to know everybody, and being with him exposed Guy to a heady cross section of New York society. They mingled with film stars, Broadway entertainers, writers, businessmen, artists and musicians.

They were at the Kit Kat Club one night. The club was crowded. Dai was expounding on magic. He did throughout their meals, talking quickly, reeling off insights and methods, stories and bits of history to his student. Though Guy had thought he knew quite a bit about magic, he quickly realized that he knew very little. Dai Vernon was an encyclopedia of the art, and when he'd had a scotch or two, quite voluble. Guy tried to take notes a few times, but Vernon stopped him.

"Don't write. Listen. Too many people don't listen. They hear, but they don't listen. Or they look but don't see. Now the most important thing, Guy, is to ask yourself, why you are doing magic. Have you ever asked yourself that?"

"Not exactly, but I …"

"Well, you gotta. Because you have to know why you are doing something. It doesn't matter if you are a magician or a surgeon or a tuba player or a plumber. Why are you doing what you're doing?"

"Well, I …"

"I'll tell you why I do magic, Guy. Now a lot of magicians poo-poo what I'm gonna tell you, but not me. I do magic because it's a gift to people.

"Let me tell you a story. I once did a show at a nursing home. Now it wasn't for the poor folks who were so far gone they'd be amazed if you just showed them a coin. No, these folks were old, but they were on the ball, if you know what I mean.

"Anyway, I did some tricks, and their eyes lit up. They looked like little kids on Christmas morning. I mean they really looked younger! For the half hour I performed, they lost themselves in a world of mystery and magic. They laughed and clapped. I'll never forget their smiles, the look in their eyes.

"What a gift to give people! To give them a few minutes of pure amazement and joy—can you put a price on that?"

"No, but ..."

"You'll find many worldly, jaded magicians who sneer at this. They think it's a cliché, a bunch of sentimental hogwash. But they're wrong. If we can light up the eyes of a child, or turn an old man into a kid again, however briefly, we've done a worthy, noble thing. If we can make someone forget their troubles, we are giving them a gift.

"That's enough for me, Guy. I don't need to show them I am clever or have fast hands. So what? Who cares? My job is simply to make them smile in wonder. That's all. Don't forget that."

Guy remembered what he had told Reverend Dowd. He thought Dai would be pleased with what he had said. Their takes might be a little different, but their basic beliefs were the same.

Vernon waved at someone across the room.

"That's Lady Barnett. Very rich. I did a show for her husband's 60th."

The club was swank and the waitresses very pretty, as were a lot of the women. It was hard to concentrate on what Vernon was telling him with all the distractions. Maybe that was why Vernon liked to work the clubs of New York. Plenty of distractions. Guy could imagine a pretty girl walking by and Dai taking a rabbit out of a box and stuffing it in a hat right out in the open and nobody ever noticing. Then he'd pull it out when the girl was gone and everybody would say: "Where the hell did that rabbit come from?"

Dai noticed Guy looking at the waitress.

"Never underestimate the power of a pretty girl," said Dai. "Great misdirection. You have a slinky assistant in your carnival act?"

"No, but I always invited the prettiest girl in the audience to help with a trick."

"Smart. Very smart. You have a girl here in New York?"

"Not exactly. There's a girl from the carnival who is here, I think. Her name is Irena. She wants to be in my act."

"Sweetheart?"

"Not exactly."

"Lover?"

"She was."

"Hmmm. I don't know, Guy. Sounds like it could be trouble. You don't want trouble in an act. So no sweetheart, huh?"

"Well, I do have a girl I love, but she doesn't live here."

"No? Too bad! Where is she?"

"Liberty, South Carolina."

"That's a ways away, Guy. It would be better if she was here."

"Yes, it would be."

"What's her name?

"Rachel. Rachel Dowd."

"What does she do?"

"She helps take care of her father, and she loves to design clothes. She has a real knack for it. She could do better than some of the gowns these women are wearing," said Guy, sweeping his hand across the Kit Kat Club.

"Is that right?" Dai dug into a slice of cheesecake. "Where are you living?"

"At the Sutherland Hotel."

"That old fleabag? It's a dump, isn't it?"

"Well, sort of …"

"Well, maybe you can do better." Vernon lit a cigarette, fiddled with the matchbox a minute, then asked: "Can you do any tricks with matches?"

"No, I don't know …"

"You should learn some tricks with matches. You should *always* be able to do a trick, so you should learn some tricks with matches and salt shakers and spoons and cigarettes and dollar bills and coins and …"

"I can do coins. Remember my Retention Vanish?"

"Right. I do. You do that very well. But if you can do magic with anything, you can do magic anywhere, anytime. In a way, that's the best type of magic. No strange little boxes or odd-looking cups or bright red silks suddenly coming out of your pocket. You know what I mean?"

Guy nodded.

"Try to use stuff that is naturally a part of where you are." Vernon paused, waved to someone at a nearby table, then turned back to Guy.

"Have I talked to you about being natural?"

"You mentioned I should …"

"Very important, Guy. Very, very important. Now listen: when you do a trick, do it naturally. Each move should have a motivation. Nothing should look fishy or forced or odd. Bury your prowess. Don't do coin rolls and card flourishes that show off your dexterity. Why would anyone believe in magic when you have just rolled two coins down your knuckles, simultaneously? If people think you have incredibly fast, tricky hands, they will think of you as a juggler, and no one thinks juggling is magic. Technique is crucial, but hiding it is even more crucial. Of all the things a magician makes invisible, his own skill should be the first and most important. Do your tricks naturally, slowly, with grace and elegance."

"That's what I try to do with my Retention Vanish."

"Yes, I like that trick of yours. It's beautiful, elegant and clear. Have I mentioned how important it is for the effect to be clear?"

"Well, you did say …"

"A true magician knows what effect he is after, Guy. The magic is clear, not confused. Anybody can confuse somebody moving coins and cards around. Confusion is not magic. No, when you are done, somebody ought to be able to say in a sentence or two exactly what happened: 'I signed a card and the magician put it in the middle of the deck. Then he snapped his fingers, turned over the top card and it was my signed card.' See what I mean, Guy? That's simple. That's magical. That's something people will remember. And you want your magic to be memorable."

Dai waved to an attractive couple who had just come in, the young woman swathed in mink, the man natty in an impeccable suit.

"That's Dr. Falk and his very young, very lovely sweetheart. She's fresh out of Wellesley. Twenty years younger. There's talk they're getting married. It won't last six months."

As if on cue, the band began playing "That Old Black Magic," and the singer started to sing.

That old black magic has me in its spell, that old black magic that you weave so well.

"She's got him in her spell," said Dai. "He's got no choice in the matter."

Looking at the young beauty, Guy said: "Sometimes choice is overrated."

For you're the lover I have waited for, the mate that fate had me created for.

Vernon winked. "Leave it to fate."

In a spin, loving the spin I'm in, under that old black magic called love.

49

Vernon turned out to be a very good mentor for Guy. To say the least, Dai was obsessed with magic. When he wasn't performing at clubs or society parties or hanging around Tannen's, he took road trips. If he heard a rumor from someone who knew someone who had seen a guy do an amazing deal or sleight, Vernon wanted to go and see for himself. He was always on the trail of card cheats. He figured they were the best at tricky moves. After all, if a magician screwed up, he might get laughed at. If a card cheat screwed up, he might get shot. So they tended to be very good. It didn't matter where the man might live. Vernon, and sometimes Charlie Miller, would get in the car and go.

One rainy Saturday morning at Tannen's, Dai gave Guy his business card. It read: "*Dai W. Vernon, the New York Card Magician*" An address was written on the back. "6 Mott Street."

"It's an apartment. Go check it out," said Vernon. "I heard about it from someone. I don't know anything about it, but it's bound to be better than the Sutherland."

It was a quiet morning at Tannen's. Not many of the boys were in the back room. Guy took the subway to Chinatown and began to wander around, looking for 6 Mott Street. He found it. It was the home of the Ping Toy restaurant. A little confused, he went in to make sure he had the right place. At the counter was a tiny old Chinese woman reading a newspaper.

"Table for one?" she asked, looking up.

"No, I'm here about an apartment."

"How you know?" she asked.

"Someone told me. A magician friend, Dai Vernon."

"Magic man like Houdini?" she asked.

"Yes."

"I am Madame Gai Pan. Own lestaurant and apartment too. Upstairs. Nice place. Has exotic chalm of Olient. You like see?"

She spoke English about as well as Irena did. Guy felt right at home.

"Yes. I like see."

Gai Pan had mischievous eyes and a gap in her top teeth when she smiled, which was often. She took him up a stairway at the back of the kitchen. When he was shown the place, it had the strong odor of the food being cooked downstairs. Guy mentioned this to Gai Pan.

"Yes," she said. "Like I say: 'exotic chalm of Olient.' Smell good, no?"

The apartment was pervaded with the aroma of soy sauce, garlic, and onion. It made him hungry. He had never been to the Orient, so he had no idea if these smells were part of its exotic charm, but he liked Madame Gai Pan and he liked the little apartment. It was clean, and its windows looked out onto the street, not a dark alley. He agreed to take it.

"Good," said Madame Gai Pan. "You like. You eat well! Evelybody be happy!"

The Ping Toy was a simple place that served simple, good food.

There was a glass case at the front crammed with teacups and teabags, incense burners, and other stuff, though it was hard to see because menus were taped to most of the glass. Gai Pan sat behind the counter on a stool. She was surrounded by Chinese newspapers, a cash register, phone, a small lamp, and a carved wooden Buddha with his arms up. Behind her was a beat up old typewriter, a teapot with pencils and scissors, a porcelain figurine of a smiling cat, a small model of the Statue of Liberty, some carved walnuts, and a rubber ear with acupuncture points marked on it and a few thin needles sticking out. Gai Pan ran the Ping Toy from her little office behind the front counter.

The rest of the Ping Toy was cozy, almost dark.

There were booths with worn red leather benches, a few with tape patches over tears, and faded Formica tabletops.

There were paper placemats bordered with red geometric patterns. The animals of the Chinese Zodiac circled the mat, listing the years and qualities of the Rat, the Dragon, the Ox, the Monkey and others. Metallic teapots, small porcelain cups, a bottle of soy sauce and a sugar dispenser completed the table settings.

The decor was typical. There was a large faded photograph of a tranquil lake with undulating mountains and a lone fisherman standing on a narrow low boat. Before it had faded to a uniform purple, the photograph might have been quite spectacular. There were watercolors of misty mountains and tiny figures making their way through them. Yellow lanterns hung from the ceiling like glowing fruit. The walls were adorned with gold Chinese calligraphy alternating with wooden lacquered sculptures of Buddhas and dragons. Here and there, potted bamboo plants added some color to the shadows.

Next to the front counter was a murky aquarium where koi swam lethargically. Whether they were supposed to be relaxing, or good luck, or a menu item Guy did not know. At the back of the restaurant, two swinging doors with round porthole windows led to the kitchen.

All Chinese restaurants seem to look the same, as if they were manufactured on an assembly line and shipped to their locations.

Guy had never had Chinese food. He tried it his first night at his new apartment. "We keep you happy," Gai Pan said, bringing him a free egg roll. He drank oolong tea, pungent and with a sediment of leaves at the bottom of the porcelain cup.

Throughout the meal, Madame Gai Pan sat in her little warren, reading her Chinese newspaper and sometimes turning to type something. She had taken a liking to Guy, and looked over at him and smiled when she caught his eye, beaming like a mother, which she would sort of become.

At the end of his meal, Madame Gai Pan went into the kitchen and returned a few minutes later with a small tray bearing three fortune cookies. Not wrapped in cellophane. No, these were fresh and handmade by Madame Gai Pan herself.

"You choose," she said, "you must have choice. That way fortune is up to you."

Guy mused over the three. He felt like it was a magic trick "pick a cookie, any cookie."

He picked the one on the far right.

"You pick. Sure? Change mind? No? Okay." She sounded just like a magician, always trying to be fair, always giving someone a chance to change their mind, to make another choice (when, in fact, there could never really be another choice.) But these were fortune cookies, not cards. Life was not always a trick.

She took away the tray and left him with the fortune cookie he had chosen. He cracked it open and read the thin strip of paper with its typed message:

"Darkness cannot drive out darkness; only light can do that."

Guy wondered what the fortune meant. He knew they were usually not literal but metaphorical. So, what darkness in his life would be driven out by what light? It was indeed a riddle.

He looked over at Madame Gai Pan, who looked back at him from her perch behind the counter. She nodded and smiled, showing a gold tooth that glimmered in the dim light coming up from below.

A few nights after he'd settled in, Gai Pan asked him what he did. He told her.

"You cut woman in half? Pull bunny from hat?" she asked.

This sounded familiar.

"No, no. Neither."

"Why no girl? You no have girl?"

"No, I'm afraid not. At least not here. There is a girl I like, but she's far away. Down south."

"She need come to New York. Be with you. Saw in half. Make little Guys."

"Maybe someday."

"Why no bunny? All magicians have bunny. Bunny good: look at menu. Means long life."

"I don't have that kind of act, Gai Pan."

"What kind of act you do?"

Guy explained he didn't have a big stage show, that he did mostly close-up or parlor magic. No sawing women, no bunny.

He took out his Morgan dollar and did his Retention Vanish for her, using a fortune cookie instead of a roll for the revelation. Gai Pan loved Guy's trick. At the climactic moment, she squealed like a kid, her wrinkled old face suddenly a beautiful soft frame for her twinkling eyes.

"Not possible!" she exclaimed. "Gone. Poof. Thin air. Then in cookie? Not possible! I make all cookies. No coin. Impossible. 'Mazing. Do again!"

Guy smiled, bent over, and kissed Gai Pan on the forehead.

"Is possible," he said. "Your eyes don't lie. I'll do it again. But not tonight."

She smiled back and tried to ruffle his hair, but she was too short. Instead, she squeezed his nose.

"Guy, you good. You should do show! Bloadway! 'Maze the world!"

"Someday, Gai Pan. Someday maybe I will."

The next night, his fortune cookie read:

"You can't build a reputation on what you are going to do."

50

Guy ate at the Ping Toy most nights if he wasn't meeting Vernon at a nightclub. What money he had saved up and recouped from Arrigo the Monkey was about gone. Guy needed work. He needed to pay his bills. Though Gai Pan had let him put his meals on account, sooner or later, that account would come due.

"Why so glum?" Gai Pan asked.

"I need a job, Gai Pan. I'm running out of money."

"Magic job?"

"That would be nice. But I don't have any prospects yet. Right now, I'll settle for anything."

"How 'bout bar? You make drinks?"

"I can mix a few."

"Bar a few blocks away needs man behind bar. You go see."

"Why not? What's the name of the bar?"

"The Litz. Here address." Gai Pan scribbled it on the back of a fortune that read:

"You will receive many words of wisdom. Don't fall asleep."

Guy went to the address Gai Pan had given him. There he came to a bar, but it was The Ritz, not The Litz. He smiled. It was those accents again. The Ritz hardly lived up to its name. It was a shabby little place sandwiched between a cleaners and a secondhand bookstore. Its front window was cracked, and one of the letters on its neon sign flickered. Its name was a triumph of wishful thinking over crummy reality.

"Oh, well," sighed Guy.

Sure enough, they needed a bartender at The Ritz three nights a week. Guy signed on.

The Ritz was a sleepy place. Guy worked there, earning a bit, biding his time. At least it helped pay his bills. A few weeks after he started, the owner, Chuck Freedman, told Guy he wished they had some entertainment. Something to liven up the place a bit. Maybe draw a few people in. Something to differentiate it from all the other sleepy bars in New York City.

The next night, Guy brought in some tricks and gave the owner a show. Freedman was amazed by what he saw and said he'd pay Guy a little extra to do magic at the bar. He even put up a hand-lettered sign: "Featuring the magic of Guy Borden." Guy mused that when he imagined his name on a sign in New York, he thought of a glittering marquee on Broadway, not a hand-lettered sign on a dirty window, bathed in the glow of neon, at a bar on the edge of Chinatown. At least he had a place to perform.

Guy was now a bartender who did some tricks on the top of the wooden bar, a stage awash in beer and cheap whisky, for an audience of depressed people drinking away their woes, easy to fool because they were already fooling themselves, easy to misdirect because they had already lost their direction. Sometimes, there were women who came in trolling for men, and if the night was slow, which it usually was, he would dazzle them with a few tricks before they did theirs. Magic at The Ritz was not much, but it gave him a chance to try out routines and keep in practice.

Guy led two lives. He tended bar and worked on his close-up routines. And he went to clubs with Vernon and mingled with New York celebrities and high society. While Dai thought it was good for Guy to keep doing his magic, he wasn't too happy about his doing it at a bar.

"Jesus, Guy, anybody can fool a drunk. Working there won't sharpen your skills."

Guy just shrugged. "For now, it's the best I can do."

Vernon frowned. He didn't like to see his student squandering his talents in a dark bar.

A few nights later, a man walked in to the bar. He had a slight limp and his fedora hat hid half of his face, not that Guy could have seen it very well in the dim bar.

"Whisky," he said quietly, hunched over the bar.

Guy served him. The man's old hands shook as he cradled his shot glass.

"Would you like to see a magic trick?" asked Guy.

"Nope. Don't like magic."

The man took a sip of his whisky. After a minute, he asked: "You do magic at the bar?"

"Yes."

"Pretty small stage. Why don't you do magic someplace bigger?"

"I hope to someday."

The man thought this over for a bit, slowly twirling the shot glass in his hands.

"Now you didn't ask for advice, so I won't give it to you," the man said after a while, still looking down at his glass. "But I will tell you this: if you are good at something, try to do it where you can go far. Don't park your railroad car on a siding that's a dead end."

"Good advice," said Guy, thinking of Archie's warning not to get stuck in the carnival. "Sure you don't want to see a trick?"

"Don't like magic."

There was silence for a while. Guy fiddled with the radio trying to get the station to come in. He wanted to listen to The Shadow.

The man spoke again: "Now you didn't ask for advice, so I won't give it to you. But I will tell you this: time flies. Don't waste your time waiting for things. Carpe diem."

"Carpe diem?' asked Guy.

"Seize the day," said the man.

"Good advice," said Guy.

"Yes it is," said the man. He finished the last of his drink, then put his money on the bar, climbed down off the stool, and limped his way out of The Ritz.

"What a strange man," thought Guy. But he had to admit, his advice was good. Vernon would agree. He wasn't going to build a career parked at The Ritz.

* * *

Things drifted along for a month until one night, as Guy was cleaning glasses behind the bar, he heard:

"Hi, Guy. Find you much difficult looking for me."

Guy knew the voice. He knew the tortured English. Irena!

Sure enough, when he looked up, there she was, perched on a stool at the bar, her hair longer, her outfit cheap but fashionable.

"Irena!"

"Yes, Guy, is me. Happy?"

Not exactly. Guy had been happy that Irena had disappeared into the oblivion of the city. While an excellent lover, she was hardly a soul mate; not like Rachel. And wherever Irena was, Ivan was never far away, and Ivan was trouble.

"I'm so happy to see you, Irena," Guy lied.

"So you work bar." A statement muttered with a trace of disdain.

"For a while."

"No magic?"

"Oh, a little. Here and there. What about you? Are you still soaring in the air, walking the tightrope?"

Irena snorted. "No. Salesgirl. Lingerie. Big store."

Guy's imagination started to wander. He reined it in.

"So how did you find me here at The Ritz, or is it just my luck?"

"I hear from somebody who know somebody who hear from somebody that young magic guy at bar. I wonder so I come. It you!"

"Yes," thought Guy, "Just my luck."

"Irena have idea, Guy."

"What's that?"

"Act."

"Trapeze? I'm not strong like Ivan, and ..."

"No, fool, magic!"

"You and me do a magic act?"

"Yes, why not? I handle your bunny. You cut me in half. Float me up. I dress like sexy and be your girl."

"I don't know, Irena ..."

"Why, you scared? You want to be at bar with drinks mixing all days of your life? This New York, Guy. Big town. Fame to be had. You need act. You need stage, not bar."

"Let me think about it, Irena. Let me ask a magician who has been helping me."

She shrugged. "Okay. Ask. Irena ready to be sexy magician girl any time." She looked at Guy. "You got girl in city?"

"Oh, yes," Guy lied. "Several of them."

"Good as Irena at love?"

"No, Irena. You are one of a kind."

She smiled. "Maybe again we make love?"

"Maybe, Irena. But not tonight. I'm working very late."

She shrugged.

"You ask magic man about act. Here my number for calling. You want to make act, Irena your girl. On stage. Off stage. Whatever you want."

She smiled, leaned over the bar, gave Guy a kiss, and left.

Guy stared after her. What had Bogart said in "Casablanca"?

"Of all the gin joints in all the towns in all the world, she walks into mine."

An act with Irena. He'd see what Vernon thought.

51

"An act!" Dai said. "With a sultry Russian assistant. Now you're talking. It will get you out of that crappy bar."

"Yes. It would give me a chance to do something bigger."

"She any good?"

"On the tightrope and trapeze, yes. I don't know about magic, Dai. She's never been in a show."

"Hmmm. You'll have to teach her. Holding trays and handing you props is one thing, Guy. But you start putting her in boxes and sawing her in half and all that illusion stuff—it's hard work. The girl does it all, really. You just wave your hands and smile a lot and try not to kill her with the swords you're jamming in the boxes. I don't know ..."

"I wouldn't do all that, Dai. I can't *afford* to do all that. I'd keep it simple. Parlor stuff. Like what I did in the carnival. Bigger than close-up, but not a stage show like Blackstone's."

"He's coming to town, you know," said Vernon.

"He is?"

"Yes, in a few weeks. He's been touring Europe for the USO. He wants to settle down a while. He's got a long run scheduled for the Morosco."

"The Morosco! I worked there once."

"Really? On stage?"

"No, back stage," said Guy.

Vernon shook his head. "Wrong place to be."

"I'd love to see Blackstone again."

"Well maybe you can," said Vernon. "Anyway, back to you. If you're going to start an act, you need a stage name."

"How about Guy Borden?"

"No, too boring," said Dai.

"Please don't tell me to change it to Guydini."

Vernon snorted.

"No, no! Everybody adds 'ini' to their name. They think that's clever, that it makes them a magician. Did I ever tell you I knew Houdini?"

"No, but I ..."

"Yes. Harry and I go back. Or at least we did when he was alive. You know, I fooled him with a card trick once. He said he could watch any trick three times and figure it out. Well, one night in Chicago I showed him a trick *seven* times and he was fooled. I got to be known as the 'Man Who Fooled Houdini.' It was good for business. Well, at least for mine."

Dai waved at another couple sitting nearby. At the Kit Kat Club, jammed as it was, everybody was sitting nearby.

"That's Pete DiNardo and his wife. Nice folks. Now, where were we?"

"My name."

"Right, Guy, let's see what we can do for you." Dai pulled out a piece of paper and a pen. "Maybe we can rearrange the letters in your name to come up with something." Vernon started jotting names down.

"How about Yug Nedrob?" he asked.

Guy didn't like that one. It sounded like a curry dish at an Indian restaurant.

"Ugy Denbor? No, that's no good. Sounds foolish. Dunge Roby? Roy Bunged?"

Guy needed to pee so he left Vernon working on names and went to the bathroom. He stood at the urinal and as he peed, he looked at the NO SMOKING sign above it. He wasn't sure why there would be no smoking in the bathroom, but there it was. He stared at the sign and, his head still full of letters and names, idly played with it. And it hit him like a flash: NO SMOKING ... NOSMO KING! It sounded great.

Thrilled, Guy finished, washed up and went back to Vernon.

"Hey Guy, here's a pretty good one," Vernon said as Guy approached the table.

"How about Engy Dubor? Has an exotic ring to it."

"No, Dai! I have a better one. How about NOSMO KING?"

"Nosmo King? How'd you get that out of your name?"

"I didn't. It's an inspiration: NO SMOKING."

"What?" Vernon looked at his cigar.

"Just space the letters differently"

Vernon wrote it down on his piece of paper and stared a minute.

"I see! Not too bad, kid. Not too bad. But not quite right. Hmmm. I know. How about you reverse it? How about KING NOSMO?"

"Yeah, Dai, that's it! King Nosmo!"

"Sure, kid. King Nosmo. Maybe King Nosmo the Mystic. Perfect! Let's drink to it, Guy. King Nosmo the Mystic. I like it. Sounds exotic as hell. Like some ancient pharaoh. Maybe you dress up like an Egyptian. That'd be different. You got Chinese and Indian magicians, but I've never heard of an Egyptian one."

"Me neither."

"You'll need a magical phrase, too, Guy. Something you say that sounds exotic. Like 'Hocus Pocus,' or 'Sim Sala Bim.' It can be gibberish, but they have to believe it has magical powers."

Guy though for a moment.

"How about 'Oed Zem Boujad'"

Vernon looked baffled. "How on earth did you come up with that?"

"Oh, just a memory. A place I was. I was doing a trick for a guy. One on one."

"Yeah? How'd it go?"

"Not so well, Dai. Not so well."

"Sorry to hear that. We all have days when our magic isn't so magical."

Guy relived the moment, so far away, seeming so long ago, when he was mystifying Butch with his coin trick. "Do it again. Do it again." He shook his head. He was back with Vernon, who was writing his name in bold letters.

"KING NOSMO, The Egyptian Mystic."

So Guy had his stage name inspired by a visit to a urinal, and he and Dai drank to it. Both men would smile whenever they saw a NO SMOKING sign.

"What about Irena?" Guy asked. "We have to include her somehow."

"We do?"

"Yes," said Guy, remembering Irena's temper and how she tended to deal with men who had upset her.

"How about King Nosmo and Irena?" said Vernon.

"It seems odd, Dai. Not very Egyptian."

"I suppose you're right." Vernon started writing names on his slip of paper. "I've got it: 'Irea' Just drop the 'n'."

Guy considered it. "King Nosmo, the Egyptian Mystic. And Irea."

"I like it, Dai. I'll see what she says."

"You do that. Work up an act. I'll ask around, see if I can get you a gig. No promises, but I know a lot of folks in this town."

"That would be great, Dai."

"Is this Irea going to be a speaking assistant or silent?" asked Vernon.

"Oh, silent, Dai. She's Russian. Her English is terrible."

"Make sure she's slinky, Guy. Not trashy, mind you. But pretty and a little sexy. That'll do worlds for you. You can get away with a lot with a pretty girl nearby."

Guy nodded in agreement. Vernon waved to a pretty girl nearby.

52

To put together an act, Guy dusted off his old carnival props and added some new ones he'd bought at Tannen's. He developed a show, and he and Irena practiced it over and over. After, they made love. She was as good as ever, but she did not make Guy forget about Rachel.

Vernon was good to his word. He had asked around and found Guy a gig. It was for the Spellman bar mitzvah. Another bar mitzvah. Guy would never forget his first one. He went to meet Hiram Spellman.

Hiram was a little concerned about the name of Guy's act.

"Don't you know we Jews suffered under Pharaoh and had to follow Moses into the desert to escape? Have you ever heard of the parting of the Red Sea?"

"Yes. That was a great trick," said Guy.

Spellman frowned. Shook his head.

"You can be King Nosmo," said Hiram Spellman. "And your girl can be Irea. But lose the Egyptian Mystic stuff if you want to perform for us."

"Sure," said Guy. "No problem."

"And I hope you don't hurt any Jews in your act."

Guy blinked. "No, sir. No Jews will be hurt. I promise."

"Okay. You go on at four. Keep it to thirty minutes. Keep it clean. These are kids, you know. Though, today, my Michael is a man!"

They went on at four.

Vernon was there, at the back of the room, watching.

The next day, Dai invited Guy to dinner. He got right to the point.

"I saw your show, Guy. You had a nice mix of tricks. It went okay. Spellman seemed to be happy. But I need to talk to you about Irea, or Olga, whatever her name is."

"Irena."

"Right. The Russian. Listen, Guy, she's pretty, and would be good misdirection if she didn't look constipated. What a face! She looks in pain. Maybe it's a kind of misdirection, but not the type you want. The point of a pretty girl … well, hell, you know the point of a pretty girl.

"You are natural and engaging, and she stands there like a statue, grimacing. I'm surprised she didn't frighten the kids. She may have been a great tightrope walker or whatever she was, but as a magician's assistant, she's no good. You need a gal who's pretty and smiles. A girl you have some rapport with, know what I mean? You two might be lovers but you sure aren't in love. It shows. Find yourself a pretty girl to love who wants to be in your show and you're all set. Or go solo. But that constipated Russian has got to go, unless you want to stick her in a gorilla costume." Dai, as always, had a strong opinion.

"Maybe we just need to work more. Let her get comfortable."

"I don't think so, Guy. A few more shows with her and you won't be doing shows. And I couldn't recommend you to any of my society gang. She'd bring down any party."

Guy thought about telling Irena. Guy thought about Irena getting angry. Guy thought about Irena kicking him in the groin. Dai saw his pained look.

"It's never easy, kid. But it has to be done. Do it quickly, like pulling off a Band-Aid. Just get it over with."

As Guy rode the subway home that night, he reflected on the show. He realized that Irena didn't like being an assistant, walking on and off carrying trays or handing him gaudy boxes. She liked to fly through the air with the greatest of ease. She liked to be the star, the one in the spotlight. Their show didn't work. Not when played in front of a live audience. Vernon was right. Irena had to go.

As it turned out, Irena had already gone. He got home and found a note slipped under his door. It was a struggle to read and understand, but he got the message:

"Guy: Is no good for Irena. Magic not me. Russian proverb say: 'Bird in cage never sing, but bird on wing happy.' We had fun, but time for Irena to move on with tears and heart of breaking and memories for times. I hope you do without me show. Is better. Maybe paths someday cross when not now. Bye and love, Irena."

Guy breathed a sigh of relief. Relief that she was gone. Relief that he didn't have to tell her. Relief that she wouldn't kick him in the groin. Maybe she would go back to Ivan and they'd become perilous performers again. Maybe she'd walk the tightrope in lingerie. He'd like to see that.

He went downstairs to the Ping Toy. He told Gai Pan what had happened. She smiled, her gold tooth glinting under the light of a Chinese lantern.

"Now what?" she asked.

"I don't know, Gai Pan. Maybe I'll continue on alone. Or find another girl. I'm not sure."

He pulled the Jack of Diamonds from his wallet and looked at it as he ate spare ribs, dim sum and sweet and sour chicken.

"Patience" he thought. "Patience."

At the end of his meal, Gai Pan appeared with her tray of three fortune cookies.

"Pick one," she said.

Guy did. She left and he opened it.

"Failure is a dress rehearsal for success."

"Let's hope," Guy said to himself.

53

Guy was on the subway, on his way to the Stork Club to meet Vernon for dinner. He sat with his head against the window, lost in thought. At the Bleecker Street station Guy looked up and saw a big man standing on the platform, just a few feet away, on the other side of the glass. The man turned toward the train. He held a pocket watch in his hand, checking the time. He looked at the train, right at Guy's window. Guy saw his face.

It was Willie Jenks! Jenks! Here in New York!

Guy sat up straight, jumped up and headed for the doors, but they had already closed and the train was moving. Jenks slid out of view. Yet again, Guy had spotted Willie Jenks a moment too late. He slammed his hand against the window.

"Damn!"

Guy was stunned. The man who had stolen his watch halfway across the country had been just a few feet away! And he still had Guy's watch! All his anger towards Jenks came flooding back. Jenks was in New York. Maybe he could track him down. Get his watch back from the son-of-a-bitch.

He was still reeling from his close encounter with Willie Jenks when he joined Vernon at the Stork Club.

"What's wrong, Guy? You look like you've just seen a ghost."

"I have."

"What?"

"I spotted a guy in the subway. I met him a year or so ago on a train in Texas. He conned me out of my watch."

"No kidding? How did he do that?" asked Vernon.

"Misdirection."

"Was he a magician?" asked Vernon.

"No, Dai. He was a thief."

"Well, Guy, you saw him once. Maybe you'll see him again."

"Maybe. Maybe not. It's a big city, Dai."

"Let me get you a drink, Guy. You need one."

The drink helped Guy forget about Jenks. So did the club's distractions. Guy's head swiveled left and right as suave gentlemen in tuxedos strutted around with beautiful women on their arms. The women had jewels on theirs. The air was thick with smoke and the sounds of clinking glasses, laughter and music. Ella Fitzgerald was singing, and Guy was in a world of entertainers and entertainment—the world he had longed to inhabit for years.

Vernon waved to a couple a few tables away.

"That's Winny and Benjamin Poltergass. Look at them: the loving couple."

Guy looked over. The man was holding the woman's gloved hand, stroking it. She had a cigarette in a long gold holder and was gazing adoringly at him.

"The truth is, Guy …" Vernon lowered his voice, "They are both having affairs. She's sleeping with the manager of the Shubert Theater, hoping to get a break, and he's got a chorus girl he's breaking in and hopes to manage. What you see here is misdirection at its best."

Guy looked at them again.

"Don't stare, Guy. You don't have to be a magician to create an illusion. Everybody does it. You never know if somebody really is who they say they are. Or doing what you think they're doing. You take them on faith, but you know, faith can be a fragile thing. A few lies or disappointments and faith is tested. Sometimes shattered."

Ella Fitzgerald began to sing "Love for Sale" and the crowd quieted, mesmerized by her singing.

Who's prepared to pay the price,
For a trip to paradise?
Love for sale

Dai reached into his topcoat pocket and pulled out a small square of black paper. From another pocket he produced a tiny scissors. He began to snip at the paper, looking up at Ella as she sang, then back at the paper, twisting and turning it. Snip. Look. Turn. Snip. He worked quickly. Guy had heard that Vernon was a master at cutting silhouettes. He'd earned a living doing it at Coney Island and other places before his magic career took off. Guy had never seen him in action. It was fascinating.

Ella finished the song, took her applause, and headed toward the bar. On the way, she noticed Dai and stopped at their table.

"Why, Dai Vernon! How ya doin', Dai?"

"Just great, Ella. Great. Join us?"

"Don't mind if I do," she said, sitting.

"Ella, this is Guy Borden. Guy, Ella Fitzgerald."

"Pleased to meet you, Guy."

"Pleased to me you, Mrs. Fitzgerald. I'm a fan of your music."

"Thank you."

"What can I get you, Ella?"

"Soda water's fine, Dai. I don't drink while I'm singing."

Vernon looked a little vexed. Shrugged. A waitress came by and Dai ordered a water, a scotch, and another martini for Guy.

"Guy's a budding young magician and a war hero, Ella. Got a Purple Heart for getting wounded and a Medal of Valor for killing some krauts."

Ella nodded, duly impressed.

"You in town long, Ella?" Vernon asked.

"A few weeks, Dai. Gigs here and there. Maybe some recording, too. What's up with you?"

"Oh, some nice shows coming up. I keep busy. Got to stay ahead of these young guys." Vernon pointed over at Guy. He was still snipping away at his little piece of black paper as he talked.

"Too bad Jean isn't here tonight, Ella. She'd like to see you. Look, I have something for you. I cut it while you were singing."

Dai unfolded the silhouette. It was a double, joined in the middle like Siamese twins. Carefully Dai cut it in half and handed Ella one of her miniature portraits. It was, as all his were, perfect.

Ella took the little piece of cut black paper.

"It's amazing, Dai. I don't know how you do it."

"Carefully." said Vernon. Ella giggled. She looked at the silhouette again.

"I'm always a silhouette," she said.

Vernon furrowed his brow questioningly.

"A Negro in the spotlight," she said. She tucked the black paper into a pocket.

"Show me a trick, Dai."

"Sure, Ella. You perform for me, I'll perform for you."

Vernon went to his coat pocket and pulled out his ever-present deck of cards. It was worn, the cards soft from all their handling. He fanned them out for Ella.

"All different, Ella?"

She looked over the spread cards.

"They sure are."

"Okay, pick one, Ella. Any one you want."

Ella looked at the fan and reached for one way at the edge, near Vernon's hand. She took it out. It was the Jack of Diamonds.

Guy did a double take. The Jack of Diamonds! The same card he had chosen when Blackstone had invited him on stage. He had it in his wallet.

"You sure you want that one, Ella? You can change your mind. It's your choice."

"I'm fine, Dai. I like the Jack."

Guy wondered: who knows why we choose the cards we do.

Vernon pulled out a pen and offered it to Ella.

"Okay, Ella, please sign the card so you'll know for sure its yours."

She did.

"Now watch. Watch closely," said Vernon. "I will take your card and put it in the center of the deck. See? There it is."

Ella nodded. Dai had, indeed, put the card in the middle of the deck.

"Now your card, well, it's ambitious. It doesn't want to be in the middle of the deck. It wants to be on top. Watch." Vernon snapped his finger and slowly turned over the top card. It was the Jack of Diamonds with Ella's signature.

"But …" said Ella. Vernon put his hand up.

"Watch again. I take the card off the top, your Jack of Diamonds, and again I put it in the deck. But, like I said, it's an ambitious card. Always wants to be on top." He snapped his fingers and turned over the top card. Again, it was the Jack of Diamonds.

"Dai, how do you do that?"

"Oh, it's not me, Ella. It's the card. Ambitious, like I said. Always jumps to the top no matter where you put it."

As he said this, Dai put the card from the top back in the middle of the deck. He told Ella to snap her fingers. She did, and then he turned over the top card and it was the Jack.

He did this a few more times. The last time, the card he turned over was not the Jack. Vernon frowned a moment.

"Where'd it go?" asked Ella.

"Oh, I know where it is," said Vernon. He reached over and slowly pulled the Jack out of Guy's topcoat pocket. "Sometimes, the card likes to get out of the pack for a bit."

Ella enjoyed the trick immensely. When it was done, she had a smile across her face. Her eyes twinkled. She shook her head in wonder.

"Amazing, as always, Dai. You're a master. Thanks. Well, I have to go. I'm on again." She held out a hand to Guy who shook it.

"Pleased to meet you, Guy. Thank you for serving our country. I'll sing a song for you."

When Ella left, Dai spoke to Guy.

"Did you see how attentive Ella was? Her reaction? That's why folks like a trick like this, Guy. It's not just fancy handwork. It tells a story. It has some meaning."

"Tell me one thing, Dai: did you force the Jack of Diamonds?"

"No. It doesn't matter what card they choose. It's their choice. Why?"

"Nothing," said Guy, still amazed that the Jack of Diamonds had again come into play. It was spooky.

Ella began her introduction.

"Ladies and Gentlemen, we have a war hero with us tonight. Guy Borden. Wounded in battle, and a hero. He received two medals for his bravery. I'd like to dedicate this song to him. Okay, boys."

The band began to play, and Ella began to sing:

There'll be bluebirds over
The white cliffs of Dover
Tomorrow
Just you wait and see

I'll never forget the people I met
Braving those angry skies
I remember well as the shadows fell
The light of hope in their eyes

Guy thought of the eyes he'd seen and remembered the look of weariness in Lily's and the blank stare of death in Butch and Clarence's.

There'll be love and laughter
And peace ever after
Tomorrow
When the world is free

A hush had fallen over the Kit Kat Club, just as it had at Ralph's Place years earlier when Kate Smith had sung "God Bless America." They were both beautiful songs, full of pride and promise. They tugged at the heartstrings. Two songs that, for Guy, bookended the war years.

The shepherd will tend his sheep
The valley will bloom again
And Jimmy will go to sleep
In his own little room again

Guy thought that Jimmy might sleep again in his little room but not Butch. They'd buried him somewhere in the African desert.

There'll be bluebirds over
The white cliffs of Dover
Tomorrow
Just you wait and see …

The song ended and there was a moment of silence, and then applause, a sudden release of emotion that Ella could not acknowledge and the audience could not control. Even the bandleader was applauding, and the band, too, tears in their eyes. For a few magical moments, the despair and hope, horror and heroism of war found expression in Ella's beautiful singing of a beautiful song. Her singing had been an arrow to the heart. It was a performance of perfection that only a rare talent could create. And everybody there knew it.

The evening ended then. What could possibly follow? There was a quiet murmur in the room as bills were paid, as people shook Ella's hand, and filed out, dreaming of blue skies, remembering when the shadows fell.

Ella came back to the table, subdued. She'd poured her heart and soul into the song.

"You ever record that?" Dai asked Ella, wiping a tear from his eye.

"No. That's Vera Lynn's song. I've only sung it a few times."

Vernon shook his head.

"Too bad no one recorded it tonight, Ella. It was a masterpiece. Sung for the ages."

Ella smiled. "Thanks, Dai. When you sing from the heart, it's easy. Good luck to you, Guy," she said, shaking Guy's hand. "You're an inspiration." Then she was gone. The Kit Kat Club was emptying out.

"She's one in a million, Guy. One in a million. What a gift to be able to sing and touch the heart like that. It was a privilege to hear her. I'll never forget it."

"Me neither, Dai. Me neither."

Dai led the way and Guy followed, getting their hats and coats, leaving the Kit Kat Club, Ella's singing still echoing in their hearts.

Left behind, the second silhouette of Ella that Dai had cut lay on the table, the shadow of a brilliant light.

54

About a week later, on a foggy Saturday morning, Guy was at Tannen's watching some of the guys sessioning. Vernon came in and after tossing his coat off, lit a cigarette, and motioned Guy over to a corner.

"Harry Blackstone is back in town and he's opening his show in a few days," said Vernon. "He's probably busy, but maybe you can go by and see him. Talk to him. It would be great if he'd let you help out in his show. You'd get a lot from it."

"Do you think I could meet him? Would he talk to me? It's been years since I met him."

"Who knows? I've met Harry; he's a decent sort of fellow. If he's not too busy, he might spare you a few minutes. But there's a problem."

"What's that?"

"Opening week, most magicians keep a pretty tight rein on things. They lock the place up. They don't want distractions."

"So I could wait a few days."

"No, not a good idea, Guy. If you want to be a part of the show, now is the time. Once he gets open and running, he won't want to change anything. Too disruptive. It might be too late as it is."

"So what do I do?"

"I don't know for sure, Guy." Dai paced a bit, lost in thought, puffing his cigarette. He picked up a deck of cards and did some passes and cuts. His hands were nervous, like a cat's twitching tail. After a few minutes, he said to Guy:

"You know, if memory serves me, I think the new guard at the Morosco is a guy named Russ. He used to be a magician;

now he's a night watchman. The perils of the business, you know. Not everybody makes it."

"And ...?"

"Well, if it's the Russ I'm thinking of, he's been known to like the bottle a bit. Maybe that's why he's a watchman now. I don't know for sure. But maybe, if you were to offer him a drink, he might just be willing to look the other way. Let you in. I don't know. Just a thought."

"What time do rehearsals start?"

"Seven o'clock. Late afternoon it will probably be hectic around there."

"Hey, Dai," yelled Mandrake. "Come over here and look at this Coin and Cylinder routine of Bertram's. You'll love it."

Dai drifted out of the shadows and back to the round table where Ross Bertram was sitting at the table.

Guy left Tannen's and took the subway to Times Square. He exited and walked to the Morosco Theater on West 45th Street. Guy rounded the corner and halfway down the block found the stage door. It was open. Further down the block, silhouetted in the fog, two men wrestled a crate out of a truck. They were stagehands and would be coming his way soon. Just as Vernon had said, there was a man guarding the stage door. Probably Russ. Guy was sure Russ saw him, but the man yawned and went inside. Guy approached cautiously. The man was inside the stage door, sitting on the steps, spinning some keys on his finger. Guy fingered the pint bottle of bourbon in his pocket.

"You Russ?" he asked the man.

"That's me."

"Care for a drink?" said Guy, pulling the bottle from his pocket.

"I don't drink," said Russ.

So much for Vernon's memory.

"Oh," said Guy, putting the bottle away.

"Can I help you with something?" asked Russ.

Guy's knowledge of forcing choices notwithstanding, he didn't have another plan. He said the first thing that popped in his mind. "I'm a magician."

"That so?" said Russ.

"Yes. My name's Guy Borden. I was a student of Mr. Blackstone's. Look ... he taught me this."

Guy took out his Morgan dollar and did his Retention Vanish.

"Do that again," said Russ.

Guy did. Russ whistled. "So what do you want?"

"I was hoping to stop in, say hello to Mr. Blackstone. Just a few minutes. I won't be a bother."

"I'm not supposed to let anybody in who isn't in the show," said Russ, "and you're not in the show."

"I know," said Guy. "But I think Mr. Blackstone will be happy to see me."

Russ looked at Guy. "I could lose my job," he said.

"Not if you were helping those guys with that crate and I snuck in," said Guy. "I'm not going to cause any trouble."

Russ stood up and took a step toward Guy. He looked him in the eye.

"Son, you better be telling the truth."

Then he brushed past him and called out to the stagehands: "Hey, Joe, Wilbur—let me give you a hand with that." Russ went over and grabbed a corner of the crate the two men were struggling with.

Seizing the opportunity, Guy stepped in and quickly up the half dozen stairs to a small corridor. He knew his way around. He'd spent almost a year at the Morosco. He had many fond memories of it. He walked down the corridor, past the dressing rooms, and around a corner into the shadows. As if in a trance, he walked between hanging curtains toward an assemblage of objects on stage. They were just a few of the 1001 Wonders.

At center stage, Guy looked out at the dark, deserted theater and tried to imagine the lights on, the seats filled with an excited audience. How heady it would be to have all those eyes on him, all those minds going where he took them, all those hearts full of wonder.

Guy turned to a table cluttered with boxes, hoops, canisters, balls, bottles, flowers, silks, a top hat, wand and cages. He gazed at the props almost reverently. And why not? To him, the things on the table were as much objects of worship as any in a church. Magic was *his* religion. As he had tried to explain to Reverend Dowd, religion and magic are like light and shadow. They complement each other and share a place in the human soul. They are not so different. Both offer miracles. Both embrace belief in the impossible.

A connoisseur of the exotic, Guy carefully picked up, examined, and replaced the props. Until he heard someone clear his throat behind him, down in the seats.

He spun around.

Harry Blackstone was standing in the middle aisle, about ten seats back from the stage. How long had he been watching?

"Find any secrets?" he asked.

Guy was too stunned and scared to answer. He just stood there holding a large devil's head that had the Three of Hearts dangling from its mouth. He bumped into the table and a wooden ball rolled off, hit the floor and split in half. A large flower sprung out and slowly flopped over, as if dying.

Finally, Guy found his voice.

"I ... I ... I ..."

"Your patter is a bit repetitive, young man. It needs work." Blackstone sauntered down the aisle and up the stairs to the stage. He stopped a few feet from Guy. Guy had yet to say anything coherent, and he still clutched the devil's head as if it were his salvation.

"Who are you?" asked Blackstone. "What are you looking for? How did you get in here?"

Guy put the devil's head down. He turned and looked at Blackstone sheepishly. Blackstone studied the young man, and before Guy could answer his questions, he asked another.

"Do I know you? You look familiar."

"Yes," said Guy. I met you ten years ago in New London, Connecticut. You called me up on stage and I helped you with the card sword trick. I still have the card. The next day you were at my father's barbershop, and then we met at the coffee shop of the hotel and you taught me the Retention Vanish. You even sent me a Mysto Magic Set. My name is Guy. Guy Borden."

"Yes, of course, I remember you."

Guy took out the Morgan dollar.

"You gave me this, Mr. Blackstone. You told me to use it to practice the Vanish. You told me to never lose it. I haven't."

"Show me the Vanish," said Blackstone, crossing his arms. "Over here, in the light."

Guy moved over a few steps and did the Retention Vanish. Slowly. Perfectly.

Blackstone smiled. "You certainly must have listened to me, Guy. You do that better than anybody I have ever seen."

"Thank you, Mr. Blackstone. I practiced it a lot. Until my hands bled."

"Ah, yes. I remember now."

"Mr. Blackstone, I've practiced my magic. I worked for a year at a carnival giving shows. I've done private parties. Performed in a bar. I've listened to everything Dai Vernon has told me."

"So you know Vernon?"

"Yes, very well. He's taught me a lot."

"He's a piece of work, that Vernon. But a damned fine magician. Best close-up man there is. But it looks like you are drawn to a bigger show?"

"Yes. I like the excitement and spectacle of your show. I'd like to amaze a thousand people, not just ten or even fifty. Dai has taught me how to be a magician. I want to learn how to be a showman."

Blackstone looked at the eager young man he had launched on the path to magic. First with the wonder of his show, then by teaching him the Retention Vanish, finally by sending him the Mysto Magic Set. Their paths had diverged after their hour in that coffee shop. Now they had converged again.

Guy took out the Jack of Diamonds. "We used this that night at the Garde," he said.

"The Jack of Diamonds," said Blackstone. "Symbolic of patience. One of the great things in life. We must learn to wait. We must believe that we may get what we desire, given the right place and the right opportunity."

"Maybe this is the right place and opportunity, Mr. Blackstone?"

"Maybe, Guy. Maybe. I confess I rather like the idea of someone I inspired as a boy coming to work for me. It seems right. What did you have in mind?"

"Anything. I worked for almost a year right here at the Morosco as a stagehand. I know the ropes. I love the theater and I love magic. I'll haul props. I'll fix things. Of course I'd love to be an assistant on stage."

"Ah, yes. The lure of the lights and all that." Blackstone laughed. "If they could bottle up the magic of the footlights, Guy, folks would buy it more than booze. It's the ultimate intoxicant. Once you taste it, you can't get enough."

Blackstone looked again at the Jack of Diamonds Guy clutched in his hand like it was some sort of religious talisman. Perhaps it was.

"Life is funny, Guy. Funny indeed. It just so happens I have an assistant in the show who was recently offered another job. He's stayed on until I find a replacement. Now here you are, out of the blue, a young man interested in magic, on my stage, hoping to be one of my assistants. Who am I to ignore what fate seems to have ordained?

"Even the devil there agrees. That card sticking out of his mouth, the Three of Hearts. It symbolizes opportunity, the chance for betterment one should never overlook. The evening is full of portents!

"You'll need to be trained, of course. And I make no guarantees. We'll give you a shot. If you do well, you can join the troupe. If you don't, you will have to have more patience and wait for something else to come your way. Agreed?"

Guy was so surprised, and so thrilled, he could only nod.

"Good. Talk to my troupe manager Pete tomorrow morning. He can start teaching you what to do. You do well, we'll see about letting you assist in the real magic Understood?"

Guy nodded again.

Blackstone began fiddling around with some of the props on the table, checking the loads, adjusting a few things, making sure the tools of his trade were all set and ready for him. Guy used to do the same in the carnival. Magic is magic.

"I'll treat you fair and square, Guy. All I ask is that you be loyal. Don't steal and peddle my secrets around like Robinson did, okay?"

"Mr. Blackstone, I promise you the one thing I won't do is steal your secrets."

Guy said it with such force that Blackstone looked up at him.

"A magician did that to me the first time I was in New York. Right here, in fact. A magician named Chen Woo."

"Chen Woo. I've never heard of him."

"He was a better thief than magician. I showed him an idea I came up with and he stole it. Made it the centerpiece of his act in South America."

"That's a shame, Guy. But, you know, there's a lot of that in magic. A fellow sees a trick and runs out and tries to copy it."

"Maybe, Mr. Blackstone. But this wasn't something anybody had ever done. It was a new trick, totally unique. It was my idea. Mine. And he stole it."

"That must have hurt."

"Yeah. It hurt. And I hate Woo for doing it."

"You ever tell him? Confront him?"

"No. He disappeared. I never saw him again. It's been years. I haven't seen his name mentioned anywhere lately, so I guess he's retired or dead."

Blackstone gave Guy a long look. The boy he had taught a coin trick to over a milkshake was now a young man, a young man who carried a bitter grudge in his heart.

"Well, you never know, Guy. Maybe you'll run into Woo again someday."

"Maybe. I'm patient," said Guy, looking at the Jack of Diamonds in his hand and then putting it away. Blackstone fiddled with a final bit of apparatus, adjusting a mirror.

"Well, everything looks set for tomorrow's show. I always check. One time someone forgot to put the loads in my production cabinet. I reached in and it was empty. Quite embarrassing. A magician is supposed to fool the audience, not himself."

"What did you do?"

Blackstone chuckled. "I raised my hand up as if I were holding something and said: 'Look what I have here: an invisible rabbit!'"

"Good recovery," said Guy.

"I thought so," said Blackstone. "But it taught me to check everything carefully. I'll do it again just before show time. Habit." Blackstone grew serious.

"One more thing, Guy."

"Yes?"

"While you're with my show, I don't want you performing professionally on your own. I'm the star here, and no good comes of having half my troupe out there doing their own shows, not that you'll have much time."

"I understand, Mr. Blackstone."

"Welcome to the 1001 Wonders show, Guy."

Guy shook the master magician's hand. He followed Blackstone off the back of the stage and down the corridor to the dressing rooms and exit door. Russ was sitting on a stool.

"Hi, Russ. This is a new kid in the act, Guy Borden."

Russ didn't let on they'd already met. He said a quiet "hello."

"Well, time to go home and show the missus some magic," said Blackstone with a wink.

"Can I close up until rehearsal?" asked Russ.

"Sure thing, Russ, See you later."

Guy and Harry left by the stage door. They stood on the sidewalk and looked up at the marquee, blazing bright. "1001 Wonders, Harry Blackstone, World's Greatest Magician." It was the same as it had been that night at the Garde, almost a decade earlier. The light went off.

"That will happen to my career someday," Blackstone said quietly.

The two men, master and apprentice, were left in the darkness of a cold New York night.

55

Blackstone's magic show was a time-consuming extravaganza. It was tightly choreographed and staged, a masterful production. Harry's brother Pete managed the show. There was a big cast, and the props and scenery were fantastic. It was one of the last great magic shows. It was true theater, a long way from the bar mitzvahs and carnival tent where Guy had played.

It was electric, exhilarating, challenging, exhausting. Within a month, Guy was on stage, dressed something like a bellhop, carrying out trays to Blackstone, sometimes secreting a load into a box or surreptitiously stealing away a dove at the end of a trick.

Ten years earlier, Blackstone had called him up from the audience to help with the card sword trick. Back then, Guy had been in the spotlight and the center of attention, even if for only a few minutes. Now, as an assistant to the world's greatest magician, he was at the edge of the spotlight, tantalizingly close, but not quite in it. He vowed to someday take the few steps it would take to make him the star.

Guy studied Blackstone as he performed. With authority and humor and consummate showmanship, Blackstone spun his world of wonder. Every element of the show contributed to the fantasy: the magician, the stories, the props, the costumes, the lighting, the music, the sequencing of tricks to create rhythm and texture to the performance. Though Guy had honed his acts over the years, they paled in comparison to Blackstone's. While Guy's shows had been a "regular carnival of fun," Blackstone's lived up to its billing of "1001 Wonders."

The show played to full houses night after night. Guy's schedule accommodated that of the show: up late, errands and chores during the morning, an hour every afternoon practicing his sleights and routines. He kept at the Mummy Asrah, which he had slowly begun to master and make into a trick that would not embarrass. Late afternoon he went to the theater for a cast meeting and review by Blackstone. Then dinner and the show. Some nights there was a party or a late night trip to a club. Saturdays usually found Guy at Tannen's, in the back room with the boys. On off nights, Guy often joined Vernon for dinner and more talk about magic.

After the show one night, Blackstone was making his way to the stage door. He passed the open doorway to the dressing room Guy shared with several other cast members. There was Guy, alone, standing in front of a mirror practicing a coin trick.

Harry watched as Guy did it over and over, adjusting the timing a bit here, the angle of his hands and arms there. Guy was lost in his world, oblivious to the presence of the master magician. Blackstone hoped his young son, Harry, Jr., would be so passionate about magic someday. Maybe even carry on the act.

After a few minutes, Blackstone said quietly, "Do you practice every day, Guy?" Guy was startled. He turned and smiled.

"I try to. At home. Here. Whenever I get the chance. Whenever I'm near a mirror."

Guy went through his moves again, a graceful series of gestures, sleights and revelations. Blackstone smiled. This kid had a lot of determination. A deep passion for the art of magic. He reminded him of himself. Blackstone put on his hat and buttoned his overcoat.

"Good night, Guy."

"Good night Mr. Blackstone."

As he left the theater, Harry stopped to say goodnight to Russ.

"Don't let the kid stay here all night, Russ. Kick him out in a half hour or so."

"Will do, Mr. Blackstone."

"What's that on your shoulder, Russ?"

"My shoulder?" asked Russ, surprised. He turned his head to look, but Harry Blackstone was already reaching up there. He drew his hand along Russ' shoulder and brought it around in front of the man, showing him a shiny silver dollar at his fingertips.

"You need to keep this someplace safer, Russ," Blackstone said, putting the dollar in the startled man's hand.

"Thank you, Mr. Blackstone!"

"Good night, Russ. Remember: get that kid out of here. He needs a life!"

Blackstone left the theater.

He did not notice the man across the street watching the stage door.

56

As he did many nights, Guy was setting up the props for the next show. He was alone. A single spotlight shone on center stage. Otherwise, the theater was dark. As he finished, his eye was drawn to Blackstone's top hat and wand. On a whim, Guy walked over, put it on. It fit him well. He picked up the wand and walked to center stage.

"Ladies and Gentlemen," he said to the empty theater.

"Tonight, I offer you wonder. I will present miracles that will make you believe that the impossible is possible. The common, the ordinary, the familiar will take on new meaning. I will open your eyes to the amazing, the unbelievable. Indeed, you may not believe your eyes. You may doubt, but I will convince you. I will make you believers in wonder."

Guy bowed. And from the empty dark theater came clapping.

"Who's there?" asked Guy, embarrassed to be caught in his make-believe performance. He peered into the darkness, but could see no one. He was blinded by the light.

"Who is it?" he asked again, shielding his eyes. He saw someone come down the main aisle and stop at the front row. He still couldn't make out who it was.

"You forgot to mention the shaman in Peru, the fakirs of India, the blind monk in Tibet and the world's smartest bunny."

He recognized the voice. It was Rachel!

"Rachel?" he said, astonished.

"Yes, Guy."

"How long have you been here?"

"For the show. And long enough to see you still love magic."

"I can't see you. Step closer to the stage, into the light."

Rachel stepped forward, out of the shadows, back into his life. He walked to the steps and down off the stage. Rachel met him and they hugged.

"What are you doing in New York, Rachel?"

"I live here."

"You do?"

"Yes. Just for a few weeks now. I'm still getting settled. I have a little apartment in the garment district."

"What brought you to New York?" asked Guy, delighted to see Rachel again and even more so to hear she was living in the city.

"I'm working at Anne Klein's as a fashion designer."

"Your dream come true."

"My dream come true."

"How did that happen?" he asked. "Did someone see one of your dresses and recognize your talent?"

"Maybe, but I don't really know, Guy. A few months ago, out of the blue, I was offered a job here by Anne Klein. She's revolutionizing how young women dress, you know. I took the job. I had no choice, really. An opportunity like this doesn't come along for a small town girl very often. I'm still pinching myself."

"What good fortune! And you have no idea how a fashion house in New York would have heard of you?"

"Not really. Like you said, maybe someone from Liberty happened to come to New York wearing one of my outfits. Maybe someone from Klein saw it, asked her who designed it, and it lead to the offer. I don't know. I don't care. I only know my dream has come true."

"Now you're here, Angela takes care of your father?"

"Yes, she lives nearby. She may move in with him soon. If it weren't for Angela, I never could have come here."

"So then you decided you missed me so you came to a magic show?"

Rachel laughed. "I had no idea you were in the city, Guy. I got the ticket to this show in the mail a few days ago. I don't know who sent it to me. I remembered you liked Blackstone, so I came. I was surprised and delighted to see you on stage."

"You must have a guardian angel, Rachel."

"Well, I have felt like a higher power has been guiding my destiny. It makes me think all my father's preaching about the Lord and how he looks after us might be true."

She smiled her dazzling smile.

"It's so good to see you, Guy. I've missed you. It's been two years. It seems you're living your dream, too."

"Well, I've been very lucky, too. Especially since I got to New York. Things have fallen into place for me. But I'm not the star of the show; I'm just an assistant."

"You looked good on stage. But I missed seeing you perform. You were good."

"I miss it, too. But I'm learning a lot. Getting experience in a stage show. And I'm making some contacts. I'm trying to be patient."

"Have you performed on your own?"

"Yes, a while ago. With Irena. You remember, the tightrope walker in the carnival?"

"The Russian?"

"Yes, her."

"You two had a romance didn't you?"

"Sort of. Not real love."

"What has become of the tightrope walker turned magician's assistant?"

"I'm not sure. She left the act."

"Your choice?"

"No, hers. She was terrible and she knew it."

"How did you end up here in this show?"

"Luck. Fate. Who knows? I came to meet Blackstone, and it turned out he needed a new assistant. I showed up at just the right moment."

"Well," said Rachel. "Luck seems to have smiled on both of us."

"Never more than right now, Rachel. Seeing you here is the best thing to happen to me in years."

He leaned forward and kissed her.

"I'm pretty much finished getting things set for the next show. How about dinner? We'll get caught up?"

"Sounds good, Guy."

They left the theater and walked through the city.

"This looks good," said Guy when they came upon the *Lopergolo*, an Italian restaurant. "Small, quiet. Let's eat here."

The restaurant was cozy. When they were seated and they had placed their orders, Guy looked across the table at Rachel. He was so happy she was in New York. Her mismatched eyes sparkled in the dim candlelight. Maybe they could pick up their romance. He wasn't sure, and he didn't want to rush things.

"So, how is the pastor, your mother, your sister?"

As soon as he asked and saw the sad look play across Rachel's face, he knew something bad had happened.

"It's been a tough few years for us, Guy."

"If you don't want to talk …"

"No, I do. It's painful, but I want you to know."

Rachel picked up her fork and played with it. She stared into a glass of water, glowing from the candlelight on the table. He saw her focus shift back to her memories.

"It was a nice fall day not that long after the carnival left town. We were about to have lunch. Mom said she needed some bread. She said she'd run out to the corner store and get it. She told us she'd only be gone fifteen, maybe twenty minutes. She even set the kitchen timer, smiling at her own little joke. She waved from the car when she left.

"Dad, Angela and I sat around and talked as we waited for her. The timer reached zero and the bell sounded. No ma. We waited a half hour. Still no ma. An hour. That sick feeling of dread started to creep in. A little while later there was knock on the door. It was the police.

"Mother was killed by a drunk driver who hit her head-on a few blocks from home. She died instantly. He survived.

"It was such a shock! No warning. No illness. No time to prepare yourself for the inevitable. Life can change so fast, Guy! In a blink. She went out for a loaf of bread and never came back."

"My God, Rachel! How terrible. I can't imagine."

"No, it's beyond imagining, Guy. Even when we heard, we couldn't believe it. We were sure she would walk in the door any minute."

Rachel wiped away a tear.

"Father barely spoke he was so shocked. He immediately pushed away the horror and the pain and started making funeral plans. He might as well have made it for two. He all but died with that knock on the door. He's a ghost. He never cried. He never let on how much he hurt. I tried to talk to him, but he just said: 'It is the Lord's will.' That's what he said, but I don't know. I would catch him just staring out the window, lost in thought. I think he was trying to figure out his Lord."

"I'm so sorry," Guy said again. "I only met her that once, but I liked her a lot. She seemed loving and kind and playful."

"Thanks, Guy. She liked you, too."

"And your father? How is he now?"

"He lives with his doubts. The Lord took his brothers and the Lord took his wife, and father must find it in himself to believe there was a reason. I'm not sure he will. So much of what he has loved has been taken that it's left his heart empty."

"How did he lose his brothers?'

"One died as a child. He and father were playing at a pond and his brother drowned. Father tried to save him but couldn't. I don't think he's ever forgiven himself."

"And the other?"

Guy thought he saw Rachel shudder just a moment.

"The other died in the war."

Guy was silent a few moments, trying to absorb all Rachel had told him. He shook his head.

"So terrible," he said. "And it must make it even harder that the man who did it lived."

Rachel nodded. "Yes, it does. My father's faith tells him he should forgive the man. But I think his heart, or what's left of it, is full of hate. So he's at war with himself. Forgive or hate? A hard choice."

"And what about you, Rachel?"

"Me? I never had my father's strong faith, Guy. Not every pastor's daughter is as devout as her father, you know. I think the Lord looks the other way far too much. I think He is powerless against evil. I wish the bastard who killed my mother had died. So, you see, I have hate in my heart."

"I think that's only natural, Rachel."

She shook her head.

"I have too much hatred in my heart, Guy. I wish I could rid myself of it. It's corrosive. But I've been hurt."

"By a man who took someone you loved."

"Yes." There was a long pause. "And by others," she said, barely above a whisper.

"Others?"

Rachel looked away. Sighed.

"We all have secrets, Guy. All of us. For you, it's how your tricks are done. For my father, his doubts about faith. And, I …" her voice trailed off.

A troubled look played across her face. She looked at Guy, then down at her hands, then back at Guy. When she spoke, it was a whisper.

"I have a secret, too, Guy. A painful one. I've never told anyone."

She looked at him. He saw the pain in her eyes. And tears. One escaped and made its way down her cheek. She wiped it away.

"I want to tell you, Guy. Because it's been in me so long, I have to let it out. Then it won't be a secret. It won't be a poison anymore. And I want to tell you because I like you Guy. Maybe more than like. So I want you to know."

Guy steeled himself. He had no idea what Rachel's secret might be. He knew sharing it was hard, and he wondered if she would be a different person to him once he knew. That was a risk, of course. That's why people often keep secrets, because once their secret is out, they change in people's eyes.

Rachel sighed, and, head down, began her story.

"My father's brother, the one who died in the war, was a few years older than the pastor. My father worshiped him. I think when his younger brother died as a kid, father directed all his love to his older brother. He lived nearby and visited often. Sometimes, he even babysat my sister and me."

She stopped. Looked up at Guy. He could see her jaw clench, and he noticed her hands were clenched too.

There was another long pause. It was excruciating.

"You can tell me, Rachel. Whatever it is, you can tell me."

She looked down at the table. She could not meet his eyes.

"He touched me, Guy. He touched me in ways that no grown man should ever touch a girl. And he made me … touch him. I hated it. I hated him. He warned me that if I told anyone I would be punished. By him and, worse, by the Lord. I was scared. So I said nothing. I had to sit at family dinners while father talked of goodness with this evil man at the table. He wore a mask of kindness, but I knew the monster behind the mask. I learned early that people are not always what they seem."

She gave a bitter laugh. "Most people are magicians of sorts, creating illusions. At least magicians are honest about their deceptions."

"What happened?" asked Guy quietly.

"He went to war. The Pacific. Like mother, he never came back. They say he was captured by the Japanese. I hope he was. I heard they are savages and brutalize their prisoners."

She looked up at Guy, and he saw the hatred through her tears.

"I was cheated out of my vengeance, but he got what he deserved. The monster was dead."

Guy thought about what she'd said. He wanted to ask her a question. He wasn't sure how to phrase it. He decided to make it more of a statement and see how she responded.

"I'm surprised you don't hate all men."

She dried her tears. "No, Guy. I don't. I know that most men aren't like my uncle. He was a freak."

Guy winced. He didn't like it when people used the word "freak." It was always used negatively. He knew better. He let it pass.

"If I am a bit slow to romance and intimacy, don't take it personally, Guy. I live with a memory that sometimes gets in the way."

He smiled, reached out and took hold of one of her hands. He noticed she was trembling. "Believe me, Rachel, I understand. I have some troublesome memories, too."

"Thank you, Guy. Just be patient with me."

"I will." Her confession had touched him. He wanted to hug her and try to make her forget her dark memories. Rachel shook her head as if to cast off the pain. She met his eyes at last and, perhaps seeing the compassion and love in them, smiled.

"Well, Guy, now you know the darkest secret of my life. I feel better having told someone. Having told *you*, Guy. Sharing a secret brings people together, right?"

"Yes, it does, Rachel. I'm glad you trust me so much."

"And you don't think less of me for what happened?"

"Of course not. What could you do? You were a kid; he was a grown man. He betrayed a basic trust. At least he's gone. You're done with him. Forever."

"Yes, and no. We are bound to those we hate by our hatred," she said. "I'm not sure we ever escape."

Guy recalled Willis in his cage. "True. So true."

They held hands across the table. In the short hour they had been together, they had opened their hearts and bared their souls.

"Enough of this dark talk, Rachel. Enough about the past. How about the future? Here we are, together again. Do you think we can pick up where we left off?"

Rachel gave Guy an appraising look.

"How do I know you won't run off with the carnival again?"

"A guy only does that once, Rachel. At least *this* Guy."

They laughed at his joke.

"It was hard to leave you, you know. I wasn't sure I had made the right choice. Not at all. A few times, I almost jumped off that carnival train and came back to you."

"But you didn't."

"No. My life had, I don't know … momentum. I was like the train I was on, speeding onward, locked onto a track."

"I almost followed you."

"But you didn't."

"No. I had my life, too. It's hard to change. Especially hard to run off with a carnival. A circus, maybe. But not a carnival." She laughed and Guy did too.

"Do you think we're destined to be together?" Rachel asked, her mismatched eyes sparkling now, with a hint of mischief in them.

"Let's see if it's in the cards, Rachel." He took out a deck of cards, shuffled them and put the deck on the table.

"Okay. Let's see. Go ahead, cut them."

Rachel cut the cards and turned the packet in her hand so the bottom card showed. It was the Two of Hearts. Again. Just as it had been that night she helped him in his act.

"The Two of Hearts!" exclaimed Rachel. "I can't believe it."

Guy was stunned. "Yes, the Two. Romance. The meeting and joining of two souls," he said, shaking his head in disbelief. "It seems to be our card."

Rachel cocked her head.

"Now that wouldn't be a force, would it?" she asked. "You didn't happen to do any fancy sleights to make that card come up, did you?"

"No, no I didn't. Honestly. I'm as surprised as you are."

"Hmmm. So our souls have met and our souls will join?"

"They will if I have any choice in the matter," said Guy.

Rachel picked up her wine glass.

"To the magician's choice," she said.

57

As Guy walked along East 53rd on his way to the Stork Club, he glanced across the street. There, standing in the glow of a neon sign, was a large man holding a pocket watch. Willie Jenks! Guy bolted across the street, dodging taxicabs. He bounded on to the sidewalk and ran up to the man. He grabbed him by the arm and spun him around.

"Okay, Jenks, I have you ..."

It was not Willie Jenks.

"Hey, pal, what the hell are you doing?" yelled the startled stranger.

"I ... I ... I thought you were someone else."

"Well, I'm not someone else and you better get yourself some *place* else fast or I'll call the police," the man snarled.

"Sorry," said Guy.

Jenks. Woo. His hatred for them was like those embers he had told Willis about. Still glowing hot. Still burning him.

He arrived at the Stork Club and joined Vernon at his table. Dai, as always, was fiddling with a coin. He made it vanish and turned his hands over, showing both empty. Then he closed one in a fist, waved the other over it, and when he opened his fist, the coin was back.

Guy told him about Rachel.

"So you say your girl—what's her name, Phoebe?"

"Rachel."

"Rachel is in town?"

"That's right, Dai. She got offered a job at Anne Klein, the fashion designer, so she moved up here."

"That's swell, kid. Your stars are in alignment. Is she pretty?"

"Very."

"You gonna marry her?"

"I don't know, Dai. I think so. I hope so."

"Well, don't wait too long to ask her, Guy. This is a big city. Full of wolves. They'll be after her. Don't let her get away."

Guy nodded. Without thinking about it, he took out his Morgan dollar and did his Retention Vanish—two men casually making coins disappear and reappear as they talked.

"And how's it going with Blackstone?"

"Pretty good, Dai. I'm just an assistant. But I'm part of a big show. It's exciting."

"Yeah, Harry's okay. How long have you been with him?"

"Over six months now."

"Well, don't stay too long." Dai lost control of his coin and it bounced off the table onto the floor.

"They don't like to be dropped," said Guy.

Vernon snorted. "I drop 'em better than anybody." He bent over and picked up the coin and went back to his sleights.

"Six months. Time flies! Maybe it's time to move on, Guy. Harry will understand. Kids are always leaving his show. Especially to be with their sweethearts. Take what you've learned from Blackstone and me. Work up a new act. See if you can talk that pretty girl of yours into helping. Get some gigs at swanky parties, like I told you. Maybe I can find you a few. You have talent, Guy. And dedication. And ambition. All the ingredients for success."

"And luck, Dai. I seem to have been having great luck since I came back to New York."

"Yes, there's that. Talent and ambition and all the rest aren't always enough. You do need luck. Sometimes you make it; sometimes it's made for you. They say luck is when opportunity meets preparedness. You can't always create the opportunity, but you can be prepared to seize it if it comes your way. Maybe you ought to ride your luck before it runs out."

"Something to think about," said Guy.

"Yes it is," said Vernon. He waved at a table where an elderly man was dining with a stunning young blond.

"Talk about luck," said Vernon.

"Or illusions," said Guy.

58

For the next few weeks, his conversation with Vernon rattled around in Guy's mind. As he stood on stage with Blackstone, Guy didn't want to be at the edge of the spotlight any longer. He longed to be in it.

Guy watched Blackstone perform and could see himself the star of a different kind of show. Not 1001 Wonders; maybe only twenty. Twenty amazing illusions woven into a seamless story of wonder. A story that would build, miracle upon miracle. It would be *his* show.

He had apprenticed with a master, but Vernon was right: it was time to strike out on his own. A fortune cookie he'd gotten at the Ping Toy seemed to confirm, in its oblique way, Vernon's advice:

"You cannot discover new oceans unless you are willing to lose sight of the shore."

At the end of the show's run at the Morosco, when the troupe was about to head out on the road, Guy asked Blackstone if he could speak to him. He told Harry how honored he was to be a part of the show, how much he had learned. He told him about Rachel being in New York, and how they wanted to create their own show. He shared some of Vernon's advice. Finally, he told Blackstone he wanted to leave his show.

Blackstone did not seem surprised.

"You have the passion, Guy. I sensed it that day in the coffee shop. That's why I sent you the Mysto magic set. I've seen it here. You are a talented young man. You've had Vernon and me to learn from. But Dai is right. Go out. Find your character, your destiny. Create an act that is you."

"You don't mind?"

"No, I don't Guy. Unless you steal my tricks."

"I'd never do that, Harry. I told you about Chen Woo stealing mine. The only thing I want to take from you is the desire to be great."

Blackstone studied Guy a moment.

"Magic needs guys like you, Guy. Magicians who really care about the art. Who have new ideas, but respect the past. Truth is, you're wasted here handing me trays and loading boxes."

"Thanks, Harry. I'll try to make you proud. I won't steal your tricks and I won't try to get your bookings."

"Guy, I'm not worried about competition. By the time you've developed your act, had your successes and failures, given it all up and come back, and maybe, with luck, made a name for yourself, I'll probably be retired."

Blackstone put his hand on Guy's shoulder. He fixed him with a penetrating stare.

"Promise me one thing, Guy."

"Yes?"

"No matter how it goes, don't lose the passion. Don't let the business get you down. Don't let the hacks depress you or discourage you from what you want to do."

"I won't."

"It's a tough life, Guy, no getting around that. But here's the thing: if you love what you do, you are blessed. Most folks don't. Most folks hate their jobs, or never find something in life they can be passionate about. We're lucky. Remember that when your act falters, or you don't get a booking or somebody doesn't pay you. Live for the art and the rest will take care of itself."

"Thanks, Harry. I've always admired you. Always taken your advice. That's why I got so good with the Retention Vanish. You taught me how to do it and you told me to practice it a lot."

Blackstone smiled. "That's right. Practice. Practice till your hands bleed."

The world's greatest magician walked off the stage and disappeared into the shadows like an illusion.

Guy watched him go. He looked at the tables full of props. He'd miss Blackstone and his show. Guy walked down the stairs at the front of the stage and up the long aisle. His hand brushed and lovingly caressed the red velvet seats as he passed them. He parted the curtains at the back and left 1001 Wonders behind.

59

They were having lunch and Vernon was talking.

"I've been thinking, Guy. I'm your mentor, right? You're on your own again, now. You want to perform. A parlor show, right?"

"Yes, Dai. You told me it was time for me to leave Blackstone so I did and now I'm trying to figure out what to do next."

"Well, kid, you have to think about the differences in the scale of shows. I do mostly close-up. The tabletop is my stage. Maybe five or ten people. Parlor is bigger: maybe twenty, maybe fifty. It depends on how big the parlor is, I guess. You can use an assistant. So long as she doesn't look constipated. That's important. Maybe your girl could help you. If you love her and she loves you, like I told you before, it will show. And you can turn a parlor show into a stage show much easier, too, if you really want to try to make it to the big time."

"I want to make it big, Dai. Someday. I want to see my name on a marquee, like Blackstone. Do you think it could happen?"

"Who knows? The world is full of marquees, Guy. With luck, your name will be on one. Is that really important to you?"

"It's a sign of achievement, isn't it? It shows you've made it."

"Maybe. But not for everyone. Not so much for me. Like I told you before, I like to see the wonder in people's faces after I do a trick. You can see that best doing close-up magic. In a theater, you can barely see anybody with the spotlights in your eyes. You know they're out there, somewhere in the darkness, but you can't see their astonishment or their smiles."

"You hear their applause."

"Sure, there's that. But people applaud at a dog show, too. I love to be close to people, to be close enough to look them in the eye and see that look of wonder. And that look says it better than foot-high letters on a marquee. I don't tell people I'm the 'World's Greatest Magician,' Guy. They tell me. But to each his own."

Guy wondered if he would ever be able to go beyond the allure of fame to the purity of craft that made Vernon so happy.

Dai moved on.

"You have that new girl, right?"

"Yes, Rachel."

"Good. So you are going to work up an act with her?"

"Yes, she's agreed, so long as it doesn't interfere with her work. So, nights and weekends. We need to start small and get some experience."

"Good. Patience. Patience is important, you know."

"That's what the Jack says," said Guy.

"Jack? Jack who?"

"The Jack of Diamonds. I helped Blackstone in a show when I was a kid. Got me started on magic. The Jack of Diamonds was the card in the trick. He told me the Jack of Diamonds means patience."

Vernon nodded. "Yes, it does. You have to be patient when it comes to a career. It takes time. You have to pay your dues. You've already made some pretty good down payments. All those shows at the carnival for a bunch of ogling rubes. All those nights at the bar doing your wonderful Retention Vanish for an audience of two bleary-eyed drunks and a bored whore."

"Don't forget the Spellman bar mitzvah."

"Right. King Nosmo and the Constipated Russian. Don't remind me."

"And my time with Blackstone."

"Yes, you and Harry and 1001 Wonders. You've got some experience, and you've had the best mentor in the world. So listen to me ..."

"I always do, Dai."

"Don't waste your time and talent on bars or bar mitzvahs. They'll eat you alive. Go for high society. For the rich folk. All you need is a good suit. And I mean a good one. Nothing shabby or cheap. You gotta have class and elegance to work that crowd. They judge folks by their appearance more often than not. Same with Ann ..."

"Rachel."

"Right. Rachel. She needs to dress elegantly. A little spicy, maybe, to help with her misdirecton, but not trampy. She can't look tawdry. So dress up, but don't wear costumes.

"I had a club show—the Harlequin Act—named after the costume I wore. I wore a shiny checked top and tights. I looked like a court jester. But I never liked it. It's not me, you know, and if you can't be yourself when you are acting the part of a magician, then it's not an authentic deception and you're a phony, if you know what I mean."

Vernon was starting to sound a bit like Irena. Scary thing was, Guy *did* understand him.

"So dress classy and show them your best tricks. You don't need 1001. Just eight or ten that you do perfectly. That will knock their fine silk socks off. And charge them a lot."

Vernon took another sip of his drink. Waved to an elderly woman dripping in diamonds. "Mrs. Ferciot," said Vernon. "Fine woman. Beautiful apartment on Fifth Avenue. I worked her eightieth. Quite a night. She's a rascal. What was I saying?"

"Charge them a lot."

"Right! If you don't charge enough, they won't think you're good. Rich people think that way. It's not about the money, it's about their perceptions of value. If they say you're young, ask them if they can do what you can do. But be careful. I got burned once."

"You?"

"Yes, Guy, me. I wanted a bundle of money for a fancy party Rockefeller was giving. He thought I might be a little wet behind the ears to be asking so much. I wasn't Houdini, after all. Just a guy who'd fooled him. Did I ever tell you they called me The Man Who Fooled Houdini?

"Anyway, I looked Rocky in the eye, and I said magic is not so easy, and I made him an offer. I said if he could do what I did, if he could fool me with a card trick, I'd do the party for free. Pretty ballsy, eh? Well, the joke was on me. I should have learned from Houdini. He did a card trick. I was fooled. How did I know he knew a card trick I'd never seen? He asked me how it was done. I had no clue. Can you imagine that? Fooled by John D. Rockefeller! Can you see *his* marquee: Rockefeller: The Man Who Fooled the Man Who Fooled Houdini. Unbelievable!

"Well, what could I do? I did the show for his party, for free. He loved it. Afterwards, he gave me this …"

Dai reached into his vest pocket and pulled out a beautiful twenty dollar gold coin.

"I keep this, Guy, to remind me that even the fooler can get fooled. To remind me not to make bets with people who have built empires. They know more than you think they know.

"You know what the kicker is? I asked him how he did the trick, and he wouldn't tell me! He told me you are never supposed to reveal the secret to a trick, which he knew I knew, but he was just screwing with me. John D. was like that. That's why he was so good at business. He learned your game and beat you at it.

"So here's the moral of the story, Guy. Go for the rich and the mighty. And watch out who you make a bet with."

"Can you help me get some private parties for the rich people?" Guy asked. He gestured around the club. "For these people?"

Dai stopped eating his steak.

"These people are *my* people, Guy. I work for them. I can't just hand them over to you. I'm your mentor. Not a fool."

"I know, Dai. But maybe there will be a show you don't want to do. Or you have a cold or something. Or maybe you will be out of town. Or …"

"Okay, relax, kid. Simmer down. I'll keep it in mind. There are some shows I get offered and don't want to do. Some folks I don't want to work for. Sometimes I throw a gig some other guy's way if I can't or don't want to do it. But I have to be careful. This is a tough racket. Somebody's always trying to eat your lunch."

As if to emphasize his point, Vernon speared a potato from Guy's plate.

"You've got to watch magicians, Guy. Some of them are real thieves. They'll take your tricks, your routines, hell, everything you say word for word. Damned vultures."

Guy knew exactly what Vernon was talking about.

"I'd appreciate anything you can do, Dai. I just need a break."

"Sure, Guy, I understand," said Vernon. "You gonna eat that other potato?" Before he could answer, Vernon stabbed Guy's potato and continued:

"You need a name for your act, Guy. Not King Nosmo. New act. New girl. New name."

"Any ideas, Dai?"

"Nope. Maybe you should go pee. Maybe you'll find inspiration again."

"I don't think so Dai."

"Well, is there someplace you've been or someone you've met or something that we could work with?"

Guy thought a moment.

"Well, when I was a kid, Blackstone sent me a Gilbert Mysto Magic Set. It came with a poster that said the show was a 'carnival of fun. With wizardry, legerdemain and prestidigitation.' So maybe I could call it my 'Carnival of Fun' or 'Guy Borden's Wizardry, Legerdemain and Prestidigitation'?"

"Jesus, Guy, how big a marquee are you planning on? But, wait, I have an idea: how about 'Mysto'? Then you could put under that, smaller: 'The Magic of Guy Borden and Rachel.'"

Guy smiled. He loved the name, and he loved that it would be a reminder of Blackstone's gift. Of his very first set of tricks.

"Perfect!" he said.

Vernon beamed as he finished Guy's lunch.

60

They had a name for the new act. They had plenty of tricks to choose from. Dai had met Rachel and told Guy she was not only pretty but "exotic."

"Her eyes don't match, Guy. That's distracting and exotic. You may not have to do much magic."

They got their first gig through Vernon. They had been practicing their act for weeks when he called.

Sidney Calabash was having a birthday party for his wife and wanted something different. There would be 100 people gathered in his mansion on Park Avenue. It was too big a crowd for Vernon, who also claimed he was coming down with a cold. He thought it was just right for Guy and Rachel's parlor show. He asked them to show him their act, and they did. He sat and watched it quietly, sniffling, helping out when Guy needed someone from the audience. When they were done, they looked at Dai expectantly.

"Well, what do you think?" asked Guy. "Are we good enough to get the job?"

"I think you'll kill 'em!" Vernon said, jumping up and clapping his hands together. "You two are terrific together. You got yourself a pretty girl, Guy, and she's not constipated. You two have chemistry. You work together like you're dancing. Yeah, you'll knock 'em dead."

Guy and Rachel were thrilled.

"Don't forget: charge 'em a lot. And don't make any bets!"

They arrived at the mansion two hours ahead of time. The main ballroom had been set theater style, and there was even a small stage cobbled together for them. They could hear the party going full bore downstairs in another ballroom. A band played, there was laughter, a general hubbub.

As they set up, they were nervous. They were being paid very well, and how well they performed would reflect on Vernon, who'd referred them. They would be playing to some of the biggest names in the New York social scene. This one show could make or break their fledgling career.

Guy was wearing more than a good suit. He was wearing impeccably tailored tails, white gloves and a top hat. He *looked* like what people expected a magician to look like. Rachel was stunning in a silver gown she had designed.

At eight o'clock sharp, the double doors slid open and a crowd of people swirled in.

"Show time," muttered Guy under his breath.

"What have we gotten ourselves into, Guy?" whispered Rachel.

"Just relax. And smile your lovely smile. It's the best misdirection I have. And I need it! I hope I'm up to this."

"Guy, do you remember that night when we were walking around the carnival and the calliope was playing 'Paper Moon'?"

"Yes, I do."

"And you told me the lyrics?"

"Yes."

Rachel softly sang:

It's a Barnum and Bailey world
Just as phony as it can be
But it wouldn't be make-believe
If you believed in me.

"You'll be great, Guy. I believe in you. I love you."

They exchanged a quick kiss, and waited for the crowd to settle down. Guy looked out at the people, at the men dressed in tuxedos, at the women in their stylish gowns. These weren't country bumpkins; they were the cream of New York society. He soaked up the atmosphere of the place, the opulence. They were here to watch him do magic. This was a real show. *His* show. Guy had waited a long, long time for this moment. He had practiced for it in front of his bedroom mirror, on the empty Morosco stage, behind that wall in Africa, in countless performances in the carnival tent and even at the depressing Ritz bar. At this moment, Guy was all that experience. He was poised to show them a regular carnival of fun, a night of wizardry, legerdemain and prestidigitation.

It was time to show them some wonder.

Guy Borden stepped forward. He took off his top hat, held up his magic wand, and began the show.

He floated through the act, relaxed and calm, performing his tricks with confidence, spinning tales that would have made Archie Walters proud. He milked the moment of magic as Blackstone had advised, and did his tricks naturally, following Vernon's sage coaching. He saw the wonder in their eyes, and he thrilled to their applause.

Rachel was charming, gracious and graceful. She played to the crowd, being just a bit saucy, a bit coy, and thoroughly enchanting. She was a natural. They loved her. The sparkle in her eyes and the smile on her face when she and Guy interacted was obvious to all.

They were in love, and it showed. When they finished, the audience stood and cheered them. It was intoxicating.

That night, Guy and Rachel made love for the first time. The magic they had ignited in that ballroom burned hot in the bedroom. They found their own private wonder.

61

Guy and Rachel's Mysto show was a hit. Not just that night at the Calabash's, but every time they performed it. Word spread quickly through the circle of New York high society. The bookings started to come in. They began to make a reputation for themselves.

Something else came out of that first show. Something quite unexpected. The elegant silver gown Rachel had designed attracted the attention of one wealthy woman. She wanted something unique and special to wear to the opening of an opera at the Met. She asked Rachel about her gown. When she learned Rachel had designed it, she asked if she could create one for the opening. Rachel did. It was a hit. Another woman commissioned another gown, and soon Rachel found herself creating one-of-a-kind dresses and gowns for some very rich patrons. Following Dai's advice to Guy, she charged a lot. She left Anne Klein and started "Rachel's," her own, very exclusive, fashion shop.

Guy and Rachel became a part of the society scene. They frequented the clubs with Dai and his wife, Jean. Guy spent Saturdays at Tannen's, sometimes even performing himself as the other guys looked on.

On Halloween night, Guy and Rachel were performing for Allen Kaufman at his home in Brooklyn. It was a masked ball. Both Guy and Rachel found it a bit unsettling. It reminded Guy of the eerie, disturbing masks at the strange booth at the carnival. It reminded Rachel of her uncle, who hid his sick desires behind a mask of decency and family love. Watching the partygoers, Rachel said to Guy: "No masks for us, Guy, ever. Let's be honest with each other and never hide behind lies."

"Agreed, my love. Our only deceptions will be on stage."

At the end of their show, Guy quieted the applauding audience.

"I have a final trick to perform tonight," he said. "A kind of encore." Rachel looked at him with curiosity. She had no idea what he was up to. This was not part of their act. Guy took a lump of coal out of his pocket and showed it to Mr. Kaufman.

"An ordinary lump of coal, is it not?" Guy asked.

"It is," said Kaufman.

Guy put the coal into his palm and closed his fist around it. He reached into his pocket and came out with some fine gold powder, which he sprinkled over his fist.

"Magic dust," he said. "Now watch."

Guy held his arm out and stared at it. "Oed Zem Boujad," he intoned. "Oed Zem Boujad."

Slowly, very slowly, he uncurled his fingers. Resting on his palm was a beautiful diamond ring. A gasp went through the crowd. Rachel gawked at it, stunned.

Turning to Rachel, Guy got down on one knee and said:

"Rachel, you are the magic of my life. You are my assistant, my muse, my love. This is no illusion, Rachel, it's real. I love you.

"Will you marry me?"

Rachel was speechless. The audience was silent with anticipation. Recovering her senses, Rachel smiled and said, simply, "Yes, Guy, I would love to marry you."

Guy slipped the ring on her finger and everybody applauded and cheered. As they kissed, one woman turned to another and said: "Now *that's* a proposal! When Teddy proposed to me he had just finished a polo match and came from the stables. All I remember is that he smelled like manure." She paused a moment. "Turns out, it was an omen."

Their wealthy host called for a round of champagne. When everybody was served he held his glass high and gave a toast:

"To our two young magicians. May their lives forever be filled with wonder!"

Rachel admired the ring on her finger, and as the audience began to come forward to offer congratulations, Guy said:

"The Two of Hearts, Rachel. Souls entwined. It was in the cards."

"Magician's Choice," she said and gave him a kiss.

When the evening finally ended, and after they dropped their props off, Rachel and Guy were still wound up from the excitement of their engagement. They decided to take a walk. Talking love, planning their future, giggling and giddy, they strolled through the night.

Half a block behind them, a man walked slowly, watching.

62

It was a rainy Friday afternoon in March. Bleak, cold, and windy. Thunder rumbled in the distance. Reverend Dowd unlocked the door to his church, shrugged off his coat, and made his way to the pulpit. He did not bother with the lights. The occasional flash of lightning illuminated the stained glass portraits of saints and God and Jesus. He looked out across the empty pews, the empty church.

In the gloom, he began his sermon.

"Many have been the times I have stood here and proclaimed that God works in mysterious ways, that it is not for us to question or to try to understand His plan. The arc of our lives, the events that are our fate, are His choice. Not ours.

"Brethren, I speak to you now as one who has seen the dark side, who has been tested by God as Job was tested. The prince of darkness has stolen my love, my life. And I must ask: Why does He allow the good to die and the evil to live? What God is this? I no longer recognize Him. I no longer feel the touch of His mercy. I no longer have faith that He will protect me, that His goodness will shine in my world.

"Has it ever shone?

"Where was He when my little brother died in the waters?

"Where was He when my older brother died in a dark and distant nightmare?

"Where was He when my wife went out to get bread, the very staff of life, and never returned?

"All that I have loved has been taken from me!

"My heart has been broken, broken by that very God to whom I devoted my life, to whom I have been a servant. Is this my reward in life? Death upon death upon death?"

Dowd looked down at the pulpit, his eyes full of tears, his heart full of anguish. Faith and doubt warred within him, and this was the moment of their final battle for the pastor's soul.

"Perhaps I have been deceived, and in being so, I have deceived you. I always had faith in a just and merciful God. I believed the choice was mine, that seeing His work, I would embrace Him and, in turn, He would embrace me. But I know now that that was just an illusion. He does *not* care!

"So what do I have if I do not have faith? Who shall nourish my spirit in its darkest time? Where shall I turn for hope? To the Lord who has turned his back on me? Who has given me a greater burden than I can carry, who has broken me with his cargo of grief? Where do I turn? What do I have?"

Reverend Dowd stopped. He let the tears stream down his face. He clutched the pulpit until his knuckles turned white. He grasped it like a man might hold a bit of floating debris to keep himself from drowning after a shipwreck. As if expressing his anguish, thunder boomed and rain lashed at the windows. He rested his head on the pulpit, then raised it and slammed it down again. He looked up at the ceiling and yelled:

"I have *no* God. I have *no* faith. I have *nothing*!"

The pastor was sweating and exhausted. He gazed out at the church through eyes filled with tears. It was as dark and empty as his heart.

He let out a wail, a bloodcurdling scream that echoed across the vacant pews. It was as if in that scream he hoped to purge himself of his doubt, his grief, his anger.

Reverend Dowd collapsed behind the pulpit, lost in the shadows.

63

The frantic phone call from Angela had come at night. She told Rachel their father had had some sort of breakdown and a stroke and was failing quickly. She urged Rachel to come home immediately.

Rachel called Guy and they made plans to take the train south the next morning. As Guy packed, he saw the shoebox sitting on his closet shelf. He took it down and added it to his suitcase.

By midday, Guy found himself again on a train heading to an unknown. Rachel was subdued. Worried. Lost in thought. He left her to her reflections. It took until night to reach Liberty, South Carolina.

Angela met them at the station and drove them to the hospital. She filled them in. The pastor was found in the empty church Friday night, collapsed, mumbling incoherently, stricken. He had been taken to the hospital. The doctors said he had suffered a massive stroke, and while responsive, there was little they could do for him. They did not expect him to recover. When they got to the hospital, they were met by a nurse.

"He doesn't have long," she said. "You best spend what time you can with him."

When Rachel and Guy went into the pastor's room, they were shocked. The strong, vibrant man they were used to looked old, frail, gaunt. His mouth was open, his breathing labored. Rachel squeezed Guy's hand hard.

"Rachel," said Guy, "I'll leave you and Angela with your father. You should be with him." He sat outside in a chair, his shoebox on his lap. After half and hour, Rachel and Angela came out, both with tears in their eyes.

"He's fading fast, Guy. We've said our goodbyes. He wants to see you."

Guy hugged the sisters and went into Dowd's room.

It took a moment for the pastor to realize Guy was there. When he did, he turned his head slowly and croaked out: "Hi, Guy. It's good to see you." He coughed, his chest rattling. "I don't have much time left. I guess I won't be seeing you and Rachel married."

Guy didn't know what to say, so he said nothing. He let the dying man talk.

"Promise me you will treat her well. Be a good husband. Make her happy."

"I will pastor. I love her. I will do everything in my power to give her a good life. I promise."

"Good."

Dowd closed his eyes. His breath was slow, labored. After a few minutes, he said: "Guy, I want to tell you something. Come closer."

Guy moved his chair next to the bed.

"Guy, I have a confession to make."

"To me?"

"Yes. Even a man of the cloth may have sins to confess. You're not a priest, but I believe you understand the souls of men. A rare gift."

The pastor winced with pain, closed his eyes, and let out a long rattling breath. He was struggling. His voice was a hoarse croak. Guy waited as the old man tried to muster the strength to speak. Finally, eyes closed, he began.

"Years ago, Guy, when I was only twelve, my brother drowned in a pond one summer day."

"I know, pastor. You tried to rescue him, but couldn't."

"Yes, Guy. True. But what I have never told anyone, ever, is that we were horsing around. Playing King of the Mountain on a rock, and I pushed him in. His head hit something. He went under. It happened quickly. By the time I got to him, he was gone. It was my fault. He wouldn't have drowned if I hadn't pushed him. I killed him."

"Pastor, it was an accident. You didn't mean to kill him. Didn't want to."

"What does it matter, Guy? My intent? I loved him. But I caused his death. I have had to live with that my whole life. It's why I decided to do the Lord's work. I hoped I would atone for my sin. That He would forgive me. So far, it doesn't look like He has. I guess I'm about to find out for sure."

Again the pastor gasped for breath. His eyes fluttered. He continued in a whisper.

"I've wanted to tell somebody, to confess and be absolved of my terrible sin. But I never had the courage. I always told myself I would do it someday. Well, this is my last day. My last chance. I have confessed. Thank you for listening, Guy. The weight is lifted. I can die peacefully. I don't know if there is a God. I have my doubts now. But if there is, I will accept His will, His choice for me in eternity. I pray He will forgive me."

Guy patted the dying man's shoulder.

"Pastor, I have something to show you."

Guy went to his shoebox and opened it. Inside was the Mummy Asrah. He had practiced it for years and had come to believe it could be a good illusion. He had wanted to find the right time and place to perform it, as Vernon had suggested. He never had. But when the call came that the pastor was dying, Guy had realized that maybe this was the time. This was the place.

He set it up quickly. Dowd watched him.

"A magic show, Guy?"

"Just a single illusion, pastor. A last sleight if you will. This little mummy represents a man who has died, pastor. He has been prepared for burial, for his life in the hereafter."

Guy put the small mummy on the little bench that came with the trick.

"He is buried, and covered with earth as he is laid to rest."

Guy covered the mummy with the paisley silk cloth.

"His body remains in the earth, but his spirit rises."

Guy waved his hands over the cloth that covered the mummy and it started to move. Slowly, it rose from the bench.

"The soul of the departed is light now, pastor. No troubles weigh it down, no guilt or fear. It is a spirit, and it ascends to heaven."

As Guy held his hands above the floating cloth, it continued its ascent. It was a beautiful illusion, full of mystery, as convincing as the drawings in the ad had promised. The pastor watched, a smile slowly creeping across his face.

"We who loved this man say our goodbyes."

Guy grabbed a corner of the cloth and spun it in the air. The mummy was gone.

"The person we loved is gone, gone from our lives, but not from our hearts."

"Where did he go, Guy?"

"To the same place you are going, pastor. To a place of peace and compassion and forgiveness."

The pastor smiled, and for one last time, his eyes opened wide and twinkled. They were looking past Guy, at something beautiful and embracing.

"Oh, the wonder of it," he said.

And then he was gone.

Guy stood there a moment, holding the cloth from the Mummy Asrah in his hand. He went over and closed the pastor's eyes.

"Rest in peace," he whispered to the old man.

In that small hospital room in the final moments of life, the pastor had come to understand the power of wonder, and Guy had come to understand the power of forgiveness.

64

The pastor had been laid to rest. Angela would take care of the loose ends. Guy and Rachel returned to New York. They had a wedding to plan. For them, it was one of those strange times sometimes offered up by life when happiness and sorrow mingle. As they grieved the passing of one life, they made plans to start a new one as husband and wife.

Guy had introduced Rachel to the walk across the Brooklyn Bridge. They did it often when they wanted to get away from the bustle of downtown Manhattan or get perspective on life.

As was their custom, they took the subway to Brooklyn and then ascended to the footpath on the bridge. It was a beautiful spring night. They wanted to take a last walk in New York before they headed to New London for their wedding and their first big show, a two-week run at the Garde Theater. Like so much of their lives, the show had been a surprise. It materialized out of thin air, like a trick.

In January, the manager of the Garde had called Guy. He had heard about Guy's Mysto show from someone in New York, had come to the city to see it, and liked it very much. He had an opening in the schedule in June, and liked the idea of a hometown boy performing where he had seen his first magic show. It would make for good publicity. Were they interested?

Guy and Rachel jumped at the chance. Their own show, in a real theater! The honeymoon could wait. It was a lot to think about, a lot to plan. Guy didn't even try to figure it all out. Life was simply too strange, too wonderful, too full of surprises.

They held hands and walked along, talking quietly, laughing, enjoying their love. The lights of New York glittered across the water, the thrum and chaos of the city hidden in the darkness.

Only its beauty remained, tall skyscrapers ablaze with countless lights, like rectangular Christmas trees.

As they stopped to look at the reflections of the city in the waters of the East River, a bird flew in from the darkness and landed on the railing just a few feet from them. It was a dove, glowing white in the night. The bird cocked its head at Guy.

"Lily?" Guy whispered.

The dove looked at him a moment, chirped once, and flew off.

Guy and Rachel watched it disappear into the darkness.

"Who is Lily?" she asked.

"A friend in the carnival. One of the freaks. She died in the fire. She told me she'd come back as a bird and find me. Maybe she did."

"I hope so. It would be nice to come back as a bird."

Guy put his arm around Rachel's shoulders, drew her close and they shared a long kiss.

"I'm looking forward to being Mrs. Borden," she said.

"And I'm looking forward to our life together, Rachel. I'm sorry neither of your folks will be at our wedding."

"Me, too," Rachel said. "I guess it just wasn't in the cards."

Rachel wandered away, toward the other side of the bridge. As she passed by the shadow of the enormous support tower, a figure lunged out of the darkness and grabbed her.

He had a knife.

It was Ivan.

He held Rachel to him and raised the knife to her throat. It all happened in an instant.

"Ivan!" yelled Guy.

"Yes, Ivan."

"Guy?" said Rachel, her voice trembling, her eyes wide in fear. Her hands went up to the arm wrapped around her chest and shoulders, but she was no match for Ivan. He pushed the knife closer to her neck. Guy could see it glinting in the lights of the bridge.

"Don't hurt her!" Guy yelled, frantic. He took a few steps forward.

"What do you want, Ivan?"

"Want?" said Ivan. "I want hurt you, Guy. I want teach you to no mess with me. I want show you how much Ivan miss Irena."

"You think I have been back with Irena?"

"Yes, I watch her go your place."

"We were practicing for a show, Ivan. One lousy show. We were together for a few weeks. Irena hated doing magic. She left. She went off to find herself another rope."

"I'm not sure."

"Well, it's the truth. I'm done with Irena. And she's done with me. Why don't you ask her?"

"Can't find her. Your fault. You drive her away. I make you pay. You take my girl, I take yours. You see her die. Worse than you die yourself maybe."

Rachel writhed in Ivan's grasp and the point of his knife nicked her neck, drawing a thin trickle of blood. She stopped.

"Don't be a fool, Ivan. Rachel has done nothing to you. If you want to fight me, fight *me*. Settle this like a man, not a coward."

Guy hoped he could reason with Ivan or at least challenge his masculinity enough to get him to let go of Rachel. What he would do next he did not know. He had no plan. No clever patter. This was not a performance. This was terribly real. He was just playing it second by second, trying to keep Rachel alive.

"Ivan no coward, Guy. Maybe after she die, I kill you, too."

"Ivan ..."

Ivan pulled the knife back, cocking his arm, getting ready to draw it across Rachel's throat.

"Say goodbye to her, Guy. This your fault."

Guy started to lunge forward when a shrill voice shouted from the shadows.

"LET HER GO!"

Ivan, Guy and Rachel turned their heads toward where the voice had come from.

"I SAID LET HER GO!" The voice was high and angry.

A tiny figure stepped from the shadows. It was Major Midget! He was holding a huge gun and pointing it at Ivan.

"You let her go now, Ivan, or I'll blow your head off!"

Everybody froze in a tableau. Ivan holding Rachel, knife poised to slit her throat; Guy a few feet away, mid-stride, his fists clenched; Midget with his huge gun.

"I'm waiting," he said.

"I kill her before you shoot me," snarled Ivan.

"I don't think so, Ivan. The hand may be quicker than the eye, but not a bullet." He started to squeeze the trigger.

With what sounded like a growl, Ivan loosened his grip on Rachel. She slithered away from him and scurried back to Guy.

"Are you okay?" he asked, wiping the blood off her neck.

"Yes, Guy. A little shaken, but fine. It's just a nick. I'll live."

They hugged as if they never wanted to let each other go. Rachel was trembling. Major Midget kept Ivan pinned with the gun. Ivan glared at him.

"I thought you was dead you damned dwarf!"

"MIDGET!" screamed Major Midget, the gun rocking in his hands. "I'm a midget, not a dwarf! Midget! Midget! MIDGET!"

"Midget, dwarf—whatever you are, I thought you died in fire."

"No, Ivan. Not dead. I just disappeared. Big difference. As you can see, I am very much alive. Which you most definitely won't be if you so much as twitch."

"Major Midget?" Guy said at last, recovering his senses as the adrenaline of fear faded. "I don't understand. We found your shoes. Your belt. Your St. Christopher's medallion. Some bones."

"Yes, those were my shoes, my belt, my medal. The bones were from one of Bruno's fried chickens. I put them all there in the confusion."

"Why?"

"Because of this creep, Guy. Ivan here had it out for me. Sooner or later, most likely sooner, he was going to come for me and break me in half. I had to get away. I thought about what you'd said about Magician's Choice. About having different paths to a desired outcome. The fire happened and it turned out to be my very best out. I wouldn't have been able to help anybody in that blaze. I'm just too small. I busied myself gathering a few things and in the middle of it all, I ran in, put the stuff down and hightailed it out and disappeared. And I must say, Guy, it was a nice funeral. I really appreciate what you said."

"You were there?"

"Yeah. I hid behind a grave and listened. When you are as small as I am, it's easy to hide."

"How did you know I was here? That Ivan was after me?"

"Well, hell, Guy. I told you I was your guardian midget. I've been keeping an eye on you. And old Ivan here has been, too. I guess you didn't know that. He's been following you. Waiting in the shadows. Letting his anger fester. He's a guy who carries a grudge. A whacko, if you ask me. I knew he'd try to hurt you, so I've been following him following you. He's kept me busy."

Ivan had been listening to all this and slowly, very slowly inching his way across the base of the pier.

"I told you not to move, you Russian bastard," yelled Major Midget.

"He's not Russian. He's from Philadelphia."

"Philly? No kidding? Who knew? Well, wherever he's from, he's a thug. Listen, you two lovebirds: get out of here. I've got some business to take care of with Ivan."

Glaring at Ivan, then walking over to Major Midget, Guy patted him on the shoulder.

"Thank you. That's twice you've come to my rescue. I owe you."

"My pleasure, Guy. You've been good to me, to all of us freaks. We owe *you*. Now scram."

Guy turned to Ivan. "Being bullied doesn't give you the right to be a bully. Maybe if you'd treated Irena a little better, she would never have run into my arms. You get what you give in life, Ivan."

Guy nodded another thanks to Major Midget and took Rachel's hand.

They walked off into the night, toward Manhattan, leaving Ivan and Major Midget to settle their grudge.

Midget and Ivan stood on the Brooklyn Bridge, staring at each other.

"You pull trigger, dwarf, and you be knocked off bridge by recoil. I die. You die."

Major Midget let out a little growl. His finger tightened on the trigger.

"I...am...a...midget...not...a dwarf." He spoke with calm deliberateness, trying to keep his anger in check.

"Dwarf. Midget. What the hell's difference? You're a freak," said Ivan. "Not a real man."

Major Midget glowered at Ivan.

"Asshole or jerk? Which are you, Ivan? What's the difference? Not a real man in either case. Just someone who doesn't give a damn about anybody else. You always hated the freaks. You never could see that we are not really any different."

Major Midget took a step toward Ivan, stared him in the eye, and spoke again:

"If you prick us, do we not bleed?
If you tickle us, do we not laugh?
If you poison us, do we not die?
And if you wrong us, shall we not revenge?
If we are like you in the rest, we will resemble you in that."

"What the hell you talking about?" said Ivan.

"Shakespeare, Ivan. Shylock. The Merchant of Venice."

"I don't care Shakespeare."

"Never mind, Ivan. You don't understand. You never will."

"You little shit! If you didn't have gun, I tear you apart!"

"I'm sure you would, Ivan. But I *do* have a gun. A big one. And five bullets. More than enough. What should I do to you? Blow your head off? Shoot you in the heart, if I could find it?"

David Cohen, aka Major Midget, aka the Nasty Little Bastard, paused to consider.

"No, I think I should let you live. Maybe a little diminished, like me. How would you like to be a little man, Ivan?"

Major Midget leveled the gun first at Ivan's head then slowly lowered it down his massive chest, down his belly and still lower, finally stopping at his crotch.

Ivan's eyes widened in horror. "You wouldn't!"

"Oh, yes I would, Ivan. How about you join the world of freaks you loathe so much."

Before Ivan could answer, Major Midget pulled the trigger.

Ivan's scream rode the loud bang of the gun across the glittering canyons of New York City, echoing in the night.

65

Guy and Rachel's harrowing encounter with Ivan had been a close thing. Their lives could have changed or ended on the Brooklyn Bridge, if not for a midget come back from the dead to save them.

Shaken, and grateful, they headed to New London and their future together.

Sam and Ruth took an immediate liking to Rachel, who promised to design something special for Ruth for the wedding. Over a series of dinners, the Bordens got to know Rachel and learned more about what their prodigal son had been up to since he'd left to seek his destiny in New York almost six years earlier.

After dinner one night, while Rachel and Sam talked, Guy's mother motioned to him to follow her. She took him into the bedroom and opened a dresser drawer. She took out a big leather-bound scrapbook. "This is your father's," she said.

It was empty except for the first page. There, carefully cut out and glued in was the announcement from *The Day* of Guy's upcoming show.

"He's prouder of you than he lets on," said Ruth.

Guy was touched. He had no idea.

"I'm proud of you too, Guy. You've come a long way from this." She opened another dresser drawer and took out an envelope and handed it to him. Guy opened it and took out a piece of paper that was inside. He unfolded it. It was the poster that had come with the Gilbert Mysto Magic set. It had yellowed, the tape that had held it to his door dry and brittle. Scrawled on the top was "Guy Borden," and in the box at the bottom: "Levinson Bar Mitzvah, May 14, 1938."

"Well, mom," he said, "you started it all that night you took me to see Blackstone for my birthday."

She laughed. "You never know where things will lead, do you, Guy?"

"You never go so far as when you don't know where you are going," said Guy.

"Where did you hear that?"

"A fortune I once got from the Gypsy at Ocean Beach."

"You and your fortunes," she said, smiling and shaking her head.

Though his mother might laugh at him, Guy had come to put great stock in the messages he got from both Gai Pan and the Gypsy Fortune Teller. Both had an uncanny knack for being relevant to what was happening in his life. The fortunes always gave him something to think about. And reflection, he had learned, often influenced his choices.

So it was back to Ocean Beach he went alone one afternoon to see what the Gypsy had to tell him at this moment when his life was about to change, when he was poised to step into a new chapter in his destiny.

In the arcade, a few people milled about, thinking about dropping a nickel to get their fortune, and, as before, Guy wondered about fate. Did it matter if one of them went first? Was the card he got inevitably the one he should get, or could fate be derailed? Altered? Given how his life had unfolded, he had no idea. It could go either way.

He put in his nickel. The Gypsy came to life, looking at him with her sightless eyes, breathing, nodding her head, then sweeping a card into a slot.

A second later, it appeared at the front of her cabinet.

Guy stared at it a moment.

Then he picked it up and read it.

"Things are not what they seem."

66

The Dutch Tavern was on a tiny side street near the Crocker House. It was where the great playwright and New Londoner Eugene O'Neill came to find inspiration in a glass or two of whisky.

With its wood floors, round tables, long bar and subdued lighting, the Tavern was a cozy place. Guy and Rachel decided to have a party there the night before their wedding. Guy had sent word to the carnival gang that they were all invited. So, too, were Blackstone, Gai Pan, Dai Vernon and Jean, Angela Dowd, Sam and Ruth, and a few of Rachel's friends from Liberty and New York.

Blackstone was one of the first to arrive. He and Guy had a drink together.

"A long way from a milkshake," laughed Blackstone as Guy ordered a beer.

"I've done a lot of growing up since then," said Guy. It had only been twelve years, but in that time Guy had gone from a naive boy of thirteen to a young man who had been to war, who had seen love, betrayal and death, who had started a career and seen others end theirs.

"So you have a show opening soon at the Garde," said Harry.

"Yes," said Guy. "Where I first saw you, where I first tasted the thrill of being in the spotlight. How'd you know?"

"Oh, the manager is an old friend of mine." Blackstone took a sip of his drink.

"I'm proud of you, Guy. I've sat down with a lot of boys over the years. They were all interested in magic. Very few of them ever stuck with it. You did. You had the talent and the passion. I saw that in the coffee shop that day; I saw that when you worked for me in New York." He lifted his glass. "To sticking with what we love," he said.

"Sounds like a wedding vow," said Guy.

"It is, in a way, Guy. We are wed to whatever we love."

"I hope you'll come to my show, Harry."

"I will. I have a few days free. I'm eager to see what sort of show the next world's greatest magician puts on."

The other guests began to arrive, including Archie Walters, who, as a Justice of the Peace, had agreed to perform the wedding ceremony. As Guy mingled, making introductions, Vernon and Blackstone drifted together.

"So, Harry, what do you think of my young protégé?"

"He's come a long way, Dai."

"He has. And he has a long way to go."

"Yes, I'm sure some surprises await him."

"No doubt. But what would life be without surprises?"

"That's why I bill my show as 1001 Wonders, Dai. To suggest there are many surprises yet to come."

Dai raised his glass and Blackstone clinked it with his. "To the surprises yet to come," said Vernon.

Gai Pan showed up, carrying a gift box.

"Is bunny," she said as she gave it to Guy. "Magician needs bunny. And 'member what I told you: means long life. You and girl live long, make lots of little Guys."

"Thanks, Gai Pan. People like bunnies."

Gai Pan rummaged in her bag. "I have cookies, too." She pulled out a small paper bag and showed it to Guy. It contained three fortune cookies. "Pick one," she said.

Guy reached in, picked up a cookie, then changed his mind and chose another. He took it out.

"Open," said Gai Pan.

Dutifully, Guy cracked it open.

"What say?' she asked, eyes twinkling.

"Treasure what you have."

"Much good," said Gai Pan. She winked and went to get a drink.

Major Midget hobbled in, a cast on his arm and leg. Most of the carnival crowd had heard he was still alive, but his entrance was greeted with gasps and cheers. After quieting everybody down, he explained what had happened: "Ivan was right, Guy. That damned gun had a hell of a recoil. It knocked me off my feet and head over heels along the Brooklyn Bridge. I slammed into one of the supports and broke my arm and leg."

"You were lucky you didn't end up in the East River," said Archie.

"No kidding! I can't swim. But it worked to my advantage. When the police arrived, they wanted to know what had happened. It's not every day they were called to the aftermath of a shooting between a midget and a strongman on the Brooklyn Bridge—or any bridge."

"What did you tell them?"

"I told them there was bad blood between me and Ivan from our days in the carnival. We'd run into each other in New York; things got ugly. Ivan beat me up. Broke my arm and leg. I thought he was going to kill me. So I pulled a gun and shot the son-of-a-bitch. It seemed logical. There was even a headline in the Daily News the next day: 'Dwarf Neuters Brute!'"

Everyone was spellbound at his account. Angela Dowd, especially, seemed rapt by the little man's story.

"Dwarf!" said Major Midget. "Even the damned paper called me a dwarf! Don't they know the difference?"

"Midget!" cried Archie, and the rest of the carny gang took it up as a chant: "Mid-get! Mid-get! Mid-get!"

Guy left, went to his room across the street at the Crocker House, and returned with a small box. In front of everyone, he opened it. Inside was his Purple Heart.

"Here you go, David. Wounded in action saving my life. Take it. Wear it with pride. You've earned it."

"Geez, thanks, Guy. Bravery be but a brief madness in the face of adversity."

"The Bard?" asked Guy.

"The Midget," said Midget. He had something more to share.

"You remember that gold mine I bought into that turned out to be a lead mine?"

"Vaguely," said Guy.

"Well, you know what? It turned out to be gold after all. Not literally, but it made me boodles of money."

"How so?"

"Well, there was a war on, as you well know. A big one. The U.S. needed bullets and lots of 'em. I mean, LOTS! Bullets are made of copper and lead. They needed tons and tons of lead, and the Gilmore Mines ended up providing most of it. I made a fortune helping kill Krauts and Japs. No more freak show for me!

"It's strange Guy: my father made good investments that went bad in the crash. I made a bad investment that made good in the war. I managed to turn gold into lead and then lead into gold. Now how freakin' strange is that?"

"Let's drink to Major Midget," said Guy. "One Nasty Little Bastard who has the golden touch!"

They all toasted, chanting "Gol-den Mid-get! Gol-den Mid-get!"

Angela Dowd had a dreamy look in her eyes. Not only was Major Midget scaled down to her size and a hero, but he liked Shakespeare and he was rich. He was looking like a bigger catch every minute.

"Does anyone know what happened to Irena?" asked Guy.

"Yes," said Archie. "She went back to Russia."

"Really? To walk the tightrope?"

"No, to teach English."

"Those people poor. Much with confusion will taught that be," said Guy.

Bodacious Bettie had a gift for Guy and Rachel. It was a watercolor she had done. It depicted a clown and a little monkey, sitting on his lap.

"That's Mazzucchi," she said, "the Italian clown. And Arrigo. I did their portrait when he was still around. I call it

'Buddies.' I never got a chance to give it to him. I want you to have it."

More laughter, more stories. As the drinks continued to flow, Alberto, nicely fueled by the liquor, took out his violin and began to play. Not the mournful dirge he used to play in the deep dark nights of the carnival, but a foot-tapping rendition of "Paper Moon."

Guy looked around the room, flushed with sentimentality kindled by whisky, and realized how much he loved this oddball assortment of talented misfits. They were all a part of his life, from different chapters of his story, and he treasured them, just as Gai Pan's fortune had advised. They shared a bond: they'd lived at the fringes of life, in the darkness and in the spotlight, too. Who knew where destiny would take them, where their paths might go or if they would ever cross. He might never see many of them again. No matter. They were here together tonight and tomorrow, and he would soak up every second, every smile, every joke. He suspected some of the others felt the same. He'd catch them looking thoughtful, looking around the crowded room, taking mental snapshots to last a lifetime. More than liquor flowed that night. Love did, too.

Perhaps reading his thoughts or just tuned to his mood, Rachel leaned over and gave him a kiss.

"This is wonderful," she said. "These are nice people."

"They are," said Guy. "Just a few missing." He was thinking of Lily Lavierre and Clarence the Giant, Reverend Dowd and Mae.

"They're here," whispered Rachel.

"Wait a minute, you two," said Vernon. He reached in his pocket, took out a piece of black paper and tiny scissors, and began to cut their silhouette. "Don't move, this will just take a minute."

Angela and David Cohen were lost in conversation about Shakespeare, David reciting love sonnets to her, a little slurred, but love sonnets nonetheless. Apparently, he was drawn to her, too.

Guy nudged Rachel and whispered: "I think your sister and the midget see eye to eye."

Rachel nodded and whispered back: "Not always easy."

Guy thought to himself what an interesting brother-in-law the Nasty Little Bastard would make.

Alberto finished "Paper Moon" and began a seductive dance tune. Bodacious Bettie grabbed Gai Pan's gift bunny, climbed on the bar and began to dance with it as only a hoochie girl could. Her sweetie, the old colonel Charlie, clapped and whistled and yelled out: "Johnny'd come marching home for that!"

Guy walked over to Archie Walters.

"It's so great to see the old gang together, Guy. I'm happy to see Major Midget didn't die. Ornery as he is, I like him. Streeter and Hale are rebuilding the show, getting in some new acts, but it's not the same."

"What about you, Archie? Are you going to stay with the carnival?"

"Yeah. I'm a ballyhoo man. I get to perform in my own way, and when that's in your blood, that's everything. I have my stage. Not big, but it's mine. Besides, what else could I do?"

"You'd be a great salesmen, Archie. You could settle down."

"I *am* a salesman, Guy. I sell dreams."

He gave Guy a friendly punch in the arm.

"Don't worry about old Archie. I got plenty of ballyhoo left in these old bones."

With a hoochie girl dancing on the bar with a bunny and a room full of strange drunk people, Mauritz Naughta, the proprietor of the Tavern, gave up. He hung out the "Closed" sign and turned the bar over to the wedding party. The place where Eugene O'Neill once brooded as he dreamed up his masterpieces was now a bawdy music hall. From the sacred to the profane, but what the hell? Naughta had never seen anything like it or them, and he was enjoying the show. The carnival had come to town, or at least to the Dutch Tavern.

They partied into the wee hours of the night, curiosities, oddities and perilous performers all.

67

The wedding of Guy and Rachel was held at the Lighthouse Inn in New London. Most of the guests, fresh from partying the night before, were a bit red-eyed and wobbly. Luckily, none had to walk a tightrope.

The piano player played a very slow version of Paper Moon at Guy and Rachel's request. It was their song and played slow it had a hymn-like quality. Archie Walters, the Justice of the Peace, had agreed to perform the ceremony. Guy had warned him to keep it clean and respectable.

When everyone was seated, Archie began:

"Laaaaadies and Gentlemen, step right up …" Guy glared at him. Archie stopped. "Ooops. Sorry. Habit you know." With a sheepish smile, he began again.

"Folks, we are gathered here today to witness the joining of Guy and Rachel in holy matrimony.

"Marriage is like a great carnival, full of many acts, many curiosities and perilous moments. At times, husband and wife walk a tightrope, yet their love is the net that shall save them should they fall. At times, they will be giddy, riding the carousel of love, reaching for the brass ring. At times, like mighty beasts, they will roar with passion. And at times, they will know sorrow and sadness, as when a mark cannot fell the milk bottles or crown the clown.

"We who witness their union today are but country bumpkins watching their act, knowing that they share secrets, knowing that they alone set the rules of the game they play.

"But wait! What is that? Why it is the call of the ballyhoo of love, of course! The show begins. We are invited into the tent of their matrimony, knowing that this is just the first act, knowing, indeed *believing*, that Guy and Rachel will amaze us, delight us, thrill us.

"Now, in solemnity and seriousness I say to you, Guy, and to you, Rachel:

"If you be tempted by others, turn away.

"If you find yourself in darkness, seek the light.

"If one or the other of you is sick or sad, be there for them in their time of need.

"And always remember that in the carnival of matrimony, the happiness you find is yours to make. It is your choice.

"Well, enough wisdom. Now it is time for the vows. Guy, Rachel, step right up and exchange your vows and your rings!"

Guy and Rachel, a bit bewildered, stepped forward.

"Guy, do you take Rachel as your lawful wedded wife, to have and to hold, to love and to cherish, through thick and thin, rain and shine, good attendance and bad; do you vow to forever love Rachel, as the 300 pound man eating chicken loves his fried bird?"

"I do."

"Rachel, do you take Guy as your husband, to love and to cherish, to obey as the bunny obeys the magician, to trust as the trapeze artist trusts her catcher, through sunny days and stormy nights, until death do you part?"

"I do."

"Well then, by the power invented in me, I now proclaim from the ballyhoo of the carnival of marriage that you are husband and wife, an act for the ages, a wonder of the world!

"You may now kiss."

Vernon turned to Blackstone.

"Harry, that was the strangest ceremony I ever heard."

"Dai, that may have been the strangest ceremony there ever was."

Sam and Ruth Borden had stunned looks on their faces. So did many others. Major Midget was crying. He was overwhelmed.

"So beautiful," he mumbled. Angela, who sat with him, put an arm around his tiny heaving shoulders.

Gai Pan murmured, "'Mazing"

Archie was anxious for a reaction from the newlyweds, but gave them time to enjoy their kiss. When they came up for air he whispered: "How'd I do, Guy? You know I wrote all that myself."

"It was memorable," said Guy. "Unforgettable."

Archie looked at Rachel with a questioning expression.

"It was beautiful, Archie."

Archie smiled. Guy and Rachel smiled. And why not? They had just had a wedding ceremony like none other, and, indeed, it would be unforgettable. Which, after all, is exactly what marriage vows should be.

68

"MYSTO: The Magic of Guy & Rachel Borden."

Guy watched as a man put the letters up on the marquee of the Garde.

He stood where he had stood over ten years ago, holding his mother's hand, in a crowd, awed by the glowing sign. Then it had been Blackstone. Now it was Guy. How far he had come. How unpredictable had been his path from here to here. He reached in his pocket for his wallet and took out the Jack of Diamonds. He had taken Blackstone's advice and been patient. He had stuck with his love of magic. It had worked out for him. Yet he had the feeling that very little of it had been his own doing. He had been buffeted by fate and by forces of history beyond his control. He had had wonderful opportunities drop in his lap. A mechanical fortuneteller, an old Chinese woman and a willful midget had been his advisors and guardian angel. Guy had lived his own 1001 wonders, and they had taken him back to this sidewalk below this marquee outside this theater.

He was thrilled to see his name on a real marquee. He had started by writing on the poster that came with the Gilbert Mysto Magic set. He was "Guy Borden" back then. Then he had been "Merloc" on an artfully painted sign outside a tent in a carnival. Briefly, and disastrously, he had been "King Nosmo, The Egyptian Mystic" with his ever faithful sidekick the Constipated Russian, Irea. For his high society shows in New York with Rachel they had become the "Mysto" show.

So many incarnations, so many personas. In the end, he realized the name was not important. Like a mask, his stage name was just a superficial embellishment. It was the twinkle of real eyes that mattered. The man playing the part of the magician. He smiled and walked into the theater.

In the wings, just before the show began, he took out the Morgan dollar Blackstone had given him. He did a Retention Vanish, like someone crossing himself, acknowledging his faith, not in a God, but in his own abilities. Then Guy kissed Rachel, the real magic in his life.

Top hat and wand poised, he was ready to create wonder. The curtain parted, the spotlight found him, and the Mysto show began.

69

Guy was in dressing room six with Rachel, unwinding from the show when there was a knock on the door. When he opened it, a man, woman and child stood there.

"Mr. Borden, my name is Caleb Bowen. This is my wife, Jennifer, and our son Nathan. The theater manager told us we might take our son back here to meet a real magician."

"Certainly, please come in."

The Bowens moved in. Caleb walked with a limp, his leg stiff. Guy noticed he wore an unusual amber ring with a spider inside.

"Weren't you the lighthouse keeper at Race Rock?" Guy asked.

"Yes," said Bowen. "Until the Hurricane of '38. It ended my career."

Guy turned his attention to Nathan who looked about seven. He was wide-eyed when Guy bent to shake his hand.

"Did you like the show, Nathan?"

"Yes, sir! It was great! I know a few tricks, too."

"Really? Care to show me one?" asked Guy.

Nathan looked stricken.

"I don't have any with me," he protested.

"Hmmm, I see," said Guy. "Perhaps I can fix that."

He rummaged around in a small magic case and came out with a Walking Liberty half-dollar.

"Now watch," he said. Then he did his Retention Vanish and the reappearance of the coin from his pocket.

"Wow!" was all Nathan could say.

"How about I teach you to do that, Nathan. Then, if you have a coin, or anybody you're with does, you will always be able to do a trick."

"Wow!"

"Mr. and Mrs. Bowen, I would like to teach Nathan this little miracle. However, as I am sure you know, the secret to a magic trick can only be shared among magicians. So if you would kindly wait outside a few minutes?"

Caleb and Jennifer smiled. They knew that Guy's including Nathan in the secret society of magicians was likely to be the biggest thrill of the night.

"Certainly," said Caleb. "We understand." Then he bent down to Nathan.

"Son, you watch carefully what Mr. Borden shows you. It's very nice of him to share a secret, and you must pay attention. Understood?"

"Yes, dad." Nathan was eager to get to the trick.

Caleb and Jennifer left the small dressing room. Rachel went into an adjoining room leaving Guy and Nathan alone.

"Now, Nathan," said Guy, sitting down so he was on a better level with the boy. "I am going to show you what is called the Retention Vanish. Have you ever heard of Harry Blackstone?"

Nathan shook his head. "Nope."

Guy smiled, but there was little humor in it.

"Well, he is the world's greatest magician. And when I was about your age, I met him right here at this theater, and he taught me this trick. Now I'll teach you."

About fifteen minutes later, Guy opened the door. Jennifer and Caleb were seated outside, chatting.

"Mr. and Mrs. Bowen, we're finished. I think Nathan will master this trick with time. With patience and practice. And I apologize."

"Apologize?" asked Jennifer.

"Yes. For the sound of a coin hitting the floor. I'm afraid you will be hearing it quite a lot for a while until Nathan masters the trick."

"That sound will be your legacy," laughed Caleb. "We will always think of you when we hear it."

Already, Nathan was practicing the Retention Vanish with the half-dollar Guy had given him.

"We've taken too much of your time," said Jennifer. "You've been very gracious."

"Mrs. Bowen," said Guy. "Part of the tradition of magic is to share, to pass down the secrets from one generation to the next. I am only doing what the great Harry Blackstone did for me. When we teach, we keep the art alive. Who knows? Maybe someday Nathan's name will be emblazoned on the marquee outside. It happened to me."

"Don't fill his head with ideas," said Caleb, his tone half serious.

Guy smiled. "Certainly. It's not for me to say anyway"

He looked at Nathan, playing with the coin.

"It will be the magician's choice."

Caleb, Jennifer and Nathan bid Guy goodnight and left. Guy took off his tails and put a few props away. He thought about young Nathan, and recalled the magical moments he had spent with Harry Blackstone in the coffee shop of the Crocker House. Guy picked up a piece of paper and a pen and wrote himself a note:

"Send Nathan Bowen a Mysto magic set."

70

After the wedding, Vernon had headed to Maine where he'd heard there was a man who had a unique card move. He did not. So Dai came back to New London and saw Guy's show. The next day, before he left to go back to New York, he and Guy had coffee at the Crocker House. Again, Guy was there with an older, wiser magician. A woman came over.

"I saw your show last night, Mr. Borden," she said. "I enjoyed it very much."

"Thank you."

"I just loved it when you turned that dove to gold! That was amazing." She left. Vernon had a perplexed look on his face.

"Did you do that? Did I miss something?"

"No and no," said Guy. "You may remember I put an ornate box at the side of the stage and told the audience that it would be amazing if I made it float or a girl jumped out of it or I put a dove inside and it turned to gold."

"Now that you mention it, I do vaguely remember that. But you never did anything with that box, did you?"

"No, I just left it there the whole show."

Vernon looked shocked and mystified.

"It's an old carny scam, Dai. They had a box in a freak tent and a sign that said the local doctor had determined it was too horrific for anyone to see. It was a popular attraction. People spooked themselves imagining what was in the box, which was nothing. It put them in the right frame of mind for the freak show. I just took the idea and applied it to magic."

"Clever," said Vernon. "That gal sure thought she saw you do something amazing."

Guy smiled. "Always take credit for miracles, Dai. Even when they are just an illusion."

"You know where to steal a good idea when you see one, Guy," said Vernon.

Guy bristled. "I didn't steal it. I took an idea from one thing and used it for another, that's all."

"Don't get testy, Guy. Hell, everybody steals secrets in magic. Magicians hunt secrets like cats hunt mice."

"I don't steal magic secrets, Dai. I don't because someone stole a trick from me. I hate him for it. I have for years. Someday I'm going to confront him. If I ever find him, that is."

"Who was it?" asked Vernon.

"A Chinese guy named Chen Woo. He was appearing at the Morosco Theater about seven years ago. I had come up with the idea for a unique trick. Something brand new to magic, Dai. I called it The Mysterium. Stupidly, I showed it to him. He made off with the plans and went to South America. He had the trick made, I guess, because I spotted an article in *Variety* that said he was making a name for himself with a marvelous new illusion called The Mysterium. My trick."

"You don't say," said Vernon. He sat back and slowly stirred his coffee with a spoon. After a minute, he looked up.

"I know Chen Woo, Guy. An old timer. He was okay. Not one of the greats. He comes by Tannen's sometimes."

Guy was speechless. "Woo, at Tannen's? Why didn't you tell me?"

"You never asked. How was I supposed to know you had an ax to grind with Woo? He's about as Chinese as I am. His real name is Isadore Klein. Jewish kid from Queens. Came back to the city to roost in his retirement. Quiet guy. Doesn't say much when we session. Usually just stands back in the shadows and watches. He was probably there that day you showed us your Retention Vanish."

Guy was flabbergasted. He had met Chen Woo and not even known it. At the Morosco, Guy had only seen him as his Chinese character and assumed he was Chinese. Even when they'd talked, he had played the Chinaman. He would never have recognized him out of costume and makeup. Not only was he still alive, he was in New York! And at Tannen's. He wondered how many times he had rubbed elbows with the man he hated.

"I can't believe it! Do you know where he lives?"

"No. But I'll check my S.A.M. registry and see if I have his address. What are you going to do, Guy? Go see him and break his knuckles?"

Indeed, what *was* he going to do? Guy wasn't exactly sure.

"I don't know, Dai. I have some ideas. I think we will have a very interesting conversation."

"Who knows how it will play out," said Vernon. "When you meet him, you might be surprised. Magician's are always up to some trick, you know. They like to be one step ahead."

Vernon looked at his watch.

"Time to take a stroll down to the station and get back to New York. Jean will be giving me a hard time for another wild goose chase to see a card sharp. She just doesn't understand, Guy. The man might have had something revolutionary, a move nobody has ever thought of!"

"And what would you do, Dai. Steal it?"

Vernon recoiled, stung, then smiled.

"Why no, Guy. I would just take an idea from one thing and use it for another, that's all."

Vernon called the next day. He gave Guy Klein's address. He reminded Guy Klein was old—almost eighty. He told him not to be too hard on him.

Guy went back to New York later that day. There was no Mysto show for two nights. It would give him a chance to find Woo. That night, at dinner at the Ping Toy, Gai Pan noticed Guy was preoccupied.

"What wrong, Guy?"

"Oh, I'm finally going to meet someone I have been looking for for a very long time, Gai Pan."

"Old flend?"

"Not exactly. More like an old enemy."

Gai Pan shook her head.

"No good to have enemy, someone to hate," she said. "Hate make us clazy."

At the end of the meal, she offered her usual choice of fortune cookies. Guy took one and read it as he sipped his tea.

"Embrace forgiveness"

71

It was a rainy, gloomy day. Guy took the subway to 2nd Avenue and walked a few blocks north until he found the apartment building on East 4th. The lobby was beat up, the floor tiles chipped. A single light fixture cast a dim glow. A row of small mailboxes, many with cracked glass, lined a wall. Above them a directory board with buzzers listed the tenants on slips of paper bent and folded into brass holders. Guy shook out his umbrella and folded it up as he scanned the directory and found the listing for Isadore Klein, aka Chen Woo. Apartment No. 7. Guy opened the outer elevator door and the folding grate. He stepped in, closed the doors, and hit the button for the second floor. The elevator began its creaky ascent and stopped with a jarring bounce.

Guy got out of the elevator and found himself at the end of long, dingy hallway. He walked down the hall, which smelled of cooking cabbage. The wallpaper was faded and showed the scene of a fox hunt—men, horses, and the elusive fox—repeated over and over. It was a hunt that would never end. Half the ceiling lights were out, and water stains darkened the plaster. It was a depressing place.

Guy came to No. 7 and stood in front of the door. He wondered what he would find on the other side. He had waited a long time for this moment. Though years had passed, the betrayal by Chen Woo still hurt. How many times, lying in bed, staring out a train window, walking down the street, even marching across the sands of Africa, had Guy imagined what he would do when he finally found Woo. It was not physical violence Guy sought. No, he wanted a more long-lasting, corrosive revenge. He wanted to bruise the man's spirit, wound his soul.

Guy rapped on the door. He waited. No answer. He rapped again, a little harder. He heard a muffled voice. "Just a minute." He heard the deadbolt slide. The door opened a crack, still held by a security chain. Eyes peeked out. Guy knew those eyes. The door closed and Guy heard the chain being undone, then the door opened again.

Klein stood there in rumpled pants, a stained white shirt and a tan cardigan sweater laced with holes. A white stubble peppered his wrinkled face. His hair was a little wild. He was standing in a short hallway. Guy stood on the threshold.

"Come on in, Guy," said Klein. "I've been expecting you."

Guy was surprised Klein knew him, then remembered he had been at Tannen's. Klein had had plenty of opportunities to observe him.

"Pardon the mess. I don't get many visitors." Klein said. "Actually, I don't get any."

Guy stepped in, and Klein closed the door and threw the deadbolt and chain. The apartment was very hot and smelled of burnt coffee. Guy propped his umbrella against a bench. Klein limped a bit as he led him into a small sitting room. He picked up some papers and magazines from a beat-up chair and shooed a fat cat off it.

"That's Alexander. Named after the famous magician. You know, 'Alexander: the Man Who Knows.' Though I don't think puss here is quite so talented. But who knows what a cat knows?"

He motioned for Guy to take the seat, and he did. Guy hadn't said anything.

"I'll heat up some coffee," said Klein and wandered off to the kitchen. Guy was left alone with a loudly ticking mantel clock and Alexander, eyeing him warily.

Klein puttered away in the kitchen, talking to himself as he searched for mugs and heated up the coffee. Guy looked around the cluttered room. The walls were filled with photographs from Chen Woo's career. The tables, shelves and cabinets were filled with magic props. Like Tannen's, the whole apartment was a magic set. In the corners and under tables were bigger props.

Klein came in from the kitchen with a tray, which rattled as he put it down, spilling some coffee. Was it nerves or just age that caused his tremor?

"So, you were expecting me?" asked Guy.

"Yes."

"Why? Why would you be expecting me after all these years?"

"We'll get to that later, Guy. Let's just say you didn't have much choice in the matter."

"Listen, Isadore, you don't have to ..."

Guy stopped. Out of the corner of his eye, he had spotted something half hidden in the shadows, something that made him gasp. He stood up, walked over and looked closely.

It was The Mysterium.

It was an awkward moment. The thief and his mark were together, and the object that had caused such hatred and desire for vengeance was there in front of them.

"Go ahead, Guy. Pick it up. It won't bite you."

Carefully, Guy picked up The Mysterium.

"The artisan Mayador made it for me," said Klein. "He did a wonderful job. The decorations were his idea. Helped it show up on stage, and helped conceal some of the secret workings. Making it wasn't so easy, you know. Almost impossible, in fact. It was a brilliant idea you had, Guy, but awfully hard to realize. It took a long while. Cost me a small fortune."

"But it paid off," said Guy, an edge to his voice. Klein, stung, said nothing.

Guy turned The Mysterium in his hands.

"Give it a try," said Klein. "See what you think of your creation. Here, you can use these." Klein opened a drawer in a nearby cabinet and took out a bright red silk and a golden ball.

Guy took the props. He held The Mysterium. His fingers searched for a small button and found it. As he turned the trick, he pressed the button. The Mysterium slowly and silently transformed itself. It was beautiful. He pushed the button and once again The Mysterium began its transformation, its precision gears, intricate carvings and cleverly disguised elements all working to create a moment of wonder. Even Guy was startled.

He had never seen The Mysterium performed. He could only imagine its effect on an audience. It was beyond what he had envisioned. It was beautiful. It was pure magic.

He put it down. He picked up the ball and covered it with the silk. Using sleight of hand, he made the ball vanish. He picked up The Mysterium again, opened a small door on its front. His thumb pushed another hidden button and The Mysterium came to life again.

"That's when they'd gasp, Guy. It was so different, so damned unexpected! Often there was a stunned silence in the theater. They held their breath."

Guy did too as the next phase of the trick unfolded.

"Astonishing, isn't it, Guy?" Guy started to put The Mysterium down.

"You aren't done yet, Guy," said Klein. "There's another phase."

Guy turned to him with a look of surprise.

"More? My design was for only two!"

"Well, I told you Mayador did a good job. It was his idea to take it a step further. I think your trick cast a spell on him. The Mysterium may be the most complicated piece of apparatus every created. It took him months. The parts had to be machined with great precision. He was determined. A real artist. A genius. Like you, Guy. And, as you will see, he succeeded. I half believe he made a deal with the devil to create The Mysterium. Maybe you did too."

Guy just held The Mysterium, admiring it. He hadn't done the final phase.

"When I performed it, Guy, the stage was empty. I stood alone in the spotlight. I started with just a wand and my hat, with The Mysterium on a table nearby, lit by its own spotlight. It was very visual, you see. Just me and The Mysterium, glowing on the dark stage. I had a wonderful story to introduce it. I drew it out. Let it sit there, looking exotic. The audience was intrigued. What was it? What would it do? Nothing like a mystery to fire people's curiosity. I made them wait and wonder. I built the anticipation, and I promised them that they were about to witness something of exquisite beauty. Something nobody had ever seen. Something they would remember the rest of their lives.

"I would take off my top hat, wave the wand, and do a simple production from the hat. The ball and the silk. Nothing too much. All just a set up for The Mysterium. Then, I would do it, in silence. I did it slowly. Very slowly."

"Very important," said Guy.

"Very!" said Klein. "Just like your Retention Vanish. Same with me and The Mysterium. Why rush a miracle? Let the impossible unfold. Milk the moments of magic. Let them see it. Let it sink in. It is so amazing that they couldn't believe their eyes. It took a while for belief to catch up with experience."

"It *is* amazing, Isadore. More than I ever imagined."

"It's a work of art, Guy."

Guy did the move with the silk, then engaged a small switch. The Mysterium created its final extraordinary, jaw-dropping effect.

"Ah, that final step!" whispered Klein. "That's when they realized what they were seeing was impossible. There was no explanation for it. It had them out of their seats howling. In an earlier time, it would have gotten me burned at the stake as a sorcerer!"

Guy smiled. How could he not? The Mysterium was a dream that had become reality and that turned reality into a dream.

"How I loved performing that trick, Guy. It was sheer pleasure. It was so magical. Blackstone had 1001 wonders. I had only one. It was all I needed."

Guy put The Mysterium on the table. His anger had been blunted by finally holding and performing his trick. Maybe it had secrets even Guy did not know.

"You invented something wonderful, Guy. Something utterly amazing. A visual illusion that turned the world inside out. Magic is full of classics. It's rare that something new comes along. You should be proud."

Guy stared at his creation, a thing of beauty in the dingy apartment of the man who had gained a measure of fame from it.

"Did you ever invent another trick?" asked Klein.

"No. That was it. My only child. Maybe I was fated to get this one great idea. I don't know." Guy turned to Klein.

"Once you started to perform the trick, I wondered why nobody ever copied it," said Guy, still staring at The Mysterium, still not completely believing it had done what it had done.

"Well, South America was kind of off the beaten path. And even if another magician saw me perform it, I doubt he would have a clue as to how it was done. It defies logic. It defies analysis. You just saw for yourself: even when you are doing it, it doesn't seem possible. Mayador died a year or two later. He took the real secrets of its workings to the grave. If it had ever broken, I don't think it could have been fixed. But he made it well. It worked perfectly for all the years I performed it. Still does, as you can see.

"I kept The Mysterium locked up in a trunk, Guy. I didn't trust anybody with the secret. Not a stagehand. Not my assistants. Nobody. I would unlock the trunk in the wings, take out The Mysterium, go out and perform it alone, and then return it to the trunk. No, I didn't share it with anyone. There are many spies in the magic world, you know. Lots of thieves."

Klein said it before he realized the irony of it. Guy shot him a glance.

"As you well know," added Klein, looking away. There was an awkward silence. Then Klein spoke, a quaver in his voice.

"Guy, I'm sorry I stole that trick." He paused. "No. That's not quite true. To be honest, I'm glad I took it, because it made my reputation at a time when my career was fading. It gave my act new life. There was more to that than giving a fading magician a few more years in the spotlight."

"How so?" asked Guy.

With effort, Klein stood up, grunting, holding onto the chair. He walked over to a wall of photographs. He scanned across them, across the years, across his life. Guy could only wonder what memories he was reliving. Klein stood a long time without speaking, and then, his back still to Guy, he began.

"This is my life, Guy. Captured in photographs. What is a life, anyway, but a lot of moments strung together like a string of pearls? I can remember each of these moments very vividly.

"There I am with Houdini. Thurston. Doing The Mysterium. There I am in an opera house in Peru, looking so elegant, so young. But that youth, that vitality … that's the great illusion, Guy. It passes quickly. The amazing vanishing youth trick! Sometimes it hurts to look at these pictures. To see myself that way when I am this way now.

"I was never a top-tier magician, Guy. I wanted to be. But eventually I came to realize that I was only good. Not great. Never would be. I don't know why. Maybe you are born with greatness, with a raw talent that eventually blossoms. Or maybe it's just being obsessed with your work, like Vernon. Maybe it's being more passionate than all the others guys. Maybe it's just luck.

"Still, I tasted the spotlight. Having been in it, you always want to be in it. But they never tell you how damned elusive it can be. You're only as good as your next show. And that brilliant light that giveth also taketh away. When your skills erode a bit, when you slow down, when you get a little tired and shaky, the light shows all that. They see. They turn their backs on you. They find someone younger, faster—somebody new. There's always somebody new."

Klein paused. He reached out and touched one of the photos. It showed Woo with a pretty assistant.

"Eleanor, my wife," he said quietly. "So pretty. Such a good person." He sighed. "She passed away three years ago."

Klein stopped. He still had his back to Guy, but Guy could tell from the shaking shoulders he was sobbing. He gave the old man his time, his grief. After a few minutes, Klein began to talk again, almost in a whisper.

"That night you showed me The Mysterium backstage at the Morosco, I had decided to give it all up. I was tired. The act was tired. So, during that show, I made up my mind to quit. And what happens? Out of the blue, a young man walks up to me and shows me a trick that is unlike anything I'd ever seen. Unlike anything *anybody* had ever seen! I knew it could revitalize my act.

Maybe push me into the big time. I was about to head to South America, so I would have a chance to try it out. I thought my mind was made up, but you changed everything."

"Magician's Choice," said Guy with a rueful laugh.

"Yes. Magician's Choice. You changed my destiny. The Mysterium was a blessing. It gave my act new life, and it gave my wife a few more years of travel and glamour before she took ill. When she did, we had that many more memories to share. And those memories were like medicine. They helped ease her pain."

Klein shook his head, turned to Guy.

"Then one day, Eleanor was gone. My magic was powerless to help her." Klein sat and took a sip of coffee.

"When she passed, she left a hole in my life, a hole that can't be filled. I became a ghost because a big part of me had died. Yet part lived on. That's what a ghost is, isn't it? Someone dead who still lives? That's me, Guy, that's me. No longer 'Woo the Chinese Conjuror.' Just 'Woo the Ghost.' Sadness is my companion now. My assistant. Always by my side, faithful and loyal."

He waved his hand. "Sorry. I ramble sometimes. I pity myself and that's always boring to someone else. That's why they call it self-pity. It shouldn't be shared."

Klein looked small sitting in his chair, surrounded by the painful reminders of better days.

"I'm old, Guy. Old men have plenty of time to sit and philosophize. We're not good for much else. Young men act. Old men remember."

Guy had waited years to confront Chen Woo. He had spent uncountable hours imagining his revenge. Planning the perfect comeuppance for the thief. Instead, when the moment came, he didn't have the heart to seize it. Klein's theft of his trick seemed more like the predictable act of a desperate man trying to cling to his career than a villainous crime. The sad old man deserved no punishment beyond what life had already handed him. Loss had taken his heart, and age had taken his soul. Guy had been chasing an illusion.

Maybe it was pity. Or weariness. Or meeting an enemy and glimpsing his humanity. Whatever the reason, Guy finally cast off his hatred and forgave Woo.

He stood. It was time to leave.

"Guy, stay a bit. There's more I have to tell you. Please."

Klein said it with such need that Guy knew he had no choice but to stay. He sat down.

"Guy, when I stole your trick it turned out not to be so simple. The Mysterium came with more than wonder. It came with guilt. I've lived with my guilt over taking it from you for years. Maybe that sounds hollow, but it's true. That regret weighed on me heavily. Turns out, I have too much of a conscience to be a good thief. Our lives took different paths after that night at the Morosco. There was nothing I could do to make it up to you.

"Or so I thought.

"In spite of The Mysterium, my act finally died. Then the love of my life died. I did some close-up shows for a while. That's how I met Vernon. But my heart wasn't in it. My hands shake. I drop stuff. But I never lost my love of magic. Through Vernon I got introduced to Tannen's. The guys there embraced me. They let me join their Saturday sessions.

"Then, one day, you walk into the back room. I was in the shadows. You probably never noticed me. Lou introduced you. You did your Retention Vanish. Even if Lou hadn't told us your name, I would have known it was you. Nobody does that vanish like you. You did it for me backstage at the Morosco. I never forgot it."

"Did I see you at Tannen's that day?"

"Yes, Guy. You didn't recognize me out of costume. I handed you the bagel for your trick."

Guy shook his head. He had met the man he had sought for years and never knew it.

"Guy, I went home that night you were at Tannen's and got to thinking about stealing your trick. And that's when I came up with my idea."

"Your idea? For what, Isadore?"

"For *my* greatest illusion. A trick in its own way as brilliant as yours, Guy. It was an illusion for an audience of one. You."

"I don't follow, Isadore. What trick have you ever shown me?"

Klein smiled. "Guy, I have been using the Magician's Choice in real life. In *your* life."

"My life? I don't know what you're talking about."

"No, of course not. Maybe I shouldn't tell you. I'm violating the fundamental rule of magic: never reveal the secret to a trick. But, in this case, you should know."

"Know what?"

"Know that since you arrived back in New York, I have been 'forcing' your choices. I have created situation after situation where you have been unwittingly part of a Magician's Choice. *My* Magician's Choice. You *think* you've had free will, but I have been directing you all along."

"Directing me? To what?"

"To success. To love. To me."

Guy thought that maybe Klein was mad, that his loneliness and guilt had pushed him into a world of fantasy. He couldn't imagine what he was talking about. Klein sensed his skepticism.

"Let me explain, Guy. You were living in that lousy hotel, the Sutherland, right?"

"Yes."

"Then Vernon mentioned the apartment above the Ping Toy restaurant, you remember?"

"Yes."

"I put him up to it. Vernon has been in on this since the start. Once Lou convinced him to be your mentor, I had the perfect person to help influence you. Anyway, I heard from him where you were living. Sounded awful. I wanted to help you find a better place. I knew about Gai Pan's apartment, so I asked Vernon to tell you about it."

Guy shook his head. Vernon had been part of the act!

"Gai Pan helped, too. She and I go way back. She was one of my assistants. Being Chinese, she fit right in, though her stage name was Su Lin. Look …"

Klein pointed to a photograph on the wall. It showed him in his full Chinese costume, on stage with his props and flanked by assistants. Looking closely at the picture, Guy saw that the little Chinese woman standing to his right had a gap in her toothy grin. Gai Pan to be sure!

Klein continued: "She became Gai Pan when she opened the restaurant. Named herself after a dish on the menu: 'Moo Goo Gai Pan.' In English her name would be 'Madame Chicken with Mixed Vegetables. In glop.' Gai Pan sounded better to her than 'Moo Goo.'"

Guy said nothing. He was stunned.

"That was easy, Guy. Not much of a force, really. Of course you'd pick a cozy apartment over a dump. But I didn't stop there. I kept track of your career. Whenever I felt you needed a little nudge, Vernon and Gai Pan were there."

"How so?"

"His advice and her fortune cookies. I know you put great stock in both. Vernon did all he could to guide you in your career and help you along. And Gai Pan knew what I was trying to accomplish. She knew what you needed to hear. So she wrote the fortunes and put them in nice fresh cookies for you."

"Yes, Isadore. Dai *was* a big help," Guy said. "And those fortunes always made me think and helped me make decisions. But she always gave me a choice of one of three cookies."

Klein smiled.

"Oh, Guy, do you think you really had a choice?"

"It was a force?"

"Of course. All three cookies were always the same."

"No wonder she never let me have more than one! And that explains why she was always typing away back there."

"She was working hard on your destiny, Guy."

Guy looked at Klein, who was smiling a mischievous smile. In his mind, he was rewinding his life, wondering about all sorts of things.

"You didn't happen to walk into the Litz, I mean the Ritz, one night, did you?" Guy asked.

"Well, I won't say for sure, but I will tell you this: we didn't want you to get stuck there too long. We wanted to move your career along, Guy. Time flies, you know."

"Is there more?"

"Lots. With Vernon's help, I helped you get the job with Blackstone."

"No! I snuck in, and Harry surprised ..."

Klein waved a dismissive hand.

"All planned, Guy. All planned. Russ was waiting for you and let you in. I arranged a job offer for one of his cast, so Blackstone *did* need a new assistant. He agreed to give you a shot."

"So Blackstone was part of the trick!"

"Yes, he was. He's always been helping you, Guy, even before I came to him with my idea. After all, he got you started in magic, didn't he?"

"Yes, when I saw his show, when he taught me a trick, then sent me a magic set."

"He liked you when he first met you, Guy. He was happy to join our little act. He invited you to work in his show. Later, he helped get you your show at the Garde. Harry had played there. Knew the manager. Harry suggested he take a look at your show in New York. It worked."

There was a moment of silence as Guy stared at Alexander the cat, hoping he would help him understand what he was hearing. For almost three years, his life had been a grand illusion. He had been making choices that were not choices at all.

"I couldn't change the past, Guy. But I could influence your future. You had to deliver, of course. I just managed to put opportunities in your path."

"I felt so lucky"

"I was your luck."

Guy was reeling. Then Klein dropped his bombshell.

"And then there's Rachel."

"Rachel?"

"Yes, Guy. Rachel. I heard from Vernon all about her. Sounded like love to me. But here you are in New York and there she was in … where was it?

"Liberty, South Carolina."

"Yes. Right. I remember. Vernon helped me find her address there. Listen: life is too short for two lovebirds to be apart. Vernon told me you told him that Rachel loved fashion design and was quite good at it. As it happens, Anne Klein is my cousin. She helped by sending Rachel the letter offering a job."

"Another force."

"Well, sort of. She could not have come, of course, but I was pretty sure she'd make the right choice. Like you, she had to deliver. And she did. They loved her work."

"So you got her to New York. And, I suppose, to Blackstone's show."

"Of course. I had to get you two together. If I'd have left it to chance, well, New York's a big city. You might never have run into each other."

"And the rest is history."

"Sounds like a fortune cookie, Guy."

Guy felt the room start to spin. Suddenly, his life was something that someone else had scripted. He was just an actor reading lines, but he didn't even know he was in a play. It was disorienting. He spent a few minutes thinking back over the past few years.

"So have you been forcing *everything* in my life?" he asked at last.

"God, no, Guy. There is much I couldn't control. I couldn't control Irena or Ivan or the Midget or all sorts of things. There was no guarantee I could even control you. Six or seven cards on a table, it's easy to force one by the Magician's Choice. Even fifty-two in a deck—not that hard. But life? It's a messy business Unpredictable. Full of variables. The trick was fraught with possibilities for failure. A few times, it almost went bad. We had to scramble and dream up some new options. It took a lot of luck to pull it off."

"You did all this out of guilt?"

"Yes. Well, no. Well, partly. I wanted to help you, Guy. I wanted to atone for my sin. When I saw you at Tannen's that day, I realized you were still in magic, that you were serious about making it."

"Why not just apologize to me face-to-face that day?"

"I was surprised to see you again. I wasn't ready to come clean, especially in front of a bunch of guys who had no idea what I'd done. And maybe you wouldn't have been ready to accept my apology. But finally, today, I can look you in the eye and say I am sorry. I have to confess it has lifted a great burden from me. It's been a bit of unfinished business that has haunted me for years."

"And the rest of it? Helping me?"

"After you reappeared in my life, I told Vernon, Gai Pan and later Blackstone what I had done. They were hard on me at first. Nobody likes a thief. We talked it over. When I hit upon the idea of trying a Magician's Choice in real life to help you, they all loved it. We didn't know if it was possible. It was a trick nobody had ever tried, just like The Mysterium. Fitting. We all wanted to see if we could pull it off. We did."

"You decided to play God with my life," said Guy.

"I guess I did. I was a good God. I gave you the happiness and spared you the pain."

"So much for free will."

"It's overrated," said Klein

Guy looked at Klein, then at the pictures on the wall of him as Woo.

"Things are not what they seem to be," he sighed.

"Pardon?" asked Klein.

"'Things are not what they seem to be.' It was a fortune a Gypsy machine in a penny arcade gave me. I don't think she was on your payroll. I think fate is her boss. Apparently, it's quite true. Half the people I've met aren't really who they seem to be, and half of what's happened to me isn't what it seems to be."

"Life is like that, Guy. It's complicated. Ambiguous. Full of illusions. We magicians hardly have a corner on them!"

"Wait until I see Gai Pan and Vernon and Blackstone," said Guy.

"Don't be too hard on them, Guy. They were just helping me. And they wanted to see you make it, too. You're a likable young man. A bit naive, but if you weren't, none of this would have worked."

"Were others involved in this act?" Guy asked, thinking of all the people he had met, who might have given him advice or done something for him.

Klein winked. "Why, Guy, you must leave an old magician a few secrets."

Guy smiled. He supposed he would always wonder who in his life might be one of Klein's accomplices. Though he had come to Klein in anger, once he had gotten to know him, Guy had to admit that he liked the old man. He looked over at The Mysterium. His idea, yes. But in the end, Chen Woo's trick.

"Do you want The Mysterium?" Klein asked softly.

"No, Isadore. It's yours."

Guy freely gave what had been stolen from him.

"Are you sure? I'll never have a chance to do it again."

"Never say never," said Guy.

"There you go sounding like a fortune cookie again," said Klein.

"It's time for me to leave, Isadore. Today hasn't quite played out the way I had imagined. I came here thinking it would be like a trial. I'd be judge and jury. Instead, it turned out to be another magic show. I have a lot to think about."

Klein nodded. "Fate brought you back to New York. Back to Tannen's. Then my Magician's Choice directed your life. But you're on your own now, Guy. Your destiny is in your hands. My show is over."

"No encores?" asked Guy.

"No encores," said Klein. "I have no more tricks up my sleeve."

"I don't know whether to believe that's true or not," said Guy.

"Your choice," said Klein.

"Is it?"

The old magician just smiled.

72

As he had so often, Guy went to the Brooklyn Bridge to get perspective on life and think. He had a lot to think about.

It was hard for Guy to accept that his God, the one controlling his fate, was a sad old man, a washed up magician, living in a dusty, cluttered apartment, surrounded by memories and regret.

Guy did not know whether he loved Klein for all he had done for him, or hated him for presuming to guide his destiny, for meddling in his life, *forcing* it to his own desires. Maybe he both hated and loved the man. That was possible. Hate makes us clazy, as Gai Pan had said.

There was more. Guy had waited for years to get his vengeance on Woo, who was really Klein. Finally, the time had come. And there was no vengeance to be had. What surprised Guy was that he didn't feel cheated. He had taken Lily's advice to heart. He had judged Klein not for what he had done or failed to do, but for what he suffered. Through some alchemy of circumstance, understanding and maturity, his hatred had become compassion. He finally understood the meaning of the very first fortune cookie Gai Pan had forced on him.

"Darkness cannot drive out darkness; only light can do that."

In forgiving Klein, Guy had driven out the darkness in his heart with the light of forgiveness. If he still needed someone to hate, there was always Willie Jenks, out there somewhere in the city, a ghost who might yet be brought to justice.

"You never go so far as when you don't know where you are going," the Gypsy's fortune had read.

"Embrace forgiveness," Gai Pan's cookie had advised.

Together, like destiny and free will, they had defined Guy's life.

There on the Brooklyn Bridge, thinking it all over, for only the second time in his life, Guy had a true inspiration. He had the idea for another grand illusion, one that would take a forgotten dream and make it a reality.

"The wonder of it," he said to himself.

73

The train pulled into Union Station in New London. Guy and Rachel were there waiting. Isadore Klein stepped off. He stood in a cloud of steam like a spirit, looking a little bewildered. Guy and Rachel waved, and he smiled in relief.

"I'm glad I got the right stop," he said. "There are a lot of 'News' heading this way."

"I'm pleased to meet you, Mr. Klein," said Rachel. "Guy has told me a lot about you."

"I bet he has."

"Let's get you settled into the Crocker House," said Guy. "Then we'll get some lunch." They took the old man up the street to the Crocker House.

At lunch, at the same coffee shop where Guy had met with Blackstone and Vernon, Klein regaled both Guy and Rachel with tales of his career, his travels, the adventures, the triumphs and little disasters that come with a life on the road performing. He even tried to do a coin trick for Rachel, but dropped the half-dollar on the floor.

"They don't like to be dropped," said Guy with a wink, picking up the coin and putting it in Klein's pocket.

"How about we get you a haircut and a shave?" suggested Guy. "My father has a barbershop here at the hotel."

Klein nodded. That would be fine.

They went around the corner to the barbershop. Sam's eyes lit up when he saw Guy and Rachel. He had come to accept his son's choice of magic as a career (at least for now). He had taken Ruth to the show to see for himself. He was nervous for Guy the whole show, his hands sweaty, but when Mysto was done and Guy and Rachel took their bows, those hands clapped the loudest. He was thrilled. Sam also enjoyed the many admiring comments he'd heard about the show from his customers.

"That son of yours has talent, Sam." "He's very professional." "He completely fooled me, Sam." "When that dove turned to gold—my oh my!" "Sam, we went back two times and still couldn't figure out how he does it!" "I've never seen anyone so good!"

How could a father not be proud? Sam cut Klein's hair and gave him a shave, all of them talking magic. Then, late afternoon, it was time to go up to the Garde. It was a short walk, just up State Street from the Crocker House. They took it slowly so as not to tire the old man. When Klein first saw the marquee, he stopped.

"Tonight Only: Special Performance by the Great Chinese Conjuror Chen Woo."

The big bold letters had been added to the marquee for the Mysto show on its final night. The old man stood there, enthralled. He never dreamed he'd see his name on a marquee again. It had been so long. He just stared at it. Guy and Rachel could only guess the emotions that must be swirling through his mind. When they saw the tears in his eyes, they knew they had done the right thing. They had given the old man a gift that was priceless.

Watching Klein, Guy had to wonder if he was seeing himself someday—an old magician past his prime, long forgotten. Would anyone be so kind as to put his name in lights one last time?

It was a moment full of resonance for the two men, an entwining of personal histories into a shared narrative.

"They'll never be able to take this from me," Klein said. "It'll be a wonderful capper for my career."

His voice cracked and he began to cry. He was too overcome by emotion to say more. Guy put his hand on the old man's shoulders. Rachel put a comforting hand on Guy, tears in all their eyes.

They stood there for a few minutes, three people bathed in the light of the marquee, three who understood the meaning, not just of magic's wonder, but of life's as well.

"Let's go inside and get ready for the show," Guy said softly.

74

Isadore Klein was nervous. Though he would be on stage for only a few minutes, and would do only one trick, it had been years since he'd been in the spotlight. He had practiced The Mysterium and knew it well, but still, he was tentative. He felt strange performing the trick in front of the magician he had stolen it from, but Guy had insisted. As he rehearsed backstage, Klein kept asking Guy about angles and timing and so on, and Guy kept reassuring him that it would be alright. Just go out and do the trick as he had hundreds of times before.

Though he was billed as Chen Woo, the Chinese Conjuror, Klein had shown up with a set of tails, a top hat, white gloves, and a wand.

"I'm too old to pretend to be something I'm not," he told Guy when he came out of his dressing room. "I will be my old self, Chen Woo, on the marquee. But tonight, on stage, I will be me. The real me. I want Isadore Klein to give this final performance."

"Whatever you want, Isadore."

"Let them figure out why a Chinaman doesn't look Chinese," said Klein.

"Just another illusion," said Rachel with a laugh.

Guy patted Klein on the shoulder. He was getting far more pleasure out of the old man's happiness than he would have had he taken his revenge.

Just before Rachel and Guy were to go on, Klein pulled Guy aside.

"Guy," said the old man, "after I perform The Mysterium, I'm giving it to you. It's yours. It always was. You can feature it in your act. Nobody has ever seen it in the States. I will premiere it here tonight, but it will make a name for you in the future. Finally, you will be able to perform your masterpiece."

Guy hadn't thought beyond this evening. Once again, his patience would reap rewards.

"Thanks, Isadore. I'd like that."

Isadore Klein beamed up at Guy.

The orchestra began their intro music: "Paper Moon." Standing behind the curtain, Guy did his Retention Vanish. Rachel joined him and they kissed. "I believe in you," she whispered just before the curtain parted.

The Mysto Magic Show began. Guy and Rachel did their act as they always did, with confidence and charm and humor. Guy could see Klein in the wings, nervously pacing, even jumping up and down a bit to loosen up and burn off energy. But, being old, Klein's feet never left the floor, so his jumping was more of a strange dance, as if he had a spring inside him. It reminded Guy of that damned fake bunny he had gotten as a kid. He hoped Klein would last longer.

And then their act was done. The curtains closed, and the audience applauded. After taking their bows, Rachel went off stage to bring out a table with The Mystrium, and Guy began his introduction, inspired by the ballyhoo of Archie Walters.

"Ladies and Gentlemen. Our show of wonder is not quite over. We have a special treat for you tonight. Our evening will conclude with a final effect done by the great Chen Woo, a master magician. He has never performed here at the Garde, so I hope you will make him welcome.

"He comes to us tonight after a lifetime of traveling the world, bringing wonder to people far and wide. For the first time in this country, he will perform a rare and exotic illusion, The Mysterium. You are about to see something you will never forget. A trick whose origins are shrouded in mystery performed by a master of illusion. Ladies and Gentlemen, I present Chen Woo and The Mysterium."

Guy began the applause and then left the stage. The orchestra played a mysterious tune that was perfect in the Garde's exotic setting.

Guy stood with Rachel in the wings, watching as Klein waited for his final act to begin. He held a top hat and a magic wand, poised to perform. At that moment, the old man was young again, his hands steady, his posture straight, his eyes sparkling with that mischievous joy magicians feel when they are about to give an audience the gift of wonder.

The curtains parted and, for a final time, Isadore Klein stepped into the spotlight.

Guy Borden
IN HIS NEW AND
STARTLING EXHIBITION
OF
Gilbert's
Mysto Magic
AN INTERESTING AND FASCINATING
ENTERTAINMENT FOR YOUNG AND OLD
Mystifying Illusions, Sleight-of-Hand
Card Tricks, Etc.
INCLUDING THE
Premier Acts of the World's Famous Magicians
A REGULAR CARNIVAL OF FUN
Wizardry, Legerdemain and Prestidigitation!
COME AND BRING YOUR FRIENDS!
Levinson
Bar Mitzvah
May 14, 1938

Todd Performing as "Merloc"

Todd & Marcia as "Merloc & Ybor"

Todd Gipstein has loved magic since his mother gave him his first magic set when he was ten. On family trips to New York, he often visited the Magic Center, where proprietor Russell Delmar would enchant him with tricks. Todd admits to a lifelong addiction to buying magics, and he has many boxes of discarded props in his attic, including the Mummy Asrah.

When Todd worked as a writer, photographer and producer for National Geographic, he and his wife, Marcia, performed a series of Geographic-themed magic shows across the country. They collect vintage magic apparatus and posters, and their collection includes a silhouette cut by Dai Vernon and a Jack of Diamonds used by him. Todd still practices in front of his mirror and performs close-up magic when the opportunity arises. He wishes he could do the Retention Vanish as well as Guy.

This is his second novel, following *Legacy of the Light*. For more information about these novels, book group study guides, trailers, and to see his photography, films and other projects, please go to www.Gipstein.com. You can email comments via the website or Facebook. If you liked *Magician's Choice*, please post a review on Amazon.com.

Acknowledgements

I want to thank:

My wife Marcia, for her ideas, encouragement, and all the times she assisted me in my magic acts. Like Vernon told Guy: "Find yourself a pretty girl to love who wants to be in your show and you're all set." Well, I did exactly that.

The talented and versatile Joshua Jay, for advice on magical history and the art of magic.

The amazing Mickey Silver, for an impromptu demonstration he did for me that proved the Retention Vanish can be a miracle. Look at his videos on YouTube and see for yourself.

Charlie Roby, who gave me a trick box owned by Howard Thurston and sparked my interest in magic history and collecting vintage magic props and posters.

Al Cohen, for his cozy shop in D.C., where I spent time playing hooky from work buying too many tricks that I didn't need and never performed.

Nan Shnitzler, a dear friend and preview reader of my book, who helped tweak my writing and polish my ideas.

And finally, I want to thank all the magicians I have met at festivals and conventions, on cruise ships, in magic shops and in the pages of books. I have been inspired, educated and embraced by your talent, insights and willingness to share. I treasure being a part of your fraternity. I hope this book will be taken as an homage to the art of magic and to the talented and generous men and women who have made it their life.

Also by Todd A. Gipstein

Legacy of the Light is a historical thriller. It is the story of two generations of lighthouse keepers at Race Rock Lighthouse off the shore of New London, Connecticut. The action takes place in 1907 and a generation later, much of it the day of the great Hurricane of 1938. Storms, ships at sea, and the isolated lighthouse are the stages of this drama. *Legacy* is a story of how the past influences the present, of fathers and sons, failure, guilt, love, and redemption. As the story unfolds, men and women visit the lighthouse and mysterious objects wash up on the rocks that surround it. Storms bear down on this man-made island in the middle of the sea, and those trapped at Race Rock – the keeper, his fiancée, and a mysterious stranger – must fight the forces of nature and the demons within that threaten to destroy them. All the while, they are trying to unravel a puzzle that could dramatically change their lives, and keep the light lit for ships at sea. *Legacy of the Light* takes readers into a face-paced adventure and love story full of twists and turns.

WHAT READERS ARE SAYING ABOUT "*LEGACY of the LIGHT*"

"This is an absolutely riveting, mesmerizing and spellbinding novel. Its description of the 1938 Hurricane is so lifelike that I felt like I was right there. Once I started *Legacy*, I couldn't put the book down."

— *A reader in New London, CT.*

"I started reading this book on a flight from Boston. I continued reading once I got home, and kept reading all night. I could not put it down. What a thrilling ride! Todd Gipstein's many years working as a photographer comes through in his ability to paint a picture with his words. He renders a scene so well that you can feel the wind on your face, hear the crash of the waves, taste the salt in the air, and feel the electricity on the back of your neck. This is best kind of historical fiction: well researched, beautifully crafted, and a joy to read."

— *A reader in Atlanta*

"Gipstein's prose is crisp and direct and his characters well-formed. He has clearly done his research, and the period details of life in an early-20th-century lighthouse are fascinating, adding considerable depth to the narrative. A well-wrought tale of family, duty, honor and redemption."

— *Kirkus Reviews*

"Todd Gipstein has produced a first-rate fact-based thriller that had me up all night. Thanks to Gipstein's deft fast-paced writing, crisp dialogue and well-defined characters, this tale about the lonely life of a lighthouse keeper ... is packed with drama and excitement as well as a sprinkling of humor. Legacy of the Light would make a great movie and I hope the folks in Hollywood will take note and grab the film rights. It would be a smash hit in the hands of a good director and cast."

— *A reviewer in Wisconsin*

"What a fascinating, thrilling, extraordinarily well written novel you produced in Legacy of the Light. I was very happy that I have retired because I couldn't put the damn book down once I got into it. It was like being there every moment of their lives with your central characters. Thank you for a great book."

— *A reader in New London, CT.*

"I loved it! I could hardly put the book down and the day I finished it I spent all afternoon and early evening reading it until I finished. What a great movie this would make. It was a real thriller for me right to the end. I always felt like I was in the scene you were describing. You certainly captured my attention with your unforgettable characters, and tension-building scenes. Congratulations. This is a great read. Thank you for writing the book."

— *A reader in Mystic, Ct.*

"Incredible read! It is a fast-paced novel written with stunning geographical details and enjoyable characters. A great read that will have you looking for more novels written by this talented author. One of my top five books of 2011."

— *Anonymous Nook Reader*

"A love story, a mystery, and good vs. evil, "Legacy of Light" is an engaging, entertaining read you won't want to put down. We read the book together and anxiously looked forward to discussing our thoughts on what happened and what would happen next."

— *Review on Amazon*

"Behind this riveting storyline filled with mystery, agony, hope and the power of love, is a profound intelligence that brings this novel to a different level. It is not just a thriller that keeps you turning the page, but a journey filled with poignant pauses where some little detail suddenly holds great meaning. Give yourself time to read this in a few sessions because there will come a point where it will be very hard to put it down."

— *A reader in New Hampshire*

"There is great human involvement with love, drive, devotion, concern, despair, fear, and many other emotions that give the story life. The mystery provides a treasure hunt and a battle royal between good and evil. Not to be missed for both the learning and the entertainment."

— *A reader in New York*

CPSIA information can be obtained at www.ICGtesting.com
Printed in the USA
BVOW072352130613

323296BV00001B/1/P